Steps and Exes

"Celia Henry—generous, gritty, sexy, full of lyric musings, and funny as all get-out—is who Janis Joplin might have become if she'd lived long enough to retire to Puget Sound and run a perfect (almost) bed-and-breakfast. . . . [Kalpakian is] so entertaining a writer that it takes a while to realize how smart she is."
—*The New Yorker*

"The pages fairly crackle with energy. . . . Kalpakian's descriptive powers are wonderful. Characters, landscapes, interiors, and even a bevy of small dogs . . . all lodge firmly in the reader's imagination."
—*Seattle Times*

"A delightful, offbeat novel. . . . Kalpakian writes with a verve that leaves you laughing and contemplating your own ideas of family."
—*Chicago Tribune*

"Tart and pungent reflections on the nature of family, life, and love."
—*Washington Post*

"Beguiling. . . . Kalpakian evokes the pervasive dampness, insularity, and placid beauty of island existence with pungent and sensuous detail."
—*Publishers Weekly*

Jeanne McGee

About the Author

LAURA KALPAKIAN is an award-winning novelist and short-story writer. Her novels include *Graced Land, Caveat, These Latter Days,* and *Steps and Exes.* Her stories have appeared in two collections, *Dark Continent and Other Stories* and *Fair Augusto,* which won the PEN/West Award for Best Short Fiction. She has received a National Endowment for the Arts Fellowship, a Pushcart Prize, the Pacific Northwest Booksellers' Award in both 1990 and 1992, and the first Anahid Literary Award for an American writer of Armenian descent. She lives in Washington State with her two sons.

ALSO BY LAURA KALPAKIAN

Delinquent Virgin and Other Stories

Steps and Exes

Caveat

These Latter Days

Graced Land

Crescendo

Dark Continent and Other Stories

Fair Augusto and Other Stories

Cosette: The Sequel to Les Misérables

Beggars and Choosers

Educating Waverley

LAURA KALPAKIAN

Perennial

An Imprint of HarperCollins*Publishers*

A hardcover edition of this book was published in 2002 by
William Morrow, an imprint of HarperCollins Publishers.

HarperCollins books may be purchased for educational, business,
or sales promotional use. For information please write:
Special Markets Department, HarperCollins Publishers Inc.,
10 East 53rd Street, New York, NY 10022.

First Perennial edition published 2003.

Designed by Jennifer Ann Daddio

The Library of Congress has catalogued the
hardcover edition as follows:

Kalpakian, Laura.
Educating Waverley / by Laura Kalpakian.
p. cm.
ISBN 0-380-97768-0
1. Girls—Fiction. 2. Islands—Fiction. 3. Boarding schools—
Fiction. 4. Washington (State)—Fiction. 5. Puget Sound Region
(Wash.)—Fiction. I. Title.

PS3561.A4168 E38 2002
813'.54—dc21
2001051328

ISBN 0-380-80660-6 (pbk.)

03 04 05 06 07 ❖/RRD 10 9 8 7 6 5 4 3 2 1

ENCORE FOR THE LADS

Bear and Brendan

Acknowledgments

Special thanks to
Deborah Schneider, Juliet Burton, Jennifer Hershey

Thank you too for smiles and support
Peggy K. Johnson, William Johnson, Jay McCreary,
Helen Johnson, Meredith Cary, Bob Eggers,
Connie Eggers, Judi Jones, Erica Strutz

and particular thanks to
Margaret Ann Marchioli

Part One

———

The Temp
and the Tempo

Chapter 1

Sputtering, distant and rhythmic, broke the afternoon quiet, and Nona York, trowel in hand, stopped weeding amongst the onions and paused attentively. A motorcycle, she thought. Or something like it. As the noise came slowly up her hill, she rose and stepped outside the cornstalks, beyond the gated garden, squinting into the late afternoon sunshine. The dogs, all six of them, went into nervous delirium, frantically yapping. Roused by the dogs, chickens in the nearby fenced yard cackled and clucked and ruffled amongst themselves. Nona took a dishtowel from her back pocket and began flapping it absently around her shoulders.

She was a solid, short, elderly woman with a helmet of close-cropped silver hair and a Roman nose to go with it. She pulled garden gloves from hands that were strong and brown and sinewy, not at all the sort of hands you might expect from a woman who, for decades, had supplied a jaded world with Romance. Nothing about her suggested voluptuous depths or romantic excess. She was in excellent health, tanned, by Northwest standards, a bespectacled woman who wore thick-soled, nononsense shoes, pants and an oversized tunic. Her posture was erect as a dancer's, though one could hardly imagine her dancing.

Nona's garden too was unromantic, laid out in a straightforward way, the fencing utterly utilitarian to keep out rabbits and the deer and not at all picturesque. There were no winding paths, no little grottos, just a chicken yard and long parallel rows wrested from the meadow that otherwise surrounded her house and sloped downward toward Puget Sound. From this hill Nona had a view of the shallow bay where reefnetters—made tiny by the great expanse of water and the islands in the distance—sat motionless on a calm September sea. In her garden Nona had planted vegetables. Living alone, she mostly gave them all away when everything came in at once, an occurrence that seemed to surprise her year after year. The tomatoes gleamed, shining pendulously on their thick stems, and the cornstalks were upright, tasseled and amber. The only flowers were a phalanx of eight-foot sunflowers no longer erect. They drooped, heavy-headed, as though napping. They reminded Nona of men after making love—drained, dry, sleepy, and a little saddened—which is why she had planted them in the first place.

"Hush, Biscuit, Pootsniff! Stop it at once, Basket," she admonished the little dogs. They all had silly names. They swam like furry tadpoles at her feet. "Stop!" She flapped the dishtowel more actively around her own shoulders. "It's only the temp."

A motorbike got up the hill at last and stopped in front of her. The driver turned the key off and the sputtering ceased. She took off her helmet and shook out her hair, which was red, short and curling. She looked uneasy.

"The dogs are noisy," said Nona, "but harmless."

"It's all right. I've been warned." She handed Nona the agency's paperwork and introduced herself as Rebecca Devere. Becky. "At the temp agency, they asked if I were allergic to dogs or smoke. I'm not."

Nona studied the papers. "This letter says they've chosen you because you live on the island and won't have to deal with the ferry schedule. I used to know everyone on Isadora Island."

"We just moved to Massacre last month. My mother and I. We're from Anaheim."

"Disneyland?"

"Well yes. We both worked there. Fantasyland."

Nona considered this in her unhurried fashion. "So you already know something about romance?"

"I was one of the Seven Dwarfs. Dopey, I'm afraid."

This squashed any further talk of romance and Nona motioned Becky to follow her into the house while she described her duties in the next month or so. Becky would be temporarily replacing Nona's longtime assistant, Doris Watanabe, who had gone to Hood River where her daughter was having a baby.

Nona explained that the first drafts of all her many romance novels were dictated into a handheld tape recorder. Nona recited the narrative and the dialogue (all given in breathless character) as she walked the island beaches, woodlands, and meadows with her doggies, and beat herself with the dishtowel when the doggies disobeyed. She had become an island fixture in this regard, though she was alarming to tourists. Isadorans shrugged off her eccentricities; after all, she was from Useless Point, where the population was said to be two-thirds misfit and one-third mad. People in the town of Massacre regarded the Useless Pointers as too weird for words (though not bad for business). People from Useless regarded Massacre residents as great suck-ups, slavering after tourist dollars. There was an element of truth in both of these commonly held prejudices.

Becky's job, as Nona described it, was to take these audio tapes and transcribe them into the computer, then print them up for Nona to painstakingly alter with a fine red pen. Becky would then enter the corrections. The work was never ending, and there were often several books in progress—in varying stages of growth or decay—at any given moment. Nona had found a style that suited her legion of readers and she kept to it. "People do not read romances looking for originality," she commented, leading Becky through the house, which was neat without being obsessive, old without being antique, lacking any real ambience or character, save for the view, which was breathtaking. Many clocks, large and small, peered from tables and shelves and walls, their ticking just audible, annoying and not at all synchronized. The grandfather clock kept time in a low, disapproving bass.

"Do you read romance novels?" asked Nona.

"I'm afraid not."

"People think romance is without redeeming social value, but they're wrong. Romance novels, mine in particular, take sex seriously. They take love seriously. Most people do not. Most people confuse sex with athletic achievement and love with dual incomes. My books are refreshing and indulgent. They are the chocolate truffles of literature. Naturally, you could go your whole life without ever eating a chocolate truffle, but would you want to?"

Becky said that she, personally, could not imagine living without chocolate truffles.

"When you bite into a chocolate truffle, you don't want to find oat bran."

Nona's study was clearly very much more lived in than the kitchen or the living room. Low bookshelves ran along the walls and beneath the windows, which afforded a dazzling view of the Sound, the other islands to the west. On these shelves there stood a complete set of Nona York titles, perhaps thirty paperbacks in brilliant hues; even the lettering on the spines looked lush and moist, gleaming. Nona's name was more prominent than the title. On the other shelves there were books and stacks of manuscripts, which hung over the edge like lolling tongues. Chairs, lamps, tables (and still more clocks) stood at random angles to one another, and well-chewed slippers, belonging to the dogs, peeked out from under footstools piled high with newspapers from Seattle, New York and Chicago, with magazines heavy on print rather than pictures. Everything seemed to suffer from hangover, unable to pull itself into order, except for the desk. Here the computer, monitor, keyboard, headphones, Dictaphone and empty bud vase stood neatly, almost military fashion, awaiting competent hands.

"Doris likes things done precisely," Nona explained. "She keeps me organized. A full-time job."

"I thought this was part-time."

"Oh, Doris only works part-time, but she's very good. She's been with me eight years. Now, turn on the machine and get acquainted with it. Would you like a cup of coffee and a chocolate truffle?"

When Becky bit into the chocolate, Nona again made her point about chocolate expectations, and oat bran realities. The chocolate was sweet and easily eaten, but the coffee was bitter, thick and muddy. Nona gulped hers quickly while Becky dawdled. They spent perhaps two hours, Nona showing her how and where and what she expected of a temp, Becky asking what she hoped were intelligent questions. Inside, she felt queasy. Miss York's file at the agency was littered with the names of temps she had found unsuitable. She was demanding and intolerant of error.

"You can come every afternoon then?" asked Nona, satisfied at last that Becky understood her terms, conditions, computer, and her working methods. Becky nodded. Nona leaned back, fished a cigarette and a match from her shirt pocket. "When I need a temp, the agency usually sends someone older. How old are you?"

"Twenty-two. Almost twenty-three."

"Most people your age are going the other direction, off this island. There's so little work on Isadora that most of our young people leave." She smoked like a man, cigarette dangling from her lips while she lit it. "Why would you ever move to this island from California?"

"My mother wanted to leave California. I couldn't let her go alone, could I?"

Nona seemed to consider this a real question rather than a rhetorical bid for evasion. "I don't know why not," she said at last, living up to her reputation at the agency, where it was said that in person Miss York was unsparingly blunt. "Your mother's a grown woman. You are a grown woman. Your life doesn't need to be tied to hers."

Becky gave a lilting half-laugh. "Well, Mom's recently divorced, her third divorce, so she's a little rocky these days, and she needs someone. Mom and I just thought it was a good time for change," she added with the chipper enthusiasm she had learned at Fantasyland in the Magic Kingdom.

"And why Isadora Island?"

These questions seriously taxed Becky's fund of cheer; she considered them rude, intrusive and inessential. But she was determined to placate Miss York, to make a good impression. "Mom was born here. Both of my grandparents were born here. I've been hearing about Isadora Island all my life. So well, it just seemed"—she smiled—"a good place. And I'm sure it is. Or will be."

Nona studied the young woman before her. Rebecca Devere was of average height, and with her great dark eyes, she had the sort of face that promised to mature into something striking. She spoke with the usual cadences of the young: sentences curling upward at the end, all statements fading into a smoky, implied question mark, as though nothing could be said with any reasonable certainty. She rolled her shoulders slightly forward, as if conserving energy, unlike the bouncy athleticism of most young women. Becky was personable (you had to be to work for a temp agency), but she was diffident and had a reflexive way of shrugging before she spoke, as though forever diminishing the import of her response. With a start Nona realized that it was this habit that made her distantly familiar. "I don't remember any Deveres on this island."

"That's my name, Devere. Lomax was my mom's maiden name. Sis and Al Lomax are my grandparents. Mom's parents. "

Without shedding any aplomb, Nona lowered herself into a nearby chair. She mused for a few minutes. "Is that Al, as in Alexander?"

"I think so. Yes. But I don't know Sis's real name. She's a grandmother and everyone still calls her Sis."

"And I take it they are both still alive and in good health."

"Yes, well, pretty good health. They are awfully old." Hoping to recapture the positive note, she added, "I guess they were like the young people you mentioned, people who left Isadora for jobs and opportunity. Only they left a long time ago, right after World War II."

Nona stubbed the cigarette into an ashtray, reached for the dishtowel. Reflexively, the doggies congregated at her ankles, their bright eyes expectant. "Is your mother their eldest daughter? Judith Denise?"

"Just Denise. There's no Judith in the family. Denise Hermann."

"But she was Denise Lomax."

The interview was brusquely terminated. Miss York said she would pay for a full afternoon's work, but Becky should leave now. Becky gathered up her things as the various clocks in the room beat in syncopated whispers. The doggies, sniffing and growling, saw Becky to the kitchen door and barked good-bye.

*N*ona, for her part, stayed staring out the study window. In the distance a mist had smudged and thickened the horizon. As she listened to the motorbike fire up and sputter downhill, she felt altogether new sensations stir, fresh, visceral shards of anxiety, of curiosity, anticipation, and regret. Emotions she had long since parted with.

Nona York believed herself to be immune to possibility. Too old for it. Too set in her ways. Well over seventy, she had long since passed the point where she hungered after what had been denied her, or mourned what she had lost, or regretted any particular day she had failed to seize. She lived in a comfortable perpetual present, reassuringly testified to by the clocks all over her house. All were off-time and none agreed. Some were set to standard time, some to daylight saving, some to Eastern, some to Greenwich. Some clocks were always wrong. None wholly right. The correct time (should it matter) could only be inferred or imagined.

She kept these clocks as a way of combating obsession. She was a confirmed chronomaniac, obsessed by time, struggling always against the implicit *when* of her own life and many others. Nona kept time. Her calendar of events, however, was not conventional, and had no commercial ties or values. No Christmas, no Memorial or Labor Day. None of that. But she kept the solstices and the equinox, both vernal and autumnal, the first of May, All Saints, all summers, kept them, but not out of reverence for the past (she was not a nostalgic woman). Nona cyclically acknowledged all sorts of dates and anniversaries, the trivial, the significant, the merely annoying. The past continually punctuated the present, and whether she wished to or not, she tripped over time. She kept an internal catalog of anniversaries, little vigils that obliged her recognition, just as especially low tides oblige ferry schedules to alter.

But other than these reflexive responses to the calendar, Nona kept her working days placid, shallow, even stagnant. Fine. That was how she wanted it. That was the very reason she had not retired. Change was unsettling. But now suddenly, as she heard Becky's motorbike go downhill, she had the sense of standing on a thread of land, a sliver of time that separated the past from the future, and yet was not quite the present: a moment constantly subject to erosion, to uncertain winds and ceaseless tides.

Chapter 2

*L*aughing could cost her the job. They had told Becky this at the agency. It had happened before. One of the earlier temps had burst out laughing with the headphones on because while Miss York was reciting a moment of passionate exchange between lovers into the tape recorder, she was also yelling *Biscuit! Poopsie! Basket! Pootsniff! You must not hump! No humping! Bad Poopsie!* That temp had laughed till tears ran down her face, stopping only when she smelled cigarette smoke and turned around to see Miss York leaning in the doorway. The temp had been sent packing and the circumstances noted on Miss York's file. The agency had further cautioned Becky to keep her exchanges with Miss York to a minimum lest she invite criticism. Becky had been advised to think of herself merely as a conduit for Miss York's prose, which, the agency manager said, was enough to choke a horse.

At first Becky thought this a tad unfair. True, the books were heavily salted with adjectives, exclamations, but the stories, told in Miss York's gravelly, smoke-roughened voice, could be oddly involving.

She began to wonder about Miss York's own love life. No doubt long past. Nona's home, at least those rooms Becky saw, did not testify to voluptuous experience. The few framed snapshots on the study shelves were mostly of doggies. There were pictures of girls, clearly from Miss York's youth, grinning, leaning over a balcony, girls clad in togas or artfully draped sheets, looking soulful. Girls with their arms draped over one another's shoulders, their shorn heads touching. The only man in these pictures was a stout, middle-aged gentleman, florid (even in a black-and-white picture, you could see he was florid), wearing a bow tie. He had his arm around a woman who could only be his wife, given the companionable way she leaned into him. She was almost as tall as he, big boned, with short hair, pale eyes in a pale face. Her long fingers were laced loosely in front of her.

There was no evidence anywhere of a Mr. York. Perhaps Miss York was a lesbian. The thought crossed Becky's mind, though the books gave lots of luscious attention to the bodies of men.

When she worked on these books side by side with Miss York, Becky often pointedly commented on some well-drawn character or well-done episode, mildly insincere flattery, most of it. She was desperate not just to excel but also to ingratiate herself here. This was the only job on Isadora Island that didn't require slinging hash, frying doughnuts, toting beers or gutting fish. She was happy to have it.

However, as the weeks passed, the regularity with which the heroines achieved uncomplicated orgasm began to grate on Becky's nerves. In Miss York's novels, while a man might act the bastard or the dastard, his fundamental caring was never in question, even if at the moment it might not be evident. At some level the heroine (and the reader) knew he cared. That was a central premise of the books. From what Becky had seen, men were indifferent. Not active malice, just uncaring indifference. Of course Miss York's romantic novels weren't meant to be manuals, only entertainment, but they little reflected anything Becky Devere knew about men, marriage, or love.

Other than a couple of inconsequential boyfriends, none of whom had enlisted her passion, what Becky Devere knew came mostly from watching her mother. Denise's three marriages had all ended in divorce (and the equally bitter breakups of a couple of long informal unions). Crash and smash and casualties everywhere. Denise was always the wounded one, dripping, metaphorically speaking, blood, sweat and tears. The men her mother had loved hadn't necessarily wanted to see Denise flattened, crying her eyes out, bent double with pain. Truly, they hadn't planned and plotted and then wrought this pain. They just didn't give a shit. They did what they fucking wanted and that was that. Their indifference was monumental.

Denise's last husband, Jerry, was the worst of a bad lot. When Becky had called Jerry from the hospital emergency waiting room to tell him that Denise was having her wrists bound and her guts pumped, he said that was terrible. He asked if Denise would be all right. To this Becky could only strangle out that if he meant by all right that she would live, yes. He was relieved. He would come by. Later.

Hanging up the phone, Becky had felt battered by the certainty that Jerry would indeed come by later. Denise would never be rid of him, divorce or not. She called her grandparents to tell them what happened. Her grandmother, as usual, was off at a meeting of the Realtors Board, or showing a house or some other such noble undertaking. But her grandfather was home. He did not ask if Denise would be all right. He said simply, "Leave. Get her out of here. Both of you, get out of here. Go to Isadora Island. You will be practically native there. It's a good place to go. Now. Especially now. Bring your car over," he added more typically, "and I'll tune it up, change the oil and get you some new shocks for the journey. Bring it over tomorrow on your way to the hospital. I have a map."

On the map he had circled for her the exit off Route 5 for the San Juan Ferries, there in Anacortes, Washington. When her grandmother heard of Becky's plans, she scoffed, declared it was all nonsense and Becky didn't know what she was doing, and if Denise would just pull herself together, she'd be fine. All this talk of going to Washington was silly and immature. Becky's aunts, her uncle, her cousins, and all their families, her half brother, Josh, all protested too. Even Denise fought her, argued she was better off in Anaheim. She wanted to stay in Orange County to be near her family. But Becky had given notice at the apartment she shared with her mother, packed up their clothes, sold such furniture as they had and told Denise to get in the car. Directly after the doctor said Denise was healing well, Becky got on Route 5 north at Katella and said they weren't getting off for 1,200 miles.

Perhaps she didn't know what she was doing, but she knew exactly where she was going. To Becky Devere, Isadora Island was recognizably part of her life, just as the Teacup ride at Fantasyland was recognizably a part of Disneyland. She carried the map of Isadora Island impressed in her own memory, so vivid was her grandfather's voice, his tales of the place. As the miles gathered behind her, Becky almost thought she could hear his laughter. Even his applause. He was not a man much given to laughter, a good-humored man, but reticent, not hearty. When all the family fur was flying about her leaving California, her grandfather did not speak up, did not mention it was his idea, did not publicly applaud her decision. Her car, however, was certainly ready for the journey. He gave it back to her with a full tank of gas.

But from the moment she had driven off the ferry at Dog Bay and followed the road to Massacre, she had terrible misgivings. Admittedly, the town of Massacre did not conform to anything she had heard. Certainly her grandfather had never mentioned the Blue Dolphin Motel where she and Denise rented a furnished one-bedroom apartment. The Blue Dolphin was mostly used by college kids working the tourist venues in summer, students who wanted somewhere cheap to live, where no one cared how many people were sharing the rent as long as the rent was on time. Since it was meant for summer folk, the Blue Dolphin was inadequately and expensively heated and could only be ventilated by opening the front door and the sliding glass at the back. The sliding glass gave out to a small poorly painted balcony and a view of stubbled field, a muddy lot and the back of Island Medical Center. By mid-October most of the apartments were empty, and the manager, Carlene, a bosomy, inquisitive sort, had more time to snoop and pry into the lives of her latest tenants.

Occasionally Becky and Denise had ringing rows. They quarreled over coming here in the first place. They quarreled over the phone bill when it revealed phone calls to Jerry Hermann in Anaheim. They quarreled over the fact that Becky was working within weeks of their arrival, but Denise, like a frog on a favorite lily pad, seldom moved from a great puddle of inertia. At first Becky tried to be supportive, but her mother's repetitious regret wore on her. Worse, Denise regretted all the wrong things. She regretted divorcing Jerry, and she resented Becky's reminding her that he had screwed her—in every way imaginable—right up to the end. She regretted leaving Anaheim, though the house was lost because of the divorce and she had lost her job at Fantasyland the year before. Denise had no internal fiber when it came to men, even after the slashed-wrists-and-overdose episode. Whenever the men in her life wheedled or whined, Denise succumbed and gave them whatever they wanted—sex to her ex and money to her drug addict son. Becky was certain, if she could once pull Denise from these destructive patterns, her mother would slowly emerge, a flower from the ugly bulb of all this anguish.

But it did not happen like that. Denise Hermann seemed to <u>have endured a defeat from which she could not recover</u>. Moreover, there was a prim quality to her mother's suffering that annoyed Becky. Denise seemed like a good girl wrongly banished to her room, waiting only for someone to tell her the injustice had been righted and she could come downstairs. Denise seldom left the Blue Dolphin. Early on, she would lie, and say she'd gone looking for a job. By mid-October she had quit looking. By November she had quit lying. With little else to think about (and no credit card for the Shopping Channel) Denise took up Olympic Criticizing.

She sprinted effortlessly from what Becky had done wrong to what she had failed to do at all, inflicting great dollops of guilt and feelings of inadequacy. She had been well coached in this sport by her own mother. Denise could achieve all this athletic nagging without ever taking her eyes from the Shopping Channel, where they described a lovely knit outfit that could be dressed up for an evening out with your husband, or made sporty and casual for that quick trip to the store.

"Oh, let's move to Isadora Island!" she warbled as the girls on the Shopping Channel cooed over the outfit. "Massacre! What the hell kind of name is that? What does it tell you about the vibes of a place that it's named after murdered Indians? Oh, this was just a great place to come, Becky. Spend all our money driving up here and renting this dump, and for what? There's no jobs here. No work."

"Mom, you were a ticket taker, not a brain surgeon. You can find a job."

"I suppose you think I should stand on a wet cement floor for eight hours and gut fish? And you know my knees can't take being a waitress. No one is hiring now anyway. The season is over. Of course, I'm not Miss Computer Literate like you. It's fine for you to live here. You're gone most all day. You don't have to deal with that bitch manager snooping and prying. She wouldn't even turn on the heat till October fifteenth, and then she turned off the hot water."

"Just for a few hours while they fixed the water heater."

Denise folded her arms over her narrow chest and slumped down against the plastic couch. "I never wanted to leave California."

Becky ran her hands through her short red hair. The red came from a box and it was growing out. "You wanted to leave this earth altogether as I recall. We have the unpaid hospital bill to prove it."

"You can't talk to me like that." Tears welled in Denise's eyes. "Josh would never talk to me like that."

"Josh would never talk to you at all unless he needed drug money. As soon as he's out of rehab and back into drugs, I'm sure you'll hear from him."

"How can you say that about your own brother?"

"Half-brother. Sixteen years older than me, so please don't act like we were happy toddlers together and you were Mother of the Year, baked brownies and came to our every piano recital."

"You never had a piano recital."

"My point exactly." Becky scooped up some papers and pens, a book or two, thrust them into her backpack, flung on her jacket and fled the apartment. She clattered down the metal stairs with Denise calling out recriminations after her. From the office window, Carlene, the manager, watched, a thin blue wreath of smoke encircling her face.

Chapter 3

John Mortimer

*B*ecky walked swiftly toward the center of town, perhaps half a
mile. Nothing in Massacre was too far from anything else. The
town lay on a neck of land, a low point between two sets of hills
with water on either side. On the westerly side, there was the wide semi-
circular sweep of Moonless Bay, rocky, shallow and treeless. Legend said
that two hundred years before, a marauding tribe of Native Americans
had stolen across this water in canoes one moonless night and slaughtered the peaceful tribes who lived there. Hence the name, which stuck,
despite all civic efforts to change it to something less ominous. On the
more easterly side there was a marina, well lit, whitewashed, docks all at
neat right angles to the boats, which were mostly pleasure crafts of one
sort or another. A few ungainly gillnetters still testified to the fishing,
the ancient island occupation, but for the most part, the Massacre marina was made inviting for tourists. But now, this late in autumn, the
town had shed its cute corset and relaxed a bit, ungirdled from the need
to be quite so picturesque. The geranium baskets hanging from lamp
posts were dried and dying, a few blackened altogether by early frosts.
Even the window displays consisted only of a few random leaves, the
perfunctory pumpkins and a plastic squash.

Becky walked toward Our House Books, in which she'd found a sort
of haven, using it as a library. In one display window, an arrangement of
Nona York titles lay in what could only be called abandon on a blue and
gold silk scarf. Opposite, self-help titles stood up at smart attention. Perhaps, thought Becky, self-help was for the oat bran types of this world
and Nona York romances for those who savored chocolate truffles.
Becky was neither. Belonged nowhere.

Inside, the Muzak was Mozart, and the bookstore had a few reading tables. She found a quiet corner and pulled her textbook and notes from her backpack. She had signed up for distance-learning courses through University of Washington Extension, primarily to convince herself she would not always be a temp. In high school she had been a conscientious student, good grades, nice prospects at graduation, but no money. She had gone one year to Fullerton Community College, then quit and took an office job in a bank, which oppressed her spirit. She left the bank, went back to Fullerton Community, but had to quit in the middle of the year when Denise's problems overwhelmed them both. This extension course in chemistry was her sole window to the future. Any future, any education. In these few months, Becky had decided that coming here was a big mistake: Isadora Island truly was a dead end. No career. No college. No friends. Her savings gone to heat the apartment.

"Science, hmmm," said a gravelly voice suddenly beside her. She looked up to see Miss York standing by her side. "Did you know that you can learn everything you need to know about science in general with a telescope, a microscope and chickens?"

"Chickens?" said Becky, mustering her best and most flattering tone.

"Nasty creatures, chickens, but instructive."

Becky gave a wan smile.

"Have time for a coffee and a walk? You can leave your books here. They'll be safe. That's one nice thing about Isadora in the off-season, most everything is safe."

They left Our House and walked a few blocks to an espresso stand, gingerbready and surfeited with cuteness. "Not nearly as bad as the Crystal Kettle Tea Shoppe over on the Moonless side," said Nona. "That's like walking into a wad of cotton candy." She ordered two grande lattes, double shots. "Do you mind a walk toward the marina? I'm not one to sit about. I get restless or sleepy. One is as bad as the other."

They zipped their jackets against the evening damp and wandered toward the marina, which was well lit, though most of the boats were dark, locked, and their sails tightly shrouded. A few small windows gleamed and their lights wrinkled in the black water, along with a great green neon beacon that said ICE across from the marina itself. The place reeked of low tide.

"Whew, it's pungent here." Becky winced against the scent of brackish rot.

Nona took a deep breath. "I like low tide. I like all sorts of things most people avoid, the smell of fish being smoked and bus fumes, vinegar and photographic developer, the smell of dogs and cigar smoke. I like men who sweat when they work."

"That's not very romantic."

"No, if I put cigar smoke and dogs and bus fumes in my books, my readers would flee. Sweat's all right though. Sweat's allowed as long as it's pearling between thighs."

Pearling between thighs was not a phrase Becky would have been acquainted with before her job with Nona York, but she scarcely even thought it unusual now. Taking the opportunity to be appealing, Becky observed with false cheer, "You must have a lot of faith in love to write romances."

"Oh, I have every faith in love. Not necessarily the kind of love I write about though."

"What other kind is there?"

"You'll need to find that one out yourself."

"Well, romantic love and true love, I meant, in your books, they're sort of the same thing," she went on stupidly, maundering about allying sex and true love.

"There's no hypocrisy involved, if that's what you're suggesting," Miss York finally (and to Becky's great relief) interrupted. "That's what romance is, sex and true love. People need these things, they need to know they're possible."

"Most people probably don't experience love or sex in quite that way." Becky tried to sound thoughtful and intelligent and knew she had failed at both.

"Do you think most people experience vampires? Of course not! That doesn't keep them from reading about them, does it? Why should love be any more false than death? People write about death all the time, and no one says they simplify or exaggerate or that such books are fantasies."

"Well, love doesn't always work out, does it?"

"Does death?"

Becky debated accidentally spilling the coffee right into the harbor and then saying oh dear, she had to go. But she knew Nona York now well enough to know Nona would never allow such a shallow evasion, that Nona York was actually interested in this awful conversation. There was no way out. Instead Becky asked about Massacre and how it had got its name and offered a few stale tales of her grandfather's, tired anecdotes about a boat that never sailed, that sat in front of his house. Becky was afraid Nona would return to the earlier, difficult conversation. Instead, she asked, oddly, about Becky's Lomax great-grandparents.

"Did your grandfather ever talk about his parents, Hector and Bessie?"

"Not much. But Sis said they were drunks and daredevils and not decent people."

"Well, that may be wholly true, and yet not be the whole truth." Nona sipped the scalding latte. "So is Sis still managing everything and everyone?"

"She's very good at it."

"Well, she's had a lot of experience, give her that. After Pearl Harbor when her brother Nels died, Sis's parents all but shriveled up and died. The old Torklunds quit working, and they left Sis with the running of the whole Marine and Feed. She did it, of course. She was famously competent."

"She still is," said Becky without enthusiasm.

Nona leaned against the railing and turned back to the town. "The old Marine and Feed used to be right up there." She gestured toward rows of pseudo-Victorian shops. "For a long time, all the mail and telegrams, good news and bad, went in and out of there. There were only fourteen phones on the whole island, and a couple of those belonged to Westervelt logging, so people gossiped and listened in because they all shared a party line of course. But for two or three generations everyone on this island relied on the Marine and Feed. People would get their messages there, use their phone. Any emergency called in to the Marine and Feed first. People would meet their relatives there for funeral processions to the church. The Torklunds' place was the heart of this island. And then, when the war came, the whole place died. The pastor went to be an army chaplain, so the church closed down. The men joined up, so the barber had to leave. Even the vet left. People feared for Japanese subs in Puget Sound and Japanese planes overhead, and so whole families moved to the mainland. The jobs were better there anyway. Only the old fishers and a few farmers stayed here, and even they could make more money selling their boats for scrap. The farmers couldn't hire help to bring in their crops. The whole island went back to the ghosts and the Indians really. Then, in about '59, the ferry changed everything. Who could have foreseen what the ferry would mean to Isadora? Look at it," she scoffed, "Massacre, the capital of Cute. And it's still rolling in tourist bucks. If Sis had known that, she probably would have stayed." Nona blew the steam from her coffee cup.

"You don't sound like you were very fond of her," Becky ventured.

"You don't either."

"Well I'm not. I guess." Becky shrugged in her habitual way.

"And your grandfather?"

"My grandfather is a wonderful man. He is . . . a wonderful man."

"But? There is an implied reservation."

Some blithe and crisp reply was in order, but the continued effort to be the Vessel of Sunshine was too exhausting. "My grandfather is the sweetest, warmest person in the world, and they all just ignore him. He's the only one I care for in the whole family." Becky added, "If you want to know the truth."

"I always want to know the truth. Why did you leave California? Really why. Not bullshit why."

Becky thought of the long afternoons she had spent in the Dopey costume, nodding her head up and down, holding hands, skipping around with brats whose grinning parents took pictures of the kids and Dopey. Becky was through being dopey. She said, "I left for three reasons. Drugs, drink and divorce. The drugs were Josh's, he's my half brother, and he would live with some woman or another till she threw him out, and then he'd show up at Mom's and say he just needed a job, but what he really needed was a fix. He'd stick around till he got it. With her money. The drink was Jerry's, he was her husband for a long time. Too long. Even after the divorce, Mom couldn't let him go. She would drive all over Fullerton and Anaheim looking for Jerry's truck at various bars and when she'd find him there, with his hand on some other woman's knee, she'd just fall apart and throw things. One time she got arrested, but mostly Jerry just called me and asked me to come collect her. We're not exactly the Swiss Family Robinson."

"You had no other family, no help? No one stepped in to help you, or help your mother?"

"Oh, I have family all right. Everyone there in Orange County, my grandmother, two aunts, my uncle, their spouses and ex-spouses and significant other yahoos and hangers-on. I have cousins and they all have kids and their kids' kids. I'm surrounded. And they're all the same, back-biting, gossiping, lying. My grandmother always coming over and ragging on Mom because she let her housekeeping go to hell. Never mind, her life had gone to hell! No, it was always *Denise I'm ashamed of you. Look at this place, Denise!* The rest of them, they just love to see people fail and fall and crash and burn. And Mom obliged them. Mom's own sister told her she'd seen Jerry's car parked at Aladdin's Motel in the middle of the afternoon. Mom drove out there, saw the car, drove home and slit her wrists. She took a bunch of pills too. She took so many pills, she botched the wrists. She was supposed to climb into a tub of warm water, and it would all be over quickly and painlessly, but she took so many pills, she forgot to fill the tub. I came home and found her, passed out, bleeding, and blue with cold. She was so stoned from the pills she sawed the hell out of her wrists and probably didn't even know. I took her to the hospital. I was going to call my grandfather, and then I thought, what if Sis answers the phone? I'll have to tell her where I am and why. And she'll show up and I'll have to listen to her heap shit on my mother even though I don't know if Mom will live or die. I couldn't do it. I waited alone. At least I didn't have to hear how flaky and destructive my mom is." Becky took a deep drink of her coffee. She was breathless and exhausted. "The trouble with my mother isn't even Jerry and his other women. She doesn't think she's worth loving. She doesn't think she has any value, that she's worthwhile at all. I didn't know that then. I didn't know it till we moved up here. And I have to live with it."

Nona York considered all this thoughtfully. Finally she said, "You're not the first person with a difficult parent, you know. You need to be resilient, Becky. The people who prosper in life—I don't say become rich or wildly sought after, any of that, just the people who do not fail—they are resilient."

"Is that a line from a Nona York novel?"

"Of course not. Resilience does not pearl between thighs."

"Are you resilient?"

"Absolutely. I wouldn't be here if I weren't."

"How do you know if you're resilient?"

"You don't. You have to learn by doing."

"Doing what?"

"It's a process of transformation," she replied obliquely. Nona leaned on the marina railing and watched the ICE sign reflection waver in the water. "When he lived here, your grandfather was called Sandy. Al does not suit him." She said this in her regal fashion, ending all talk of Al. "He was Sandy Lomax. Sandy Lomax. Did he ever mention Temple School? Or Sophia Westervelt?"

"Sophia's Beach. Is that the same Sophia?" Becky was pleased to see Nona's face soften and an unaccustomed smile play round her lips. "I've heard about the beach. Who was Sophia?"

"She was an immortal teacher in an eccentric school," replied Nona without a glimmer of irony. "I was her student. Sandy Lomax drove the Marine and Feed truck and made deliveries to the school. Once a week. Thursdays."

"So that's how you knew him, and Sis."

"Yes. That's how."

"He has great stories of that school. He said the girls used to dance in togas and the fishing boats would congregate in the Sound just to watch them." She remembered now the pictures on the low bookshelves at Nona's house, the girls in togas. The girls on balconies. She could not imagine Miss York in a toga. "The school is Henry's House now, isn't it? The B and B?"

"Yes. Have you been there?"

"Well, I drove out there."

"If you'd like one day I'll take you all around. It's very different now, but Celia Henry is a friend of mine and I can show you something of what Sandy would have remembered."

"That would be nice. Maybe I can even drag Mom away from the Shopping Channel. Mostly, when I'm looking for things my grandfather talked about, I just go by myself. She won't come. I've been all over this island, but there are still a few things I can't find."

"Maybe I can help you. What are you looking for?"

"Well, there's a place called Ditch Nelson."

"Oh, that's up over on the other side of the island, near Dough Bay. A long time ago, some poor sonofabitch thought he could dig a channel between Dough Bay and his own place. He died I think, and it's all but grown over, but local boaters, fishers, if you ask them, they still know where it is. Anything else?"

"Well, there's the *Waverley Scott*. I can't find that. I've looked all over."

"The who?"

"Some monument, maybe. Or a house that's long gone. Probably a boat. That's what the librarian says. With a name like that, it was probably a boat."

"What did your grandfather say about this Waverley Scott?"

"He just said when I found it, I'd be amazed. But even the island librarian told me it was probably long gone. She got out this book of old boats of the Puget Sound and I looked all through it. They were beauties, those wooden vessels. There's nothing like them now."

"No," Nona concurred.

"They were called the Mosquito Fleet, the librarian said, because they used to dart all over the Sound, and for a long time there were lots of vessels out of Massacre. The librarian told me what you did, about how Isadora was pretty much abandoned during the Second World War, just went back to the wild and the wooden boats rotted and the metal ones were scrapped. But before that, they all had romantic names. Men would name their boats after wives or sweethearts, though *Waverley Scott* doesn't sound like a wife or a sweetheart to me. It hardly sounds like a name at all. The librarian thought it sounded like the title of a book, but she couldn't find that either."

Nona felt her chest tighten, as though her heart had grown beyond her ribs, as though the congestion might kill her, and for the first time in years she suddenly feared dying before her time. She ground her cigarette out under her foot, and leaving aside the whole question of ships and boats, she asked after the motorcycle. She asked if Becky's grandfather knew she was riding a motorcycle back and forth to work.

"It's just a scooter, Miss York, not a motorcycle. I bought it used right after we got here because I thought Mom would be using the Toyota. That's my car, my grandfather gave it to me. Jerry took her car."

"Yes, well, she isn't working is she? So why don't you use the Toyota?"

"The scooter is cheaper to run." Becky gave a diffident shrug. "We don't have a lot of money and gas is expensive on an island."

Nona bent and genteelly picked up the butt, took an empty Altoid tin from the canvas bag that she always carried, and put the butt in. Like a judge after careful consideration, she announced, "I think it's safe to say Sandy Lomax would not like you riding the motorcycle on this island. Riding it at all."

"Motorbike. I wear a helmet."

"Nonetheless, motorbikes are very dangerous, and I think you should use the car. He would certainly want you to drive the car. The roads here are narrow and take unexpected turns sometimes. The road to Useless is particularly bad. People have died on the road to Useless."

"The road to Useless," Becky mused. "It sounds like a warning."

"It is."

Chapter 4

The longer Becky worked for Nona York, the less she thought of her as a chocolate truffle. With her discipline, her constant walking, her lack of flourish, her blunt ways, Nona York seemed the epitome of oat bran. For Becky, the contrast between the solid, silver-haired writer and her lissome heroines grew more marked and curious. The heroines in the act of love all had arching backs, hungry lips. The men, surly, expectant before sex, were tender afterward. The men in these books all had hard shafts and the women were enveloping sheaths. For all the talk of romance, love, the sex was physically portrayed—nipples and breasts and bellies and buttocks tingling or throbbing or wet. Becky thought these characters lived at the other end of the experiential telescope from their creator. Miss York herself was as sexless as a crash test dummy.

One afternoon, when she came to the end of one cassette for Nona's latest, *The Dusk Lovers*, and it was too late to start another, Becky stood, stretched, and strolled around the study, picking up the framed photos. Even silver frames could not make the doggies look any more than a pack of boisterous mutts, nasty, jealous, their great black eyes like saucers, their fur standing on end, their mouths taut with vindictiveness. Horrible creatures.

With nothing better to do (except work) and since Miss York was gone, Becky poked aimlessly through the desk drawers. The usual pens, pencils, paper clips and, tucked far in the back of the bottom drawer, a Rolodex. Flipping through it she found not ordinary addresses, but a compendium of synonyms, all in Miss York's eccentric hand. On each card were terms and words, clusters of expression associated with the body, with making love and lovemaking, with foreplay and afterglow. All alphabetized and carefully cross-referenced. Becky laughed out loud—then had a quick guilty look up to be certain Miss York was not smoking in the doorway. Satisfied she was safe, that Miss York and the doggies were still on their walk, she flipped through the cards. She cracked up laughing again and again. The coy "mound of Venus" was defined with synonyms and various directives, such as "see under *pudenda*." Looking in the Ps Becky found *pudenda*, itself cross-referenced. Under *penetration* were a series of verbs on the order of "lush thrust," which made her laugh all the more. Naturally *penis* was there in all its incarnations, some poetic, some of them slangy and unthinkable in a Nona York novel, some clinical as a urologist's wall chart. Penis had three cards to itself, each duly labeled, Penis 1, Penis 2, Penis 3. The last entry on Penis 3 said, "See under *scrotum*." Becky tried to picture Miss York seeing under scrotum. Impossible. And yet the swath of possibility gathered in this Rolodex suggested a vast sexual history.

She put the Rolodex carefully away and wandered those rooms in the house she had never seen. The guest room was clearly unused; here the ironing board and the vacuum lounged together in a comradely fashion. In the guest bathroom, laundry, long dry, still hung from the shower curtain rod. In Miss York's untidy bedroom, the high unmade bed was surrounded with books stacked four and five deep on the floor. Two small tables and a dresser were crowded with small lamps, more clocks, more books and more framed photos, doggies past and present. But what drew Becky's attention were three paintings hanging on a broad white wall protected from sunlight. Simply framed, elegantly matted, they roiled with color. They seemed to leap off the wall, to dance all by themselves, to suggest energy and motion, emotion that could not be contained within the frame, even within the room. Becky had never seen anything like them. She could not make out the signature, only the dates in the bottom right-hand corners, '14, '12, '34.

Shadows produced by a rustling amongst the poplars that ran the length of the back of the house arrested her attention; they flitted restlessly over a desk tucked in a corner of the bedroom. It was an old-fashioned wooden school desk, the seat ornately united to the writing surface by curling ironwork. Carved in great block letters across the top, she read WAVRIL. The letters had been carefully inked in. She sat down at the desk. The back kept her spine uncomfortably straight. Opening the lid Becky inhaled the odor of old graphite, spilled ink, must and dust. And there, at the back, she saw a pillowcase that had yellowed and cracked along the fold lines. The embroidered edges were decorated with an arch, a rounded roof held up by three pillars. From inside she pulled a white gift box with the logo of some ancient department store, Strawbridge and Clothier, and in faded blue ink someone had written across it:

Sexual Scrabble, A Game for Lovers

She lifted the lid, and from the box there wafted a peculiar scent, which she had barely breathed in when suddenly she heard the kitchen door open and Nona's voice admonishing the doggies. The doggies, their paws clacking along the floor, ran snorting, yapping through the house. Becky's breath caught in her throat and she froze. She shoved Sexual Scrabble back into its pillowcase and thrust it into the desk, dropping the lid with an unintentional thud. Dashing into the bathroom, she closed the door so swiftly, she nearly caught Biscuit's nose in it. He stood there barking and all the other little dogs joined him, a canine chorus of reproach. Becky flushed the toilet several times and washed her hands and face.

"Have you been around cats?" Miss York asked when she emerged at last into the kitchen. "Cats drive the doggies wild."

"No cats." She suppressed the squeal of anxiety in her voice. "No pets allowed at the Blue Dolphin."

Miss York put the last of the groceries away and faced Becky, grinning. "Guess what? I just talked with Doris this morning and she's going to stay in Hood River all the rest of the winter. She won't be back until January at the earliest. So I was wondering if you can continue working for me." She added confidentially, "And I've heard through the island grapevine that they're hiring at Our House Books. You can apply there. Use me for a reference. That way you'll have two part-time jobs—and enough money to pay for gas for the car, instead of the motorbike," she added pointedly. "And when this job is over, when Doris comes back, I'm sure Our House Books will put you on full-time."

"Thank you, Miss York."

"Oh, you don't have to thank me. I'm happy to have you working here. The temp agency has never sent anyone as competent as you. You really are a marvel. In fact, I'm going to call the agency and tell them how pleased I am. You're fast, you're accurate, you're on time. I can't tell you, Becky, what a pleasure it is to work with someone so trustworthy."

Becky blushed and then paled. The doggies, knowing how little she deserved this praise, snapped at her ankles. She thanked Miss York and said good night, picked up her jacket and helmet and put them on and left in the early twilight. On the little motorbike she rattled along the road, her mind elsewhere, when suddenly a bevy of rabbits darted across her path as she came up over the hill. Startled, she swerved to avoid them just before she laid the bike down in the road. She collected herself, cursed the rabbits under her breath and got back on the motorbike. She drove on home to Massacre, wondering what Sexual Scrabble was and how many could play and what you would forfeit if you lost.

Part Two

Dinner with the King of Sweden

Chapter 5

NOVEMBER 1939

*L*ike the unforgiving slap of a metronome, the windscreen wipers scraped back and forth, back and forth. Rain pounded on the roof of the limousine, which slowed, came to a stop at a broad, working dock where battered fishing boats hunkered beside the pilings and gossamer mounds of gillnets beaded brightly. Waverley Scott sat in the plush confines of the backseat beside her mother. Her dark hair had been hand-curled into ringlets that were held back with a soft bow. With her smart little hat and matching maroon coat, the Mary Jane shoes and white stockings, the overall impression created was that of a much younger child. Her gloved hands were pressed against her breasts, which were already too big for someone fourteen.

Her mother pulled a picture postcard from her purse, studied it and said again what a wonderful school this was. Progressive and on an island that was wild and had lots of animals. "You know how you love animals."

Waverley looked away.

The uniformed chauffeur knocked on the window and told Mrs. Scott he would go find the boat and take Waverley's bags on board. She thanked him, but she did not use his name. He was an anonymous hotel chauffeur who had driven them some fifty miles south and over the border from Vancouver.

Her mother held the postcard and read from it. *"Idyllically situated on Useless Point, beautiful Isadora Island in the Puget Sound, Temple School is dedicated to art, to science, to health and the transformation of North American girls into the Women of the Future."* There was a picture of a beautiful structure, high on a green and sloping lawn, boldly facing the Sound, a white house with balconies and broad arbors on either side, wisteria dripping down. The wisteria looked hand-painted, patently false. "Mr. Gerlach says that Miss Westervelt lived in Paris for years, studied there with Isadora Duncan herself. Whoever she is, they named the island after her. Mr. Gerlach says Temple School will suit your artistic temperament, Waverley."

Waverley scoffed through her nose. Before talk of Temple School, no one had ever mentioned Waverley's being artistic. "I know why I'm being banished. I know what's happening."

"Waverley." Her mother elongated her name in a pleading voice.

"I don't look like you, do I?"

She didn't. Her mother was a beauty, a delight to the eye, small and delicately boned, with light brown hair and great blue eyes seeking always some assurance from the world. She had fine-chiseled features and a mouth pursed to please. But Waverley had a big nose, dark hair, dark eyes and a straight seam of a mouth. She was the image of Mr. Gerlach, though she could not think of him as her father. She could not even think of him as her guardian, his official title. She thought of him as someone tall, wreathed in cigar smoke and dressed formally to go down to dinner in any number of hotel dining rooms, Mother on his arm. They went down to dinner and Waverley stayed in her room with her nanny or tutor or whoever they had paid to look after her. That was the way she had lived.

"I admit," her mother faltered, "it might have been easier if you'd been a boy, but it doesn't matter to me. I have loved you always."

"If you loved me, you wouldn't let him send me to this school. It's sending me to prison. Look out there—" She motioned vaguely to the west, to the Sound, where huge black land formations dissolved in the persistent rain. "It's an island and I will be a prisoner."

Rhoda Scott took a different tactic, but resolve fit uneasily in her throat. "You need a formal education, Waverley. Ordinarily we would, that is—you would have been sent to finishing school in Switzerland, but the situation in Europe is so terrible. The Germans marching into Poland, all that nastiness." This was the only word Rhoda could find to describe the Nazi invasions, the only thought she could strum up to suggest the whole of Europe plunging into war. "Mr. Gerlach wants to keep you out of danger."

"I hate you both."

"Why are you being so difficult? Be sweet. Please. You were always so sweet."

"I'm not sweet! I've been well behaved, but I'm not sweet and I won't ever be! I'll make them hate me at this school. I'll get myself kicked out and then you'll be sorry. I'll steal and break things and smoke and get in fights!"

"One day, Waverley," her mother said carefully, gulping back tears and reaching for her hand, "when you are older—"

"Don't do this!" the girl cried. "Don't! Don't tell me I'll understand when I'm older! I understand now. I understand everything! I see everything! How can you live with him like that? It's disgusting! Traveling with him! Sleeping with him!"

"Keep your voice down. What if the chauffeur hears you?"

The girl gave a long jagged laugh. "You think that chauffeur doesn't know? They all know! Every chambermaid and waiter in every hotel! They all know. They know he has a wife! He has other children! You pretend to be his secretary—"

"I am his secretary, Waverley, and you should show a little gratitude. Only out of the goodness of his heart does he allow me to keep you with me while I work. So I think you're being—"

"I am your daughter! Where else should I be, but with you? I am your daughter!" And this thought, and the fact that she would no longer be with her mother but cast amongst strangers, drove her into great sobs and she hammered on the seat with gloved fists and her shoulders shook with anguish.

The chauffeur tapped on the window and Rhoda Scott rolled it down.

"I've found the *Nona York*, Mrs. Scott," he said, ignoring the child. "I'll take the young lady's bags on board and come back for her."

"Thank you." She rolled the window back up and sat silently stroking her daughter's dark silky curls. She did not trust herself to speak. In fact Rhoda had protested Mr. Gerlach's choice of Temple School: so far away from everything and everyone, so remote, so hard to get to and from. And what if Waverley got sick or frightened? He said it was a fine school. Artistic. He said an island was a safe place for a young girl. That was the end of Rhoda's protest. It had never amounted to a quarrel.

Waverley brought her face up out of her hands and wiped her nose with the back of her glove, a gesture calculated to offend. "I will run away. You will never see me again. I will never forgive you." Then she flung herself into Rhoda's lap and cried some more. They cried together.

The chauffeur returned and said the bags were on board. He opened the door and held a huge black umbrella as Waverley and her mother both emerged from the backseat. The rain had wilted Waverley's curls, and Rhoda's marcelled waves drooped and hung over her ears. She started to say a dignified good-bye, but Waverley flung her arms around her mother, clung to her, breathing deep of the familiar brew of Shali-mar and cigarette smoke and the unpleasant damp of her fur coat. Press-ing her, holding her close, Rhoda whispered, made Waverley promise that she would learn a lot, look after her health and hygiene, be good and diligent. Waverley wept *yes yes yes*, without hearing her own voice, hearing only the shred and destruction of her life, knowing she could not forestall this death.

Finally, still weeping, Rhoda stepped back, pulled out a lace hanky and placed it in Waverley's hand. "I must get back to Vancouver. Mr. Gerlach is waiting for me at the hotel. We leave for Toronto this evening." Rhoda Scott got back in the car, her slim legs neatly crossed, her hands folded in her lap.

"What does it matter to me where you are going?" Waverley said by way of farewell.

The chauffeur closed the door, and holding the black umbrella over-head, he escorted the girl all the way down the dock till the limousine was out of sight and she could no longer look back, but must look for-ward, or at least look around her at the various small vessels, ugly tubs most of them, bobbing beside the dock. Men with thin lips and hard faces watched her as they mended nets in the persistent drizzle. The chauffeur pointed down to the end, to a small sturdy craft, paint faded and rust streaks on the hull, which sat low in the water, lashed to the pil-ings. Leaning over the rail, smoking a pipe, a hat pulled low over his eyes and grizzled hair sticking out all around his head, was an old man, rust colored, unshaven, his eyes tiny slits in his face.

"That's the *Nona York*," said the chauffeur, "and that's Captain Briscoe."

"There's been a mistake." Waverley halted. "That can't be the *Nona York*. That can't be the boat I'm supposed to take. My mother cannot want me to get on a boat with that man. He looks like a criminal."

"Everything's arranged." He walked her right up to the *Nona York*, said good-bye, and left with his umbrella.

Waverley stood in the rain. "Are you taking me to the school?"

"Not to the school. *Nona* can't hold the currents around Useless. I'm taking you to Massacre. They're waiting for you at Massacre."

"Massacre?" she strangled out. "Massacre?"

"Massacre, Washington." Captain Briscoe offered her his hand covered in fingerless mittens and said she should get on board.

The *Nona York* smelled terrible. Gradually Waverley identified the overwhelming composite odor as fish, fuel, chickens, and smoke from the captain's pipe. Cheap tobacco. There were wooden boxes of shining dead fish lashed to the railings and perhaps sixteen small crates, cages of noisy chicks lined up along either side of the small roofed cabin. They clucked and chattered under the canvas tarps that protected them from the rain. Captain Briscoe pointed Waverley into the cabin, where a stove offered some warmth and a good deal of smoke. The cabin reeked of diesel, of old clothes and old dog. Wet dog. Rufus, the Captain introduced him. "Say hello, Rufus." Rufus roused, shook himself off, sniffed her up and down, sneezed and padded away. Lines and lanterns, tools hung from hooks, and navigation charts of the San Juan Islands, the Inside Passage, were rolled and stacked nearby. Captain Briscoe told Waverley to have a seat, that it was a rough chop today and it would be a sonofabitching lively journey.

He went below, the dog after him, to start the engine of the *Nona York*, which moaned and shuddered, protested, billowed out a great stink and finally pulled away from the dock, steaming westward into the Sound.

"Lively" did not describe the journey. The pitch and heave of the *Nona York*, the rumble of the engine, the stink of the boat and the smoke and the fish quickly overcame her. She ran outside and vomited violently over the side.

"You'll get used to it," he called out cheerfully.

Waverley doubted this as she threw up again and again, though the purging was finally cathartic. The rain beat down on her bare head (her hat having fallen into the water in the first awful throes of heaving) and drenched her coat and shoes. She kept an eye on Captain Briscoe however. He could murder her, she thought, throw her overboard into the Sound and no one would ever know the difference. Her life or death had no consequence whatever. She felt exactly like those islands she could see in the distance, pulled apart from the greater landmass of her own life, of any life at all, everything she had known, and set adrift, isolated and uncared for.

When at last she'd quit vomiting and stepped gingerly back inside the shelter of the cabin, she kept her distance from Briscoe, just in case he did try to throw her overboard. He asked if she was feeling better. "If you get it all out at once," he counseled, "you're a lot better off."

Even if he was a murderer, Waverley reasoned, he did seem to be right about this. She started to feel better. She watched with some interest as he navigated passages, inlets, where, when he hugged the shore, seals suddenly popped out of the water or roused themselves from the rocks and cried out in their hoarse, coarse shouts of longing. Waverley had never seen a seal except in a zoo. These creatures, unlike those, seemed both to demand and repudiate human contact. Rufus barked back at the seals, looking very pleased with himself. Waverley moved forward with Captain Briscoe for a better view. He said if she liked animals, she'd find lots there. He said the school had a big dog, named Nijinsky after some dancer or another. He said even Isadora Island was named after a dancer, a personal friend of Sophia Westervelt's. When Waverley wasn't impressed, he said he hoped she liked sonofabitching chickens.

They plied the small islands wreathed in fog, clouds settling in great protective necklaces around the tops of thickly forested mountains. The Captain had stories of every one of these, pointing out settlements since abandoned and ghost stories of Indian burial grounds, which he said were especially prevalent on Isadora. Massacre, he said, was haunted, and everyone knew it, and the beach by the school, Sophia's Beach, that was haunted too. Everyone knew it had been a burial ground and spirits still lingered. You could just know it was a sacred place. The Indians had fished these waters forever and made gods of all the elements that balanced their world, the fish, the birds, the sea, the sky, the land. The old gods remained, even if people like the sonofabitching Westervelts ignored them and slavered after money. He pointed out a hillside that had been shaved right down to the ground, and said that now most all the island timberlands belonged to the sonofabitching Westervelts. "And that hill, you see it there, just stubble and stumps? In fifty years there'll be alder and madrona. In a hundred and fifty years, there'll be cedar again and then the Westervelts will come back and tear it down all over again. Only reason Sophia got the land for her school from her pa is that Useless is just that. Useless. No timber, no forage for stock, and the currents are too treacherous for trade or fishing. They got fresh water, though. They got to pump it, but they got water. The land's pretty good, once it was cleared, though not fit for crops. Sophia's got a few apple and pear trees though, and the school's got a garden. Oh yes, they'll have you out in that garden, sure enough, come spring. Temple School grows the best spuds you ever et." He pulled off his woolen cap and stuffed it in a pocket. She noted with some horror that he had only one ear and his skull was creased with scar tissue. "Go have some coffee if your guts are settled now."

Walking with the pitch and roll of the *Nona York* was difficult, but Waverley made her way to the stove at the back of the cabin. She took a cup from the shelf and used a rag for a potholder to unhook the blue enamel pot from brackets that held it to the stove. The coffee looked like sludge and tasted bracingly bitter. She no longer considered Captain Briscoe a potential murderer, and rejoined him. "Can you tell me about the school?" She was belatedly curious. Before now, when her mother or Mr. Gerlach brought it up, she had refused to listen.

"The finest place on the whole Sound, Temple School. In the old days, Sophia had maybe twenty, thirty students, for the Dance on the Green, all wearing little white togas and dancing down the lawn and the music coming off her Victrola. Voices and music, any sound carries over water, you know, and you could hear it miles away. There was some of us, fishers and tugs, boatmen, Indian and white alike, come every year on the summer solstice and we'd just ride anchor around Useless Point to hear the sonofabitching music and watch them girls dancing in their togas. It was a sight. It was that."

"What's a toga?"

"You know, wonna them little loose things, like a sheet tied up at the shoulders. Nothing like it in all the world, Temple School. Looks just like them pitchers of ancient Greece and whatnot. Just takes your sonofabitching breath away, it does. You come on this big white building in the middle of nothing and nowhere, and it takes your breath away. Who spects it? No one. Ain't what it used to be though. Since her pa died, Sophia's had a pile of trouble with sonofabitching Jethro, the brother who's running Westervelt Timber now. Everyone knows Jethro's cut off the money her pa used to give her, or what he hasn't cut off, she doesn't get regular like she used to. Sonofabitch. Jethro's a Westervelt through and through. Sophia, she is just a pearl in a pigpen, if you ask me. Someone musta switched her at birth, that's all any of us can figure. How else could such a lady as her belong to a tribe of pumpsuckers?"

"What's a pumpsucker?"

"A man who'll beat you to death with your own Bible. A man who'll praise God on Sunday, and evict the widow and the orphan on Monday morning, do it for their own sonofabitching good. He'll drink water, damn the devil, steal you blind, smile and know he's right. He'll be in heaven afore you ever get thought of, even if you was to die on the same day."

"Are there pumpsuckers at the school?"

"Sophia Westervelt, she wouldn't tolerate a pumpsucker in a ten-mile radius of her school."

Isadora Island rose up out of the Sound, dominated by a huge brooding mountain in the distance that Captain Briscoe said was only used for logging and threaded by logging roads where the cut timber was loaded up and taken laboriously to the water's edge where it was unloaded, dumped into the Sound, roped up and tugged to a mill on the mainland. The island was not as profitable as some because of the currents at Useless, low tides at Dough Bay and the shallow side of Massacre called Moonless. The sea was hazardous, and the land, especially once you started climbing the mountain, difficult. Mostly fishers and farmers and loggers lived on Isadora. Hardly anyone had a car, but there were some wagons and horses, mules of course. The roads were bad though, and most people boated everywhere they wanted to go, doing day trips by figuring the tides.

Fishers mostly lived near Dog Bay or Massacre. Farmers lived up higher. Loggers all worked for Westervelt. Any fisher or farmer who went bust could be a logger with a day's notice. Westervelt Timber always needed men. But everyone who lived and made their living on Isadora Island got their supplies from Torklund's Marine and Feed. He pointed it out as the *Nona York* pulled slowly landward, coming into Massacre, Washington, a ramshackle arrangement of sagging docks supporting a fleet of fishing boats with names like *Margaret Ann* and *Rose Marie*, where men, nearly as grizzled as the captain, worked, mending nets, or smoked contemplatively and waved the *Nona York* into the small, dirty harbor.

Captain Briscoe jumped off the *Nona York*, secured her to a cleat and offered Waverley his hand while Rufus dashed about the pier, peeing on the pilings. "You go on up to the Marine and Feed," the captain said, over the squawking chicks and the barking dog. "See the Packard out front. That's Sophia's and it's the only sonofabitching Packard in all the islands. You tell Sandy I got the ice and chickens and the fish on board and her radio. I got her new radio crated up and ready too."

"Who?"

"Just ask for Sandy at the Marine and Feed. Go on now, they're waiting for you."

Waverley could still feel the *Nona York* under her feet as she walked up the dock in rain that had diminished to a fine, persistent drizzle. The Marine and Feed, the largest building in Massacre, was a great barn of a place, three stories tall. The Torklunds lived above the emporium; the third floor served for storage. Other frame structures clustered nearby the Marine and Feed, as if comforted by its bulk and presence. All the buildings were clapboarded, paint peeling, and had rusted awnings over the doors of businesses. Signs—barbershop and bathhouse and beer, testifying to a largely male population—were bloated and soggy, as though nothing had been dry here since the beginning of Time. All the roofs were quilted with spongy moss. The few homes had a pointy primness to them, utilitarian and uniformly gray. Aside from the Packard only one other motorized vehicle was visible in Massacre, a 1924 Dodge pickup truck that said MARINE AND FEED on the side. Other than that, there were mules harnessed patiently to wagons and a few horses who dropped great grassy turds, which the rain washed away.

As Waverley left the dock and started up the unpaved street toward town, a thick rind of mud encircled her Mary Janes and sucked at her feet with every step. There were no sidewalks, but doors opened and people stared at her, the barber stropping his razor, a few customers at what was euphemistically called the Isadora Inn. Several of these men, holding beers, called out to each other something about the new student, that Temple School had a new student.

For the first time in her life Waverley Scott wished she had been brought up with some religion. Afraid, uncertain and alone, she longed for some chant or prayer, but she could scarcely even remember the little bedtime ditty taught her by one of her nannies. She began to murmur it now, but since it started with *Now I lay me down to sleep*, it was not equal to the occasion.

She pushed open the double door of the Marine and Feed and stepped into a high-ceilinged space. The place smelled like rope and damp burlap and cardboard, canvas, cheese, oil, pipe smoke, woodsmoke, smoked fish, and people who didn't change their smoky clothes very often. Parallel shelves made long aisles all the way to the back, and customers, bearded men and a few pale hardworking women, stepped out and stared at her. They were grim and wordless. Waverley ducked into an aisle where the shelves held pumps and rubber hoses.

At the back of the emporium, a long counter ran half the length of the store. Mrs. Torklund, a pinched and vinegary woman, knitted and somehow managed at the same time to keep a hand on the till while Mr. Torklund explained the wonders of a particular mousetrap to a middle-aged couple. Behind him a dozen postcards from Hawaii curled in the damp. The Torklunds' son, Nels, was in the navy. Seaman first class on the *Arizona* (as the Torklunds never tired of telling people whose own sons had not done as well). Their daughter, Sis, sat on a high stool working on her homework, chewing alternately on a pencil and then on the end of her blond braid. Sis watched Waverley emerge from the long aisle. No one else paid her any attention.

Sis jumped off the stool and walked round the counter. She was tall, older than Waverley by a couple of years perhaps, with a broad bland face, freckled and attractive. She fingered the lamb's wool collar on Waverley's wet coat. "Is this what they're wearing in New York?"

"I'm not from New York."

"Where are you from?"

Waverley considered this. "Nowhere. Are you Sandy? Captain Briscoe said to tell Sandy—"

"Sandy's a boy. I'm Sis. Sis Torklund."

"I'm Waverley Scott."

"Ah! Waverley!" Her name rang out, and the man who had been so attentive to the wonders of the mousetrap turned and suddenly bounded over to her, took her hand, shook it up and down, introduced himself as Professor Faltenstall of Temple School and husband of Miss Sophia Westervelt without any seeming understanding that a Miss Westervelt would not have a husband. He was balding, flushed and bow-tied. "Oh, you're here at last! We are so happy to see you! We are so looking forward to your coming to our school! Aren't we, dear?"

Sophia Westervelt moved toward Waverley in a more stately fashion. She was a big-boned woman, almost as tall as Professor Faltenstall. She wore the strangest clothes Waverley had ever beheld, a lose tunic of some close woven fabric with a fringe on the bottom and full trousers. Thick wool socks showed at the top of her rubber rain boots. Her hair was cut very short, close to her skull. Her gray hair matched her great gray eyes. She had a thin nose, high forehead and an arresting gaze. She shook hands like a man and said it was such a pleasure to meet her new student.

"Hold out your arms," she commanded Waverley, "out to the sides. Now take a deep breath and pretend, imagine that you can fly. You are a bird, soaring."

Dubious, Waverley looked around the Marine and Feed, but neither Sis Torklund nor her father and mother, nor the Professor, nor anyone in the emporium seemed to think this a peculiar request.

"Close your eyes if it helps," Miss Westervelt advised.

"No one can fly."

"I didn't ask you to fly. I asked you to imagine flying. You must defy Descartes. It's the beginning of wisdom."

Waverley mumbled something dull and her sallow cheeks flushed with embarrassment.

"Of course, it's a long process, learning, practice, discipline, but you must begin somewhere. Why not here?" Miss Westervelt looked around the Marine and Feed as though it were the Coliseum and at any moment the Christians and the lions might converge.

Carefully, so as to avoid the misunderstanding that had thickened the very air, along with the smoking stove, Waverley whispered, "I can't imagine flying."

"This is dire. Truly. We shall have to remedy this. Now—" She took Waverley's arms and held them out from her body. Waverley's coat and hair were so wet she dripped her own little puddle on the floor. "Hold your arms, there, yes, out there and now turn slowly. All the way around. Two or three times."

Waverley did as she was bid.

"Hmmm. You seem to me a syncopated sort of girl, but you do not have the balance or the body of a dancer. Your guardian said you were a dancer."

"Mr. Gerlach? How could he know what I am?"

"And what are you?"

No one had ever asked Waverley this question before. No one had cared, except in low, unkind whispers. I'm Mr. Gerlach's bastard, Waverley wanted to say (for so she had heard herself described by gossiping hotel staff). I have no family at all except for Mother, and I see her maybe three times a day, my favorite being in the evening when she sits at the vanity getting ready to go down to dinner with Mr. Gerlach, screwing earrings into her earlobes and smoking a cigarette while she tries on necklaces and powders her face and puts Shalimar along her shoulders. I have no friends and have never made any. I get sent outside to amuse myself in the hotel garden or dutifully take in the sights with the nanny or the tutor. I have been all over North America, less like a traveler and more like a chess pawn moved from place to place to please or protect other people more important than myself. Everyone is more important than myself. Mr. Gerlach, president of the Allegheny Shipping and Freight Company is the most important of all. My mother and I travel with him everywhere, staying in the finest hotels as he inspects his shipping empires, all along the Great Lakes, the Mississippi, the freight and rail centers in Chicago and Omaha and Denver. Canada too. I remember nothing of these places. But I know when chambermaids are laughing at me, disapproving, though they are poker-faced. My room is always on another floor, but my mother's room is adjacent to Mr. Gerlach's. She is his secretary. She carries a pencil, a pen, paper and takes notes of all his important meetings. She eats with him. She sleeps with him even though there is a Mrs. Gerlach in Pittsburgh. Everyone knows it. Even me. There are Gerlach daughters. Mr. Gerlach detests his wife, but on certain ceremonial occasions he must return to his family. Then Mother and I go to spas in the mountains of North Carolina for the restoration of her health. Mother favors the Grove Park Inn in the hills above Asheville. On New Year's at the Grove Park we always wear funny hats and stare at each other across the table as the hotel orchestra plays "Auld Lang Syne" and Mother smokes. We hardly ever smile. We wait for Mr. Gerlach to return and bring Mother back to life. If you can call it life. I wouldn't. But what do I know? I'm only fourteen.

"I'm fourteen," said Waverley. "That's all I am."

Miss Westervelt put her arm around Waverley's shoulders and drew her toward the stove in the corner of the Marine and Feed. "You are more than the sum of fourteen years, Waverley. You may count on that. Now, you dry out by the stove. We're almost finished and then we'll take you to the barbershop and get your hair cut—"

"My hair cut?"

"Of course. All Temple girls have sensible, healthful haircuts. Like mine." Miss Westervelt gave a brief affectionate tussle to her own incredibly short gray hair.

"But your hair is cut like a man's."

"Women are also allowed healthy hair," she declared. "Then we'll go to Temple School and get you out of those foolish clothes."

"What's wrong with my clothes?" She fingered the lamb's wool trim on the expensive maroon coat. "My mother bought them in Chicago. They're fashionable and useful."

"Nothing is fashionable *and* useful," declared Miss Westervelt. "Besides, look at them. They constrict you at every turn. Constriction and congestion are the great enemies of freedom. At Temple School, the first rule is freedom. Without freedom there can be no discipline. Without discipline there can be no discovery. Without discovery there can be no achievement. Without achievement there can be no advancement. Form follows function and transformation lies within the reach of all."

She returned to the counter with Professor Faltenstall to consider the merits of the mousetrap.

Standing by the stove, Waverley grew so warm she could all but feel her coat start to steam. Then through the swinging doors leading to the back came a boy pushing a wheelbarrow piled high with cans of peaches. Perhaps he was not a boy. He was certainly older than Waverley. He was tall and broad-shouldered, with dark hair and hazel eyes, wide against his pale skin. He wore a moth-eaten sweater too big for him. "Are you the new student?"

Waverley nodded. "Are you Sandy?"

"Yes. So, the *Nona York*'s down at the dock?"

"Yes. The Captain says he has your chickens and fish and your ice and the radio."

"Not mine. The school's. I'll be bringing them out to the school along with your bags later on."

"How much later on?"

"It won't matter. You won't be wearing anything you brought with you. None of the girls do." He pushed his wheelbarrow to the end of one of the long aisles where he began building a pyramid of canned peach tins, working with the concentration and intensity of a man building a bridge.

Suddenly in Marine and Feed a woman's voice rang out. "I seen it! I seen that goddamned Packard! Where are you, you murdering bastards! Where!"

She burst through the aisles, her gait awkward because she wore men's galoshes, unfastened, and they flapped around her ankles like panting dogs. She was hatless, her fists raised, and she lurched toward the counter where Mr. Torklund, mousetrap in hand, might have leapt over and stopped her, but his wife's hand stayed him.

"Ma! Ma!" Sandy implored, coming up behind her. She struggled against her son and went toward Professor Faltenstall, who had stepped in front of Sophia, his great girth protecting her.

"Thank you, Newton, for your sense of intervention, your gallantry," said Miss Westervelt. She emerged from behind her husband and stood shoulder to shoulder with him. "But I am not afraid of Mrs. Lomax. She is misguided, that's all."

"You murdering bastards killed my husband and cheated me out of my rightful claim and no one on this island will raise a voice against the goddamned Westervelts. No one! No one! No one will help Bessie Lomax." She wept and sagged against her son. Then she looked up and saw Waverley. Bessie's eyes narrowed and her whole expression knit into a knot at her mouth. She wriggled out of Sandy's grip and advanced toward the stove. "You're the new student, aren't you? Well, you oughta know you're living with murderers."

Waverley looked wildly past Bessie Lomax, hoping that Professor Faltenstall would leap in to protect her, but Bessie bore down. "Hector was coming home, it was a Friday night and he was coming home—" She stopped and turned evilly to the people in the store, who were watching, not horrified, just interested. "I don't care what any of you bastards think, Hector Lomax was on his way home. He was going to get into the truck with the last load of logs to come down the mountain, but no, they tell him, no, there's no room for my Hector in the cab. No, Mr. Westervelt's lickspittle foreman, he has to ride in the cab, don't he?" She jabbed her index finger into Waverley's chest, pressing her back closer to the stove. Her breath was thick with alcohol and plumed in front of Waverley's face. Her teeth were brown and little bits of saliva flew. "So he says to Hector, get on top! Go on! Get on up top of them logs on the truck, Hector, and tie yourself there and you ride downhill! You hang on! Like it was funny, he said it. You know how I know all this? There was a regular inquisition, not here in Useless, but over at Friday Harbor, but what's it matter? Everyone in the San Juans they lick the feet of the Westervelts, they—"

"Ma." Sandy reached for her shoulder, but she flung him off.

"So my Hector"—she jabbed Waverley again—"gets up on the top of the log truck and ties himself to one of the trees and they're coming down the good logging road, fifty miles an hour and—there's this low-hanging branch and—" She made a swoop across her neck. She was nose to nose with Waverley. "It tore off his head. That's the fact of it. Clean off. Tore his head off his neck!"

Waverley, to her own horror, could all but see the blood, the flying projectile of Hector Lomax's head, the inert body still tied to the logs, the truck screeching to a halt. She shivered to dispel the terrible vision. "That's t-t-t-terrible."

"That's murder! Murder." Bessie's voice reached a high keening wail. "Hector went to his death without a prayer. Not a chance to ask the Lord forgiveness for his sins."

"Ma—" Sandy tried to hold her. "It was a swift death, Ma. He never felt any pain."

"But I feel pain!" she wailed again and again. "And then you know what they done? Huh? Do you know?"

"No," Waverley admitted.

"Those murdering Westervelts, they said it was all his own fault. Said Hector was up there against regulations and he was drunk and the company ain't going to pay the Lomaxes a goddamn penny." She swiveled and pointed a long finger at Sophia. "You murdered Hector and now you want to starve us, me and my son—"

"Ma, no one's starving," Sandy protested.

Sis Torklund slid around the counter. "You are so right, Bessie." Sis put her arm around Bessie. Sandy stepped back, away from his mother, and cast Sis a look of inexpressible gratitude. "They are, all of those Westervelts, dogs, Bessie, and no son of yours will ever work for the Westervelts again."

"Never. Oh, Sis, you understand, donchu? Oh Sis!"

"Hector Lomax was a good man. A good father and a good husband."

"Yes, yes he was, Sis. You know that's true."

"Course I do. And you miss him. We all miss him, don't we, Sandy?" Sis regarded Sandy, who nodded while she went on about Hector Lomax. A good man, steady man, who didn't drink but now and then, who wasn't foolhardy, only brave. Very brave. A charming man. Good to Bessie. He died in vain. Sis lured Bessie out of the Marine and Feed with the promise of a hot drink at home.

A farmer in the emporium chuckled, and turned to his wife. "She didn't say what kind of drink, did she?"

Sandy gave the man a look of tired aggravation, but he said nothing.

"That Sis," declared her father, "she can handle anything. She could wrestle the devil to the ground."

"And one day she will," retorted his wife sourly as she put away the mousetraps. "When you finish with stacking them peaches, Sandy," she called out, "you can collect the school's order and put it in the truck."

Sandy returned to building his pyramid of peach cans, but he bent under the task, and Sophia Westervelt, on her way to the door, touched his shoulder.

Professor Faltenstall paused as well. "You'll keep the chicks sheltered won't you, Sandy? Keep them in the cab of the truck? They mustn't get chilled." Sandy nodded, but he looked drained. "Come, Waverley," cried the Professor, "we're ready!"

Waverley was not at all certain she was ready, thank you, but she followed them out of the emporium. They all three dashed along the muddy street till they came to the barbershop. Sophia introduced her to Mr. Hulbert, a dapper man with a walleye and a waxed mustache and a dirty smock. He had a chair all ready for the new student. He gave it an extra dust off.

By the time Mr. Hulbert had finished cutting Waverley's hair, perhaps half a dozen islanders had come into the barbershop, some just to have a look at her, others, men who reeked of fish and diesel, for a shave. Captain Briscoe himself came in, had a merry conversation with Miss Westervelt and Professor Faltenstall while he was waiting. Waverley had never heard anyone use the term "sonofabitching," much less in the presence of a lady, but oddly Miss Westervelt took no offense. She patted Rufus, who nuzzled her feet.

"Well now!" exclaimed Captain Briscoe when Waverley's curls had been brutally shorn and she felt all around cold and naked. "That's a fine haircut. I'll have one of those myself, Edwin!" He sat down in the chair, removing his hat but not his pipe.

Miss Westervelt and Professor Faltenstall bid him an affectionate good-bye, cheerily told Edwin to put the haircut on the school's bill and ushered Waverley into the pouring rain. They made a quick sprint to the waiting Packard where the professor gallantly opened the back door for Waverley. He got in behind the wheel, Sophia beside him, her arm draped casually over the back of the seat, her hand resting on his shoulder.

"You mustn't mind Sandy's mother," she said to Waverley. "Her telling of that story isn't altogether accurate. In fact, most of it is out-right rot. There was an inquiry at Friday Harbor and it was found that Hector Lomax was indeed very drunk, that any number of people, including the foreman, tried to talk him down off the logs, but he wouldn't hear of it. Nonetheless, I still believe the company should have paid her something. I even wrote a letter to my brother, Jethro, protesting their treatment of the Lomaxes. That was probably an error. I probably did more harm than good."

"You tried, dear," Newton Faltenstall soothed as he bounced out of Massacre. The Isadora roads had been wrested from the land, trees torn up, gravel thrown down, rain-rutted mud paths that required the car to rock sometimes to move forward. Progress would come though, Newton assured Waverley. One day Isadora would have ferry service, he was certain of it.

Miss Westervelt laughed at the very idea of ferry service for Isadora. Then she turned to Waverley. "Have you heard much about our school?"

"No, Miss Westervelt."

"You must call me Sophia. All the students do."

"Yes, Sophia."

"Newton likes to be called Professor Faltenstall, but all the girls call him Quizzer. You'll find out why."

"Now, dear, I only quiz in the interest of mental acuity and to strengthen the students' brain waves."

"You will find our school unlike any other you have ever been to."

"I have never been to school, not really. I've been tutored though. I know lots of things. I can recite the times tables up through twelve." Ordinarily Waverley expected to be commended for this achievement and then commanded to do just that, recite the twelve times tables, but instead, Sophia laughed, peeling laughter, genuine and uncolored by irony or condescension

Newton, laughing too, explained. "Math as it actually applies to this world, as it relates to building, to physics, to chemistry, to science, that's fine. Excellent. But the twelve times tables? Math for math's sake?" He chuckled heartily. "Nothing could be so far from desirable. Math is no different than science or art. It must be put to use to be valuable. It must be used to fathom. *Fathom* is my particular favorite word lately."

"Newton has many and they all connect."

"*Fathom* implies depth, a deeper understanding. You see?"

Waverley did not, but apparently it didn't matter, as Sophia and the Professor rattled on, speaking a weird and unintelligible language, words and phrases wholly foreign, though presumably English. Waverley understood almost nothing, but she agreed with everything. She bounced around in the backseat as the Packard lurched and rocked along the rutted road, and she wished Professor Faltenstall would keep his eyes ahead and not turn so often to talk to her. He was not a very good driver and the roads were very narrow, scarcely more than ditches.

Professor Faltenstall and Sophia extolled at great length the school's avant-garde curriculum, and the achievements of their four resident artists. The Austin-Smythes taught flute and cello (. . . *marvelous musicians. The finest in all Winnipeg. Duets—oh, duets to make you weep. They had been part of the All-Alberta Chamber Orchestra . . .*). Morton Dahlgren taught art (. . . *exhibited in Chicago and Duluth, three years in a row. Not perhaps the most daring of painters, but thoroughly grounded. A fine sense of line and color . . .*). Agnes Kauffman taught voice (. . . *she comes to us from the Denver Opera Company and what an outstanding soprano! Oh, to hear Agnes sing Mozart! Verdi! Bizet!*). They went on about the many successes, rattling off names that meant nothing to Waverley. References to music and art and literature were flung about the Packard, allusion to tides, and True Foods, progress, tempo and defying Descartes. Their words were almost incomprehensible, but their voices lulled her and she nodded off, despite the rough ride, rousing only at the sound of her own name. She opened her eyes to see both of them looking at her, asking her something that she had failed to understand.

"No one reads Scott anymore," said Newton, returning his attention, mercifully, to the road.

"He's very passé, of course. One outgrows him," replied Sophia, "but we have a whole set of the Waverley novels in the library. Red leather bindings. Marble endpapers. Long red ribbons to keep your place. Your mother must have adored Sir Walter Scott."

"My mother?" she asked.

"Well, that's your name, isn't it? Waverley Scott." Sophia turned her head to smile. "She named you after Sir Walter Scott's novels, didn't she?"

In fact Rhoda Scott scarcely read anything more taxing than *Photoplay*. She would not have known Sir Walter Scott if he had leapt out of her cocktail glass. Waverley had got her name because she was supposed to be a boy, because her mother was so unprepared for a girl, she had not secured so much as a pink bootie, much less a girl's name. In giving Mr. Gerlach a son, Rhoda would give him what his wife could not. Mr. Gerlach already had girls. Girls were redundant. A boy would have been named for Mr. Gerlach. A boy would have secured rights and privileges, adoration, affection no one else had.

To have her inconvenient baby Mrs. Scott had gone to a small, exclusive private hospital in the mountains near Asheville, North Carolina, and when the baby arrived, the mother was so disappointed in its sex she wept openly and did not want to hold her. When finally Rhoda telephoned Mr. Gerlach with the news, she was unable to conceal her own chagrin and failure. She asked if he had a suggestion for a name. He did not. He had to go. He was busy. Rhoda put down the phone. In the small hospital library, she saw the Waverley novels, all thirty or so of them. Beautifully bound, she later told Waverley, with thick paper and looking complete and unto themselves there. She said she was struck because the name was the same as their name, Scott. (The late, mythical Mr. Scott, however, was so very vague a personage as to suggest smoke or shadow or mere good intentions.)

"My mother needed a name," said Waverley bluntly, wondering what the truth would finally taste like. It felt funny and foreign on her tongue, like a great chocolate toffee. "She took the name off the books. She never read them. She wanted a son. She was so certain she would have a boy, she didn't even bother with a girl's name."

"Well then, your mother must be a great booby," commented Professor Faltenstall to Waverley's complete surprise.

Sophia concurred. "She ought to have been delighted to have a girl. From what I know of men—Newton aside, of course, dear—boys are a lost cause."

"Boys are a vile lot," Professor Faltenstall said. "Give a girl half a chance, a good education, physical exercise, opportunity and a diet of True Foods and she will outperform a boy every time. Girls will save the world. And of course, at Temple School we have a unique curriculum and regimen to give girls these chances. We school our girls to equate form and function, to effect transformation."

"At our school," said Sophia, "you will be educated to have dinner with the King of Sweden."

Waverley, not at all certain what a king would be doing on Isadora Island, asked, "Does he come here often?"

"One has dinner with the King of Sweden in Stockholm when one wins the Nobel Prize."

"What's that?"

They both turned to her, amazed. Newton shook his head and concentrated on his driving. Sophia waxed on about the Nobel Prize. "Awarded to honor the best and most lasting achievements in the world."

"Not always," Newton corrected her. "After all, Sinclair Lewis won in literature."

"Yes, and he writes like a goat. So, of course there is the occasional error, but never mind. Our point is that our girls are educated to make lasting contributions, to be amongst the best, the very finest, to win the Nobel Prize."

"Can girls win the Nobel Prize?"

"Girls can't. Women can, and have. Women of the future most certainly will. At Temple School we will be educating you, grooming you to be a North American Woman of the Future."

Waverley settled back against the Packard's plush embrace and imagined herself grooming for dinner with the King of Sweden, sitting at the vanity and screwing in her earrings and dabbing Shalimar along her shoulders; she was lovely, naturally, self-possessed, accomplished, trying on one necklace after another. She fell asleep with this pleasant picture. The rain relented and a swift dusk descended and mist floated up from the fields as the road wound westward toward Useless.

Chapter 6

The King of Sweden wafted over Temple School, ever present, ever vigilant. He hovered in the muraled practice room where Sophia taught Music into Movement, in the music room where the Austin-Smythes taught flute and cello, in the art room where Morton Dahlgren taught the elements of watercolor, in the dining room, which (now that there were so few students) served as Agnes Kauffman's classroom for voice. He occupied the library where literature and history were taught. The King of Sweden lurked in the garden and roosted in the poultry yard, where, under Newton's supervision and according to his theories, the girls maintained a flock of leghorns. He lingered over Newton's labs, outbuildings near the chicken houses where Newton magnetized water and conducted brain tests by placing on his students' heads little crowns of lights and wires to ascertain whose brain could stimulate the most current. Waverley sometimes pictured the King of Sweden, stout, jowly, short-legged, clad in royal blue, his crown gleaming, his expression dismal, the king deeply saddened because none of these errant girls would ever come to dinner. The king knew all too well their failings. How could he not? The King of Sweden was called upon to prod, to point to their every deficiency. His name was invoked in cases of bad manners, nail biting, movement poorly executed, for unswept chicken houses and uncandled eggs, for uncollected specimens and failure to grasp the principles of physics, natural selection, the poetry of Keats, the genius of Byron, the import of Debussy and the inability to reach high C, for faulty handwriting, beds left unmade, uncertain hygiene.

Waverley sometimes thought she could see the King of Sweden frowning at her when her attention wandered away from Sophia and up to the library ceiling beams where the school's mottoes were emblazoned in bold gold letters, one motto for each of the six beams, abstract injunctions to greatness. Some more abstract than others. *Form Is to Function as God Is to Nature*. What did that mean? *See the Unseen, Hear the Unspoken*. What was that about? When she actually asked Sophia (who was unduly fond of metaphor) Waverley didn't understand the answer, though she nodded sagely throughout the ten-minute disquisition and tried to look enlightened.

In the library-classroom, the six students' desks lined up in a semicircle facing the front. (The arc was Sophia's favored geometric configuration.) Sophia taught history and literature as well as Music into Movement, and she stood before a great map of Europe and the huge new radio that had come over on the *Nona York*. Gleaming in its wooden case and newly installed, the radio sat there like a wheezing god, making shrieks and squeals and pulling in, finally, a crackling signal from Vancouver. On this radio, every afternoon they listened to the war news from Europe, and each day students in pairs took turns moving the pushpins across the map. Black for the Germans, red for the British, blue for the French. Sophia took the War very seriously.

"As long as there is war," Sophia had informed the students, "we will endeavor to understand history, the past, by fathoming the present. These are dire and perilous times, girls."

"I thought we didn't care about Europe," said Marjorie, a chubby, ungainly student with a great moon of a face and a sweet nature. "I thought Europe was full of people gagging on sausage."

"North American Women of the Future live with a spirit of inquiry and make every attempt to understand the world they live in, Marjorie," Sophia reminded her.

Waverley tried to think of Marjorie by name and not as the fat one. The other students were easy enough to remember. The one with the long neck was Florence. Violet wore little round glasses, her jaw slack, her listless eyes downcast. Ginevra had a heart-shaped face, a widow's peak and a perpetually wistful expression. There was no mistaking Irene, who was imperious, beautiful, older than the rest, and especially hateful to Waverley. The others all followed Irene's lead, cool unto hostile. But since Waverley had lived most of her life in the company of people who didn't especially like her, and except for her mother demonstrated no fondness for her whatever, the other students' chill neither eroded her confidence nor broke her heart, though this was undoubtedly their intent. She rubbed her hand over her short-cropped hair and tried to care about Poland.

Irene's hostility to the newcomer was clear from the beginning, that very first night. Irene had led her to the room that Sophia had decreed they would share. Irene had taken a piece of chalk from her tunic and drawn a line down the middle of the floor. "Don't cross that line. Ever. Or you'll be sorry. Understand?"

Waverley nodded. The two sides were exactly the same: narrow bed, prim dresser, desk with a lamp, and a basket for dirty clothes. There were no pictures and everything was in its place.

"What did you do to get sent here?" Irene sat cross-legged on her bed, pulled out a mirror from under the pillow and studied her face, pulling and tugging at her skin.

"What are you doing?" asked Waverley.

"I'm looking for old-age deposits, mineral deposits from Untrue Foods if it's any of your business, which it's not. I'll ask the questions. Now, everyone gets sent here for some reason, some punishment. What did you do?"

"Nothing." Except breathe and be, she thought. "Mr. Gerlach chose it."

"Who's he?"

"My guardian."

"Don't you have parents?"

"Just my mother."

"I suppose you'll be crying all night for her."

"I don't think so. I would be very surprised if I did."

"Well, just don't keep me awake."

Waverley tested the bed. "What did you do?"

"What?"

"To get sent here. You said everyone here was being punished."

"I spent the night in a New York hotel room with a man. I am not a virgin. I have experienced sexual intercourse. I have known what it is to love a man, to see him naked. My family sent me here to this godforsaken island to separate me from my lover. He adores me."

Waverley considered all this for a moment. "What did the others do?"

Surprised at how little reaction her scandalous declaration had evoked, Irene continued in her haughty way. "Violet wanted to be a nun. Her family thought it was fine she was at Catholic school, but when she started talking nun, they shipped her off. Marjorie is fat and ugly and retarded, as you can see. No one wants her around. Ginevra is the bastard brat of someone or another, I forget who, and Florence's mother was a Temple alumni. She graduated back in the days when this school was really something, back when there were thirty or forty students and scads of resident artists and lots of money, back in the beginning when the school first opened. I suppose you got the picture postcard—*Temple School on beautiful Isadora Island*—something like that."

"Yes."

"They've used the same picture, the same come-on for twenty years. I suppose you heard something about artists and music! And painting! And all that?" Irene sounded bemused.

"Yes."

She gave a trilling laugh. "I don't suppose it said that there's only five of us now, six with your sorry presence, and we have to do the work that twenty used to do. Didn't say that, did it? Oh, no. When Florence's mother went here, they had whole bunches of girls and staff and teachers. Now, there's just us. I wrote my parents, I said, you really want me here, cleaning out chicken coops? You really think it helps me be educated to look at Morton Dahlgren's ugly mug three times a week?"

There was a short silence till Waverley asked what her parents had said.

"They said they were just sure Temple School was the very place for me. They hate me." She put the mirror down. "I told them Mr. Austin-Smythe made an indecent overture to me. Really indecent."

"That's awful."

"It was a lie, of course. Mr. Austin-Smythe wouldn't recognize an indecent overture if he pulled it out of his own sphincter. Then I said I was sick. Really sick. Did they know the only medical man on this island is a vet? That's right. If you get sick, Dr. Oland, the vet, comes to look at you! And he drinks!"

"It sounds terrible."

"It is terrible. You're going to hate it here."

"I already do."

"Good. Just don't snivel and weep all night." Irene turned out the lights and got into bed, leaving Waverley to unpack and get undressed in the dark.

"What is a resident artist? I didn't quite understand when Sophia and the Professor were telling me."

"That's because you're stupid. The resident artists fornicate, masturbate, intoxicate, play bridge and smoke cigarettes most of the time. Sometimes they pretend to teach. Now if you're going to share a room with me, you'd better learn to shut up."

"Irene?"

"Don't say that! I hate my name."

"I hate my name too," Waverley confided. "Sophia tells me I have to read all of the Waverley novels in the library in honor of my name. There's about thirty Waverley novels and they're all a thousand pages."

"Shut up. I had this room to myself before you came, so you can imagine just how I feel about you." She farted resolutely.

"Why do we have to share a room anyway? There are lots and lots of bedrooms up here."

"Because Sophia believes you can only learn to live with other people by doing it. You know, Learn by Doing."

The very next day Waverley read *Learn by Doing* on a library ceiling beam. This was a good deal easier to understand than *Form Is to Function as God Is to Nature,* and not nearly as stern as *Waste Not Thy Hour.*

Nearly every Waste-Not-Thy hour in the day was accounted for. And for a place dedicated to freedom from tradition, the liberation of the intellect through art and science, the overthrow of constraint through expression, Temple School ran on an absolutely disciplined schedule that would have pleased the King of Sweden. The students were up each morning at six, performed their ablutions, made their beds and gathered in the kitchen with clean hands, clean nails, clean faces, dressed in the school uniform: tunic, trousers, wool socks and sandals. They sat with Sophia and Quizzer at the oval table in the center of the spacious kitchen and ate a breakfast prepared the night before by the school cook, Mrs. Foltz.

Along with the housekeeper, Mrs. Huey, Mrs. Foltz (both wives of fishers) rode over from Massacre every morning in the Hueys' old Model A. They arrived when they damned well felt like it. They always said the roads were bad, which was true. After the breakfast dishes were cleaned up, and a broom wafted over a few rooms and a dozen potatoes put in to bake for lunch (all school meals, True Foods, were bland, monotonous fare) Foltzy and Huey—monuments of inefficiency, both of them—spent most of the day in the laundry shed. In a haphazard fashion they put clothes through the wringer while smoking cigarettes (which were forbidden inside Temple School) and discussing the shortcomings of their husbands and children. Labor was scarce on Isadora and few people had the means, a vehicle, to get them all the way out to Useless, so of necessity Sophia tolerated their lapses.

But she gave her students no such leeway. Their days were disciplined: classes, practice, meals, leisure, chores, everything regularly scheduled, though she had been known to syncopate the schedule for what she called "natural causes." Particularly sunny weather, for instance, that would call for syncopation. Particularly snowy weather. But never particularly rainy weather, as that was the norm. Especially low tides meant that Newton needed more time syncopated for science and nature. The equinoxes and solstices, these called for reflection and celebration, and syncopation, holidays in lieu of the ordinary ones. Temple School did not recognize Christmas, Easter, Passover. Sophia would have none of it.

"I started this school to educate North American women, to bring forth a generation of leaders who were not steeped in prejudicial tripe and inherited bile," Sophia explained. She and Waverley walked the halls of the school, Sophia wafting her personal, peculiar scent, something fresh and woody. Waverley breathed deep and listened. "That's why we do not celebrate traditional holidays. We despise tradition. You will find no missionaries amongst Temple alumnae." Sophia pointed to certain outstanding students in the framed photographs that lined the walls. These earlier girls, Florence's mother amongst them, were all in togas, poised, posed, their limbs gracefully arranged, their expressions serious, their eyes on the future. Sophia explained that she regarded her students as beacons of her vision, each unique, and worthy. Some more worthy than others.

Waverley peered into the faces of the alumnae in the grainy photographs, trying to discern those qualities that distinguished them.

Sophia pointed to a solemn-faced, toga-clad girl and told Waverley this girl had grown up to be a well-known philanthropist, and then, farther along, there was a newspaper woman, an author and a poet among these long-ago girls. "Never say poetess," cautioned Sophia, "nor authoress, nor any of those demeaning diminutives. They sound affectionate, but they are the very bitterest denunciation. They reek of subjection, of women made from the rib of a man, and so, a lesser being. Fight such dogma, Waverley, always. If ever you hear of an authoress, ask that person, ah, does she write for a readeress?"

"I don't know, Sophia. I've never heard of a readeress."

"And with good reason. There isn't any such thing. Why not just have teacherettes? How would you like to be a studentess?"

"Never, Sophia," declared Waverley, having now got the hang of the discussion. "A North American Woman of the Future would never consent to that. I am going to be a teacher, like you."

Sophia smiled and said that Temple would one day be famous for the teachers and reformers it produced. She brought her level, gray-eyed gaze to another framed photograph and pointed out a Temple student who was a famous birth control advocate. "Reform must come from the North Americans. Even without this terrible war, this new war, it's obvious that Europe must, shall sink of its own tragic weight. Oh, I admit, there was a time when Paris was the center of the universe. A transforming experience, I don't deny it. I was there. Isadora Duncan! Gertrude and Alice! Pablo Picasso! Juan Gris! Apollonaire! Denis Aron! I was able to breathe the very air of these artists, Waverley! They advanced human understanding with every piece they wrote or painted, with every day they lived. But that is all the past." Sophia paused in front of a set of pictures, all featuring a single Temple student whose limbs were so stylized, her expression so intense, she looked as though she might leap out of the frame. "That is Lydia Fraser. One of our best students. Lydia now teaches Delphic Dance at the most prestigious girls' school in Philadelphia, Miss Butler's. Look at Lydia Fraser and you can see Isadora Duncan's tragic mistake."

All Waverley saw was a narrow-shouldered girl with a pointed chin and a magnificent forehead.

"Isadora should have used her genius to teach North American girls how to transform Music into Movement. Isadora Duncan was an American. She was from California, Waverley. Imagine that. A Girl of the Golden West. She should have opened her schools here. But no, she took her genius to Europe. How could those European students possibly absorb what she had to teach? From the beginning, her task was impossible. They were freighted, weighted, made leaden by religion, history and tradition. They could never Express! Emote! As Lydia Fraser could Express! Emote!"

"Has Lydia had dinner with the King of Sweden, Sophia?"

"Alas, not yet. None of my students have yet. But there will come a day. . . ." Sophia rested her hand on Waverley's shoulder as though surely she would fulfill her hopes, though nothing was said. Sophia, always sparing in her praise, drew from Waverley the passionate wish to be worthy. A compliment from Sophia was the sweeter for its being so rare.

Newton Faltenstall, on the other hand, slathered praise and recognition, rained joy on every student endeavor. Newton Faltenstall questioned and exhorted and complimented his students, everything in excess. Newton was indiscriminate in his zest for teaching, for learning, for life and health and science. He never rested. He tested their brains for creative impulses transformed into current, and he magnetized water for the relief of pain. He dedicated his life to teaching his theories, and writing his book, still in progress, the great tome *The North American Life-Enhancing and Perfecting Diet of True Foods*. If Newton's practices were followed (as they strenuously were at Temple School) no student need ever die of disease. Indeed, following a regimen of True Foods and Double-Range Breathing, you could avoid debility, senility, pain, disease, and die only when you felt like it.

Moreover, and in keeping with his theories and his scientific principles (streamline, distill, simplify), he believed that students could comprehend all science using only two instruments: the telescope for the unseen cosmos, the microscope for the unseen particulars. He had the girls spit into a petri dish, let it grow for a few days and see on a tiny slide what teemed within them. They were revolted to see squirming germs.

He believed his students could fathom all nature by growing a vegetable garden, by understanding the accumulating tides and the eliminating tides, by raising poultry. He had limitless faith in chickens.

He had earned the name Quizzer because he was in the habit of stopping a student any time of the day or night, on her way to the library or the music room, the practice room, or even the bathroom for that matter, and in his curious way pause, his index finger pointing heavenward, as though testing the wind for knowledge, and demand: What is Rule 44 of the *North American Life-Enhancing and Perfecting Diet of True Foods*? Or, what fourteen things are on the List of Nevers? (Also a feature of the diet.) How does Double-Range Breathing prohibit pneumonia and stop tuberculosis? Sometimes he would ask who wrote a particular piece or book or poem that tumbled into his head at that very moment. He would recite random lines and ask, Who wrote that? Sometimes he knew the answer. Sometimes he didn't, and he told the student she must look it up and write it down. When the student reported back to him with an answer, his face would flush with pleasure at her genius.

One morning he snagged Waverley in the hall, pulled from his pocket a tiny packet, strange and suspended by a string, and demanded that Waverley tell him what it was.

Waverley peered more closely. "It's a tea bag, Professor."

"Oh, Waverley! Waverley! You've been here for two whole months!" he despaired, "and you still have not grasped the fundamentals?" At that moment Ginevra was walking by, and he stopped her, dangled the tea bag in front of her and asked what it was.

"That is a packet of paralysis, incontinence and death, Professor! Rule 14." Ginevra gave Waverley a superior smirk and moved on.

"Excellent. Now, Waverley, you know that tea is on the List of Nevers, don't you?"

"Yes, Professor."

"Well, then, go in the library and look the rest up and write them down."

This phrase, Look It Up and Write It Down, was not on the library ceiling beams, but it might as well have been. Sophia and Newton used it all the time. More often than not, when Waverley did go into the library to look up or write down, she was distracted by all the books, and forgot what she was supposed to look up. She pondered instead one of the school's mottoes on the ceiling beams: *Fear Nothing Save Ignorance, Untruth, Ugliness.*

The meaning of this strange phrase only gradually emerged as Waverley adjusted to the school's peculiar speech. An entirely separate language, so it seemed to Waverley, constructions that refused euphemism but embraced metaphor. Euphemism was rubbish, rot, and Temple students were forbidden the obvious *pee, poo* and *tinkle.* Curiously, though, while Sophia, Newton, and the students referred to bodily processes with the words *urinate, constipate, fornicate, menstruate,* and the same for body parts, they metaphorically described evacuating the temple. To defecate. The body was a temple. But women routinely had vaginas and men were encumbered with penises. Everyone had a rectum and a sphincter. Thus, ignorance, untruth and ugliness were negated, avoided altogether, and there was no profanity. In fact the whole notion of profanity was laughed off at Temple School because according to Professor Faltenstall, profanity resulted from congestion of the stomach and could be cured by diet. Any student overheard suffering from congestion of the stomach was immediately put on the antiprofanity diet. This cured her.

"How can the body be anything but beautiful?" Sophia asked Waverley as they strolled through the garden one afternoon. The school grounds were no longer immaculately maintained, nor much maintained at all, but still one could turn the unsuspected corner and come upon statuary, always nude. Sophia paused in front of Mercury, a god perhaps, but a man in every feature, save for the little wings at his feet. "He is beautiful, isn't he?"

Waverley would ordinarily have been embarrassed to comment on the contours of his perfect body, but in growing into the Temple curriculum, she said yes, he was beautiful.

"We have bodies in order to use them," counseled Sophia. "What is sexual intercourse but a means to transform men and women from solitary vessels into units of mutual responsibility and affection?"

Waverley wondered momentarily if this is what sexual intercourse had done for her mother and Mr. Gerlach, but they seemed so long away

and far ago, so distant and diminished in time that she could barely remember, nor scarcely imagine them.

Given the war in Europe, Mr. Gerlach spent the holidays in Ottawa
renegotiating shipping contracts. His secretary stayed with him. So Waverley did not see—and did not miss—her mother at Christmas. Temple
School did not recognize Christmas but celebrated instead the winter
solstice, not the dark, but the coming of the light.

In the school kitchen with Sophia and Quizzer and Nijinsky, the
dog, Waverley helped prepare the True Foods feast. Sandy Lomax delivered ice that day, fish, coal and flour and agreed to stay for a celebratory
meal before returning to Massacre. In the school kitchen amidst the
good smells, the geniality, the warmth, Waverley held her cup of mulled
bran-ade in her hands and smiled. The Victrola on the shelf offered up
tinny waltzes, and later, Quizzer stood and recited "The Convergence of
the Twain," and Sandy sang "The Minstrel Boy," and promised to teach
Waverley, who knew no songs at all. Sophia got them all laughing
through a round "Sur le pont d'Avignon," and their voices counter-
pointed the Indian ghosts moaning in the Useless trees. Everything else
flowed away on an eliminating tide.

Chapter 7

She had grown into the freedoms of the school uniform and out of the clothes she had brought with her. Waverley liked not having to fuss with her hair, which was only slowly curling back in. Good weather or bad, she loved to take Nijinsky down to the beach, just the two of them, where she flung sticks endlessly and Nijinsky happily retrieved. The otters never minded her, just came out to play as if she were not even there. She knelt down on the rocks to adore the nudibranches, limpets, sea stars and other low-tide life. Quizzer had taught her these wonderful names and Waverley recited them like poetry.

Slowly too, the other students warmed to Waverley, the painfully shy Marjorie, myopic Violet, the prim Florence and pretty, vacant Ginevra. She even elicited words of comfort from Irene one afternoon when Dahlgren had stood before Waverley's easel, frowning at her still-life and muttering. Waverley's use of color, perspective, relationship, form, volume, everything was off. "Look at that still life," Morton carped, "it's supposed to be still, Waverley, not dead."

Despite the school's fearless attitude toward the body, Morton preferred the students to paint a long, phallic-looking bottle with its tiny aperture, and fat, round-bottomed pears. He was a bony, graying man in his forties, tall and stoop shouldered, exuding some metallic odor, or perhaps that was just the Lucky Strike smoke imbuing his clothes, his yellowed fingers and teeth. "And are you equally inept at everything else?"

"That's what the Austin-Smythes say about my playing," Waverley confessed.

"And Agnes? Miss Kauffman?"

"She says I can't sing at all. And never will." She brightened a bit.

"But Quizzer says my brain tests well. He says I have a lot of electro-magnetic impulses."

Dahlgren snorted audibly as he wandered among the other students, each at her easel. He frowned at Violet's pathetic bottle and pear, and shook his head at Marjorie's efforts, but for the full weight of his disapproval, he returned to Waverley. "The less talent you have, the harder you must work." Then he left to have a cigarette.

Waverley bit her lip, dawdled with her brush.

"What do you care what he thinks?" asked Irene in a burst of camaraderie. "He's a moron, a has-been. They all are. The Austin-Smythes? Failures. Great musicians from *Alberta*? Don't make me laugh. And Agnes Kauffman? She likes to think she is Nellie Melba, but she's a third-rate chorus girl from Denver. If they were any good at all, do you think they'd be stuck on this rock?"

Florence offered, "My mother says when she was a student here, they had really fine visiting artists. They were taught by the best."

"That was then," Irene scoffed. "These people take the free rent Sophia gives them, and the money she pays and pretend to care about art. I tell you, they're ridiculous. I don't know why Sophia tolerates them."

"Who else is she going to get?" asked Ginevra. "Who would come here but second-raters? Is her old friend Pablo Picasso coming to teach here? Is Denis Aron? Not likely."

"They couldn't come here anyway. They're not North Americans. Everyone at Temple has to be part of the New."

At that moment Sophia passed by the art room. She frowned to see them idle. "Waste not thy hour," she reminded them. "Without discipline, there can be no discovery, without discovery there can be no achievement. Without achievement, how can you be Women of the Future?"

Fortunately for Waverley there was no Nobel Prize in Music into Movement, which was Sophia's specialty. Someone else might have referred to this exercise as the dance, but Sophia took a broader view. She would place the Victrola on the shelf in the practice room, wind it up and bring the needle down carefully on the music. She favored the composers of her long-ago French acquaintance, Debussy, Saint-

Saëns, Ravel, Fauré, Satie. She was partial as well to Dvořák's *New World Symphony*.

"Transform!" she commanded her students. "Transform music into movement!" She clapped her hands and moved amongst them. "Tempo, tempo! Advance—accelerate! Allegro! Internalize the tempo, express the emotion! You are works of creation, animate! Not clods of dirt! Animate! Bring the inward out! Express! Emote! Ginevra, tuck in your buttocks! Marjorie! Lift those knees. Violet, your chin, your chin! Waverley! Your spine! Your Corinthian column!"

And even if Music into Movement was not—and would never be—Waverley's venue, still she was more adept than the chunky, ungainly Marjorie or the timid Violet. Violet wore heavy glasses to correct her myopia, and the glasses fell to the end of her nose because her head hung down, her shoulders rounded. Violet kept always close to the walls when she walked, as though she might at any moment have cause to melt into the wainscoting.

Sophia blamed this cowering on Violet's earlier improper education at a Catholic girls' school run by nuns. Sometimes Sophia would take Violet's elbow and pull her into the center of the practice room, jab her in the back, to Violet's visible pain. "Come now, Violet, you need to find your pride."

"But the nuns told me humility—"

"Nonsense. Why on earth would a woman need to practice humility? What rot! Humility is forced upon women. You don't need to practice it. On the contrary, girls, practice confidence! Confidence needs practice. How can nuns teach girls anyway? To teach is to engage with the world on the most fundamental level. To teach, a woman must know something of the world, of heartbreak and happiness and possibility. Girls will not live in a sexual vacuum when they grow up. They need to know something of men."

Irene turned, gave all the rest of them a sly, knowing look.

Irene's love affair, her having slept with a man in a New York hotel room, was a beloved tale at Temple. Irene told it often and well: how at a tea dance hosted by a cousin, the fifteen-year-old Irene Ames had met the dashing Richard, who was perhaps twenty-two. Richard worked in banking, had a degree from some lackluster college in the South, the manners and bearing of a gentleman, and an old family name. But he had no money. He was a fortune hunter, declared Irene's wealthy Philadelphia family, who, once they'd caught wind of the courtship, forbade her to see him. But Richard had fallen truly, madly in love with the beautiful Irene (and who wouldn't? Irene seemed to imply; she was blond and insouciant and fancied herself another Ginger Rogers). Irene returned Richard's passionate love. This wonderfully romantic tale, like Romeo and Juliet, replete with peril, even tragedy, continued as, after months of secret assignations, Irene lied to her parents and went with Richard to New York. Richard had bought her high-heeled shoes, hose, a sophisticated hat with a veil so she would look older than her years. They spent the night in a hotel. As husband and wife. "Certainly," Irene loved to add, "as man and woman."

But the forces of Fate and ill fortune were all against the lovers, and on their return from New York, there in the Philadelphia train station they were greeted by her father, two policemen and a private detective her father had hired. Richard was ordered never to see her again on pain of being charged with statutory rape. (Whenever Irene told the story she had always to stop here and explain again the concept of statutory rape because Marjorie never did quite get it, or when she did get it, she could not remember.)

Word of Irene's escapade and New York assignation reached Miss Butler's, and Irene was expelled. Moreover, she had been banished to Isadora Island at the suggestion of the dreaded Lydia Fraser, Temple alumna and teacher of Delphic Dance at Miss Butler's Philadelphia School for Girls. Lydia Fraser had suggested to Irene's wealthy parents that Temple School and a diet of True Foods would transform her from a wayward student to a Woman of the Future. Also, from Mr. and Mrs. Ames's perspective, Temple was on an island, far away from opportunities for men or misadventure, and Irene's tarnished past could be overlooked.

Marjorie too was the daughter of rich people, and though untarnished, she was a reproach to them: ungainly, painfully shy, afflicted with a stammer, her inherent sweetness preserved in the amber of lassitude. Florence's father was in the foreign service, posted someplace exotic, Hong Kong, Ceylon, Burma, places where the stamps on her parents' envelopes were lacy and colorful and enviable. Ginevra seemed even less connected to the world beyond Temple School. She got almost no mail and was, Waverley gathered, ignored by both her mother and father. They had all been sent here because they were unsightly or inconvenient to someone. Waverley wondered if Sophia knew this, fathomed or even cared. The girls themselves did not seem to care. No one wept for home. Everyone was content to learn by doing.

"Learn by doing, girls. Tie your blindfolds. When I put the needle down, you must express, emote and transform this music into movement until I take it up again. Then, you must hold your pose with poise. We do this exercise in the interest of expressing individuality, just as we clean the chicken coops in the interest of enjoying community. Now—" Sophia put the needle down on Fauré's *Pavane*.

Blindfolded, Waverley clung to the bar, afraid to release. She stood there, bouncing rhythmically up and down, hoping this was satisfactory, knowing it was not. The other girls created drafts and currents all around her, so much so she was certain they were all swooping and soaring and she alone earthbound. In fact, only Irene had any of the grace and ease that Sophia had so hoped for with her students.

Sophia came up and spoke to Waverley, her voice soothing, strengthening, a rich whisper. "You must transform! Ingest this music. Emote. Express it as movement."

"What if I run into the others? What if I go into a wall?"

Sophia removed Waverley's hand from the bar. "What if you do? Experience augments talent and corrects error." Sophia led her into the middle of the practice room, stood behind her and whispered, "Hear the Unspoken. See the Unseen! Effect Transformation! Defy Descartes."

In educating Waverley, Sophia was the first person to treat her as though she had some intrinsic, if undiscovered, merit. That Waverley's gifts did not readily present themselves meant only that they had to be sought out rather than automatically encountered. In the lexicon of Temple School, this was a positive attribute: the more unsung the individual, the greater her achievement.

For the rest of her life Waverley Scott heard Sophia's voice behind her, the whisper of implicit challenge, the expectations of courage, the admonition to intuition. She was fortunate, really, that Sophia prized imagination over consistency, and energy over direction. Direction and consistency could be learned. Imagination and energy were givens, Sophia maintained, gifts with which Waverley could hew her way through the world toward Stockholm and dinner with the King of Sweden.

Chapter 8

Waverley loathed Sir Walter Scott, and her ire against her mother grew with each one of the Waverley novels she was obliged to trudge through. Why not choose the name of someone simple who had done something easy? Why must it be stinking Sir Walter, who wrote great turgid tomes of history, full of unsayable Scots dialect and no kissing? Sophia had pointed out to her that if the books were easy, there would be no point in the exercise, would there? There's no point in it now, Waverley thought, throwing *Old Mortality* across the small room and making Irene jump and drop her mirror.

"If that mirror had broken, you would have been sorry," Irene growled, returning to her undertaking. Each night she sat cross-legged on her bed, critically regarding her face in a mirror, looking for old-age deposits.

"Why do you bother?" asked Waverley. "How can you have old-age deposits when you're not old?"

"They can start anytime. You ought to know that."

"Not if you eat True Foods. With proper rest, Double-Range Breathing and True Foods, and if you stay away from overboiled water and mineral matter, you can fight off old-age deposits. Rule 99," Waverley added reflexively.

"Fine, but did you eat True Foods before you came here? Did you know Double-Range Breathing before you came here? Of course not. No one did. You probably spent thirteen years eating mineral matter and catching old-age germs and you don't even know it. I used to eat foods on the List of Nevers. Often," Irene added wistfully. "Crisp fried potatoes. Sausages. Marmalade. Chocolate."

Waverley went to the mirror, searching for her own old-age deposits, but all that greeted her was her well-known face: dark eyes, olive skin, Mr. Gerlach's hateful nose and mouth. "I don't remember what I ate. I ate in hotels."

Before she came to Temple, Waverley had never even seen a meal cooked, and so had no concept of what transpired in a kitchen, believed that food appeared always on trays, with no notion of how it might have got there. Taste and texture were utterly lost to her, of no possible interest or value then. The only thing she could remember with any clarity was dessert.

"Chocolate," she said, exhaling with Double-Range intensity. "*Chocolate*. Napoleons. Those pastries with chocolate sauce and custard filling? Chocolate sauce on burnt cremes. Chocolate truffles all set around cheesecake dribbled with chocolate sauce and whipped cream topped with chocolate shavings and little thin spirals of caramel sauce, all sort of soft and hot and—"

"Don't," Irene cautioned her. "Don't do this."

"Chocolate orange torte. Chocolate raspberry tart." Waverley sank down on the bed. "Chocolate-dipped strawberries on chocolate ice cream. On strawberry ice cream. Chocolate almond ice cream baked in peach cake and chocolate-cream-filled soldiers lined up in the confectioner's window at Christmastime and chocolate eggs at Easter filled with those gooey, sugary, sticky candies that leave sugar all over your fingers so you have to lick it off again and again."

"Chocolate is number one on the List of Nevers, and it will infect you forever, so you had better just shut up about it." Irene put her mirror down and clasped her hands to her bosom. "But there are times when for one piece of chocolate cheesecake, one chocolate truffle, I could say, never mind old-age deposits! Never mind mineral matter! Never mind dying when you want to."

"What's the good of dying when you want to if you can't live the way you want to?"

Irene was uncharacteristically pensive. "You know what I'm going to do when I can finally get off this awful old rock? I'm going to have chocolate every day."

"I'm going to worship at the Church of the Chocolate God," said

Waverley. Not to be outdone, she added, "To go back and worship at the Church of the Chocolate God."

"Back where?"

"To the Church of the Chocolate God."

"There's no such thing."

"Yes there is. Of course there is. How do you think I know all about chocolate?"

"Well, there's no such thing in Philadelphia."

"Too bad for you. I used to go all the time. I used to worship there. If you weren't so hateful, maybe I'd tell you about it."

"Don't be an oaf," snapped Irene with her usual superiority. But later, when her search for old-age deposits was concluded, she murmured, "A chocolate church, a church for chocolate, can't you just imagine?"

The truth was, Waverley could imagine. This pleased her, surprised her. She had always regarded herself as a talentless lump of unshaped human dough: the bane of her tutors, a burden to Mr. Gerlach, a source of chagrin to her mother. So it was nice to think that Sophia was right. Perhaps talent of some sort lay dormant within her.

January 30, 1940

Mrs. Rhoda Scott
c/o Mr. Gerlach
President, Allegheny Shipping and Freight
Pittsburgh, Pennsylvania

Dear Mother—
    Thank you for the postcard of the Peabody Hotel in Memphis. I re-member it but only because of the ducks. No other hotel has ducks in the lobby. I am writing this on my side of the room just before bedtime which Sophia says is a good time to put your thoughts in order just like you would put your dirty clothes in the basket, though thoughts of course can't be dirty except for ignorance, untruth or ugliness. And why would you think about them anyway?
    You ask if there's anything I need. It would be very nice if you sent me a five-pound box of chocolates. I could use that. But when you send

it, it must be transformed, Mother. You must pack it so it doesn't look like
chocolates. It must seem to be a metaphor. Here at Temple School we are
very partial to metaphor and we do not like things to be too obvious.

Waverley counted on the fact that all the Temple School instructions, injunctions, rules and the like had been explained to Mr. Gerlach.
Very likely, Rhoda would not know that chocolate was first on the List of
Nevers and parents were forbidden to send chocolate to their daughters.
Other things on the List of Nevers didn't seem worth addressing directly,
since it was unlikely parents would be sending sausages, pickles, cranber-
ries, orange rind, radishes or anything included in French cooking.

Radishes came in for Newton Faltenstall's special ire because they
looked so innocent. Waverley had never considered the guilt or innocence of radishes. It was an interesting concept, particularly when
Quizzer would hold one up in front of the class by its little leafy head.
Quizzer pointed to its little white root, hanging down low, exposed, vul-
nerable as a penis. "What is this before you, girls?"

"A killer, Professor Faltenstall! A cause of untold suffering and
death, the font of congestion which leads to constipation, which allows
poisons to gather and accumulate and infect with their toxity and death.
Rule 56."

"Correct," said Quizzer with a smile. "The King of Sweden would be
proud of you."

Regularity in all things was one of Newton Faltenstall's many scientific principles. Chickens require regularity. Temple students of the past
had built the chicken houses and roosts (thus learning the elements of
architecture and engineering, a bit of geometry and a good deal of frus-
tration). In those early days some twenty or thirty girls had maintained
the flock, but now only six students assumed the chicken chores, on ro-
tating days, working two at a time, keeping the runs and houses clean,
the chickens free of lice, and their feed free of mice and rats. The students raked the chicken yard; they cleaned up feathers and dung daily.
They fed them grain and mash and grits and sprouted oats and dried
peas. They kept timers carefully set and monitored so that the lights
would come on and the unknowing chickens would lay on schedule.
The eggs had to be candled and separated. The new chicks had to be

kept warm, and old ones had to be culled. Those hens that had gone broody and those that had turned cannibal had to be segregated from the rest of the merely stupid. These candidates for the axe were chased round the chicken yard, caught and taken to a stump behind the henhouse where Quizzer did the honors. He had a killing collar, a sort of giant funnel into which he quickly shoved the chicken, pulled its head through and chopped it off. Headless, the chickens ran all over as though frantically unable to believe their own bad luck. When they fell over, the students had to pick them up by their awful feet, to scald them in great tubs kept in a separate shed for that purpose, to thrust the carcasses in cold water, to hang them from a cord and to pluck them naked. To Learn by Doing. These chickens, however tough and stringy, were a True Food as long as they were not boiled.

To further Learn by Doing, Quizzer kept the girls at work in the vegetable garden from late February through November, absorbing the rhythms of nature, he said: planting, thinning, watering, weeding, and keeping the fishing nets spread over and between fence posts to discourage the deer and rabbits. The island was overrun with rabbits, so many that if they got into the garden, they could destroy six months' work in a single night. There was, at Temple School, no misplaced affection for Peter Rabbit. Everyone was on the side of Mr. McGregor.

Three times a week, rain or shine, Quizzer marched the students down to Sophia's Beach. Carrying their notebooks, pencils, buckets, spades, scrapers, slides, microscopes and little bottles of tincture, they followed him single file down the threadlike path beaten out by years of Temple students, marching and whistling. The whistling was obliged of them because it helped in Double-Range Breathing. Whistling and marching and Double-Range Breathing (especially uphill) were good for your diaphragm, larynx, your lungs, and helped clear congestion.

When they had whistled themselves down to Sophia's Beach, he sat the girls on long parallel driftwood logs that had bleached and lay like nature's own pews. The beach was his favorite pulpit. He preached to them of the sin of human pride (though he did not call it that because Temple School did not believe in sin, which Sophia maintained was for pinch-lipped Presbyterians like her brother Jethro Westervelt, whom she despised).

"But," Quizzer cautioned the six of them, "never let it be said that we here at Temple School shirked the truth. Even without sin, we are often afflicted with overweening human arrogance. And that is very much to be avoided, just like chocolate and radishes. Human beings are but tide pools ourselves. And like these small silent, wordless, wishless, soundless creatures, events wash over us and leave us altered. In the scientific sense, the historical sense, like these creatures, we share cyclic requirements, we too live by two tides. An accumulating tide and an eliminating tide. All the processes of life can be thus understood, changing food into vitality on the accumulating tide and the residue washing away on the eliminating tide. We are but mollusks ourselves. On the accumulating tide, we human mollusks take food into our bodies and on the eliminating tide, we eliminate, we evacuate the temple of our bodies, purge them of toxins and poisons. It is a process"—Newton beamed, and threw open his arms—"of *Transformation!*"

This word—also emblazoned on the library ceiling beam—was always invoked with ardor at Temple School. In the course of her education, Waverley Scott was transformed. She learned to whistle and march uphill, to regard the sky with wonder and the humble mollusk with respect. She learned to pluck chickens and to candle eggs. She finished six of the Waverley novels that first year at Temple School; she read Jane Austen, Mrs. Gaskell, Gene Stratton Porter (weeping through A *Girl of the Limberlost*), both of the Brontës and Willa Cather. She grew a full inch. And if she still remained artistically hopeless as far as Morton Dahlgren was concerned, Agnes Kauffman nonetheless eked out a bit of praise for Waverley's's husky contralto. Mrs. Austin-Smythe said she did well (all right, anyway) on a simple flute piece after hours of practice, though the same could not be said of the cello. These teachers mattered less to Waverley than Sophia, whose praise, regard and approbation she labored to earn.

She did not, however, bring to Sophia's attention her talent for invention with the Church of the Chocolate God. In creating the Church of the Chocolate God, Waverley absolutely transformed her relationships with Irene, Ginevra, Marjorie, Florence and Violet. She went from pariah to high priestess.

The Church of the Chocolate God began with a simple act of worship shortly after the five-pound box of metaphorical chocolates arrived. Like a penitent, Waverley took her candle, knelt on the floor beside her bed, earnestly praying over the box. Irene watched and listened. Slowly Waverley opened the box, chose a chocolate, ceremoniously nibbled one end, and in a lavish display of unworthiness put it back and completed the prayers she had written. Irene, struck with the solemnity of these devotions (and the fragrance of the chocolate) asked to be taught the proper words, the prayers to the Chocolate God, and Waverley, after due consideration and cajoling (and a bar of Irene's own lavender soap), consented.

The next day, subdued, and yet elated, Waverley and Irene were a reproach to the other students, who soon invaded the church. Thursday nights, long after lights out, one by one the other communicants stole into Waverley and Irene's room, and kneeling in a semicircle on the floor around the box of chocolates, their hands folded, their eyes closed, they prayed, conducted services.

As a Catholic, Violet provided Waverley with considerable liturgical help in how communion worked. One piece of chocolate nibbled by all six, made holy by scarcity and the words murmured over it. And when the original five pounds of chocolates were gone, Waverley used the empty box as altar, the lid lifted for wafting scent. (Incense, said Violet.) The services, as Waverley conducted them, required that each worshiper recite—in dripping detail—a dessert they remembered or imagined. All desserts had to use chocolate in some form or another and if the dessert did not of its own include chocolate (as peaches melba, say, did not) chocolate sauce could always be added. Since the dessert recited could never be the same one twice, worshipers soon left the realm of memory and moved into imagined delights. These often taxed the worshipers' powers of description. All except Waverley. Waverley achieved a kind of passion in reciting these rich concoctions and found it liberating to describe in ecstasy what had never actually transpired in life. She became, in effect, the Saint Teresa of Chocolate.

These services both assuaged the hunger for chocolate and created new hungers. Worshipers in the Church of the Chocolate God had faith that chocolate existed and would be made manifest to them. It made them rather sick, confessing their past truffles, imagined soufflés, chocolate caramel cakes, sicker than if they'd actually gorged on them, vomited and been done with it. Once enunciated, these hungers left them dry-mouthed with Chocolate Thoughts. Those Chocolate Thoughts, once articulated, awakened them to other denied delights. Irene was frequently called upon to wax eloquent on her doomed affair, on her knowledge of men and her vast experience with love, with caressing, with kissing, which she demonstrated on the back of her hand. After the evocation of the Chocolate God, the forbidden accosted them, often and without warning, uneasily.

Walking through the school's garden, say, Waverley found she could come upon the marble Mercury and find herself stroking his marble thigh, touching the cold scallop of his buttock. Or she might find herself in the practice room, not absorbing the tempo, or thinking even about music or movement, but regarding the murals painted on the practice room walls. Beautiful men, lithe, naked, save for (strategically placed) garlands, dancing with pearl-breasted maidens. At Temple School, they did not fear the human body. Artwork everywhere testified to this. In expensive frames, there were nudes, not merely in the art room but in the library and music room, the dining room, bedrooms, even the kitchen. At Temple School the human body was held to be a thing of beauty and a joy forever. Wasn't it?

The students might not have agreed if Quizzer's human body were under discussion. Or Mr. Austin-Smythe? He was soft and pink, with little piggy blue eyes and pale lashes; he was querulous and had a long nose, which quivered with indignity whenever a girl hit a sour note. Morton Dahlgren? Though younger than Mr. Austin-Smythe, Morton Dahlgren was bony, gray, morose-looking. He had long hair, vaguely greasy. He was narrow chested. He was not at all like Sandy Lomax. Now, there was a human body that might truly be said to be a thing of beauty.

On Thursday afternoons when Sandy Lomax came to Temple School, the time allotted to chores had a festive air, something like the Church of the Chocolate God without its secrecy. Helping Sandy Lomax was as beloved a duty as chicken chores were despised. The girls waited in the kitchen for the sound of the Marine and Feed truck grinding up the hill and into the yard at the back of the school. Then they raced into the mud room and put on boots and ponchos, if it was raining, and pulled up the hoods and waited to see his beautiful face behind the windshield wipers. Sandy had dark curly hair and hazel eyes, and for all the hard lessons that life had dealt him—the death of a difficult father, the burden of a drunken mother, long hours, hard work—he had a bright smile, a fine smile. Waverley, for her part, when she saw him smile, felt her heart (or something very like it) leap up into her mouth, under her tongue to be precise, and melt there like a lozenge.

Sandy made deliveries, did minor repairs and chopped wood. On Thursdays he brought coal, ice, flour and fish (a True Food if not fried or boiled). Salmon lay shining in the back of the truck, their scales in the rain looking like coins of some foreign country. These poor sightless salmon did not know that Sandy Lomax had, with one perfect slit up the middle, reached his hand in and cleaned them out. They did not know that Sandy Lomax lifted them from the truck and put them, one by one, into the waiting arms of girls. The fish, thick and muscular, were slick, and so the girls had to press them close against their tunics, closer than they might otherwise have held a dead gutted fish.

Carrying the salmon into the kitchen, they flopped them into the soapstone sink, pumped water and washed them off, dried them and wrapped them in thick paper, tied it and put them at the back of the icebox after Sandy had put the new ice block in and rinsed out the tray that held the old water. After the ice and fish came in, if there were repairs, Sandy took the list that Sophia left on the table and went to work. He kept a toolbox in the truck and could fix a drain, a pipe, a drafty sash in no time at all. Then he cut wood and the girls hauled the short, even logs into the kitchen, the library, music room, dining room. Finally Sandy burned the trash at a site up by the pond they called Frogtown and then loaded what wouldn't burn in the back of the truck to take to the garbage dump near Massacre. With the work done, the girls always asked if he would like a cup of coffee. Fresh coffee was a True Food, they told him, though boiled coffee was toxic. Ditto tea. Tea would kill you in no time at all.

Sandy Lomax liked his coffee strong and sweet. Just like he was, Waverley thought. As winter settled on Isadora Island and a smoky dusk enveloped Temple School, they gathered in the kitchen, speaking inconsequentially, drinking coffee, the clock ticking, early darkness pressing against the windows, all of them breathing in that elixir compounded of fish, rain, coffee and drying sweat on Sandy's flannel shirt and the girls' tunics, that cordial brewed of unspoken longing, unfilled hunger, unassuaged curiosity.

That was Thursday afternoon. Thursday night the Church of the Chocolate God met. Inevitably on Friday, Sophia found her students subdued, weakened, dreamy, depleted, peevish.

Oddly—for a woman who had experienced both men and chocolate—Sophia failed to understand exactly what had transpired, what had transformed her students. Herding them into the practice room, she put Bach on the Victrola and told them to find the tempo, internalize and abide by it. No need to say *express the emotion* because with Bach there was no emotion, only tempo, which she thought would cure them. And if this exercise did not rouse and restore them to the discipline required of a North American Woman of the Future, then she sent them out to the chicken coops, trusting the grit and shit, the gravel and feathers, the clucking and cackling of half a hundred witless chickens to bring them to their senses.

Chapter 9

*D*affodils, promiscuous for twenty years, clumped in great congregations all around Temple School where, untended, they nodded and applauded and swayed with the spring wind. Not long after, winter vanished altogether. Volleys of rhododendrons burst, pink and scarlet and lavender, like floral fireworks down the sloping lawn to where the currents, seasonally stirred, frothed about Assumption Island, a pile of rocks just off Useless Point.

Waverley Scott ingested this particular spring, 1940, whole and intact, unlike anything she had ever experienced before: these waves of change and rebirth, the lush thrust of buds popping up like fists, unfurling, flowers in colors so tender and fleeting, they looked edible. The school vegetable garden—which the students tended and tilled, readied for planting under Quizzer's direction—was to Waverley a revelation. Once turned, the soil reeked of clay and mold and mulch, tangy and deathish. In her Wellington boots, she sank slightly into the damp earth, planted her seeds with a sense of expectation, fulfilled when their tiny green caps sprouted.

But inside the school, gloom deepened with every passing day. As war news on the radio worsened, students moved the pushpins to conform to the tempo of marching feet, a broad, black swath of Nazi triumph. Obliterating Poland. Occupying Norway, Denmark, Holland, Belgium. Till at last in May, the British and French pushpins were massed, coiled in a tiny corner at the coast called Dunkirk. Sitting very straight at her desk in the library, Waverley sometimes pictured the King of Sweden: isolated, sulking about his palace, eating dinner alone while sad waltzes played on his Victrola.

These bleak broadcasts made Sophia suffer visibly, so much so that Quizzer fussed over her, with True Food prescriptions. Sophia followed his instructions absently, but they did not effect any real change. All Temple School came to a halt for the war news. The Austin-Smythes, Dahlgren and Agnes abandoned their afternoon bridge game. Foltzy and Huey left off smoking in the laundry shed to join Sophia, Newton and the students in the library and listen.

Every aspect of a Temple education registered the Allies' persistent defeats. Agnes Kauffman no longer trilled Bizet and Verdi arias, but requiems. And when the Austin-Smythes practiced their duets, the cello seemed to be wrung dry and the flute weeping. Only Morton Dahlgren never veered to a darker palette but kept his students painting the same bottle-green still lifes, the same yellow pears.

As the Germans marched through the north of France toward Paris, Sophia would listen with her hands knotted before her, her composure forced. She flinched when the announcer solemnly named the towns that had fallen: *Cambrai, Arras,* her pain so plain that Nijinsky looked up from the floor beside her desk and whimpered. Sophia Westervelt had always instructed her students to express the emotion, but she could not do this, and her suffering did not allow for their intervention. Even Newton could do little more than place his hand on her shoulder as she recoiled at *Abbeville, Verdun* under the names of towns fallen to the Nazis. When the broadcaster announced that the Germans had occupied the cathedral town of Reims, she wept openly.

Waverley, the other students, the Austin-Smythes, Dahlgren, Agnes, even Newton, looked away from such grief.

Sophia accepted Newton's offer of a hanky. "I'm always telling you to use your imaginations as well as your cognitive processes, girls." She collected herself, her posture impeccable, and faced her students with a dignity they could but emulate. "And so, I am moved to tears when I hear these things not just because they are terrible things, but because I *can* see the Unseen. Imagination's ally is memory, and together they are powerful. Terrible. I can see Cambrai, Arras, Abbeville"—she gulped— "Reims, because they are mine. They are mine in the way that a place where you have suffered is yours forever. It's yours by virtue of what you endured, and because you can still picture the morning light there."

Sophia crossed her beautiful hands, one over the other, and squared her broad shoulders. "During the last, great war, I was living in France, in Paris, as you know. I could have stayed in Paris, but to remain idle when so many others were making sacrifices, well, such inaction is beneath a North American woman. And besides, it was terrible in Paris. The bombs, the air raids, the forced gaiety. I knew I must do something. After all, I spoke French. I had a car. So I signed on as a liaison between the French and the English Red Cross. I drove and fetched and carried and ferried, I did whatever was needed of me, all across the north of France, in all those towns where the Germans are marching now. But in Reims . . ." She looked around the library as though it were a train station and she sought the timetable. "I had other reasons to remember Reims, but our lives are syncopated in mysterious ways, girls, and . . ."

"Tell them the story, Sophia," Newton urged her. "The students should know how powerful and unlikely were the forces that brought you here, dear, to build your school in this miraculous place. Before you came here, Sophia, it truly was Useless."

She put her hand over his. "In Reims I was catching a little sleep in the field hospital and the French nurse came and woke me, said I must help them with a Canadian, who was screaming, swearing. They thought he was dying, but they didn't know what he meant or wanted. So I was brought to this soldier. He had lost an ear. The bullet had taken part of his skull as well. We had no morphine. He was screaming out *massacre massacre,* and swearing love at the same time he was cursing a girl named Nona York. Swearing love and cursing God as well." Sophia paused, listening for the screams across the time and miles. "But this patient was not a Canadian. He was an American, and when I told him my name, Sophia Westervelt, he seemed to rouse, to lift from the abyss of pain. He left off cursing God and Nona York and cursed my family. And finally, I realized the Massacre he was crying out was not an event, or at least not a recent event, but a place. Useless Point, Dog Bay, Dough Bay, Massacre, Chinook Lookout, all those places, he called after them, as if his heart would break if he died before returning. I promised him he would not die. I promised him we would see these places again, he and I, we would live to do that." She sipped her bran-ade quietly while Newton hovered nearby. "I did not think it was a promise I would keep. I thought Eugene Briscoe would die, but he didn't."

Morton Dahlgren twisted uncomfortably in his chair. He gripped his own shoulders, as though desperately embracing. "I was amongst the first American doughboys to go to France in 1918, and what I saw there . . . What I saw there, there are no words for that. What I lived through there . . . I thought I would not live." Morton's long, unlovely mouth twisted and then clamped shut. "If Sophia hadn't rolled me over in the field hospital, I would have strangled on my own vomit."

Agnes Kauffman looked up, alarmed. In the little clapboard behind the school, Agnes had lived with Morton in what was not marriage (artists scorn marriage) but something very like it for three years. She had never heard him speak of the Great War. No, no longer great, merely the last war. She had not even known he'd been a soldier.

"And for what?" scoffed Morton. "What did it all come to twenty years ago? All our hooray and sacrifice? All that suffering. Look at these black pins on the map. It came to nothing. We didn't know what the hell we were getting into. We went over there and fought and bled and died. Why? So the Frogs and Krauts can blow hell out of one another again. They're doing it all over again! Americans should never again fight in their stupid European wars. Let them rot, the Frogs, the Krauts, the Limeys. We are well out of it. It's like the Professor is always saying, Europe is nothing but a lot of stained glass and sausage."

"I may have been hasty in that judgment," Newton cautioned. "Rash and overstating the case."

"So you think we should get involved?" Morton sneered. "Go save La Belle France? Again? Let them go to hell. Americans for America."

"That's very crass and narrow," objected Mr. Austin-Smythe.

"Just because you cheesehead Canadians sing 'God Save the King,' does that make it your fight? Well, fine. Go die in France. Send your sons." Mrs. Austin-Smythe began to weep. Their young nephew had recently joined up. "Even Churchill knows the Frogs are going under. It's just a question of time before the Nazis march into Paris, occupy the whole bloody place, the whole stinking continent."

"Perhaps the French can hold," said Agnes.

"The Frogs couldn't hold water in a bucket."

"I speak only for myself"—Newton glanced at Sophia—"but if France falls to the Nazis, then England is in very grave danger. I think the rest of the world will suffer too. Yes, I do. I think America should come to the aid of the Allies. Now and in every way possible."

Sophia ran her hands through her rough, short hair. "This is a very dark hour, and it would be a disservice to our students to pretend otherwise, or to ignore it."

"I thought the whole point of this school was to prove that we don't need Europe!" cried Morton. "That we're free of all that trash and tripe and tradition. You're a hypocrite, Sophia."

Waverley jumped up from her desk. "You take that back! You're lucky to be in the same universe with Sophia!"

"Please, Waverley," Sophia remonstrated. She waited for Waverley to sit down and then, in her own stately fashion, addressed Morton. "Call it what you will. What sort of person would I be if time did not move or touch me? If I failed to respond to the tempo of everything around me? What sort of person remains always the same, and invincible? Tides—accumulating tides, eliminating tides—wash over people as they wash over Newton's limpets and sea stars and barnacles. We cannot remain impervious to them. We must respond. A supple mind is allied to a supple body."

"That's just another way of admitting defeat."

Sophia looked directly at Waverley, perhaps not seeing her, but holding her gaze nonetheless. "Sometimes the ability to let go of a dream is as important as the ability to hold on to it."

Chapter 10

There had not been a proper graduation at Temple School in years. No proper graduates for that matter. There would not have been a graduation in June 1940, but Mrs. Ames wrote announcing that they were looking so very forward to seeing their daughter Irene take her diploma with the class of 1940. Lydia Fraser had told them how stirring were Temple School ceremonies.

Sophia slid the letter back in its pale blue envelope and put it in the pocket of her tunic. It crinkled there ominously as she walked all over Temple School, seeing it with the eyes of Irene's parents. The various economies she had practiced over the years were painfully evident, on the buildings, the gardens, on the sheds and statuary. The front gardens had gone rampant with blackberry brambles and belladonna, bracken. The walkways were clogged with moss and covered with thick ferns whose scent underfoot was peppery, damp and peculiar. In the house itself, stained rugs, scuffed floors, unmended cracks in the walls and little islands of damp greeted her in every room. Upstairs, one by one she opened the doors of rooms that had remained long shut up, unheated, unventilated, unvisited for years. The walls were crawling with damp. Long festoons of cobwebs hung in the windows, and fat spiders woke with alarm at her footfall. In one of these bedrooms she would have to put Mr. and Mrs. Ames.

When she told Irene her parents were coming, Irene groaned and wept and gnashed, forgetting every sophisticated thing she had learned from Ginger Rogers. "Tell them I won't graduate. Tell them anything. Tell them I've failed. That's it. I'm not transformed enough to graduate."

"You are eighteen. You should graduate. You are our only graduate this year. Our only graduate in quite a while."

"Sophia, they've never been west of Pittsburgh! They're, well they're, they're Philadelphia. They're full of notions of, they believe in—oh, Sophia you'll hate them! I hate them. You don't know what they're like!"

"I soon shall," Sophia replied, her lips pursing.

For the next three weeks, all education halted in favor of the massive cleanup campaign. Except for chicken duty, and the evening radio broadcasts, which could not be ignored, Temple students dedicated themselves to learn by doing with the broom, the trowel, the scrub brush, the mop and bucket, the paintbrush and whitewash. Foltzy and Huey complained endlessly of the work, the hours, their knees, backs, and bursitis.

In an effort to enlist the faculty's help, Sophia appealed to the loyalty of Mr. and Mrs. Austin-Smythe, of Dahlgren and Agnes, but they were having none of it. Cleaning, painting, repair, scrubbing, sanding, these were not artistic enterprises. They had been hired as artists. Moreover, since their students were in the throes of this work, the four artists played an interminable bridge game in the clapboard house where Morton and Agnes lived.

The trouble with all this energy expended was that every attempt to paint, plaster or mend led Sophia to further unwanted discoveries. The wainscoting in the dining room, for instance, that had buckled slightly because of the damp, fell off and was found to be a hive of carpenter ants gnawing at the innards of the wall. The sight of them sent Violet screaming from the room. The work taxed the nerves and bodies and spirits, and finally any semblance of goodwill amongst the students. Irene continually protested it wasn't her fault her parents were coming; she hadn't wanted them, but the other students blamed her just the same. There was sulking, name-calling and hard words tossed about. Even in the Church of the Chocolate God.

Even relations between Sophia and Newton strained. For the first time in their years together, their long marital accord, Newton declared that Sophia was being disloyal to his ideas. Sophia thought Newton was being pigheaded. He refused to consider that the True Food diet should be mitigated while Mr. and Mrs. Ames were their guests, that Irene's parents might think it strange, even unsavory (given the very high fees they were paying) that their daughter should have been fed a diet primarily of stale biscuits, baked potatoes, raw vegetables, fish, oatmeal, eggs, and corn pudding for years.

Sophia arranged for Captain Briscoe to collect Mr. and Mrs. Ames at the citizens' dock on the mainland and bring them to Massacre. Irene must accompany him. "If you are not on the *Nona York*," Sophia explained, reasonably, no panic, "your parents might be, well, alarmed at Captain Briscoe, though he has promised me his language will be, well, exemplary. Maybe not exemplary, but conventional."

"They'll hate him no matter what. No matter who's there. This is going to be a nightmare."

However, the day of Mr. and Mrs. Ames's arrival was fine and bright, warm with only a lilting wind. Waverley talked Irene into letting her come. This was not difficult. Irene was happy to have someone help her absorb the dreaded reckoning. On the roof of the *Nona York* cabin, the two girls lay stretched out in the sunshine while Captain Briscoe grumbled and heaped imprecations on Rufus, who alternately whimpered and growled. The coming of Mr. and Mrs. Ames brought out the worst in everyone.

Irene chewed on her fingernails. "I don't care what Sophia says about the King of Sweden," she declared, "and the Nobel Prize. Out there, in the big world, all a girl really has to do is find a husband."

"Maybe I'll marry Sandy Lomax," said Waverley dreamily. "Here at the little church over on Cutlass Road."

"Don't be a dolt." Irene knocked on Waverley's head. "Sandy Lomax is an island boy. He'll never have any money. You want someone rich."

"Do you think that's really that important?"

"Of course it is! How can you be so stupid, Waverley? You just astonish me. You need to marry a rich man. Only money can make you free."

"I don't believe that," Waverley stated with a firmness that cheered her. She felt brave and very much a Woman of the Future.

"Well, when you're ready for a rich husband, you come to Philly and live with me, and I'll introduce you to the boys I know. They're dull and usually drunk and they're bores and they'll grope your breasts and thighs, but they have money. They have good families." Irene snorted. "For what that's worth. And do you know what I'm going to do as soon as I get back to Philly? I'm going to grab one of them right away and have sexual intercourse. Often." Irene sat up and took an unladylike swill of Coca-Cola, untrue food that it was.

"But Richard, your lover, " Waverley protested. "Richard has waited for you all this time. He's waited faithfully while they sent you into the wilderness thinking they could becalm your passionate heart. Just like the Lady of Shalott." In Waverley's mind the Lady of Shalott had Irene's beautiful face. Waverley closed her eyes to better enjoy the image. "They didn't care how miserable you were as long as you were parted from your lover."

Irene burped. "He was after my money."

Waverley thought she misheard, opened one eye and squinted at her friend.

"He was a fortune hunter just like they said. I was glad to be sent to Isadora, if you want to know the truth. I never once asked my parents to bring me home. It would have been too humiliating to stay in Philly."

"But I thought you said—"

"I know what I said. What have you got, bran-ade for brains? It was a lie. It wasn't romantic at all. It was really pretty vulgar and disgusting. I hate Richard."

"The hotel room? The hat with the veil? The consummated sexual intercourse?" Waverley stuck with Temple terms, which was the only way she could actually picture these events, the act of love itself.

"Oh yes, all that's true. The New York part. The intercourse. But coming back to Philly, we stepped off the train and I saw my father and the cops, and I flung myself against Richard, and I held him and I told my father and the cops that I would live for Richard, love him, that he was the man I loved. Forever." Irene hugged her knees.

"So that part was true."

"Yes, and you know what Richard said? Right there, in front of every-one, he said, *'I've dishonored you, Irene. You'll have to marry me. No one else will have you.'* "

Waverley took this confession to heart, more to the solar plexus. She had to sit up to breathe. "Not that. He didn't say that."

"He did. I had never felt dishonored until that very moment. I had felt loved and ennobled because I loved him and he loved me." Irene hiccupped. "But after that, I felt ugly and dirty and disgusting, even to myself."

"Oh Irene, that's terrible. I've never heard anything so awful. Oh, I can't believe that of Richard"—who, after all, had got ensconced as the amorous element in the services of the Church of the Chocolate God. "Why did you never tell me before?"

"Why should I ruin the romantic story for you? It sounded good, didn't it? Dramatic."

"Like the Lady of Shalott."

"Yes, well, I didn't go downriver like she did. No. The cops came up and took me from Richard's arms. And then he said the same thing to my father, that I was sullied and not a virgin and my father needed Richard to marry me. No one else would have me. Damaged goods. After that, I didn't care where they sent me. Honestly. I was already in hell."

Shorn of her sophisticated cynicism, Irene seemed to Waverley a stranger, an altogether foreign girl.

"I was glad to come here, truthfully, far away from all that humiliation. I bless Temple School and Sophia Westervelt, whatever else you can say about this place, I've had three years here to figure out that form is to function as Nature is to God—"

"God is to Nature."

"Who cares? To figure out that and a lot else. My parents think they're coming to collect little Irene, headstrong Irene, the baby of the family, the spoiled girl. But I'm not that girl and I never will be again. My parents think I will go home and be just like Miss Butler's girls. Like my sister Babs. At eighteen they stuffed Babs in a ballgown and put her on the block like a steer in silk, a piece of debutante property with a FOR SALE sign and an orchid corsage. And then they waited for someone to fall in love with dear old Babsie and marry her. And someone did. Arthur the Odious. She married Arthur and now she's popped out three little Arthurs, odious little ferrets, just like him, and everyone's applauding."

"No North American Woman of the Future could live like that," Waverley concurred.

"Well, you are my witness, Waverley"—Irene clasped Waverley's hand in both of hers—"you have my solemn vow, and if you see me departing from this solemn vow, I want you to remind me of this day on the *Nona York*. Do you promise?"

"I promise, Irene."

"I swear by the Chocolate God, when I get to Philadelphia, I'm getting a job and an apartment and a lover. In that order. I'm not living with my parents and I won't be trussed like a chicken just waiting for the first pair of pants and a penis that comes looking for a bride. It's just an exchange. They call it love, but it's like turning one currency into another. You're striking a bargain. I swear to you, Waverley, I am going to get the best of that bargain. Every time. You go into it looking for what you can get and you have to decide what you're willing to give or give up. That's the great lie and the great secret about love."

"I don't think I believe that," Waverley repeated, more insistently, not feeling quite so brave.

Irene got to her feet and began halfheartedly waving to people as they came in sight of the mainland dock. "Look, there they are. They've seen us. Oh, hell and damnation, they've brought sonofabitching Hercule. The dog. You see him? The sonofabitching poodle."

*H*ercule had been named after Agatha Christie's detective. Mrs. Ames adored Agatha Christie. Just adored her. Mrs. Ames adored many things. Certainly she adored her daughter, and once introduced to her daughter's best friend, she adored Waverley Scott. Droll name. Mrs. Ames wore gloves, a hat with a veil, and silk stockings, her seams perfectly straight. Mr. Ames wore a hat, gloves, a vest, tie and coat, all this despite the beating waves of June heat and the sticky little pools of tar on the dock, sending up their own pungent fumes. Mrs. Ames admonished Hercule not to step in the tar. Mr. Ames cleared his throat, often, as if persistently about to say something vast and important, keeping them all in suspense.

Mrs. Ames did not adore the *Nona York*. Emphatically did not adore Captain Briscoe, particularly when he took off his hat and she found he was one ear short of the more popular pair. She would not have adored him even had he left his hat on, or had he removed it as a mark of respect. That wasn't why he removed it. He removed it to beat Rufus, who had tried to mount Hercule, a poodle with fluffy high-heeled feet and great black eyes, a pom-pom on his tail, his gray body elegantly shorn in places and poofed up elsewhere. The Captain locked Rufus in the cabin, and he howled and shrieked, protesting this injustice all the way back to Massacre.

Which Mrs. Ames also did not adore. Particularly as the Packard was not there to collect them. Irene's heart sank at this and Waverley stepped up briskly to offer the Ameses a tour of the Marine and Feed, and see if perhaps Sandy couldn't drive them in the Marine and Feed truck. The Ameses emphatically did not adore the thought of riding in a feed truck. No, the Ameses must have a cup of tea or they would expire. They marched, Hercule in tow, to the Isadora Inn, which they also did not adore.

Isadora Inn, the rather too-grand name for a place where men like Captain Briscoe would come when they felt the need of a hot bath, a hot meal and a bed that didn't rock with currents, was low-beamed, smoky, and smelled of sweat and fish and cigarettes and things cooked in grease. Here, over a pot of tea, Mrs. Ames launched into a long, lyrical tirade, chiding Irene, for starters, for her sunburnt complexion, her short hair, the muscles in her legs. Mrs. Ames made her way, trilling through Irene's numerous other shortcomings. And these were only the obvious ones.

Waverley watched, horrified, spellbound to see the Ginger Rogers of Useless Point shrinking, succumbing to this silly woman. Just then, Dr. Oland entered the Isadora Inn. He called out something to the effect of his kingdom for a cold beer. He saw Irene and Waverley and strolled over to the table, delighted to make the acquaintance of Irene's parents. He extolled the virtues of Temple School, especially on the health of the students, which he pronounced excellent.

"And are you their doctor, then?" inquired Mrs. Ames.

"I'm the vet hereabouts." He smiled to see his beer appear on the bar. "It comes to the same thing. We're all vertebrates. A vertebrate is a vertebrate is a vertebrate—Gertrude Stein."

"I do not approve of Miss Stein."

"Except that horses can't vomit. And more's the pity." He made his way toward the beer.

Mrs. Ames bristled, turned and wreaked her wrath on Irene, asking why she hadn't mentioned all the vulgar people here.

Waverley, feeling protective and brave, put herself between Irene and Mrs. Ames and asked for a cigarette.

"Smoking at such a young age! Why, that's terrible. You'll stunt your growth." Mrs. Ames's indignation foamed into a long tirade, heaped, all of it, on Waverley. Finally she demanded, "What kind of school lets their students smoke?"

"Oh no, ma'am," Waverley replied. "They don't let us smoke. And they won't let you smoke either."

This was true. And the Ameses were not delighted that Newton persisted in giving them dramatic descriptions of what their lungs must look like, corroded, crusted with carbon, veritable tar pits, all their little pink air sacs shriveled and gasping. They did not adore Sophia's edict that they could not smoke inside Temple School. Smoking outside, declared Mrs. Ames, made her feel like a bum on a street corner. A lady never smoked outside.

A compromise was struck in that Mr. and Mrs. Ames could go over to the clapboard house and smoke with Morton and Agnes. There they could also play a quick rubber of bridge. This ended up not delighting them either, since Morton cheated. Moreover, they ascertained that Morton and Agnes were living in vulgar sin, particularly as Morton remarked that marriage was for suckers.

Dinner in the Temple School dining room with all the artists was equally not very delightful. And despite Newton's enthusiasm for the stringy, just-slaughtered chicken, baked potatoes and cornmeal dumplings, Mr. and Mrs. Ames could hardly gag down these True Foods. Later Mr. and Mrs. Ames and Hercule were led to a bedroom aired out, even painted in their honor, and no one got any sleep because Hercule yapped all night long.

He yapped all the following day as well. The island's burgeoning rabbit population drove Hercule into a canine frenzy, from which at last he sank, exhausted, just before the Dance on the Green, also known this year, 1940, as graduation.

The audience arrived at the school to join the teachers and students for the celebration. Mr. and Mrs. Torklund, Miss Torklund, and Sandy Lomax came in the truck; Dr. Oland, Captain Briscoe (minus Rufus), and Mr. Hulbert, the barber, came in the vet's car. The guests (none of them delightful to Mrs. Ames's eye) milled about, moving amongst wicker chairs and lounges set at artful angles. The Victrola provided music. Mr. Torklund sweated profusely in the suit he was not accustomed to wearing, and Mrs. Torklund mentally totted up the cost of everything she saw. Sis had unbraided her hair and pinned it up; she wore a voile dress, very becoming, and her fair skin pinked in the sun and she looked quite lovely. Sandy, equally unaccustomed to a suit, asked permission to remove his jacket, which Sophia freely gave. The white of his starched shirt contrasted nicely with his tan. All the men had fresh haircuts. The barber had evidently nicked himself getting ready for the event, and Dr. Oland, whose wife had left him the year before, had dog hair all over his clothes.

The weather cooperated, bringing a glorious day, and out in the Sound boats bobbed in the treacherous currents off Useless Point, fishers standing on their decks to watch the Temple girls. Tables, draped in cloths embroidered with the school logo, were laid with the best cutlery and china, washed and pulled into service. True Foods were hastily tarted up to look more appealing than they actually were, a task to which Foltzy was not quite equal.

When it was time for the actual Dance on the Green, the students went inside, and on Sophia's cue, Newton wound the Victrola up and brought the needle down on Saint-Saëns's *Improvisation for Sampson and Delilah*. Sophia (who looked stunning, regal in her toga) clapped her hands, and the girls streamed out from either side of the arbors, toga clad, barefoot, running, each with a long silken banner, a scarf held high overhead, blue scarves, turquoise, green and gray, and these they lay down in a silken heap and gave themselves over to *Samson and Delilah*. Irene played Delilah because she could actually dance. Waverley assumed the role of the hulking Sampson, all brawn (with or without his hair), and no brains. The other girls were sprites and spirits, both good and evil. The next dance again showcased Irene's grace in *Clair de Lune*.

Sophia and Newton wept openly throughout these performances, so moved were they, wiping away tears and applauding their students. Mr. and Mrs. Ames put down their glasses of bran lemonade and applauded too. They declared themselves pleased. But they emphatically did not adore it.

The climax was the *Rite of Spring,* in which Irene led the other toga-clad dancers, her arms tanned and graceful in the sparkling sunlight as she ran and dipped and leapt, ingested the music, expressed the emotion. For this dance, this moment, Irene Ames kept time as she would never again keep it in all her life. She and the others finished their dance to wild applause, which rang out all over Useless Point and well beyond. Even the seals of Assumption Island seemed to applaud, barking in the distance.

Then, solemnly, the other girls lined up on either side of Irene for the Transformation ceremony (which Newton and Sophia had cobbled together, racking their collective memory for what they'd done in the days when Temple School had had many students). They conferred upon Irene Ames—her posture impeccable, her gaze straightforward—a Certificate of Transformation. She was a North American Woman of the Future. Irene, Quizzer, Sophia, all started to cry and embrace one another; all the students cried and embraced one another and their teachers.

Captain Briscoe was so moved he had to go inside. He could not be seen weeping. To take his mind off emotion, he turned on the radio, which protested, wheezed, and the signal came in at last, the voices urgent, anxious, distraught. Eugene took a nip from his hip flask while he listened. Then another.

When finally Eugene returned outside, he found the girls all clustered around Irene, Sophia and Newton, the other celebrants awkwardly nibbling their True Foods, Mr. and Mrs. Ames like stick matches beside the Austin-Smythes, who chatted about their Edmonton successes. A little unsteadily, Eugene touched Sophia's arm and asked to speak with her.

She turned to him, sniffed alcohol on his breath, and frowned. "Is this confidential, Eugene?"

"No."

"Then tell me." She gave him her unfaltering gaze.

"The Germans have marched into Paris, Sophia. France has fallen to the Nazis. They say the German army marches through the Arc de Triomphe."

Sophia walked away from him, from all of them, absorbing the news as if she had been hit, but expressing it the only way she knew how. She improved her already stately posture, lifting her chin so she more than ever resembled the figurehead on a ship, proud, alone, her whole body taut and prepared to meet the cresting waves. She blinked into the afternoon sun beating molten across the Sound, and the brightness made her eyes water. Over the strains of Debussy's *La Mer* rasping out of the Victrola, Sophia heard the march of black-booted troops through the streets she had known and into the lives of the people she had loved, the imagined tempo, marching, marching.

Chapter 11

Paris
28 Juin 1940

Madame,

You are surprise to have this letter from me. You know who I am though we have never meet. I am the woman who marry your lover, Denis Aron. I am Judith Aron, the mother of his daughter, our daughter, Avril.

You know too, as does all the world, of the terrible things that have come to Paris. The invasion of the enemy, the German Occupation of our country. There have been since these days many suicides in Paris.

When the Nazis have occupy other countries, those peoples escape to Paris. These peoples, they have bring with them terrible stories. Many Jews and Communists, certainly have bring with them stories so brutal you cannot believe, but they are true. In Saint-Antoine, my cousin have many foreign neighbors who carry these stories like the bad smell in their clothes. How the Nazis shoot peoples in the street, women, old men, babies, little children. How Nazis march peoples from their homes and into ghettos and keep them there without food or water. They tell of peoples who become like cattle, worse than beasts. Beasts are not left to freeze and starve. These are stories peoples bring with them, foreigners who have flee their cities, their lands to come to Paris to escape the Nazis. Now the Nazis have come to Paris. These stories, they are like swift rats running through the sewers and you can hear their little feet.

I have fear, Madame. I have beg Denis that he, that we will leave France, but he refuse. He say he leaves France once before and he will not leave again. Denis say the Germans dare not come near to us here in the rue de la Grande Chaumière. Denis is a great artist. One of the most great in France. All the world knows this. France is our country, says Denis. He have won the Croix de Guerre in the Great War. We are citizens. If France suffer, then we must suffer with her.

I have accept this for myself, but I have fears. Denis will not leave and I must stay with him. It is my duty. But I have fear for my daughter, Madame. This is why I write you now. My daughter, our daughter, Avril, she must come to your school. You must take her. She must live with you at your Temple School till this war is finished and France is free again.

My cousin by marriage, he say he and his family, they leave France. Now. Soon. He say they will take Avril if I have, am finding the proper papers for her. The passport, the exit visas. All she needs. The wife of these cousins have peoples in Montréal. They will go to Montréal. Those peoples have peoples, family in Vancouver. I have found the map and your island is very near to Vancouver. You can go to Vancouver and bring Avril to your school. My daughter is my life. I cannot bear that any danger or harm or sorrow come to her. I can live, or die, endure everything if I know Avril will be safe. At your school she will be safe. With my daughter, I trust no one but you.

I trust you, Madame, because you and I, we have love the same man. You love him like no other woman and you have been to him as no other. Denis love you. He love you still. Denis have always love you. He have never love me. He have many other womens too, Madame, I tell you this, though sometimes I am sad for it, but I do not believe he love them. In his heart, he never love anyone but you. I share my husband with you, Madame. I share him not with his other womens, no, but you and I, Madame, we know what it is to love this man. And so I am certain you will love too this girl, my Avril.

29 Juin 1940

I have hear your story, naturally, Madame. Denis himself have tell me some. Maurice Fleury tells me some. Charming, amusing Maurice, *who admires you still, speaks fondly of you still, who still makes the magic with his camera. Sometimes our whole building smells like his photographie chemicals.*

Over these many long years Maurice have been my friend, he have tell me stories of the great days in Paris, you and Denis and all your friends. Your adventures. Crazy with love and art and wine and youth, Madame. How you and Denis meet at the duel. You live together. Denis paints, you are his model. You are body and soul the same and together. Then come the war. You try to make him stay, but no, he must go to fight. This war is the great adventure for all young men and he must be part of it. Later, the war is over. All the young men are dead. Maurice lives. Maurice bring you the final words that Denis is dead.

These stories, the stories of Maurice and Denis, the great time before the war, they are fine stories, Madame, but they are to me as the fables of La Fontaine. So far away. They are as the tales of the Red Sea parting for the Jews. So far away.

They are far away also from the man who returns to Paris four years after the war. Denis returns from the dead, to Paris, to Montparnasse. You are gone, long time before. Perhaps fortunately, Madame. Denis, on his return, he is not the man you know. He is not the man any of his friends know.

Sometimes Denis is not even knowing his own self. Denis have suffered terrible wounds and he have been a prisoner of the Germans. He is crazed and in pain. When finally he returns to Paris, he have a soldier's pension and the Croix de Guerre and no place to live. He comes to the rooms of his friend, Maurice, in the rue de la Grande Chaumière. My widowed mother, she is the concierge in this building. I am a schoolgirl.

Denis who comes to live with Maurice is mad. Everybody say so. Denis Aron return to Paris to find Sophia Westervelt is gone and he is mad with rage and passion. He writes to you. You tell him you have marry someone else. You are teaching in your school. You will never return to France. Denis swear and rages and cries (all the building hears him, Madame, my mother she tells Maurice, if your friend don't shut up and let us get some sleep in this building, you are both to leave). I have never think Monsieur Aron is crazy. I have never think he is mad and raging. I think he is very sad. When I say this to Maman, she slaps me.

Tells me to stay away from these mens. Most of all to stay away from crazy artists who have the Croix de Guerre and no money.

But how can I? One thing leads to another. I am pregnant. Seventeen, pregnant, and no husband. My mother rends her clothes for the shame, cries out to God and all the rue de la Grande Chaumière that I am a whore and I deserve to die in the street like a dog. But I am not a whore, Madame. I have fall in love with Denis Aron. Like you.

It is not my fault that war takes him from you. It is not my fault that you think him dead and leave Paris. It is not my fault that he lives and returns. It is not my fault that he rages and cries out and swears against you. He goes mad with loving you, but he lies with me.

I have make him a good wife. I have make him a beautiful daughter. My mother despise him still, but we live here in her apartment. Denis paints in a studio in the rue Delambre, but he return home here. To me. Most times. Sometimes. Not always. He is a difficult man to love. He is sometimes cruel.

They say he is a great genius. I hope he is. But I have no faith in art, Madame. I believe in God. But I do not trust Him either. I will stay in Paris. My mother is sick. My husband believes he can fight the Germans with his paintbrush and his French citizenship and his Croix de Guerre. Fine. I will stay too. But not Avril. I will not take these chance with my daughter.

Why this letter is so long, Madame? Because Avril have already gone. She is coming to you. There is no time for anything else. I have this chance. The Saint-Antoine cousins, they go. I can say no more for fear of—fear. Avril is with them. She brings to you things you will treasure. She brings to you somethings of great value. After the war I swear to you on my soul, you will have pay. After the war, you bring Avril back to me, I will reward you your kindness. I swear.

Denis gives me the last letter you write him from your school, Temple School, Isadora Island. So I have this number of telephone and I give this to Avril. She will telephone your school from the home of the family in Vancouver.

She have fifteen years my girl. She is beautiful. She have very good English. Denis insist on it. Sometimes when times was good, when Denis have no pain in his head and his work goes well and he don't drink too much, and the money comes in from the gallery in the rue Luxembourg, Denis say to me and Avril and even to Maman who don't like him, he says, Come, ladies, put on your hats, and we will go to the café and practice our English. Maurice is there. He practice his English too. We all speak English because Denis says we must. One day, he says, the Americans will rule the world. But it is not to be. It is the Germans who rule the world. There will be no more café days for Denis and me.

Do not reply to this letter. To any letter. It is enough with God's help that I find you. That this letter find you. It is too dangerous for me and Denis and Maman if we receive post from America. Denis is artist and they have always trouble. We are Jews and we have always trouble. The Germans have spies everywhere. Someone don't like you, someone want your apartment, think you maybe cheat them on the payment, this or that. Who does not have enemies? There is always hate and anger, jealousy, and people have so little hearts. War makes it simple to be cruel.

I have give you my daughter, Madame. The daughter of Denis. I have release my beloved girl like a bird and I watch her to go high over the rooftops and into the clear blue sky. This journey she must make is very long, very terrible, very dangerous, and she is young and alone. But for all the dangers of this journey, of what we do not know, I prefer to release her to that. Go into the unknown, Avril, better that than to remain here. Accept my daughter, Madame, the daughter of Denis. I ask you to do this in the name of love, Madame. My love for Avril. Your love for Denis.

Judith Aron

Part Three

Maid of
the Isles

Chapter 12

September sunlight fell in thick, buttery slabs through the tall windows of the Empress Hotel dining room. Uniformed waiters made their way amongst the tables with the circumspect reverence of undertakers. For all the waiters' bustle, their to-ing and fro-ing, their trays aloft, bearing pots of tea and coffee, meaty breakfasts, and for all the many people filling the vast, high-ceilinged room, there was nonetheless a pervasive somber spirit here. Nearly every guest was ensconced behind the pages of a newspaper, frowning at the long gray columns of print with their dreary news of the war, the ongoing defeat, destruction, casualties, the unchecked Nazi advance through Europe.

Rhoda Scott's newspaper was still folded neatly beside her fork. Soon she would join Mr. Gerlach. She would take her opinions of the war from him. In the meantime though, she sipped her coffee and glanced at the headlines. "Mr. Gerlach has always said the Germans were the only ones prepared for war. Their transport systems are the best in the world and they value efficiency in a way that gives them an advantage."

"The war in Europe has nothing to do with Mr. Gerlach." Waverley finished off her eggs with gusto. "Europe is succumbing at last to centuries of tradition and religion and sausages that have led them to congestion and despair." She slathered jam on her toast with her knife, which made an odd scraping sound that annoyed Rhoda.

Almost everything about Waverley annoyed Rhoda. They were coming to the end of their summer holiday together, touring western Canada, the best hotels at Banff, Lake Louise, Harrison Hot Springs. Rhoda found all of these marvelous places overwhelming, the lakes too blue, the sky too wild, the mountains too big. Not like North Carolina.

The Empress Hotel, here in Victoria, was their last stop. From here, this very morning, Waverley would return to Temple School and Rhoda would leave for Minneapolis.

In their long weeks together, Rhoda had found her daughter altogether changed. Waverley had acquired a patina of certainty, enthusiasm and a straightforward gaze utterly unlike her old self. For a child who had never much demonstrated strong affection, Waverley had new, passionate attachments and had spent much of the trip scribbling letters and postcards and running to the front desk to post them to half a dozen people, names that Rhoda could not quite keep straight. Waverley lacked all decorum. Though her posture was improved, she moved with a freedom unbecoming in a young lady. A young lady ought to be more conscious of keeping her ankles neatly crossed, her knees pressed together and her arms close to her sides. Rhoda said so. Gently, but said so. It was her duty as a mother.

To Rhoda's chagrin, Waverley laughed off these admonitions and advice, scorned the whole notion of being a young lady and declared herself instead a North American Woman of the Future. Women of the Future would never succumb to such rot. (Waverley had perfected her use of the word *rot* so that to Rhoda's ear it sounded downright profane and certainly vulgar and irritating.) If you wanted to dance, Waverley declared, then you did it. When Rhoda protested that a girl needed a partner to dance, Waverley laughed that off too. To dance you needed only music and your own body, to find and abide by your internal tempo.

Rhoda thought it unlikely that Waverley would be asked to dance in any event. She did not have beauty to recommend her, and youth was not enough. Many people had youth. Rhoda was, of late, increasingly aware of those who had youth. And those from whom youth was ebbing.

Temple School, Rhoda thought, was not preparing her daughter for life. Rhoda might have approached Mr. Gerlach about changing schools, but Temple also seemed to have softened Waverley's attitude to Mr. Gerlach. She no longer heaped abuse on him. In fact, Waverley never spoke of Mr. Gerlach at all. When Rhoda brought him up—his views, his thoughts, his wisdom, his preferences—Waverley only looked vacantly elsewhere. Now, after weeks together, Rhoda knew that Waverley had not accepted Mr. Gerlach at all. She was simply indifferent to him. She did not give a damn.

"Sophia says we'll have to save Europe again, just like the last war," Waverley commented as she mopped jam from her lips. "Europeans are mired in their own historical trough. That much is clear. It's disgusting what goes into sausage."

"What are they teaching you there?" asked Rhoda.

" 'Waste not thy hour.' " Waverley beckoned the waiter for more coffee. "May I be excused after this cup? I need to finish packing."

"Packing what? You refuse to take anything except chocolate and underwear."

"That's all I need." She ruffled through her very short hair. "At school we wear clothing against constraint."

However, for the journey back to Isadora Island—by chauffeured limo hired in Victoria, and the ferryboat—Waverley wore the conventional if constraining gored skirt of a forest green with a batiste blouse and matching green ribbon at the Peter Pan collar. She wore saddle shoes and socks instead of Roman sandals, which she kept in her suitcase. The journey took the better part of the day. On the ferry Rhoda stayed inside, smoking and reading *Photoplay* while Waverley stayed outside, windblown, watching for whales, chatting with other hardy young people, even (much to Rhoda's dismay) several young Canadian soldiers. Waverley ought not to be so chummy and easygoing with men.

This journey was entirely different from the year before. This time when the chauffeur pulled his limo to a halt, parking near some waterfront sheds and machine shops, Rhoda braced herself for the pangs of parting. But Waverley wrapped Rhoda in an enormous hug, planted a fat kiss on her cheek, promised the very things she had promised the year before, and leaped out of the limo. She told the chauffeur to hurry up, bring the bags along while she found the *Nona York*.

She ambled down the long dock calling out, "Hallo there! Captain Briscoe of the *Nona York!*" And when he climbed up the ladder and into view, Waverley broke into a run, bounded on board the old boat, asked the captain all the latest from the island while the chauffeur, sweating in the September afternoon heat (there had been no rain for two weeks), hauled her valises on board.

Once the *Nona York* was under way, Waverley poured herself a cup of the captain's chewy coffee and took her place beside him as they moved westward through the islands, steering clear of those few pleasure crafts dotting the Sound and evading tugs and barges pulling log booms. Waverley commented on the traffic, the tankers and steamers, their thin lines of smoke piping against the sky, but Briscoe was in a sour mood. He resisted Waverley's attempts to cheer him. He said it was the war. In the last war his comrades had died for nothing. He rubbed the place where his ear had been shot away.

Waverley left him to his miseries to go up on deck, to take a Double-Range breath, look out over the Sound and the islands as though they were all her very own. She was the first student to return to Temple, the Captain had told her that. The sky was an unambiguous blue and the waters calm, and in the distance a pod of orcas, gracefully plying the waters, leapt, catching the light, pluming spray, their bodies as elegant as dancers. Waverley applauded.

The late afternoon heat had not abated by the time they came in view of Massacre, and Waverley helped the Captain secure *Nona York* to the rickety dock. She aye-ayed him sharply, but when she looked up to the Marine and Feed, she was disappointed that the Packard wasn't there.

"Sonofabitching Packard busted last week," he said. "Sandy's been out there, took it apart for them. He says it's the carburetor. I got a new one for him." He rummaged about in one of the tool bins and came up with a bag, a heavy bag, and handed it to her. "He can take it out there when he takes you. Sophia'll be needing the Packard soon for the rest of the students. You'll be having a new student this year. A Froggy orphan is coming to the school."

"Froggy orphan?"

He scratched his palm on his stubbled chin. "Maybe she's not an orphan. But she's a Frog. She ain't there yet. No, you're the first."

He gave her his old warm smile and bade her good-bye as Waverley hoisted her suitcase and the bag with the carburetor and sauntered up the dock, nodding to the fishers who were smoking and mending nets.

Isadora Island had been so long without rain that the waters of Massacre Bay were sluggish and the boats rocked in what looked like seaweed soup. Everything in the town lay clotted under a rind of dust. Even the dogs, panting on porches, couldn't be roused to bark, and horses tethered to wagons stood listlessly immobile. Every window in the town was open, and at the barbershop, Mr. Hulbert stood in the door, fanning himself with *Time* magazine while the pomade on his mustache melted. He waved to Waverley in a halfhearted fashion.

Once inside the dim and silent Marine and Feed, Waverley blinked. She walked to the back and found Mrs. Torklund, alone, frowning over a long sheet of figures and muttering to herself. "Hello, Mrs. Torklund," Waverley said brightly. "Is Sandy here?"

She regarded Waverley, reflexively totting up the cost of her clothes, from the saddle shoes to the blouse with the Peter Pan collar, and said no.

Waverley's breath seemed to stab lightly just beneath her heart. She had not heard from him all summer, though she'd sent half a dozen postcards from her travels. "He didn't join the navy. Did he?"

"The navy? You've confused him with Nels." She turned proudly to the postcards from Hawaii on the wall behind her. "No, Sandy's mission is a little less dramatic than that!" Mrs. Torklund's mouth cinched up.

"Ah," said Waverley, casting about for some euphemism, never minding the Temple injunction against them. "Has his mother had another seizure?"

"Another seizure of gin. Bessie's costing Sandy money, too. If he thinks I'm paying him for hours he's not working, he's got another think coming. And I don't count taking you to Temple School as part of his working hours either. And you can tell him so. You'll have to go out to the house to get him. He's there with Bessie. He can't leave her and he can't handle her either. Only one who can is Sis, though why she bothers, I don't know. If you ask me, the world will be no worse off when Bessie Lomax croaks. But you go on. Oh, and by the way, when you get to the school, you can tell Miss Westervelt, it's cash from now on. Her check bounced this morning. I got a note from the bank at Anacortes and you can tell her that her credit's worthless here. Cash or no goods."

Embarrassed on Sophia's behalf, Waverley shrugged.

"Leave your bag here and go on and get Sandy. The house is on the Moonless side of Massacre. You'll know it. The boat is still there."

"What boat?"

"The *Maid of the Isles*. Hector built it for Bessie, a thousand years ago, lots of big talk about sailing her away but it's never moved." Mrs. Tork-lund snorted. "You can see what dreamers come to."

This seemed to Waverley rather venomous and emphatic merely to describe an unfloating boat, but she nodded, left her things, and ran outside.

At an indecisive angle facing Moonless Bay, a boat set high on sup-ports floated on a sea of weeds. A sailboat without sails crested corn-flower waves, and a tiny tattered pennant lay, windless, at the top of its single mast. The boat and the house beside it, a two-story clapboard with a steeply pitched roof, were the same mottled gray as the rocks on the beach. A gaping, low picket fence stood straggled amongst the weeds. Oddly incongruent with the rest of the dilapidated house were those places where Sandy had made repairs, new wood, blond and smooth, contrasting with the worn porch, the steps, roof supports.

From inside there came cries and wails, weeping, a woman's sobs, sloshing water and a flushing toilet. She heard swearing, a man's oaths, Sandy's. Another voice, low, emollient, Sis's, tolled just beneath his. Waverley knocked gingerly at the screen door several times. Through the screen, blackened with age, Waverley saw, emerging from one room and vanishing into another, Bessie Lomax, hunched, haggard, Sis's arm around her, Sis's soothing voice mixing with Sandy's continued oaths, almost a sort of duet, long practiced, well known.

"What do you want, Marjorie?" said Sis, coming at last to the door. Her broad face was pinched, her blue eyes drained.

"I'm Waverley."

"You all look the same to me. Rich delinquents."

"We are not delinquents."

"You're not debutantes either, are you? I guess you're looking for Sandy."

"I guess I am," Waverley retorted with some bravado.

"Wait here."

But Waverley left the porch, the wretched sounds and meandered out toward Moonless, which was scummy and shallow and locked in a wide terrestrial embrace. The heat seemed to have dried up the very wa-ters of the Sound and they peeled away from rocks and shallows, leaving the beach pocked and awful, the roots of old madrona exposed like the veins on old men's legs. She imagined the cries of enemy Indians who stole over this water 150 years before, the massacre, creating the still-unquiet atmosphere.

Suddenly Sandy called out and came through the weeds, holding a clean shirt in one hand. Waverley had never seen him shirtless. Suddenly she realized the indelible truth of the old expression *to feast one's eyes*.

"Sorry you had to hear all that."

Waverley shrugged and said it did not matter.

"It was my fault this time."

"How could it be your fault?"

"When I came home last night she was sloshed and trying to light the stove, so I dumped out all the gin before I went to work this morning. Pretty soon, there comes word to me that she's out on the porch naked, flapping around. She had drunk the whole bottle of her medicine and some cologne my father got her one Christmas. Could have killed her, but we got her to puke it all up. Sis and me. I don't know how I'd manage without Sis. She's putting her to bed now. Just like a baby. Like a little sonofabitching baby."

Anything more said of Bessie would just wound or humiliate him. So Waverley remarked that maybe Sis would be a nurse when she grew up.

He put his shirt on and sat on the rocky beach beside her. He seemed to relax. She could feel the ease of him. "What about you, Waverley? What will you be?"

"I don't even know what I am, much less what I'll be."

"I know what I'm doing. Soon as I can, I'm getting off this island, that's for sure. I'm going to build things that move, planes and cars and boats, anything with a motor and some speed."

"The *Maid of the Isles?*" She nodded toward the stationary sailboat.

He laughed, lay down and flung his arm over his eyes. He said the *Maid of the Isles* had no motor. "Anyone can sail. I want to fly."

"Sophia will like to hear that." Waverley fought the impulse to rest her hand on his shirt, over his heart, to feel his heart beat. The heat radiated up from the rocky beach, uncomfortable through her green skirt. She tossed a few rocks toward the stagnant water and asked what he'd done all summer.

"You want to see? Come on."

She followed him through dense knee-high weeds, to his house and around the *Maid of the Isles* to the very back of the property, where there stood a small shed, whitewashed once, yellowing now. He lifted the latch and swung the heavy door up, and there arose the odor of metal and old newspapers, motor oil soaked into the dirt floor. And in the dimness, relieved only by one tiny window, she saw a motorcycle, polished, but not gleaming, the leather seat well worn, the front wheel cocked at a jaunty angle.

Sandy ran his hands over it, as if he expected it to purr. "Classic, Waverley. A classic 1915 Vickers-Clyno. Six horsepower, V-twin engine. They used it in the last war. They used lots of these." He rolled it out of the garage and into the sunlight. "See here where the sidecar would have been fitted. These motorcycles are so tough they used them against the enemy. They'd put the sidecars on, mount machine guns on the sidecars and take them right into battle. They could go over anything but land mines and barbed wire. Indestructible. A beauty, huh?"

"A beauty, Sandy."

"Look." He knelt by the front wheel. "A bullet hit here, dented it, but didn't pierce. And look, here's another bullet hole. If this machine could talk, it would have some tales all right."

"Does it run?"

"It does now." He grinned. "Took me all summer though. Captain Briscoe found it for me over in Anacortes. It hadn't run in fifteen years and the guy was just about giving it away. Me and Captain Briscoe, we practically had to carry it back to Isadora in a sack, that's how bad it was. And parts are hard to come by, so I had to make a lot of adjustments."

"Can you start it?"

He went into the shed and came out with a small key, fitted it into the ignition and turned the motor over several times until at last it sputtered, farted out a great cloud of exhaust and then chugged along like a panting dog.

"Can you drive it?"

"Now what kind of mechanic would I be if I couldn't drive it?"

"Can you give me a ride?"

"It's too dangerous."

"Temple girls are not afraid of anything. I am ready to embrace experience."

"What about your bag?"

"It's at the Marine and Feed anyway. I'll just leave it there and you take me to the school on the motorcycle."

"You'll be my first passenger ever." He threw his leg over the worn leather of the seat.

"Hasn't Sis been for a ride?"

"Her mother won't let her."

This pleased Waverley, and in a single swift motion she flung her leg over the seat and settled herself, smoothing her skirt down over her thighs.

"Rest your feet on the pipes and keep them there. Don't let the pipes touch your skin. They get very hot and they'll burn you. Now, hold on."

She didn't need to be told twice. To her shock and surprise, the motorcycle leaped to life, metal vibrating wildly between her thighs and reverberating all the way down her legs and up her spine, out along her arms to her very fingertips. They roared out of the garage and toward Massacre. She put her arms around his waist, gently at first, more tightly as he gathered speed. Rattling through Massacre, the unexpected noise and speed startled dogs and roused mules and horses broiling in the heat. He drove down along the waterfront, passing through swift gusts of scent, smoke and fish, tar and stagnant water, all brewing in the September heat. The exhaust of the motorcycle trailed after them like a grainy banner as they left town and climbed toward the Useless road. As he picked up speed, her skirt flew up. She pressed her cheek against his back, breathed in his salty scent and felt his warmth against her face, delighted to feel the delicious shiver of the motorcycle through her whole body. She could feel the engine's percussive staccato along his spine and where her arms touched his ribs and where her hands met over the hard muscles of his belly. She responded to his every shift in weight, leaned when he leaned into a turn, where the road dipped and rolled, plunged here and there, rutted, dry and dangerous, but to Waverley, completely liberating.

Such speed and freedom! She understood at last what Sophia had asked of her a year ago when she had bid Waverley to open her arms and imagine she could fly, suggested that in the expansion and release of the body there was possibility for the spirit and the soul. Oh *yes, yes, yes, yes!* Waverley slowly released her hold on Sandy Lomax's body and opened her arms wide, palms to the wind, head back, legs apart, mouth open, the tempo internalized, the emotion expressed, the rhythm accentuated by the gold light shuttering through evergreens as they moved through the great broth of afternoon, stewing all summer to achieve this nonpareil moment.

"Hold on," he yelled back to her, "don't let go."

Sandy, avoiding a rut in the road, lifted the bike. They bounced and Waverley thought they might actually defy gravity and fly, but she quickly brought her arms back around his body, held him close to her as he crested a hill. Apple orchards lined either side of the road, the trees so thick with fruit, their boughs were braced with beams, and the fruit, windfalls, clustered all over the ground, along split rail fences. Looking over Sandy's shoulder, Waverley could see in the distance Isadora's own huge mountain curling out toward the north. The other islands, the Sound itself, spread out before them like all the possibilities of life. And Waverley Scott, the Maid of the Isles, eyes closed, enjoyed one of those moments of unalloyed joy which she knew she must savor, keep, press into memory.

And so she did not see a tribe of island rabbits feeding on the windfalls, startled by the sputtering engine, dart frantically across the road in front of the bike, felt only Sandy lurch, swerve quickly, swear, hit a rabbit, bounce over another, the rabbits squealing, and then the flying Waverley had imagined briefly came to pass. The dream of flight. The flying. The resolution: a thud. She had hit the ground with a thud, painful and yet physically brilliant.

Grass, dirt, earth. Her nose and mouth seemed to be full of grass, dirt, earth. Between her very teeth. She wanted to grunt, to groan, but there was no breath to push through her lips. Her breath had deserted her. Gone elsewhere.

With some difficulty, pain, she turned her head so her cheek rested on the ground. She kept her eyes closed and sought her own breath. Slowly she brought a hand to her face, her bruised lips. She brushed them, and spat. The dirt remained grainy on her tongue, the grass sharp in her nostrils. Rising up too, all around her, the winy rot of windfall apples long cooked in the heat, the scent of yarrow, crushed, red clover flattened, dog fennel and rabbit pellets all protested her weight, and sharply these odors overcame her. Her whole body hurt. Her thighs were damp and cold. Her lips were sticky and warm. She could not breathe. She heard her name.

An arm came up underneath her and gently rolled her over. Sandy, on his knees, bent over her, the whole right side of his face alight with abrasions, beading with blood, a seam of blood down his cheek and blood on his shirt and shoulder. She held his hand. Her breath came back slowly and she pulled his hand close between her breasts. Sandy. And knowing it was Sandy, she closed her eyes again. He said he would go for help. She clutched his hand more tightly. "Don't leave me."

Sandy brushed the blood and dirt and grass from her lips. Waverley opened her mouth, closed her eyes and concentrated on the taste of his fingers across her lips, her mouth, her teeth, her tongue, till there was no more grass or dirt taste, just Sandy's taste, and she puckered her lips to better hold his finger between her lips, against her tongue, savoring the pleasure of the kiss he would give her before he gave it. Gentle at first. His lips, like his fingers, were gentle at first, insistent but not demanding, mingled the taste of him with the grass and clover. She had wind knocked out of her. Again. Mingled with the surge of energy that radiated from her whole torso as she took him gently into her embrace and he eased his body on top of hers, and when he whispered, asked if anything was broken, she said yes, though she wasn't sure just what, knowing only that nothing would ever be the same.

Chapter 13

*I*sland opinion on the accident was divided. With only fourteen telephones on Isadora, all sharing party lines, certainly everyone knew within hours of the vet being summoned to Useless Point. Sophia had asked the central operator to ring Dr. Oland's house, and unable to find him there, rang the Marine and Feed, telling Mrs. Torklund she was desperate, that Sandy and Waverley had been in a terrible accident. Mrs. Torklund sent her husband over to the Isadora Inn, where, this late in the afternoon, Dr. Oland was inebriated, very happy, but unfit to drive. Mr. Torklund took him to Useless Point in the Marine and Feed truck. When they passed the motorcycle still in the road, they stopped and put it in the truck. They saw the dead rabbits, their guts strewn everywhere. Dr. Oland remarked that the island ought to put a bounty on rabbits. They were a menace. Mr. Torklund was silent.

"Who's first?" inquired the vet brightly as he and Mr. Torklund came into the school's kitchen where Newton and Sophia tended the victims.

"Waverley," Sandy insisted.

"Up on the table with you, Waverley!"

Waverley did not want to move. By now she realized that the impact of the fall had loosed the contents of her bladder, and her skirt, her clothes in general, were a mess. But Dr. Oland led her to the table, helped her up. Once he had her laid out there, without a thought for modesty he had a practiced feel up and over her body, pushing here, pulling there. Waverley yelped.

"Sorry," soothed the vet, "I keep forgetting I can just ask if it hurts. I'm not used to patients who talk." He had her bend her knees, and gave a twist to her ankles. He waved his hand in front of her eyes and asked if she felt like puking. He announced that Waverley had a concussion, probably slight, some significant bruises, but her organs were all still in place. He ordered her to bed. "Good thing for you, you bounced instead of breaking." He patted her haunch as he might have a cooperative horse. "Time and nature," he prescribed, "time and nature."

"And three raw egg whites a day," added Quizzer.

"That won't kill her either. Must be wonderful to be young. Next patient!"

Turning his attention to Sandy, who could only get on the table with considerable pain, Dr. Oland tore what was left of his shirt, muttered over his abrasions, and doused them with a splash of antiseptic so powerful that Sandy almost passed out. Oland smeared him— bloodied shoulder, arm, chest—with a horse salve that stank. Sandy yelped when the vet pressed his low ribs. Dr. Oland said that Sandy's corduroy pants had protected his legs for the most part, though turning both ankles rather more roughly than need be, he said the right was probably sprained, and a couple of ribs cracked, maybe broken. "Like your heart, eh Sandy?" And Dr. Oland gave a wink to Waverley as he taped up the ribs.

Then he asked Sophia for a pot holder and told Sandy to put it between his teeth and bite down. He daubed some antiseptic on the cheek and cheerfully sewed up half a dozen stitches on the right side of his face, chatting all the while.

"Half an inch closer," he concluded, snipping his thread, "and you would have left your eye there in the road with the rabbit guts."

"Rabbits darted into the road," said Sandy, after spitting out the pot holder. "I swerved to avoid them, hit a rut and we went flying." He looked over at Waverley. "I think that's what happened."

"We went flying," she repeated.

Dr. Oland asked if there was anything to drink.

"Alcohol is not a True Food," said Sophia.

"Not for me," the doctor protested. "For them. They'll be needing it. Both of them."

"Let's go, Sandy," said Mr. Torklund. "Time is money."

They gently helped Sandy to his feet. He draped his arms over their shoulders and limped toward the door, fearing he might faint. He had to stop. He turned and brought his gaze to rest on Waverley. "I'm sorry, Waverley. About everything. Really sorry."

"I'm not."

These remarks were repeated all over Isadora, provided fodder for gossip that went round the island, ringing it like the tides and currents. Even those people who had no phones soon heard that Sandy Lomax had laid his motorcycle down on the dirt road and injured himself and one of the Temple girls. Many people said that Sandy was as bad as his old man, a reckless daredevil like Hector. Mrs. Foltz and Mrs. Huey were both of this opinion. In this matter, Foltzy and Huey were fonts of knowledge. After all, Foltzy and Huey had come upon the wreck of the motorcycle as they rattled along the Useless road on their way back to Massacre after working at the school. They had found Sandy and Waverley and taken them back to Useless.

People who disliked the Lomaxes believed that just like Hector, Sandy would come to no good. But those Isadorans who disapproved of Temple School believed that Waverley had distracted him. Perhaps worse. Led him astray. It was probably the girl's fault. Almost certainly the girl's fault. It usually is the girl's fault. Waverley wasn't even sorry (judging from what she'd said, oh yes, Mr. Torklund himself had been there to hear it and Mrs. Torklund repeated it word for word). And when it further emerged (Foltzy and Huey did not gossip, mind you, but this was the truth) that as their car came up over the hill, they had found the victims in a weird sort of state. Together. The boy lying on top of the girl. Her arms around him.

Some people, Dr. Oland amongst them, blamed the rabbits. To anyone who would listen, he put forth again his plan of a bounty on rabbits. Shoot to kill, that was his philosophy, and a lot of farmers concurred with him, but nothing came of the scheme.

The penance that Sandy bore for his ill-fated escapade was to wear the shopman's apron. For months while his injuries healed, Sandy stood behind the till. He loathed the job, but he was lucky to have kept it, since he could neither lift nor carry. In this new, inglorious capacity behind the counter, Sandy had to listen as Isadorans, some of whom seldom talked to anyone but the seals, would stand with their purchases, not moving, not paying till they had said their piece: rattled at length

about their health, the tides and weather, the fishing, the farming, the
logging, their sheep, their pigs, their mules and motors, their thankless
children, their complaints against the Westervelts, or God, whoever had
treated them worse. But the really unbearable part of his new duties was
that Sandy was in the almost constant company of Mrs. Torklund. She
was as astringent as Dr. Oland's antiseptic. He began to better understand Mr. Torklund's thin-lipped grimness.

Sandy could only tolerate the work when Sis was around. Sis often
relieved her mother, and Mrs. Torklund went upstairs to iron or scrub or
sweep. Sandy and Sis could hear her incessant activity. When Sis was
there, she would step in and free Sandy from the rigors of listening. She
could effortlessly absorb some farmer's or fisher's long-winded tale, and
usually sell him something at the same time. Sis Torklund was a marvel,
everyone agreed, smarter even than her brother, Nels, though not as
good-looking. She had an insatiable fund of efficiency, energy and good
health, patience and competence, and she was nowhere near as grim as
her parents, both of whom were slightly in awe of her.

The elder Torklunds considered themselves by far the most injured,
however much damage the accident had wreaked on Sandy. After all, they
were stuck with the consequences. Sandy Lomax would not be able to do
any heavy lifting for six to eight months, nor could he bounce around in
the old Dodge. So Sandy's lift-and-deliver duties fell to Mr. Torklund, who
complained nightly of sore muscles and a bad back. He said he wasn't getting any younger. Mrs. Torklund said that Temple School had brought
them nothing but trouble. And no wonder. The whole place was godless,
did not celebrate so much as Christmas or Easter, much less keep the Sab-
bath. And what sort of woman kept her maiden name when she was de-
cently married?

"Perhaps they aren't married," said Sis as they ate supper one night.
She cut her fried fish with a fork. "Those two living in the clapboard
next door, Dahlgren and Agnes, they're living in sin. No one thinks anything of it out there. They call themselves artists, but if they were artists,
what are they doing at Useless? And those students, they're nothing but
rich delinquents."

"Godless," said Mrs. Torklund. "They're all a godless lot."

Sis's parents kept their eyes on their plates, and ate, for the most part, without conversation. The Torklunds did everything efficiently. For a time there was only the sound of cutlery on the tin plates, the thud of thick cups of sugared tea moving to their lips.

Sis finished her fish and returned to her thought. "If those Temple students were decent girls, they'd be living at home."

"Like you," said her father.

"Like me." Sis buttered her biscuit with a brisk finality. She remarked that Sandy was repairing his motorcycle, and he would be riding it again when he was able to.

"You had better not be on the back of it," cautioned Mrs. Torklund.

"No one should be on the back of it. But you know what those Temple girls are like."

"Godless." Mrs. Torklund further ruminated. "Trouble. They're all trouble."

"Once his ribs mend, once he's got the motorcycle working again, Sandy will just get back on and go out to the school and one of those girls will throw her leg over"—she bit the biscuit and chewed for a bit before continuing—"the motorcycle, and off they'll go."

The Torklunds all considered this wordlessly.

Mrs. Torklund reached across the table for the pan and ladled herself up another helping of hot sauerkraut. "I told that girl cash, the one who was in the accident with Sandy, I said, tell Sophia it's cash from now on. She didn't do it. On purpose. I'll have to tell Sophia myself, I guess, 'fore I send out November's billing."

"Doing those deliveries is hard on Pa's back," said Sis. "As long as Pa's having to do all that lifting and hoisting, I think we should double the school's delivery fee."

"Do we charge a delivery fee?" Mr. Torklund asked his wife, who gave him a cryptic look encoded with twenty-three years of marriage.

Sis saw this look. She attended to her supper. She put down her fork. "We do charge them a delivery fee, don't we? All that gas all the way out to Useless? All the wear and tear on the delivery truck? All the time it takes? And it takes even more time when Sandy does the delivery than when Pa does it."

"It does?" Her father pulled a fish bone from between his teeth.

"Sandy always delivers the school's goods last. He spends hours out there. Keeps the truck tied up at Useless for hours while he, well, who knows? Sophia pays him to do repairs, but that's probably not all he does."

"Not on my nickel, he won't," said her father. "He's supposed to be working for me."

"What else does he do?" asked Mrs. Torklund.

Sis finished her supper and pushed her plate away. "There's a lot of rooms at that school and a lot of woods nearby, and a lot of girls all throwing themselves at Sandy. He's only human. He hasn't exactly had the best upbringing, either, not from Bessie and Hector."

"Bessie Lomax had a child before Sandy. Before she and Hector were even married," Mr. Torklund offered. "Only, it wasn't full term, this child."

"It was a child of sin," said Mrs. Torklund. "And that's why God didn't let it get born."

Sis picked up a green apple, and with her knife she pared it in one long undulating peel. "The girls at that school think nothing of taking off their clothes and wearing togas. You wonder what they wear under them. Oh, for their performances they wear underwear, but you wonder about the rest of the time. You just wonder."

"I don't," said Mr. Torklund, who indeed had wondered this very thing on more than one occasion.

"Sandy shouldn't be spending time out there," said Sis. "Not time we're paying for anyway. Our time. Any time, really."

Mr. Torklund adopted Sis's point of view, even Sis's tone of voice and her very words when he spoke with Sandy about Temple School. Then, to prove he was the man of the household, he forbade Sandy to go out to Temple School at all. Except to deliver. When he once again could drive the truck, he must deliver and return to Massacre immediately. Sandy could not stay for any reason. He must not spend time with any of the Temple girls, who were, all of them, trouble. Sophia and Newton and whoever was living in sin out there, they were all trouble. Mr. Torklund was emphatic, direct, but when he was done, he wished he'd let Sis deliver the message because Sandy didn't seem to understand the full implications of his speech.

Sandy, pushing a broom, replied, "I can't be lifting and hoisting and driving for months yet, so I don't—"

"I'm not talking about when you're driving for us. I'm talking about all the time." This thought cheered him, and he laid down the law. "You stay away from those girls, from that school."

"I don't think you can tell me what to do with my time," Sandy replied recklessly.

"You work for me. You follow my rules." Satisfied, Mr. Torklund walked away.

Sandy pushed the broom and the dust danced before him. Perhaps the Temple girls were trouble. The physical pain he still lived with served only to remind him of the physical pleasure he had known in that moment; the pain and pleasure were indissolubly connected. Hadn't Waverley Scott brought his hand to her breast? Hadn't she brought his body to lie on hers. Hadn't he—never minding the abrasions, the sliced-up cheek, the cracked ribs—felt from and for Waverley something desperate, urges, emotions that could not be suppressed? He knew he was to blame for the accident, but that was not what he had apologized for. At least not entirely.

$\mathcal{S}$ophia put through a call to the Marine and Feed to protest the delivery fee when the bill came.

"New policy," said Mrs. Torklund. "You want delivery. You pay extra. In fact, Miss Westervelt, you pay cash. I told your girl months ago. In September. The day of the accident. I told her, you tell Miss Westervelt it's cash and cash alone. No more checks. The school's checks have come back, Miss Westervelt. Insufficient funds. But I don't suppose she gave you the message."

"Well, how could she? I mean—there was an accident."

Mrs. Torklund harrumphed. "Accident indeed."

"It was folly, of course, but not fatal. No one died."

"It will never happen again, Miss Westervelt."

"Of course not."

"My husband has forbidden Sandy to go near your school. Everyone knows about him and that girl the day of the accident. When they found the two of them, he was on top of her. Lying on top of her! She had her arms around him and her legs—"

"Let's return to the money, Mrs. Torklund."

"Fine. Cash."

"But there is no bank on this island. I would have to go to the mainland, and often. I can't take that kind of time from my work. It's a terrible hardship."

"It's a hardship for us when goods aren't paid for."

"We are your most reliable customers. We have been for twenty years."

"Our most reliable customers pay their bills. If you can't pay cash, take your business elsewhere," declared Mrs. Torklund, and hung up without another word.

Sophia went into the library, where she found Waverley deep into a novel by Sarah Orne Jewett. "Follow me." She led Waverley into her small, semiprivate study at the back of the library. She sat behind her desk and beckoned Waverley to the chair across from her. Sophia folded her powerful hands in her lap and leveled her gray-eyed gaze on her student. "I understand that when Mrs. Huey and Mrs. Foltz came upon you and Sandy after the accident, you were discovered in some sort of compromising position."

Waverley moistened her lips. In the months since the accident, she could think of little else, but she could not say it. Not to anyone. She knew though that she and Sandy had shared something that had fundamentally altered them, set them apart from the others. She felt none of Irene's superior delight in her sexual experience. But then, Waverley wasn't altogether certain hers was actual experience. It was sexual. That she knew. She grew warm, moist even, just thinking about it. She flushed now.

"Is this true, Waverley? What were you and Sandy doing?"

"Nothing."

"You know I dislike evasion as much as euphemism."

"We got thrown off the motorcycle. What could we be doing? We were thrown to the side of the road, and it's lucky we didn't hit the fence. Or a tree. We could have been killed." She paused, expecting a volley of sympathy, but Sophia's features did not alter. "Huey and Foltzy have low minds."

"I did not hear it from Huey and Foltzy."

"Oh." Waverley squirmed in her chair. Since the accident she had seen very little of Sandy Lomax; she had gone into Massacre with Quizzer a couple of times to pick up the returning students at the Marine and Feed. Sandy would not meet her gaze directly. And so Waverley too had looked away.

"I heard it from Mrs. Torklund. They've forbidden Sandy to come here."

"Dr. Oland said he can't lift things."

"At all. Sandy's not to come here at all. Even after he can lift."

"I swear, Sophia, Mrs. Torklund is just spreading vicious rumors. There's nothing in them. I swear on the Choc—" She gulped and cast around. "Chalkboard."

"Why on earth would you swear on a chalkboard?"

"I wouldn't lie, Sophia."

Of course you would, Sophia thought. She understood both passion and foible, folly and farce. After all, she'd indulged in all of these in her youth. In this regard Sophia Westervelt had certainly learned by doing. "We will continue this conversation later. Perhaps you should make yourself useful to humanity and go help Marjorie with her lessons."

"Yes, Sophia."

November wind throttled trees outside, and the rain beat against her window. Sophia turned on the lamp at her desk and got out her spectacles, her pencil and paper and the school's ledgers. She began checking her figures to see where she had gone wrong. Figures were not her forte. She pored over the long columns. Sophia was painfully aware that her school had been funded entirely by her father. The vision was hers, but without Pa's money, it would never have existed. Dear old Pa had lavished on Sophia—his youngest and best beloved—money. Pa could never deny Sophia anything. For years he had supported her in Paris, though the whole family gave him grief for his indulgence. He had given her the land at Useless for her school. He had built the school with Westervelt money, timber, labor. He had endowed it with a trust fund. He didn't understand Sophia's passion for art and artists, for the dance and dancers, for imagination and education at all, but he was always there to applaud and sign the checks.

And then, four years ago, he was not there. Pa died. From the moment Sophia and Newton had gone to the funeral (she had not been informed in time to say good-bye) she felt her siblings' collective wrath: theirs and their spouses and their children, their children's children. The whole Westervelt tribe, down to the last mewling, puking infant. And her brother Jethro, having succeeded to the head of the family business, found ways, slowly, certainly, to strangle Sophia's funds, to meddle in the trust, to deny payments, to drain her assets. He did these things without notifying her. Funds for Sophia's school diminished, dried up, seemingly blew away.

But her situation had never been as dire as it was this fall. This fall she had raised student fees, and in doing so, deprived herself of a student. Florence. Her mother, a Temple alumna, wrote that Florence would not be returning, the underthread in the letter suggesting that a Temple education was not what it had been. This was true. Sophia also cut the artists' salaries in half, hoping they would take offense and leave. She knew they would not: Agnes and Morton, the Austin-Smythes, where could they go? Who else would reward their meager talents or recognize their frail reputations? They were a contentious lot, failures as inspiration. But Sophia needed them. She had conceived her school from the very beginning as a place where the arts and artists were supreme, and without that vision, Temple School was but a building. She had never once entertained the notion of failure. Sophia did not entertain it now, but it came to her, unbidden. The disparity between her ambitions for the school and its current sorry state left her feeling weak, queasy.

"What's wrong, dear?" asked Newton, bouncing in, Nijinsky beside him. "Bad news?"

"No. Just a little headache."

"A glass of magnetized water. That's what you need."

"Yes, Newton, that's what I need. Thank you."

Off he went to the lab to siphon a glass of magnetized water. When Newton came back, he would sit with her, tell her some new advance with electromagnetic brain waves, describe some new observation link-ing universal rhythms in the universe, extol the new chapter in his book. She would smile and be pleased for him. Sophia cleared the figures from her desk. She would deal with all this later. The bank. The money. Mrs. Torklund. She had long since given up discussing the school's financial problems with Newton. His response was always the same. He declared that to save money she could quit paying him a salary. And Sophia always gently reminded him that he had not been paid a salary for years.

Chapter 14

*N*ewton packed his bag, kissed his wife, bade farewell to the students and left on the *Nona York* when the call came from Vancouver to collect the French refugee. Amongst themselves the four Temple students had already named her the Frog, but they were careful to refrain from this in Sophia's hearing.

Quizzer was gone for days, several of them windy, icy, the chop on the waters of the Sound visible for miles. On the fourth day a thick fog set in, and Sophia moved Newton's telescope up to their room to keep watch. In twenty years she and Newton had never spent a night apart, and without his comforting bulk beside her she did not sleep well. As thick and unrelenting fogs enveloped the island, she could not think or work, and she taught her classes absently. The devotees of the Church of the Chocolate God on the other hand were certain that Quizzer had discovered the chocolate shops of Vancouver, that he had been seduced from True Foods into the arms of the Chocolate God. Services that week were particularly enthusiastic.

Not until the sixth night, as the students were all in the kitchen, Marjorie reading Mary Wollstonecraft in a halting and lackluster fashion as the others set the table and peeled apples, did Sophia come flying downstairs. She ran through the kitchen, pulled on her wellies in the mudroom and flung a heavy coat over her shoulders. Only then did the students hear the sound of the truck making its way up the hill. The Marine and Feed truck.

Given the possibility that Sandy might be the driver, there was a collective dash for the mudroom door and all five of them stood, shivering, watching the headlights gleam through an icy rain. The truck stopped and Newton got out and Sophia flew to his arms. Newton planted a great kiss on her lips and told her to get inside or she'd catch cold. He greeted the girls effusively and in general raised the temperature of the surrounding area by about ten degrees just with his personal warmth.

Waverley, peering past Quizzer, saw Sandy at the wheel. He had not been to Temple School since the accident in September. He got out of the truck and went to lift two valises from the back when Newton stopped him and asked the girls to get them out, that Sandy's ribs were still mending. Waverley took one, Violet the other. Sandy went inside carrying nothing.

As Newton nattered on about the lack of proper heat in the truck and the laws of physics, warm air rising, he offered his hand to the girl still inside the cab. He tugged at her hand and pulled her out of the truck, through the mudroom and into the warm kitchen. He released her hand. He beamed at her. "Girls, allow me to introduce to you our new student, Avril Aron."

Sophia reached out, as though to touch Avril's face or hair, but the girl stepped back, turned away. "Of course," Sophia murmured, "of course it's all very new and strange here. *Soyez la bienvenue*, Avril."

"I speak English," she replied defiantly.

Waverley guessed Avril to be about her own age, chunky, though her legs were skinny. Her stockings and shoes were filthy and her hair matted, dirty, long, very thick, coarse and curly. Her face was thin, her skin gray and the eyes huge and dark and set too close to the nose. She smelled bad. She shook herself off like a dog.

"Poor Avril," declared Newton, "she's been sick since we set foot on the *Nona York*, vomiting the whole way here. It was a brutal crossing. Brutal, even with the steady hand of Captain Briscoe."

"Can you hold your arms out, Avril?" asked Sophia wistfully. "Imagine you can fly?" But the girl only folded her arms resolutely across her chest. A most unlikely candidate for flight. "You must look like your mother, Avril."

Avril shot them all a nasty look and her lip curled and she shrugged.

"I'll be going," said Sandy.

"Oh, now, the least we can do is offer you supper," said Ginevra. "Don't you think, Sophia? Sandy must be cold clean through."

" 'Clean through' betrays vulgarity, Ginevra," replied Sophia, her old equanimity restored, "but yes, of course, Sandy must stay." She clasped Newton's hand, said again how she had missed him.

Shedding his great coat, Newton took the lid off the pot of cornmeal pudding, a staple of Temple fare. He bent over the stove and breathed deeply and satisfaction lit his face. "Oh, you girls cannot imagine how glad I am to return to health! And what I had to eat while I was away! I tell you, it was dreadful!"

"How dreadful?" asked Violet, as they all took their places.

Waverley was the server that night, and she heaped a great ladleful on every plate and took her place between Ginevra and Marjorie and across from Sandy and the Frog. Unfair, she thought, that the Frog should get the coveted seat beside Sandy Lomax. The Frog had bitten her lips raw, and her red-rimmed eyes were ringed with great dark circles.

Quizzer explained to the Frog that though Temple School did not subscribe to the old outmoded religions, they were committed to the life of spirit and so before each meal there was a moment of soul silence. Then they would partake of the food of the gods. True Foods. "Heads bent, girls, hearts lifted."

Waverley looked up and across at Sandy. He winked at her.

They passed around the sugar and cream for the cornmeal pudding and the stale biscuits and pitcher of milk. Newton in particular fell to his supper with gusto, asking many questions about the chickens and the school. He quizzed each girl about something: who wrote "Ode on a Grecian Urn," and the spiritual implications of isosceles triangles. He asked after Sandy's ribs and how they were mending. He said he'd send some magnetized water back with Sandy for Captain Briscoe's dog Rufus, who was afflicted with mange and flatulence. And in the midst of all this noisy reunion, Avril silently jabbed at the cornmeal in her bowl. Sophia leaned over to Avril, placed a hand lightly on her hand and bade her eat something. Avril shrugged, pulled her hand to her side.

Sophia guided the conversation away from themselves, the joys of homecoming, and to their guest, no, not guest. Student. A new Temple student. From Paris. "From the rue de la Grande Chaumière, Fourteenth Arrondissment. You have lived there all your life, Avril?"

"Yes."

"I know that street very well. I once lived nearby. On the rue Notre-Dame des Champs. You know that street?"

Avril picked up her spoon and excavated a hole in the cornmeal pudding where the cream had soaked in.

Sophia turned to the rest of them. "There was more talent in Montparnasse than any place on earth. Those streets were the center of the universe, though that was a long time ago."

Avril lifted her spoon, nibbled her pudding and put the spoon down, swilling a gulp of milk, wiping her lips with the back of her hand. "No, Madame. That is still true. Still the center."

"More sugar and cream for Avril," cried Quizzer.

Avril doused her dinner in sugar and scraped it off the top, licking her spoon.

"It's not her fault," Quizzer informed the rest of them. "French food is Number 18 on the List of Nevers. She's been eating it all her life."

"You have been traveling long, Avril?" asked Sophia.

"I leave Paris in July. Now it is what? December? November?"

"Your mother said you left in June."

Avril shrugged. Her shrug was cosmic: her whole body rose up into her shoulders and she rolled them forward and she made a face that said *so damn what?* She did not need English to do this.

Sophia sipped her coffee. "Was it a dangerous journey?"

"They are all dangerous now." Avril kept her eyes on her dish.

"You traveled with some relatives."

"Cousins."

"Was it difficult?"

Avril regarded them all, one by one. "We crossed the Pyrenees on foot. Is that difficult enough for you? Dangerous, Madame?"

Undaunted by the implied contempt, Sophia continued. "You left your relatives and traveled to Vancouver by yourself?"

"It was on a train. On a train there are many peoples."

"And your relatives in Vancouver, how did you find them?"

"They are not my relatives." Avril brought her eyes up from her dish and glared. "They are some peoples of my cousins' peoples. I find them filthy. Pigs."

"They were horrible!" cried Newton. "It took me the longest time to find them and when I did—oh, it was just awful. They're furriers and they live above the shop. Everything, absolutely everything stank of formaldehyde and deadness, death and preservatives." He glanced meaningfully at Violet. "And what are preservatives?"

"The fifth great enemy of life. Rule 65."

"Tell us about Paris, Avril," said Ginevra with killing sweetness. "I just know we can learn so much from you."

Perhaps Avril recognized the thread of malice in her voice because she refused to answer.

"Is Paris terrible now?" Sophia asked. "With the German Occupation, it must be terrible."

"Paris is never terrible, Madame. Cruel. Perhaps cruel, but never terrible. I have no wish to leave. No matter the Germans. I leave because my mother tells me I must go. She takes me across the river and says, go. My grandmother says I must go. But I will return to Paris. If the Allies win, fine." She gave her insolent shrug. "If the Germans win, fine. I return."

"But while you're here, you must think of us as your family," declared Quizzer. And to the other girls he offered, "Avril is our part of the war effort. She is our contribution to the men and women fighting Hitler. Having her at Temple School is an act of solidarity with the Resistance and on behalf of the Allies."

Waverley rolled her eyes. Never in all her life had she heard such rot. How could a pitiful, hunched-up, dirty-haired, silent, surly girl carry on her narrow back the whole weight of the Allied cause? She glanced at Sandy and felt sorry for him sitting so close to the Frog. Waverley could smell her from across the table.

"I'm sure Avril is exhausted." Sophia rose and lit a small lantern. She picked up one of Avril's suitcases. "Come with me. We're going to give you the little room, the one we save for when someone is sick and needs some time to be alone."

"I am alone, Madame. I promise you that."

"You will be happy here, Avril."

"Never." She stood, pushed her stool back and sullenly followed Sophia out of the room without a word to anyone else.

Sophia led her through the dining room and into the long hall, which was dark except for the light at the very end, and up the stairs, also lit by one bulb. She explained to Avril that they were just now practicing economies. She explained in French till Avril mumbled again that she could speak English.

Sophia opened the door to the small room which, like the rest of the upstairs, was chilled, heating being another economy the school was practicing. "Did your father teach you English? His English was quite beautiful. As he was beautiful." She turned on the electric light. Avril blinked against its brightness. "It's so gratifying to see your father receiving at last, really, the acclaim and recognition that his genius deserves. He is a genius."

"He is not my father."

"Pardon?"

Avril tucked her hands in her armpits. "Denis Aron is not my father."

"But your mother's letter said—well, she said you were the daughter of Denis Aron."

"I cannot answer for her letter."

"You are Avril Aron?"

"Yes."

"And your mother is Judith Aron?"

"Yes. Judith is the wife of Denis Aron. He lives with her and with me and my grandmother. He sleeps in my mother's bed. He sleeps with lots of other womens too, but he is not my father."

Sophia opened the dresser drawer and took out a Temple regulation white flannel nightgown. As she shook it out, the scent of creeping damp wafted from its folds. She laid it out on the narrow bed. "Then who is your father?"

Avril gave a shrug that suggested her cosmic indifference. "Men come. Men go."

"That is a very unkind thing to say about your mother."

"You asked about my father. Not my mother."

"Did she send something for me? When she wrote, your mother said you would be bringing something for me. Something particular."

"And what was that?"

"She didn't say precisely. But only that you would have something for me."

"Money?" Avril reached down between the bulk of her layers of clothes and pulled out a silken bag. "I have nothing left. Some Canadian."

"Not money. Something more important than money. Something of great value."

"I have nothing for you, Madame. She gave me nothing."

"Wait here."

Sophia crossed the broad hall in the dark and turned on the electric light in the bathroom. A square of light fell across the floor like a boat of brightness on a sea of black. She returned to the little room where the girl still stood, the valise beside her on the floor. Avril's eyes were on her shoes.

"That is the bathroom. You should have a bath. It looks to have been a very long time since you've had a bath."

Avril sniffed her own armpits and made a face and shrugged again.

"Your mother's letter said you left in June. Now you tell me you were still in Paris. Why would she have said that if it was not true? I could not have objected to your coming. She told me not to write."

"She told me nothing at all, Madame. Your quarrel, if you have one, is with her."

Some old remembered ache pierced Sophia, darting around her heart, plummeting through her bowels. Though a long time had passed, she recognized the pain that only Denis Aron could inflict. She felt his hand in this as surely as if he had struck her. Sophia knew what it was to be included in his anger, his arrogance, in his presumption that his talent, his drive, his charm, ambition, passion, intensity, that all these things forged for him a ticket, and with this ticket he was exempted from the ordinary obligations. With this ticket, Denis Aron assumed he could go through the world doing exactly as he pleased, neither asking permission nor begging pardon. In this remembered fashion, and with his casual assumptions of superiority, Denis had foisted this girl upon Sophia. And Sophia upon the girl. A sad match. A sad and bitter match.

Well, it was done and could not be undone. She bade Avril good night, and added, "You see the light down the hall. That's the bathroom. You remember where it is. You know where you are?"

"I only know where I am not," she replied without looking up from her shoes.

Chapter 15

*A*vril waited until the footsteps had died away altogether and
even then she did not move. She waited to cry. She thought
she might cry at last. Wanted to. She should have been able
to. Only old women have used up their allotment of tears. Only very old
women are left tearless in the face of tragedy. That's what her grandmother always told her: *Save your tears. One day you will need them and
you will have used them all up if you weep over petty trifles. So shut up.*

For Avril's grandmother, tears were to be hoarded. Like everything
else. Like bread and soap, like laughter for that matter, tears were to be
kept, pressed close to the bosom, parted with only for some worthy
event: the death of a husband at Verdun, say. Yes, weep for that. You
could weep for that. Avril's grandmother had. Tears for the disgrace of a
daughter, pregnant by a penniless madman, weep for that. And her
grandmother had. For the marching of German boots into your city. Her
mother and grandmother had wept for that. Even Denis Aron had wept,
but Avril had not. Avril had not truly understood what awaited her city
when the Nazis marched in.

Life had changed. Swiftly. Her mother and grandmother retreated
behind the doors and windows of their apartment, keeping everything
closed, locked, stifling in the heat. Avril's piano lessons ended. Her
friends were not welcome. She was not allowed to go anywhere. And for
these things Avril had cried and protested, stomped her feet, yelled bitter things. Her grandmother carped at her, *Save your tears, one day you
will need them.* And then, one day she did need them. One day her
mother told her she was leaving Paris.

Now Avril did more than cry and protest. She screamed and

slammed doors, bellowing insults, refusals, so that all their building could hear her. Her mother slapped her soundly, not so much so that Avril should stop crying, but that her tears should have a physical basis. A cause. Anyone might slap a noisy child. Everyone did. *Save your tears*, cautioned her mother. *Keep your mouth shut.*

And then one night, while her grandmother had packed her things, her mother dressed Avril from the skin out, bundled her up despite the summer night and marched her across the river to the cousins in the rue Saint-Antoine. After a last passionate embrace, she told Avril to save her tears and left her there.

Avril had saved her tears. Now, where were they? Had she used them all up? She needed them now, here. Her grandmother would have scoffed. To weep for loneliness? To squander your allotment of tears on behalf of something so elusive and ephemeral as loneliness? Even a lone-liness so vast and empty that Avril felt untethered from her own flesh, as though she and her body might wave at each other from a long dis-tance, and could only be united under the duress of pain, hunger, fatigue or seasickness, the festering of her skin and blood consumed by ver-min—all of which she had endured on this wretched journey, first to last. Why could she not cry?

If her grandmother was right, it would be a terrible thing to be fif-teen and to have used up all your lifelong allotment of tears. Avril's nose ran. Her lip trembled. A single sob gathered deep in her chest and burst from her like a bubble, but the feast of tears did not materialize. There was nothing but silence.

Perhaps her failure to cry was the fault of the silence. How could one weep in such silence as this? How did people live in such silence? This terrible island-silence. The quiet pressed around her. Never in her life had Avril heard such deafening silence. Always in the rue de la Grande Chaumière there were voices and calls and quarrels and errant laughter, cars and cries, horns and grinding wheels from the street. The noise dimmed at night, but never was it entirely still. And in all this terrible journey, except for the long walk across the Pyrenees, there was not such silence as there was on this island. At the furrier's stinking shop in Van-couver, noise had surrounded Avril. Had she allowed herself to cry (which she did not) the tears would have been submerged, insignificant, all but inaudible drops in a great vat of noise. But here, in this stillness (save for the wind in the trees outside) the sound of her own tears would only make her more alone, more lonely. So Avril saved her tears. No doubt she would need them later.

She lifted the valise to the prim starched bed and looked around the room, harshly lit from above. A bed, bedside table, bureau, laundry basket, bookshelf, a tiny grate unlit despite the chill, a desk, a washstand with soap, towels and a tin of talcum powder, which she sniffed for its fragrance. Lavender. It made her sneeze. A plain rug covered the floor, and the walls were dotted with framed fine-arts prints: surprised maidens and happy cavaliers, fat cherubs, bosomy goddesses, earnest young gods, all of them half clad. Stupid reproductions of the sorts of pictures Denis Aron despised.

Opening the valise, Avril took from it the picture of her mother, a small framed snapshot, and she leaned it against the silent clock on the bedside table. In this picture, taken in a café, Judith Aron looked relaxed and happy, and in that regard alone, it was remarkable. Avril dug down amongst the clothes and found a packet of cigarette papers and a tin of tobacco and these she put in the drawer. The rest of her clothes she collected in a single scooping armful, and dropped them in a drawer and slammed it shut. One by one, she undid the buttons on the sweaters that she wore, four sweaters, five if you count the pullover sweater with no buttons. She dropped them on the floor. And she dropped the three blouses, one after the other. She took the little silken bag with what was left of her money and flung it in the suitcase. Three camisoles, two skirts, two underslips later, Avril stood in her underwear. There in front of the mirror she beheld her unlovely self. She was pale, dirty, her lips chewed to pieces. Her limbs were splotched with scabs and sores, spider bites, the bites of bedbugs, fleas, lice.

She lifted her arms high over her head, not as if she could fly, but as if she might dive. Tied in parallel lines around her rib cage were three rows of twine: under her arms, just beneath her breasts, and at her waist. These held the linen wrappings against her body. She pulled each knot loose with some difficulty and then put the twine in the valise. So completely molded to her body were these linen wrappings that even untied, they did not immediately fall. Avril unwound them slowly. They crackled and crinkled in the oppressive silence as she unraveled them from her torso, canvas by canvas, each protectively swathed in soft linen.

She put the valise on the floor and opened each painting across the bed. Their brilliant colors leapt to the eye, a mélange of blue and orange and green, black, thick crisp yellows all seemed to swim up, to impress themselves on the viewer, a sensation like ice water or intense heat against the skin: color first, shape after the experience of the color itself had cooled. They were signed Aron, one dated 1934, one dated 1912, and the last, smaller than the others, a blue nude dated 1914.

Shivering with cold Avril scrambled into the nightdress Sophia had left for her, a white flannel utilitarian thing, too long for her. She rerolled the canvases, each in its linen shroud, and put them in the valise, closed it and pushed it under the bed. From her little handbag she took a comb and a toothbrush, and removing her shoes she made her way in stocking feet down the long quiet hall to the bathroom.

Avril wished she could be invisible. And then she thought, since I am wishing to be invisible, why not wish to be invisible somewhere besides this wild island with these awful strangers? The man who had come to collect her was so terrible, so fleshy and breathy and excitable, so eager that his enthusiasms should be infectious. The girls with their hostile stares. The woman, Sophia, who had been the lover of Denis Aron. Avril did not care who he slept with. Now or then. She cared only to be home. Home. So, why not wish to be invisible in Paris? There in her own apartment in the rue de la Grande Chaumière, to be invisible so she could move about the building like concealed dust. Even the cat, Choufleur, would not notice her. Her grandmother could not see her. Her mother either. If her mother could not see her, then the Germans could not see her. Safe from the Germans. Wasn't that what her mother had said? She wanted Avril to be safe from the Germans. Very well then. Once invisible, Avril could move with sweet impunity, anywhere in Paris, anywhere at all.

Chapter 16

The following morning the students, Sophia, and Quizzer had nearly all finished breakfast when finally Avril appeared. Sophia had told them all that the first few days, Avril's schedule would be syncopated. She had had a long and dire journey and needed the rest. Still, Sophia was surprised to see her come into the kitchen dressed in the same filthy stockings, heavy shoes, the same stained skirt and sweater she had on the night before, the sweater buttoned against the cold.

Waverley whispered to Ginevra, "She must have left twenty pounds of dirt in the tub because she looks a lot thinner and more pathetic."

"If that's possible," Ginevra murmured back.

Sophia turned to Waverley. "I thought I asked you to put a complete school uniform on the floor in front of Avril's room and knock gently to wake her."

"I did, Sophia."

"Did you see the clothes there in front of your door, Avril?"

"Yes."

"But you're not properly dressed."

"No."

Sophia scanned Avril's face as though it were a map and she had lost direction, then she said, "Temple School is not like schools in Paris. It's not like any school. We do things differently here. We wear these clothes because they are healthful, clean and easily washed. They will keep you warm while allowing your body to breathe and your blood to circulate without constriction. So please go put on your correct clothing, Avril."

But Avril replied only that she was hungry, and to Waverley's surprise, Sophia relented. Quizzer heaped a plate with oatmeal and gave her a bowl with a couple of soft-boiled eggs and poured some milk in a glass stuffed with stale biscuits. Beaming above his bow tie, he extolled the virtues of the North American Life-Enhancing and Perfecting Diet of True Foods. Avril toyed with her spoon while Quizzer exhorted her to eat.

How hard can it be to eat a glass of stale biscuits, Waverley thought, a bowl of oatmeal and a couple of eggs? Waverley was embarrassed for Quizzer, making such a fuss. Let the Frog starve if she didn't want to eat.

Suspiciously, the Frog took a couple of bites of oatmeal, gagging them down. She poked at the milk and stale biscuits with her spoon and when the biscuit came up dripping, she put it down. She turned her attention to the soft-boiled eggs and poked at their little quivery golden eyes in the middle of gelatinous white while Quizzer waxed on about the manifold goodness of egg whites, especially raw. The egg rolled over and Waverley involuntarily thought of an eye cut from its socket. Avril made a face.

"You need never fear adulteration here, Avril. We raise our own chickens," Quizzer consoled her. "You can learn all you need to know about the natural world by raising chickens. We feed them our own special mash and do not allow them to eat slops, slugs, bugs, flies or other filthies." He paused momentarily and looked skyward. "What are the three filthiest things in the world, Violet?"

"A pig's snout, a chicken's feet and a sheep's buttocks."

Avril darted from the table out to the mudroom door and vomited noisily off the porch.

Waverley put her napkin back in its ring. "Eventful, for breakfast."

Sophia glared at them. "Everything is very new and strange to Avril. I'm sure you can all remember how you felt when you came here." She rested her gaze on Waverley. "It will take time. She has not your advantages in being a North American woman. She comes from a culture that is freighted with old loyalties and hatreds and it will take time for her to throw these off and embrace the new. Each of you will take one week in which Avril will be your special charge. It will be your responsibility to see that she is happy."

"She'll never be happy," remarked Waverley. "You can look at her and know that."

"We'll begin with you, Waverley."

So after breakfast, the Frog followed as Waverley, dutifully, carried her dishes to the sink, rinsed them, followed her upstairs and stood at the door where the uniform, neatly folded, still lay on the floor.

"You go make up your bed," said Waverley. Then she went into the room and yanked the covers around. "Make up the bed, see? And you put your uniform on. It's time for me to evacuate the temple and when I come back, you better be dressed right."

But when Waverley returned from the bathroom, Avril sat on the unmade bed in her ugly old clothes and shoes, her arms crossed. "You must be stupid," said Waverley. "I know you're not deaf."

They walked into the library and Avril took a seat at the very back, her arms still tucked in her armpits. Waverley said to Sophia, "I did my best. Take it up with her."

In a low persuasive voice, Sophia again explained the importance of proper clothing.

Avril heard her out and then she said, "I will not do it."

And that was just the beginning of what she would not do.

She wouldn't eat oatmeal, boiled eggs and stale bread in the morning, only toast and coffee. She wouldn't clean the chicken houses, nor collect the eggs, nor rake their yards, nor feed and water them either. She would not lift her hand to clean out the last of the garden, even when Sophia and Quizzer both explained to her that war could come to the Puget Sound as well, and that the school might very well need to be completely self-sufficient. Avril shrugged. Avril would not have her brain tested or her eyes or hearing tested. Quizzer shouted at her like she was deaf. When he quizzed her, she refused to answer; she shrugged. Sophia and Quizzer urged her to play the school piano, but no, she sat with her back to the instrument. In class she would not open a single book. She listened to the war news from Europe, but refused to move the pins around the map. She stood beside the map, hunched over, her hands in her armpits. This was her favorite posture. When Sophia asked her about the Germans or France, or the war, she shrugged. She had a lethal shrug.

She refused as well all Music into Movement, and stood at the bar, stolid and unmoving. Sophia blindfolded the students and put on Saint-Saëns's "Valse mignonne." The Frog tore hers off and stomped on it. In the first six bars, Ginevra ran into Avril and Avril pushed her down and away. Ginevra fell and hit her head. Ginevra cried. Avril cursed her. In French, but cursed nonetheless. Sophia knew what she had said and told Quizzer. He tried to put her on the antiprofanity diet, though he confessed to Sophia he wasn't at all certain that the same diet worked in French.

Sophia did win the clothes war, however. Swiftly and without comment. One night as Avril lay sleeping, Sophia went into her room, making no attempt at stealth or silence. She picked up all the clothes lying on the floor where Avril had flung them, including the shoes, put them in a bag and took them away. Avril shrieked at her to bring them back; she swore at Sophia too. But Sophia just closed the door behind her. The Temple clothes were still there on the dresser and the next morning Avril had to dress like the rest of the students or go naked.

She was of course excluded from the Church of the Chocolate God, but there, in whispers, the worshipers talked of nothing but the Frog. Indignantly they recounted the things she had got away with, behavior that would not have been tolerated of the rest of them. There was always some new affront to the teachers, to the school's routine, to the chores assigned. Her long hair alone marked her as benighted, unhealthy—in some fundamental way, not clean. And yet, neither Sophia nor Quizzer made any attempt to take her into Massacre, to Hulbert's barbershop. Worshipers at the Church of the Chocolate God knew why too. Avril would have fought them tooth and nail. Physically. She was rude and crude, hateful and silent. She actually growled. They thought her not merely Froggy, but the incarnation of everything North American women were not. Moreover, it was painfully clear to the other students: Avril understood perfectly that she could do whatever she wanted at Temple School (or refuse what she didn't want to do). Avril could hardly be punished. Certainly she could not be expelled. Sophia could not send her back to Occupied France. Waverley offered the whispered opinion one night that Avril had occupied Temple School as the Germans had occupied Paris, altering the entire place and changing it from the inside out.

Hostilities escalated on both sides. Avril would mutter at the other students in French when Sophia was not nearby. They, for their part, imitated the way she stuck her hands in her armpits and flapped her elbows. Like a chicken. Observing this performance in Music into Movement, Sophia dismissed the rest of the class but asked Waverley to remain behind. She fastened on Waverley her steely gray-eyed I-have-seen-the-Unseen stare. "I would ask you to imaginatively reconstruct, Waverley, your own earliest days at Temple School. How did you make friends with the other students?"

Waverley could hardly say she'd founded the Church of the Chocolate God. She said she couldn't remember.

"It would behoove you," Sophia advised, "to consider, to think how you might have wished to be welcomed."

Waverley promised that she would consider this, but it made no difference to the ill will they all bore the Frog. When Avril stuck her hands in her armpits and hung her head, the students squawked or cackled and then cleared their throats, thinking that Sophia wouldn't immediately guess. Quizzer would never have guessed in any event.

Quizzer would lock his arm through Avril's so that she had to keep up with him on their scientific expeditions to the beach at low tide, marching and whistling. She refused to whistle and would hardly lift her feet, much less march, but Newton dragged her to the beach on his arm. He sat her down on the logs while, with his back to the water, he railed on for her sake, extolled the great unifying principles of the universe. The other students sighed, gazed stupidly out to sea. They had heard it all before. Avril ignored him, remained hunched up, bent over, staring at the stones. Sometimes she just wandered away, down to the tide pools, where she poked sticks in the little anemones till they squirted translucent jets of anger at her.

When Agnes Kauffman directed her to join the Verdi chorus, Avril called her a cow, then pointed at the other students and called them all cows. She said they sang like dogs. Like cats who have got the itch. She made a lewd gesture to indicate what the itch was and where it was to be found. Then put her hands in her armpits. This incident was reported to Sophia.

Though Avril's attitude was no different in Morton's class—she would not pick up so much as a brush—Dahlgren tried to rise above her insidious sneer. He never reproached Avril. Instead he adopted a sort of world-weary air, as though he and she were the true sophisticates. He rattled on extensively about Paris, how he had gone there to fight for La Belle France, one of the doughboys who had saved Europe. Such was his unique appreciation for French art, for culture (he insinuated), he'd returned to France after the war to study painting in Montparnasse. He knew well the work of Denis Aron, knew the gallery that carried the work of Denis Aron. Morton had met Denis Aron there, briefly to be sure, and also in a café here and there, a studio perhaps, Picasso's he thought. Yes, and the studio of Modigliani, everyone called him Modi, of course, some party that Kisling threw. Morton would toss out names like eggs, waiting for Avril to catch one. Her expression never altered. Morton gave them all the benefit of his vast acquaintance as he walked from easel to easel criticizing and correcting. Sometimes he would pick up a pear and comment on a series of still lifes that Denis Aron had done, adding that he had once heard Denis Aron remark that the pear was the most artistic of fruits.

Eventually Morton's tactic elicited from Avril some response. Morton glowed to see the brush in her hand, to see her execute strokes across the paper. "I can't tell you, Avril, how I have always admired your father and how I look so forward to having his daughter as my student."

"He is not my father."

"He lives with you."

"So does the cat. That doesn't make it my father." Avril put down her brush and tore off her page, holding up to Morton a cartoon of Hitler with a dynamite in his carefully detailed, rosy rectum, the fuse lit and smoking.

With Sophia, Avril was more circumspect, more cautious, cold and grim. Sophia herself maintained her distance from the girl. All Sophia's theories of teaching, of instilling discipline in resistant young minds, were useless to her with Avril. Sophia felt like a hypocrite, chiding the other students for not liking Avril. Sophia did not like her. She could only admit these ungenerous feelings to Newton, and he soothed her, but he did not fully understand. Not her guilt and anger. Not her fear. Whenever there was mention of Denis Aron,

Avril denied he was her father, cruelly suggested that he slept with thousands of women and cared for none. Not even for Sophia. Moreover Avril (with her shrug, her curled lip, a few significant vulgar gestures) indicated that her mother did not even know who her father was, that the artists (yes, even those Sophia had known and loved, maybe especially those people) were crude and vulgar. Not men and women of spirit and talent, but little whores with swaggering egos. Honor and art and discipline did not exist. There floated round Temple School an unpleasant whiff brought by Avril, that the Paris and the people Sophia had extolled were brutal, specious. That Sophia's own glorious Montparnasse past was tawdry. In short, Avril made Sophia look like a liar, implied, with her lethal shrug, that Sophia's every value was a lie. Avril tainted the past. She undermined the present. Avril mocked Sophia's aspirations, everything she had worked for in her school. Most terrible was the doubt, the fear. Lying sleepless beside Newton, Sophia feared her whole curriculum was indeed pretentious. Not visionary. Just the pretensions of a rich woman who had failed to marry the man she had loved.

The Austin-Smythes took the North American high road with Avril. They said that even if she had had piano lessons, she couldn't possibly properly learn the flute or cello because she was a European, bent and bowed under with the weight of centuries of wretchedness. To this, Avril remarked only that the Austin-Smythes were pigs. That all their ancestors were pigs. She made obscene gestures and pointed to Mrs. Austin-Smythe. Mr. Austin-Smythe, his long nose twitching, went directly to Sophia and offered their resignations. He would not be dissuaded, nor cajoled—no, not even an apology from Avril would suffice.

Secretly, Sophia was, if not pleased to see the Austin-Smythes go, at least cheered by the thought that she would no longer have to pay them. She suggested that Avril apologize to them in any event. But she did not insist. After all, the Austin-Smythes were leaving. Why should Sophia pitch a battle on their behalf? Avril would never apologize; Sophia knew this, and she was glad to be spared the ordeal of punishing her. What could she do? Send her to her lonely room? Avril preferred the lonely room. Feed her cornmeal, eggs, baked potatoes and stale bread? This was the school diet. Should she inflict the standard Temple punishment and double her chicken duty? Avril would not pick up so much as a feed bucket in any event. And when Quizzer tried to teach her to candle eggs, she had flung them down on the candling shed floor and put her hands in her armpits.

But Sophia did call Avril into her study as Quizzer was loading up the Austin-Smythes' belongings, putting them into the Packard for the journey to Massacre. Sophia lectured her on the rude, vulgar and ill-considered nature of what she had done.

The girl raised her dark eyes to Sophia. "I have done nothing. But I know what you have done. You were the mistress of my mother's husband. You brought him grief. You brought him sorrow. He visits this sorrow on my mother and my grandmother, on me. And now my own mother sends me to be your prisoner. It is cruel."

"It is," Sophia agreed, "but not in the way that you think."

After the departure of the Austin-Smythes, Sophia and Quizzer redoubled their efforts to integrate Avril into the life of the school. To Quizzer, in particular, the French student was a test of all his theories regarding history, sausage and an education comprised of universal principles. As Avril resisted, so Newton worked harder, his own oratory often sending him into a froth.

The students lined up before him on their driftwood pews, listened listlessly as Quizzer extolled the tides and rhythms, the unifying forces of the universe. Waverley expected any minute now the well-known injunctions about greatness and dinner with the King of Sweden.

Finally Quizzer walked round to Avril, who kept her hands thrust in her armpits. "And how fortunate you are, all of you, to be students here, not just on this beautiful island, but at a school where the whole being is educated, where art and science and nature all work in unison in a place that itself is a temple to achievement." He shouted at her as though she were deaf. "A temple is a sacred place, isn't it, Avril? You wouldn't allow filth to accumulate in a temple nor dirt to corrupt or degrade? You must keep the temple clean. As it is with the mind, the body and the heart. Thus, the eliminating tide! Release the past, Avril! Purge! Evacuate the Temple!"

For the first time, Avril looked up at him, looked directly at him—not as if she might respond, but as though Quizzer were mad. Blathering complete gibberish. Absolute rot.

Ginevra turned to Avril and said quite clearly, "*Merde*. To evacuate the temple is to make *merde*. That's shit, Professor Faltenstall."

Avril burst out laughing. In all the months she had been at the school no one had ever heard her laugh. It was a strange sound, coaxed from some unexpected place within her and sounding raw and rusty, unrehearsed, braying. Her whole face altered and her mouth opened, and she threw her head back, and into this pool of laughter the other students tumbled laughing. Waverley, Marjorie, Ginevra and Violet were suddenly all united: their youth against Quizzer's uncomprehending age, their girlish high humor against his poor masculine lack of understanding. Quizzer looked from one girl to the next, perplexed and undone.

And suddenly, with a stab, Waverley knew that it was all rot and rubbish. The North American Life-Enhancing and Perfecting Diet of True Foods was all Quizzer's own ridiculous notions. Rot. Avril had seen that everything they were being taught at Temple School was fatuous, ridiculous and pathetic. Dinner with the King of Sweden was pathetic. Quizzer was pathetic. Sophia would never teach anyone to imagine they could fly. No one would ever be transformed. Waverley looked around at all the others on the beach. Did anyone else have any inkling? They didn't seem to. Did Waverley alone guess that Temple School was a fool's paradise? Surely that did not mean that Sophia was a fool. Did it? Sophia was brilliant and beautiful; she understood everything. She had a great mind and a great vision. Didn't she? Waverley suddenly felt sick and alone, as alone as she had on that first awful day. As alone as if, say, she had crossed the Pyrenees on foot and been plucked from an apartment reeking of preservative and formaldehyde.

In the Church of the Chocolate God that week there was some dissension, when Waverley announced she wanted Avril to join them. Waverley was finally reduced to simple expedient tyranny, declaring that the Chocolate God had been her idea and she got to choose who was in the church. Marjorie began to blubber because she had always thought the Chocolate God was real.

"Of course it's real. Quit crying, Marjorie. Why do you think we're here every Thursday?"

"I don't like the Frog," Ginevra sulked. "She'll ruin everything."

"She still smells bad," said Violet.

"Churches have to have new members, or they die," Waverley insisted. With this point she carried the day.

She listened carefully to be certain neither Quizzer nor Sophia was stirring, and then took a candle and went softly down the hall, knocked on the door of the small single room that was Avril's. She knocked again, softly, and Avril opened the door, looking pale, frail in her nightgown. She frowned and drew back, her hands flying up to tuck in her armpits.

Waverley put a finger to her lips. She pulled Avril's hand out, opened it and put in her palm a well-nibbled bit of chocolate. Avril cupped her hands in front of her face and breathed deep of the forbidden odor. Waverley beckoned that she should follow her back to Waverley's room where the other communicants waited.

It was quite the ceremony, inducting a new member. Everyone got to think of something that Avril must answer and then swear to. The others required eloquent forswearing, but Marjorie was blunt and to the point. "Can you think of new desserts? We've used ours all up. There's no more."

"French desserts are permitted?" asked Avril gravely.

"Oh yes. We don't care if they are on the List of Nevers. Do we?" Marjorie asked her cocommunicants. They agreed they didn't care.

"Very well then," said Avril, keeping her cool, superior air. "I can give you French desserts that are from the List of Never Ever." Holding her hands out, just above the candle, she smiled in its flickering warmth. "Let us begin with the pâtisserie at the corner of the rue de la Grande Chaumière and the boulevard du Montparnasse."

Chapter 17

*A*vril began to move. Not music into movement, perhaps, not to transform. But like a paper doll long folded, her limbs slowly extended, and she took up motion, uncertainly, awkwardly, lacking all fluidity and ease. Sophia did not alter her standards for Avril, did not unduly praise Avril's fledgling efforts any more than she would have praised another student. Sophia corrected Avril's posture and her poise and told her to think about her spine, her Corinthian column, but she was pleased secretly to see Avril emerge from her protective hunch. She knew the change had less to do with her own splendid teaching practices than with Waverley Scott.

One morning, in the dance room, Sophia passed out the blindfolds to each student and brought the Victrola needle down on Satie's "Trois gymnopédie." As each student, except Avril, tied hers on, Waverley peeked out from under her scarf and reached out, across to Avril, took the blindfold and tied it around her eyes. "Go on," Waverley said, holding her shoulders, echoing Sophia, "find the tempo. It's there. See the Unseen. Hear the Unspoken."

As Avril slowly roused to her new environment, Sophia could relent on the need to include her. Presiding over the evening radio broadcasts and the increasingly Nazi-engulfed map of Europe, Sophia no longer asked Avril to stand up by the map, to move so much as a pushpin. Often, when the war news was especially grim, Sophia excused her altogether. Avril returned to her small room and stared at the photograph of her mother, the one from the café, the one where Judith was smiling, her hat at a jaunty angle.

When Newton halted Avril in the hall and held his quizzing finger to the sky, she no longer gave him her contemptuous shrug. Speech crossed her lips. Newton was happy all day when Avril replied, no matter what she said. At least she had quit swearing in French. Unlike Sophia, Quizzer rained down praise on Avril's every halfhearted attempt to remember the Rules of the North American Life-Enhancing and Perfecting Diet, to remember the List of Nevers, to describe the difference between a barnacle and a sea urchin. She got them all wrong. Quizzer thought this was marvelous.

More marvelous yet, Avril slowly, gingerly, with great misgivings, took up some of the chicken yard chores. "What can you expect?" Quizzer told the others. "Of course she would hate the chickens! Why didn't I think of it before? She's from the city, girls! She cannot possibly have been exposed to the learning implicit in keeping chickens. She would not know a rooster from a fox."

Violet reminded him they were all from cities, a fact Quizzer chose not to comment on. Instead he retreated to his meteorological equipment, barometers, thermometers, a weather vane for winds and a rain gauge with funnel of his own devising. For twenty years Quizzer had measured precipitation on Isadora Island, but in the course of about six dismal weeks it rained so much, his gauges were unequal to the task. The rain drove the chickens mad, the incessant pounding on their tin roofs. Some of them turned cannibal and crazy and beat their own heads against the wall.

In the unremitting cold and rain, tempers frayed. Foltzy and Huey threatened to quit unless they were paid in cash. Agnes and Morton, deprived of bridge partners after the departure of the Austin-Smythes, grew especially snappish and cross. Their domestic quarrels floated over to the school's yard and echoed while the students did chicken duty.

Though Avril slowly integrated with the other students (and even got her hair cut short), for Sophia the doubts she had unleashed had not abated. Doubts about the school, the curriculum undermined Sophia's certainty, her steadfast vision. Though she could admit this to no one, not even Newton, Sophia suspected that the students themselves had begun to doubt the wisdom of Seeing the Unseen, Hearing the Unspoken, that in truth, they cared nothing that Form Is to Function as God Is to Nature. Even the King of Sweden had lost some of his panache.

All Sophia's fears congealed late one afternoon when she happened on Violet in the library, happily shuffling a deck of cards. "What are you doing?" she asked.

"Practicing. Shuffling." In Violet's hands the cards snapped with a tap-dancer's perfect percussion.

"You're very good at it."

"Thank you. I've been playing bridge with Agnes and Morton. They're teaching me and Ginevra. I've picked it up quite quickly. But no one wants to be Ginevra's partner."

"Why is that?"

"She can't seem to get the game. Ginevra says she understands the concepts, but she doesn't. She plays her every hand predictably, and since everyone knows what she'll do, the element of strategy is lost." Violet lost control of the deck, but smoothly collected the cards and tried again. "Agnes says this element of strategy is the best part of playing bridge. Do you play bridge, Sophia?"

Sophia just shook her head, without saying that the thought of afternoon card games gave her hives. It was the sort of thing her mother would have done, the undertaking of an underemployed mind. Sophia fathomed that if playing bridge with Morton and Agnes was absorbing the efforts, the energy, the time and imagination of her students, then the complete failure of her vision could not be far behind.

Violet observed, "Morton says that playing bridge is absolutely necessary for a North American Woman of the Future."

"I don't think I'd go that far," replied Sophia, mesmerized by Violet's uncanny skills with the cards. "A certain type of woman perhaps. A club woman or a . . ." She couldn't think who else might play cards. She knew that many former Temple girls were now resolutely club women. A stagnant life, by Sophia's standards. "A woman with not enough to worry about."

"Well that's what Waverley says. She says playing bridge is rot. She refuses to learn. And of course Marjorie's retarded and can't learn."

"You know I dislike descriptions like retarded. They betray a narrow mind."

"Sorry."

"And Avril? Did they enlist Avril to play bridge?"

"No, Morton detests Avril. And besides, she'd just shrug at it. She'll never play. But Morton says I have a genius for bridge, and that Ginevra is a card-playing cretin."

"He called Ginevra a cretin! How could he? I will not have such—"

"He apologized to her, Sophia, honestly. Ginevra ran outside crying and Agnes made Morton go get her and apologize, and then when he brought Ginevra back, Agnes made him apologize to all of us for his bad taste and bad language."

"I should hope so. I shall still speak with him. This, this game should not interfere with your studies, you know. Nor with your health, nor your obligations to the rest of the school."

"Oh no, Sophia." Violet fanned the cards expressively; they snapped to their own tempo. "Waste Not Thy Hour."

Something had to be done. Something new added to the curriculum. Something radical, without seeming to be desperate. Sophia pondered this dilemma the whole month of December. Waverley, Avril and Ginevra remained at the school over the holidays and celebrated the solstice in the kitchen with Sophia, Newton and Nijinsky.

Avril, of course, had nowhere else to go. Ginevra's guardians had no plans for her for the holidays, but sent (at her request) a five-pound box of chocolates for a Christmas present. Since Sophia did not believe in Christmas, Ginevra could quickly hide this parcel and donate the contents to the Church of the Chocolate God. Rhoda actually rang the school and treated the entire island party line to her apologies to Waverley: Mr. Gerlach's contributions to the Allies were invaluable. He must work the whole month of December. She must remain with him in Toronto. There would be no Grove Park Inn New Year's celebration for Rhoda and Waverley. Rhoda grew sniffly just saying good-bye.

"Don't cry, Mother," Waverley said cheerfully, patting Nijinsky. "Don't cry. Yes. Good-bye, Mother! Good-bye." She hung up the phone, knelt and rubbed her nose against Nijinsky's. "Stinky old North Carolina anyway, huh, Nijinsky? Good dog."

In January, at the very first breakfast when all the school had reconvened, Sophia had an announcement. She had labored over the vacation, considered, contemplated and she could now, with great firmness tell her students, "Temple School is going to expand its curriculum."

She rose to make the statement, indicating its import. At the other head of the table, Newton beamed at her as if her remarks were addressed to the Swedish Academy. "We are to become something the world has not seen in many ages. Warrior Women."

"What kind of women?" asked Ginevra.

"Warriors."

"Will we paint our faces like the Indians, like the Indians who stole up on Massacre?" asked Waverley. "Will we have spears and shields? Bows and arrows?"

"Swords?" asked Violet.

"This is not a matter for levity. This is a matter of the utmost gravity. An undertaking, an endeavor, a challenge that Temple students must meet. To make you better prepared for the world you will inherit. I have developed a new curriculum that will make of you Warrior Women."

"No one will marry us then," protested Ginevra.

"No one will marry you anyway," Waverley jibed.

"Maybe there won't be any men left to marry," said Avril with Gallic resignation.

"Whatever the world may bring you, the tasks, the training of Warrior Women will serve you well in the future." Sophia seemed to look into the future, the Unseen, while Newton nodded, inspired by her nobility and genius. "We are going to learn to sew." She sat down,

"What sort of warriors would sew?" Waverley protested. "Warriors would be slashing enemies and throwing spears, marching."

"Real warriors," Sophia corrected Waverley, "would be doing whatever the cause obliges of them. If the cause obliges them to sew, then they will sew. And that is what's needed right now. We are very near to Canada and Canada is part of the British Empire and they are fighting with the Allies, so it behooves Temple School students, in support of our Canadian neighbors, to sew blackout curtains for the emergency."

"What emergency?" asked Marjorie, mystified.

"Any emergency that might occur."

Ginevra pointed out that she did not know how to sew. It turned out that no one did.

Sophia declared, "We will learn. Tomorrow. Tomorrow we begin. We will scour this island and find treadle machines and bring them back here and set to work."

"Why not get electric sewing machines?" said Violet.

"We will stick with treadle machines," Newton explained, "because then you can always work on your own power. You are beholden to no man. Even if the enemy cuts the power supply, you can go on sewing blackout curtains."

"If the enemy cuts the power supply," Violet pointed out, "no one will need blackout curtains." Since she had begun playing bridge, Violet had developed a new asperity, a cold clear-eyed approach to all her undertakings, whether it was chicken duty or the Church of the Chocolate God.

Driving the Packard all over Isadora Island, and taking students with her, two at a time, Sophia collected sewing machines with the same spirit and vigor she brought to every endeavor. In Massacre, she put up signs at the Isadora Inn, the Marine and Feed and the barbershop saying she would pay cash for old treadle sewing machines. When he read this, Mr. Hulbert said that if she was paying cash for them, he would have to ask her to settle her account with him. He colored to the peak of his receding hairline and asked for cash. No more checks. Drawing herself up to her full regal height, she assured Mr. Hulbert he could have cash. Soon. Not just this minute. But soon.

At the wheel of the Packard, Sophia lumbered over tiny threads of roads, crunching over ice, digging the Packard out of ditches when necessary, stopping at remote farmhouses and clusters of fishing shacks near the beaches. Her students saw parts of Isadora Island that few white people had ever seen. Those homes she couldn't get to by land, Sophia asked Captain Briscoe to approach by boat. He made the rounds as well of some nearby islands, collecting in all, four treadle machines. Particularly since the offer was for cash, islanders hauled old Singers out of their attics and back rooms, secretly laughing at the folly of buying machines so completely outdated, and chuckling over the island party line, *What did you expect from Sophia Westervelt and Temple School?*

All four machines suffered from some malady or another, the wooden cabinets bloated with the damp or green with mildew, the treadles rusted, the needle frozen. But Newton took them out to his scientific shed, went to work on them with nothing more esoteric than some oil and grease, pliers, a screwdriver and coaxing. One by one, the machines hummed. Sophia set them in a semicircle in the library by the windows. Two library tables had been pushed together to spread out the oceans of black cloth.

"Since we have only four machines, the student who is not sewing will read to the rest." Sophia went to the shelf and selected a book. "*The Iliad*, I think. That will make Warrior Women of you. But of course you'll have to take turns. Now, let's see. Violet, you read first and the rest of you take your seats."

They did as they were bid, faced the machines and regarded the spools of thread, but no one moved. No one had the slightest idea where to begin. Avril said her grandmother could sew, her mother too, but Avril had never learned.

"Well, it can't be that difficult. Many people do it." Sophia took her place at one of the machines. She rocked the treadle with her feet. "The first rule is obvious, isn't it? Keep your rhythm consistent and unflagging. In sewing, as in life, tempo, timing is everything."

Not quite everything. There was for instance the bobbin and the foot and the needle and the drive wheel. There was a proper way to thread the needle and to wind the bobbin. All of which eluded Sophia. She lifted the machine and peered under it. The underworks were all clean and simple looking, but did not testify to their immediate use.

"Form is to function, Sophia?" asked Waverley.

"Something like that." She tried again, but the thread got hopelessly caught and had to be snipped. She nearly sewed through her own finger. The machine was a Singer, and while she struggled with it, she told the students the story of Singer, how the heir to this fortune had been the lover of the Great Isadora and the father of her son. How Singer had put his millions in service of Isadora's art and vision and built a school for her right there in Paris. How Sophia had gone there many times. She had studied with Isadora and observed her methods, her choreography. How Isadora's liaison with Mr. Singer had come to tragedy when her two little children died, their car plunging into the Seine. Isadora herself was never the same.

She told the story and told it well, but at the close she was no nearer understanding the sewing machine or operating it, much less teaching someone else to do so. Sophia folded her hands. What good was it to strive always to some standard of temporal perfection that would in all likelihood never be tested or realized, or useful in a world where her students were unequal to fundamental tasks? The old unpleasant whiff of defeat floated past Sophia, a stubborn scent, made more pungent by her financial woes.

"Girls," Sophia declared, "a Woman of the Future, if she does not know the answer, at least can frame the question." She excused herself and went out to the laundry shed where she found Foltzy and Huey, bundled up in sweaters and contentedly smoking while the laundry sat in a great dirty lump. "I wonder if I might have a word with you," Sophia asked.

In the end, it was not the visionary Sophia who taught the students how to sew, but Foltzy and Huey, who between them had raised seven children, and made or mended all their clothes. They were brief and businesslike about it, how to measure the materials, to cut and baste and stitch and bring the whole together, an enterprise for which none of the Warrior Women had any particular talent. But these were blackout curtains, after all, not haute couture. Blackout curtains began to stack up on the library shelves while the treadles whirred, counterpointing the girls' young voices reading the old words of *The Iliad*. The thump of their iron resounded to the voice on the radio.

The war widened. The map of Europe hanging in the library could no longer contain it. Sophia had to order a new map, a map of the whole world. The students were obliged to wrap their tongues around the names of difficult places, Asian places, Pacific places, Balkan and desert places ancient and far away. Sophia ordered as well new pushpins in different colors, as the menace spread. The whole world map teemed with black pushpins for the Germans, white pushpins for the Japanese, like beetle larvae crawling over the whole vast expanse of the earth.

An uneasy blight settled on the school at Useless Point. Newton kept antianxiety concoctions on hand at all times, egg whites and bran-ade and magnetized water to relieve Sophia's headache pain. Sophia dutifully ingested them, but they did no good, and as the war news darkened, even her Warrior Woman convictions faltered, though her posture did not.

TEMPLE SCHOOL
ISADORA ISLAND, WASHINGTON
ISADORA 123

January 1941

Madame Aron,

Twice yearly I write a summary and evaluation of each student and I send a copy to the parent or guardian and keep one in the student's file. Though I cannot send this to you, yet shall I write.

Your daughter no longer pines here. Her posture has improved. She has grown physically. She has absorbed the rudiments of Learn by Doing, though she is not transformed. She has improved at Music into Movement, and voice. Her skills in art remain undeveloped and untested. She responds in a far better fashion to science, where she works with Newton, my husband. Newton brings out the best in everyone. He is the dearest of men and he would not admit defeat with Avril, though she has tested his resolve. She has tested everyone's resolve, Madame Aron.

When she first came I despaired that she would ever be accepted by the other students. Friendship must be forged on both sides and Avril made no overtures herself. But I am happy to tell you that Avril has moved closer to being a part of our school community. It is a very small community. Only five students. Of those, she has struck up the closest friendship with Waverley Scott, a young woman, bookish and boisterous at the same moment, who has gifts still undiscovered. Waverley is an exemplary student here, though immature and full of potential. Waverley can offer Avril the contagion of her exuberance. Avril can offer Waverley some depth perhaps. At the winter solstice, a good moment for change, I asked Avril to move out of her solitary room and in with Waverley. At our school we believe you learn to live with others by doing just that.

However, your daughter still refuses to come into consciousness of the school and our mission. Still, here at Temple School we educate the whole woman, not simply those elements for which one may have talent. Avril so alienated the music teachers that they have left altogether. In art, she continues recalcitrant and sulks. Her continued conduct in this class has to do with Monsieur Aron and his gifts, being known here as his daughter, which I must in candor tell you, she denies. She has many harsh words for him. She has many harsh words for you, Madame. Her attitude toward me remains formal and not forthcoming. Cool, though no longer hostile, an attitude I feel certain is allied to my old, long-ago affection, in truth, my love for Denis, for whom I now feel of course admiration and respect for his work. I am pleased that the world has finally thought to honor him, to recognize the genius I so vividly saw thirty years ago.

I have, at every turn, shown restraint with Avril, more restraint than I would have shown with a North American girl. Most of our students are not especially homesick, but Avril suffers this affliction. I believe that she misses you terribly and this is the root of her unhappiness. I hope you have done the right thing in sending her so far from home, from you, from Paris.

Of course her situation is the more difficult because there is no word from you. There is almost no word at all. Since the fall of France, we hear little from Paris itself. But we hear a great deal of other defeats. We hear so much defeat that I myself am defeated. I often imagine your life there, Madame Aron, yours, Denis, Maurice, the friends of such a long time past now. The streets I see are through a veil of memory, populated with the faces of the dead, or the faces of young people now grown old. The streets I see have no Nazi soldiers.

Avril can see what I cannot. In this sad regard, Avril can see the unseen and hear the unspoken and I cannot. Have the last twenty years of my life been spent in the service of illusion, and all my works and efforts futile? Has my insistence, my certainty that form will follow function, that discipline leads to discovery and discovery to achievement, is all that rot? Is transformation impossible? Madame, these thoughts, these fears steal my sleep and though I try to concentrate on my students (and they are my beloved students), still I had wished, hoped to teach them more than merely to keep time. I set out to develop women unbowed by tradi-

tion, unconstricted by convention, women who would not sit and suffer the metronomic days to pass, but recognize the universals and apply them to the particulars of their lives. My students must not be the pawns of men and armies, the dupes of cruel fate. Have I sent my work, my students, out into the future, to be simply swallowed into the past? What good have I done? Shall I—

But Sophia took this last page, and wadded it into a ball, flung it into the fire burning in the library. She put the cap on her fountain pen, rose and walked to the window, where rain tumbled out of broken gutters, cascading in ruts and rivulets.

Chapter 18

The spring was false, of course, but like untrue love and Untrue Foods, it was the more valued for that very reason. The days were cold and clear and cloudless and the forsythia curled in tight yellow fists, and when the students cut them, brought them into the classrooms in scrawny bundles, they burst into blossom.

To Waverley this change—forsythia from nubby sticks to clouds of yellow—was easily as important, if not as thoroughgoing, as the departure of Foltzy and Huey. Foltzy and Huey declared there was better paying work on the mainland, real work with real wages, and with their men (their children were grown and living on the mainland), they were leaving Isadora forever. They asked for cash. Sophia said she would mail them checks.

Though Foltzy and Huey were ineffective and generally surly, their departure left the burdens of laundry, cooking and cleaning to the students, burdens more tedious than any of them would have guessed. Sophia declared it was yet another lesson in being Warrior Women, that it was altogether good that the school was now wholly self-sufficient.

Sophia also invoked the tenets of self-sufficiency in requiring the students to unload the Marine and Feed truck when Mr. Torklund made deliveries. He stood and watched, reminding anyone who would listen that his back was not what it used to be, and he saw no reason to further debilitate himself on behalf of Temple School. Helping Mr. Torklund unload was not a pleasure. To bring in the ice, four of them made a sling of the ice blanket and hoisted it while Mr. Torklund smoked beside his truck. He also demanded cash.

So on that false spring afternoon, no one paid any attention to the grinding gears of the Marine and Feed truck as it rattled up the hill. Then Sophia called out, "Come, girls! Sandy shouldn't be straining his ribs."

For Sandy's well-being, Temple School stood ready to oblige. The return of Sandy Lomax warmed the whole of Useless Point, all the way down to Assumption Island, where, Waverley thought, even the seals joined in the general chorus of applause.

He had changed in these six months. Waverley had scarcely seen him at all, except now and then, a jaunt into Massacre, and he looked different from how she remembered. Though he was pale—the winter, his months behind the emporium till—he still seemed to her broader, brighter, altogether older than he had before. His looks were barely tarnished by the scar where Dr. Oland had sewed him up near the eye. There was only a slightly downcast tug, which contrasted with his bright smile. Waverley remembered all over again the flying, the fall, the thud, the thump inside her body, the tingling, the scent of windfall apples, the branches gnarled overhead when she had looked above Sandy to the sky, as he brushed the dirt from her lips and brought his own mouth to hers. Today, she could tell, he was happy to see her. No doubt he was happy to see all of them, but Waverley knew he was especially happy to see her.

"Been doing any flying lately?" he asked as he loaded into her waiting arms a five-pound round of cheese.

"Not lately. Been riding on your motorcycle?"

"No. But I will. It's almost fixed. Not quite."

"And your ribs? Are they fixed?"

"Better than ever." He winked at her and strode out into the yard as Quizzer offered him a manly handshake. Sandy commented on how good all the girls looked. "Lots of True Foods, I guess, Professor. I guess these girls must really prosper on the North American Life-Enhancing and Perfecting Diet."

"As will all mankind one day, Sandy. Now, let me give you a couple of jugs of magnetized water to take to your mother. How is she? Still . . . grieving?" Newton thought that surely, in this instance, euphemism was in order.

Sandy said she was fine, turned away from further discussion of

Bessie, and greeted Avril. He put into her arms great skeins of black yarn and boxes of knitting needles. "I wouldn't have known you with your hair short."

Avril shrugged and patted her short dark curls. She looked expectantly toward the sack that said US MAIL. Her face brightened. "And is there a letter for me? From Paris? From . . ."

"Mrs. Torklund puts the mail up, Avril, not me. So I couldn't say."

"You could say, but you are kind not to."

"Well, Sandy." Sophia strode into the yard. "How nice to see you recovered from that regrettable accident, and I hope, truly, you will never ride that motorcycle again."

"Can't promise that, Sophia."

"Well I can promise you"—she cast a serious look around at her students—"no Temple girls will henceforth or ever again be riding with you. Is that clear, girls?" Sophia addressed the whole student body, all five of them. "Waverley?"

"It's clear, Sophia," Waverley replied, without taking her eyes from Sandy Lomax.

"Very sensible," Sophia observed. "There are some things one can learn by Not Doing."

"You going to stay and have coffee, Sandy?" asked Marjorie, her round face alight. "It's a True Food. It won't kill you."

"I can't today." Then he explained rather sheepishly to Sophia that the Torklunds had declared that he could not help out at the school. "But soon as I get my motorcycle running again, I'll be back. I'll have that cup of coffee. Just like we always did, Marjorie." He grinned at them all, got back in the truck, and put it in gear. "By the way," he called out, "what's all the black yarn for?"

"Warrior Women," Sophia announced to the puzzlement of everyone except Newton.

Sophia next tried to make a moral lesson out of knitting. Since they now had enough blackout curtains for the whole of the San Juan Islands and the Upper Canadian Peninsula and all of British Columbia, Sophia next turned her Warrior Women to knitting socks for Allied soldiers. Knitting class, like the sewing machines, was set up in the library. She had ordered six set of needles and enormous quantities of yarn to be

Transformed, all of it into socks suitable for the Allies. She maintained that anyone of moderate intelligence could knit.

Though they spent weeks at it, their needles clicked and clacked to no purpose. Sophia could not knit, and this proved something of an obstacle to teaching the others. Finally, after fruitless weeks, Sophia looked overhead and beheld *Waste Not Thy Hour* on the ceiling beam. She dropped her knitting needles in her lap. "This experiment is at an end. We'll find some other avenue of service to the Allies."

"We could build lookout towers on the beach," offered Quizzer, glancing up from his book. "To scout for Japanese subs. Well, maybe not towers. Huts. Yes, I'll have Sandy bring us up some lumber and we'll start with huts. We'll move on to towers after we have managed the dynamics of the huts. Lookout huts . . . ," he went on dreamily, seeing the Unseen.

When Sandy next came to Temple School, Sophia had gathered all the wool and knitting needles and thrust them into bags. "Take this back to Mrs. Torklund," she instructed him, "and tell her to give it to anyone she likes, to someone who can use it. Herself or anyone else who knits. I can't. More's the pity, but I can't. But you must tell her she must give it away and not resell it."

Sandy shifted his weight uncomfortably. "Maybe you should write that down and I'll deliver the note. Mrs. Torklund doesn't take orders. Especially not from me. She isn't fond of me."

"She isn't fond of anyone, except Nels. I doubt she even much cares for Sis."

"They all look up to Sis."

"Yes, and I can see why. Sis is smarter than either of her parents. One day she will either be a general or make some poor man's life a misery. Or both. Sis has no imagination." Sophia took a piece of Temple stationery from the kitchen desk, scribbled the note and handed it to him. "Others must knit for the Allies. We here at Temple, we will do something else."

"Mrs. Torklund says she prays."

"Mrs. Torklund and I do not share the same gods."

Chapter 19

Such prayers as were said at Useless Point were mumbled in the Church of the Chocolate God. Even skeptics had to admit it had been rejuvenated by admitting Avril Aron. However hateful she might have been at first, Avril's contributions to the Church of the Chocolate God were manifold and many, delights that needed not simply names, but wholesale descriptions. If Waverley was the St. Teresa of Chocolate, Avril Aron became Notre-Dame de Chocolat. No one interrupted Avril, however long she spoke. Her voice, low, wafting over the single candle that illuminated the faces of the Chocolate God worshipers, floated over the near-empty chocolate box. Even more lively than the desserts Avril concocted for her listeners (not all of them chocolate; the embrace of the Chocolate God had widened to include vanilla, strawberry, marzipan, raspberry, and best of all, meringues, this latter, as Avril described them, somehow defying words altogether and existing as pure spirit) was the world she was able to revisit, if not re-create.

Avril gave her listeners not just chocolate, but context. Beginning at the corner of the rue de la Grande Chaumière and the boulevard du Montparnasse, she rambled through her whole *quartier*, describing those cafés and pâtisseries and which were best for which chocolate creations. And in doing so, Avril would retrace her routes, describe the café near her piano teacher's apartment and the street singers who sang on the corner, what they played and the songs they sang. Eventually she even shared the picture of her mother, the photograph Maurice Fleury had taken: Judith in her jaunty hat that afternoon. She talked at length about her mother, candidly, affectionately, about her grandmother, the tart-tongued concierge. Sometimes she even spoke of Denis Aron.

Waverley, sitting close by the others, hugging her knees and listening to Avril, had the peculiar sensation of being in two places at once. She watched the candle in the center of their circle flicker. She listened to the wind coming up off the Sound, bending boughs of ancient trees, tearing the cries of ghosts from their limbs. But she also heard the Unspoken: Avril's noisy life in the concierge's *loge*: the domestic quarrels of the upstairs neighbors, the laughter of the tenants, the sad guitar player on the second floor, the acerbic wife on the third. She could see the Unseen, Chou-fleur, Avril's white cat, who had somehow fallen in love with a red geranium, Chou-fleur and her geranium, in the kitchen window, companionably silent, peering out into the street, communing with each other. When Violet questioned that a cat and a geranium could be lovers, Avril assured her, assured all of them: you had but to see Chou-fleur and her red geranium together to know they were in love, the cat's adoration requited, the geranium in love too. Waverley never doubted this.

Years later, Waverley went to Paris, to Montparnasse. She went on Avril's behalf. She began, as Avril had, at the corner of the boulevard du Montparnasse and the rue de la Grande Chaumière, and from there Waverley went into every café, however low and unlikely, every bar and every pâtisserie she could find. And at these establishments there were red-armed matrons behind the counters, wondering at this American woman weeping to see the meringues lined up, like clouds marshaled for the angels' inspection. All those years later, Waverley recognized the places she had never been, the things she had never seen, the Unseen: the shops and studios, street singers on corners, the curve of a café table. She heard the Unspoken: Avril's voice. Déjà vu: Waverley repeated experiences she had never personally had, only heard about there on the floor of her room in the Church of the Chocolate God.

But in that false spring, the mighty Chocolate God succumbed. And his death signaled a turning point in Waverley's life, and the life of Sophia and Newton and Temple School altogether. The Church of the Chocolate God fell as the result of unscheduled greed.

Always, on Thursday nights, the services once concluded, the worshipers returned to their rooms one at a time to avoid detection. Altar duties revolved amongst them. This particular night Marjorie had the honor of blowing out the candle and putting the sacraments away. The candle blown out, Waverley and Avril got into their beds and said good night. Marjorie, just before she put the communion box in its sacred hiding place, reached under the lid, and snatched a whole chocolate.

She popped it in her mouth for luck and tiptoed out the door without murmuring the usual Chocolate God Farewell. After all, she could not talk with her mouth full. Marjorie darted out the door, only to find herself in the hall face-to-face with Sophia, holding a lantern on her way to the bathroom. Marjorie froze in its light like a deer blinded by a torch.

"Why, Marjorie! You startled me! Are you ill?"

Marjorie shook her head, her eyes still wide with shock.

"What are you doing coming out of Waverley's room so late at night?"

"Noffink." Marjorie made a great effort to get her tongue round the chocolate and in doing so, it bulged in her cheek.

Sophia bent closer, sniffed. "What's in your mouth?"

"Noffink." Marjorie swallowed the chocolate in one great gulp and smiled. Little flecks of chocolate clung to her teeth.

The next morning before breakfast, everyone assembled in the kitchen. At the head of the table Quizzer sat, pale, his eyes red-rimmed, his hand clutching a mug of bran-ade made with magnetized water. The students were ordered to take their accustomed places, but no food would be served until a matter of the gravest discipline had been broached and settled.

"It has come to our attention—" Sophia began brusquely.

Quizzer interrupted her. "I am betrayed." His bow tie trembled under his Adam's apple and he swallowed his emotion with difficulty. Quizzer lifted his chins and looked into the distance (foreshortened by the huge stove that ran along one wall). "The work of a lifetime is betrayed."

"No, Quizzer . . . ," Waverley protested, but Sophia told her in no uncertain terms to hush.

Marjorie started to weep, tears dribbling down her pale cheeks, her lower lip trembling.

"You mock me," Quizzer went on. "What else is it but mockery that you should all so blatantly forswear your vows of chocolate chastity and flaunt the List of Nevers? The congestion. The toxic torment to your livers, your intestines. How could you!"

In a limp whisper, Waverley offered that it had seemed a good idea at the time.

"And will death, unbidden, seem a good idea? You have courted death under our very roof." Quizzer was pale, unshaven, disheveled. Dark circles garlanded his eyes, which were muddy with anger and anxiety. "Who among you is guilty, besides Marjorie?"

Five hands slowly raised and five heads slowly bent, studying the grain in the table.

"Though you are all guilty, there is one among you who is utterly undeserving. Unworthy of Temple School. And that is the girl who brought the chocolate into this school in the first place. That girl will be expelled."

"Newton," Sophia remonstrated softly. There had been no talk between them of expelling anyone. Temple School could not afford to expel students; there were too few to begin with. "Newton, perhaps—"

"No, my dear. I will not allow you to be mocked as I have been. Whoever smuggled this chocolate into the school is not to be trusted. Without trust there can be no loyalty. Without loyalty a school dies. Even a great school like Temple. This girl must be expelled. Who is this guilty person? Speak. Do not add cowardice to your catalog of error."

Waverley's heart seemed to tighten in her throat. The thing she had invented in order to be accepted at Temple School would now get her expelled. Life in another school? Life without Temple at all? She thought of the pictures she had seen in books in the school's library, Adam and Eve weeping, gnashing, expelled from the Garden of Eden, expelled forever and only themselves to blame.

"It is me," said Avril, standing, her hands at her sides. "I bring the chocolates. I bring them from Vancouver."

"Oh, Avril!" cried Quizzer. "Ever since you've been here? You've been defying the North American Life-Enhancing and Perfecting Diet? You brought chocolates? You brought others into this—this outrage! And have you also been seducing the other students with pastry, with pickles and sausage?" Quizzer suppressed a shiver. "Pork, new bread, bacon, cucumbers? The rinds of oranges!" Quizzer raised his eyes to heaven. "Radishes?"

"Yes. I have spoken of all these things. I have said how wonderful they are. I have made many wish, all the students wish they could eat Untrue Foods. French foods on the List of Nevers."

"But you actually provided them with chocolate?"

"Yes."

"The first item on the List of Nevers!"

"Yes."

"And why, may I ask, did you do this?"

"So they would like me."

"You think you will be liked, admired for breaking the school rules?"

"Well, they called me the Frog, and I thought, well if I am the Frog, then I must do some things that are, well, Froggy."

"You would risk your life and theirs to be liked?"

"Yes."

"And were you better liked?"

"They no longer call me Frog. At least, I don't think so." She kept her gaze on Quizzer, not on the other students.

Marjorie began to sob openly. Waverley half feared she would blurt out the truth. And half feared she wouldn't.

Sophia demanded that Avril go upstairs and return with the offending box of chocolates.

The silence was stifling, save for the tick of the kitchen clock and the rooster in the chicken yard. Marjorie quit crying, though she continued to hiccup. Waverley could feel all eyes on her, though no one lifted their heads. Shame flooded through and over her, gushed from her very pores, but she remained silent, and so, the more ashamed.

Avril returned and gave the box to Sophia, who lifted the lid. Out wafted the odor of the demon chocolate. Quizzer began to breathe heavily through his mouth, not wishing to smell the offending substance. His bow tie trembled as he controlled his emotions.

"I think," Sophia said, after she had put the box of chocolates into the kitchen fireplace and lit it, whereupon the whole of it burst into untrue flames, "that we shall have to devise some particular punishment for Avril, Newton, but we cannot expel her."

"We could send her to the furrier's in Vancouver. They breathe preservatives and eat formaldehyde. I'm sure she'll be very happy with them."

"We can't do that. I have given my word to her mother. Whatever else Judith Aron will suffer, she should not fear for her daughter's safety. She has sent Avril here for safety and we will not disappoint her."

Avril regarded Sophia with a quizzical affection.

"But Sophia! Look at what she has done to the school!"

Sophia fastened her level gray-eyed gaze on Avril, on the downcast other students and knew very well, if not where the chocolate came from, at least where it had not come from. "Well, what can you expect Newton, dear? Avril is not a North American. Think of it, centuries of sausage have gone to make Avril Aron what she is. She has had only a few months here. We need more resolve, dear. More training. More exercise and Double-Range Breathing. I think they all need that. The other students are not blameless." Sophia let the implication lie undisturbed before continuing. "After all, if they have called Avril the Frog, this suggests to me they need more chicken duty. More cleanup duty. Fewer bridge games for those who enjoy such things. Fewer trips to the beach with Nijinsky for those who enjoy such things. Fewer pleasures all around and more hard work. A little transformation, Newton. That's what's needed here. To transform a bad experience into a good one."

The rest of the day was altogether grim, Newton so ill, so sick at heart that Sophia urged him to go back to bed. This he would not do. He had never been ill a day in his life, he reminded her with a touch of pique. However, he did escape to his lab, where he remained, refusing to come out at all.

The incessant rain finally dwindled to a drizzle, but the clouds did not part and the wind came up from the west. Even the chickens seemed downcast, Waverley thought. Her chicken duty was doubled immediately after breakfast and shared with Violet, so she had no opportunity to thank Avril. (And Violet said she wasn't sorry the Church of the Chocolate God was closed; it was boring. Certainly compared to bridge, it was boring.) Anyway, Sophia imposed silence on Marjorie and Ginevra and had banished Avril from the company of the others.

Not until art class were they all five together, and at that, Morton, apprised of the situation, admonished them all to silence, the better to hear his own wonderful voice. From the music room, Agnes warbled out a trilling *Lucia di Lammermoor,* warming up her vocal chords.

Waverley sat at her easel, halfheartedly rendering Morton's same wretched still life: the yellow pears, the candles, the arrangement altered by the addition of a blue scarf and a spent candle in a single sconce.

Despite the injunction to silence, Morton must have been in a rare old mood, Waverley thought, because he praised everything, including even Waverley's efforts. He strolled up and down between the easels, three on each side, a dry paintbrush held behind his back. He chatted cheerily, the same old stories about men and women so dedicated to art that they had hungered in cold garrets while they painted their fruit instead of eating it. The garrets were kept cold because the fruit stayed chilled and lasted longer.

"These artists painted against time. They had to finish their pictures before the fruit rotted. Only then could they eat it. Timing is everything, even in painting."

"Rot," whispered Waverley, hoping to inject some levity. "Morton is flatulent and full of rotten fruit."

Ginevra hushed her. Morton returned to Ginevra's easel to praise and linger.

At Avril's painting Morton paused critically. Avril had taken to splashing a bit of color here and there and then regarding it with exaggerated affection. If Morton criticized or inquired, she said she could not help it, that was her artistic vision of the pear, the scarf, the candle. In this oblique fashion she dared him to criticize. Denis Aron was an unspoken presence in the art room of Temple School.

But two could play at this. Morton studied Avril's work, and remembering his own glorious artistic acquaintance, he trotted out once again his story of his afternoon of absinthe in Picasso's studio, with Picasso's dog, Picasso's mistress, Picasso's model.

Avril took up her brush and put a patch of purple on his nose.

Morton swore under his breath. He wiped it off. "Very funny."

"Yes," she conceded. "You are very funny. You are a funny little man." Avril took the brush and put a great blob of purple on her own nose, one on each cheek and her chin. She grinned at him.

"You have lived amongst the greats, and yet you give art no respect. Your father would be ashamed of you."

"You know nothing of my father." She slashed her paper with purple and green and yellow and flung down the brush. "I detest hearing you speak of him."

"He has discipline. Talent. Genius. You are nothing. You will never—"

"Have dinner with the King of Sweden? I care nothing for the King of Sweden! Or for you. You are not an artist. You are a moth." The thought evidently gave her pleasure because she laughed.

Waverley laughed too. Avril glanced over at her. The gray cloud canopy shadowing Isadora lifted. Swiftly, dramatically, not as if dissolving, but as if rising, a curtain pulled by some unseen cosmic stagehand, the sky went suddenly blue. Through the French doors and windows, the art room flooded with light. Raindrops poised on the leafless wisteria lit up golden, gleamed, prismatic before they splashed, shattered on the stone below. The moment, so unexpectedly gorgeous, took Waverley's breath away, as though she had been stabbed by the beauty all around her, an understanding she could not articulate. She dropped her brush.

"Get back here this instant, Avril!" Morton shouted as Avril got off her stool and sashayed toward the French doors. "You will never learn anything if you walk out on everything that is difficult in life."

She turned and gave him a look of consummate contempt, unnerving on a face so young. "You think this is difficult? This?"

And with that she stepped to the still life tableau and yanked the scarf from the table. The bowl and the bottle crashed, broke, the spent candle overturned; the pears all fell to the floor and rolled. Avril flung the scarf over her shoulder and walked away, stooping down to pick up a pear. She dusted it off, bit into it, chewed, with no particular haste on her way out through the French doors. Her laughter echoed as she crossed the terrace. She flung the half-eaten fruit behind her.

The pear rolled into the dust. To Waverley's eye the dust and shadow and rocking pear all became animate, and the sudden sunshine choreographed. I have just seen the Unseen and heard the Unspoken, she thought, struck, amazed, appalled, joyous that she recognized Transformation when it happened to her. She jumped off her stool and pushed past Morton. She ran out calling, "Avril! Wait for me! Wait for me, Avril!"

Chapter 20

Using a penknife, the pointed end of a compass and a nail file as tiny chisels, Avril elegantly defaced their desk at the back of the library. They had a new name, *Wavril*. One created out of two. The old isolated "I" subsumed, blended, even obliterated into the broader, brighter "We" of *Wavril*. Wavril was a single being composed of all their pasts and preferences, their lives, their new language. Their very dreams melded on the pillow because they pushed the two beds together so they could lie close beside each other and talk till they fell asleep. Sitting across from Avril in the library, Waverley watched, chin in hand, as the little curls of wood, tight as pubic hairs, peeled out of the desk. Avril's progress was painstaking, unhurried, carefully done, crafted.

By the time Avril had finished the first letter, *W*, she and Waverley had developed a wordless parlance, a language that superseded Avril's basic English and Waverley's nonexistent French, silent communing like that of Chou-fleur and her lover, the red geranium. Theirs was a grammar based on a wrinkled nose, a raised eyebrow, a pursed mouth, or some complex combination of all three, a lexicon that allowed them to be both silent and expressive. As a result, the two girls started to resemble each other. That they both had dark eyes and the same close-cropped dark hair and school tunics mattered less than the way they held their bodies. Waverley (short, solid, sturdy) imitated Avril's shrug, her insouciance. Avril (small and slender) began to imitate some of Waverley's physical exuberance.

* * *

$\mathcal{B}$efore the A was finished, their pasts had melded, their secrets collapsed. Avril had opened the suitcase and laid out the paintings her mother had asked her to bring to Sophia. "I have disobeyed my mother in this. I will give them to Sophia. One day. Not yet."

"Does your mother hate Sophia because Denis loved her?"

"No. Never. She could not hate anyone, my mother. She is so gentle. So kind. Everyone orders her about. Do this, Judith! Listen to me, Judith, says my grandmother. My father says, Ignore the old woman, Judith. My mother keeps the peace between them. But inside, here"— Avril touched her heart—"she is stronger than all of them. Even stronger than my grandmother. And my father—oh yes, he is my father, more sorrow for us all—his is false strength. But there is nothing false about my mother. She has"—Avril sought the words in Waverley's eyes—"a dignity and a spirit, *l'esprit.* She has both together. You do not often find together, these things."

"Sophia," said Waverley. "That's what Sophia has, together and at the same time. Dignity and spirit. Maybe that's why your father loved them both."

"No. But perhaps that is why they love him. My father loves no one, Waverley. Perhaps not even himself. He knows not even how to love. They say he is a great artist, but he is not a great man. A great man would be more kind to my mother. She is a great woman, though no one will ever know this of her. What do I care if people say he is a genius?" Avril smoothed the paintings on the bed.

"They are dazzling paintings." Waverley moved from one to another. "They are like nothing I have ever seen."

"No one has. They are the best of him. He has great passion for his work. To watch him work, it is obscene, it is like watching someone make love. Maybe he loves the work. Maybe he loves, not this"—she touched the corner of the canvas—"the thing itself, but the doing of it. When he works, he hears nothing, sees nothing else, cares for nothing. He is like a man going under the water and not caring. And that is when the work goes well. When it goes badly, he swears. He drinks. Sometimes he strikes my mother. He leaves the apartment and stays in his studio, or perhaps there is this woman or that. My mother cries, but I do not. I hope he will find some woman and stay away. But, no."

"Is that why you always say he is not your father?"

"Of course." Avril shrugged. "No. That is not the truth. I am jealous. My mother stays with him, but I am the one who loves her. I want to stay with her. No, she says I must leave Paris. Then, I want her to come with me. No. She loves him more than me. I love her best of all and she loves him."

That one's mother would love a man better than she loved her daughter was not, to Waverley Scott, any sort of surprise at all. She was puzzled that Avril could be so hurt, could feel such loss, love and resentment all at once. And, never having lived in a family, Waverley was amazed at the potpourri of passion and affliction, affection and resentment that looped and bonded and separated the three generations of Avril's family. When, in bits and pieces, Waverley offered up the tale of her parents' liaison, her own unlikely name and her hotel childhood, her past seemed, in the telling of it, scarcely even strange, only rather pathetic. For the first time, Waverley felt pity for Rhoda. A new sensation.

Avril thought it strange that Rhoda should tell such vast lies to conceal her relationship with Mr. Gerlach. Of course men have mistresses. They all do. Many women have lovers.

"That may be true in the world you come from," whispered Waverley, brushing Avril's short hair from her forehead as they lay on the pillow. "But here, in America, it's all husbands and wives. Mr. and Mrs. before you can travel together."

"Like the ark."

"What ark?"

Avril laughed. "The ark in the Old Testament. To travel two by two on the ark. Did you never read the Bible?"

"Of course not. I am truly a North American Woman of the Future. I am spared all that weight and freight of religion." Waverley felt deprived. "So tell me the story. Tell me what everyone else knows."

"In the Bible, God is angry. Peoples have been very wicked and God is disgusted with his creations. God tells Noah, I am going to destroy all the world with a Flood, Noah, but you are a good man and I will save you. Build the ark, Noah, says God, and take on that ark two of each creature, each animal so that when my anger is spent and the flood is no more, and the waters . . ."

"Recede. The eliminating tide."

"Yes. Then, the world can go back to the way it was. So Noah builds his ark, and two by two, all the animals go on and live there, forty days and forty nights of rain." Avril sighed and rolled on her back, her hands beneath her head. "Poor Chou-fleur, she never can take her geranium on the ark. They are not two by two, one of each, though they are constant. Chou-fleur and her red geranium are faithful to each other. Even when the geranium has no flower, Chou-fleur is faithful and sits beside her in the kitchen window and . . ." Avril used her hands to try to describe how the cat would nudge the potted plant, to draw its attention to something entertaining in the street. "Still, for all their fidelity, Chou-fleur and her geranium, they cannot go on the ark. Theirs is a love like no other."

*B*ut before the V in *Wavril* had been completely etched into the desk to Avril's artistic standard, Temple School itself had altered. Both discipline and schedule lapsed almost entirely. Except for chicken duty, the radio broadcasts, and garden work, the other stringent daily patterns tattered, partially because the war news was so dire. So ongoingly dreadful. The war, so far away, crept up and over Useless Point. The German bombers pounded England, and Sophia was certain the Japanese were in the Puget Sound. Every overhead noise from a plane sent her outside with her binoculars. She scanned the Sound, looking for the Japanese invasion. Finally she took Newton's telescope up to their room and aimed it out the window, sweeping the waters for hours at a time, convinced that Japanese subs were silently menacing British Columbia and all the islands.

Once Sophia's unerring hand on the tiller of the school faltered, Quizzer's energetic convictions of correctness wilted too. In truth, after chocolate had been discovered in their midst, Quizzer never did regain his old equanimity. His attitude toward all the students remained distant, and he didn't seem to care if they marched and whistled or not. The girls all wished he would stop them in the hall, asked him to quiz them on the List of Nevers, but he seldom did so.

Agnes and Morton taught when they more or less felt like it, and played bridge with Violet and Ginevra for vast tracts of time. Sophia did not seem to notice, nor to remark when Violet took over the kitchen duties, cooking and cleanup, allotting chicken duties and setting up shared responsibilities, getting things done in a timely fashion so she would have more time for bridge. Marjorie did the laundry with her usual goodwill, though there was considerably less clothing than in the old Temple days, since the standards for personal grooming lapsed. Sophia seldom offered comment when tunics were no longer spotless, when students wiped their hands on their clothes, or bit their nails or wiped their noses. The King of Sweden had deserted Useless Point.

On their unstructured afternoons, Violet and Ginevra played bridge. Marjorie listened to the radio, not the news, but the music. She bounced around the library at the behest not of Debussy or Saint-Saëns, but Artie Shaw and Benny Goodman, dancing often, with the broom whom she called the groom. Sophia, when she came downstairs from her submarine vigils, smiled to watch her, sometimes showed her how to find the underlying tempo even in the most jazzy tune. Waverley and Avril and Nijinsky syncopated their days by crashing down the path to the beach to throw sticks to annoy the anemones, and on those rare, hot afternoons, to peel off their clothes and splash, screaming, into the icy waters to the delight of the otters and the dog.

Before the *R* had been fully carved, Waverley had shared with Avril her only truly prized possession: the afternoon on the back of the motorcycle, flying, and then falling, and then Sandy's lying on top of her, kissing her. Avril agreed that any injury she might have suffered was well worth it for such an experience.

"And since then?" she asked.

"Nothing," replied Waverley. "How could there be? Sandy couldn't even drive the truck for months and the Torklunds have forbidden him to spend any extra time at Temple School."

But there came a day, an afternoon in May when the Torklunds had all put on their best clothes and ceremoniously departed for the mainland, for the Greyhound bus station in Bellingham where they were going to meet Nels, home on leave from Hawaii. For today, the truck belonged to Sandy Lomax. And as he unloaded the school's bags of cornmeal, he asked in a low and confidential voice if Waverley could meet him at the bottom of the hill. He had the whole afternoon. He had something she should see. It was then that Waverley knew she truly had become *Wavril:* she could not imagine seeing without Avril's eyes, hearing without Avril's ears, experiencing without Avril to share, to validate.

The three of them bounced in the cab as the old truck groaned and rattled over roads that gave way to paths, the transmission straining toward this place Sandy was taking them. Few white people had seen this place, at least from the land. But Sandy knew all the legends that clung to the island. His grandfather, Hector's father, had arrived on this island long ago, just ahead of the law for a forged check, perhaps a murder, or a barroom brawl where knives were flashed—the charges varied according to who told the story. He had married an Indian woman and divided his days between logging and fishing. Farming he could not do. He had died in a fishing accident. From his grandmother's side of the family Sandy had heard the tales of the island's original peoples, passed, told, retold, one generation to the next, never quite the same, accumulating, eliminating as the tides.

They left the truck and climbed single file, threading through the pathless ferns and fallen trees. Waverley and Avril behind Sandy crashed through thigh-high bracken and stately disapproving cedars. Their footsteps roused deer, who bounded before them and just out of sight, and whole armies of rabbits, who skittered underfoot. Trees burst into cacophony as their limbs seemingly lifted off, and flocks of birds, unaccustomed to any human intrusion, rose in ragged unison against the blue. Underneath the leafy canopy the air was still, cool and damp, though overhead the sun burned in the afternoon sky. Their voices rang out, Waverley and Avril pulling each other up the hill. Then suddenly, as though they had stepped from behind a curtain, the forest ended. They found themselves suddenly on an outcropping of rock, cliffs, perhaps two hundred feet above a broad shallow bay.

The effect, coming so swiftly from the shady forest to the sun-streaked cliff, was dizzying, and Waverley had to sit down on the rough grass that clung to the cracks between the rocks. Tiny tough daisies protruded from moss. Far below them seals barked and hooted. In the distance, the mountains of the Olympic Peninsula, still covered in snow, rose above and behind the sparkling Sound. An eagle swooped overhead, studying them, no doubt as oversized prey.

"It takes your breath away," said Waverley.

"This place was sacred to my father," said Sandy. "He said that this place, and lots of others, that they had their own gods and their own ghosts and you must not disturb them."

"You can feel the eye of God here," said Avril. "Any god. Many gods."

The eagle flew off, out of sight, but its presence seemed to have alerted the gulls, and in their gossiping way, they called out to one another and dipped and soared, gray streaks in the blue sky. The three sat silently, in a row, plucking out the tiny daisies, listening to the water lap at the rocks far below, and the seals' noisy protests, feeling the sunshine pink their faces. Giddy still from the height, the bright wind, Waverley felt too some exquisite pressure at her heart, that this day would be hers always, and when Avril lay down, put her head in Waverley's lap, she savored such an exquisite sense of well-being that it sufficed for a holy peace, until Sandy announced he would be leaving in the fall, joining the navy.

"All those months behind the Torklunds' cash box, looking at the postcards Nels sends from Hawaii, I had a long time to think about it. What am I doing on this island? I could be on the island of Oahu. If I don't get out of here soon, I'll end up busting my guts for some Westervelt logging crew, bringing timber down the mountain. I can't stay with the Torklunds, driving their truck, stacking their cans, counting their change. Anyway, we'll get into this war, it'll happen and then they'll be drafting anyway. I might as well join up. I haven't told anyone else yet," he added. "Not Sis. Not my mother. So I don't want you to tell either."

Waverley and Avril promised they would not.

"It will be dangerous," commented Avril. "You think it is romantic, but the war will come and the danger is real."

"At least if you live with danger, you know you're alive. All I fear now is that one day I'll wake up and I'll be thirty years old and I'll still be driving the Dodge and stocking the shelves and listening to the Torklunds bicker and snipe. That's a kind of death right there. Or logging? Working some gasoline donkey skidding logs down to the water? Living your whole life around men and timber? Not me. That's all there is on this island."

"What about Bessie?" asked Waverley. "She can't—well, she can't really live alone, can she?"

"My father was the only one who could make Ma laugh." Sandy leaned back on his elbows. "He was a daredevil. He wasn't reliable or responsible. He drank too much, but he knew how to live. You wouldn't think that would be a gift, knowing how to live, but it is. Ma doesn't have it. I don't know if I have it. But if I stay here, I'll never find out. Pa died and Ma's going to cry and mourn and drink. I can't stop her. I know that now."

"Maybe Sis will look after her, after you leave," offered Waverley. "She always has."

"Whatever happens, Ma's made her choices. I'm making mine. I'm leaving," he said, biting down on the finality of the last word. "I'll send you postcards, and you can put them up in the school, just like Nels's postcards from Hawaii. Beautiful Oahu. Beautiful Honolulu. Beautiful Pearl Harbor. There are other islands besides Isadora."

"And will you come back here after the war?" Waverley stroked Avril's forehead.

"Hell no. I'm going to be an engineer. Make things move. I can't do that here on this rock. There's not even any roads on Isadora, except for logging. There's nothing with an engine, except the log donkeys, the pulleys, the winches. Nothing here but mules, horses and sailboats. I want to hear motion, motors."

"Tempo," offered Waverley. "The thump-thump of the motor is a kind of tempo."

"Yes."

"Then you must make a motorboat or fly an airplane and come to Paris. After this war," Avril declared, "Waverley and me, we are going to Paris, to have a school, to teach the French girls to be North American Women of the Future. Warrior Women!" Waverley smiled as Avril tickled her chin with a daisy.

"We are going to put Debussy and Satie and Saint-Saëns on the Victrola, and blindfold the students and tell them to Hear the Unspoken!

See the Unseen. Ingest the music!" cried Waverley with Sophia's exact inflection. "Express the emotion!"

"Have dinner with the King of Sweden."

"And fly?" asked Sandy. "Sophia's always asking you to imagine you can fly."

At that moment, such was her happiness that Waverley thought perhaps she could fly, though it was not at all the same experience as on the back of the motorcycle, with the pistons throbbing between, through her thighs, her pelvic bones. This was not physical. This was a leap of the imagination, a leap as recognizable as if she had leapt off the cliff, Sandy and Avril with her, if she had taken their hands and brought them with her, carried them over the water, the Sound, the summer, their cries of wonder falling to the rocks where the accumulating tide rhythmically bathed, fed, refreshed, and finally obscured all that silent unseen life below.

*B*efore Avril had carefully carved the graceful *I* into their name on the desk, Temple School had lost every vestige of educational decorum and Agnes Kauffman had involuntarily reached a high B-flat, a note she had unsuccessfully sought all her life.

Late one afternoon Agnes had gone into Massacre shopping with Quizzer, and returned earlier than expected. Agnes meandered through the dappling sunshine and apple trees toward the clapboard house, Verdi ringing pleasantly in her head. Humming, she put her packages on the bridge table and flung her summer hat on the chair and slipped out of her shoes. Her feet had swollen in the heat. She unfastened the buttons of her blouse as she went upstairs, but *La Forza del Destino* in her head was interrupted by other, less musical sounds. Agnes stopped humming.

Treading on tiptoe up the stairs, she put her ear against the bedroom door, where grunts, thumps and little squeals sounded from within. She flung open the door to an utterly unobstructed view of Morton's well-known buttocks heaving up and down encircled by a pair of legs. Agnes screamed, hitting a high B-flat, a note so strong, so piercing, it was virtually a chord, not altogether tonic, but heard all over Useless Point. Heard by the seals on Assumption Island and beyond.

Ginevra and Morton joined in this operatic moment. As Ginevra screamed, Morton scrambled off of her, and she rolled out of bed and onto the floor. But with Agnes filling up the door, there was no escape. Agnes threw a lamp at Morton, the lamp thudding against his hairless chest. Ginevra, in true Warrior Woman fashion, stood up and flung herself, naked, before her wounded lover, putting her own body between him and his assailant. For her pains she got belted across the mouth by Agnes and shoved down the stairs.

Their shrieking roused Waverley and Avril and Violet, who were in the school's garden, and they came running through the orchard, Newton following at a little distance. They all four burst into the clapboard and found Ginevra, naked, dazed, splayed at the foot of the stairs.

Newton, out of breath, astonished, sent Violet to get Sophia, took off his jacket and told Waverley and Avril to cover Ginevra. Bravely—though admittedly not very quickly—he went upstairs, calling out, "Agnes! Morton, stop! Stop at once!"

Upstairs the battle raged. Agnes beat Morton with his own framed paintings, torn from the walls of their bedroom. First she put her knee through the canvas and then, using the shards of frame, especially the ends with nails, she attacked him again and again. He wrested the weapons from her and they fell to the floor, rolling over each other, slapping, kicking, screaming.

Newton stood in the doorway. Then, with a deep breath, he entered the fray and pulled them apart, holding the struggling Agnes in his arms. Morton, naked and bleeding, tore past him and ran downstairs. Agnes doubled her fists and beat on Newton until, bursting into tears, she sobbed, her face in her hands. Newton patted her shoulder.

Downstairs Ginevra wept and called out for Morton, who ignored her. Naked and shameless, Morton searched about the ruins of the bridge game for a cigarette while Waverley and Avril fell into paroxysms of laughter at the sight of his penis. This was the situation when Sophia arrived, with Violet and Marjorie right behind.

In an instant, Sophia had assessed all. To Waverley and Avril, Sophia said, "Shut up."

To Morton, she said, "You old fool."

To Newton, she called, "Please bring Agnes down."

To Ginevra, she said, "How long has this been going on?"

Ginevra, clutching Quizzer's coat against her nakedness, blubbered and bawled. "It's not what you think! Is it, Morton? I love Morton and he loves me! We're going to get married! Tell them, Morton, tell them!"

Morton found a Lucky Strike, a butt, and lit it. He smoked and assessed his wounds as Agnes wobbled downstairs, Newton's steadying arm at her elbow.

"Are you going to marry Ginevra, Morton?" asked Sophia.

"Tell her our plans!" cried Ginevra.

"Tell us," said Agnes through clenched teeth. "Bastard."

"Bitch," he retorted.

"Get out of here, all of you," commanded Sophia. "We will leave Morton and Agnes to settle their domestic differences between themselves."

"Don't leave me, Sophia," cried Morton, "she'll kill me."

"I don't care if she does. In all the years I've known you, I guessed you had few scruples, but never—never!—would I have guessed you'd stoop to this! You have— You have—" Sophia trembled. "Betrayed my vision! You have until six this evening to leave Temple School. Both of you."

"Me?" cried Agnes. "Why me? What did I do? I am innocent!"

Sophia regarded them all—Agnes, Morton and Ginevra—with a monumental disgust. "There is no innocence here. You're all leaving, all three."

"Me?" cried Ginevra. "You're throwing me out of Temple School? Expelling me? Morton and I will leave together then. He and I—"

"Oh, shut up," Morton snarled.

The island party line crackled that afternoon as everyone listened in on Sophia's call to the Marine and Feed to arrange for Captain Briscoe's services to take the three miscreants off the island. Two separate trips. At least two: Morton and Agnes would have to make their own arrangements (and pay their own fares). The school would be responsible for Ginevra's fare, and she would travel alone. Then Sophia put in a call, long-distance, to an attorney's office in San Francisco. This was the attorney who made all Ginevra's arrangements with the school. When the attorney called back, Sophia explained that Ginevra would be leaving, that she had been expelled from Temple School. And when Sophia bluntly told him why she had been expelled, every island matron hanging on the phone line gave a tiny audible gasp. Sophia knew she had fulfilled, at last, all the island's worst suspicions about her school. For all her years and maturity, Sophia Westervelt had not much moved beyond being a girl whose every notion was an affront to propriety. She blamed Morton for the incident leading to the demise of her school, but she knew it would have come to this. In some guise or another.

And so the eliminating tide bore Morton, Agnes and Ginevra away from Isadora Island and out of Waverley's life forever. Out of one another's lives for that matter. Their leaving was the effectual end of Temple School, its rigorous curriculum, its vision put into practice. At the end of that spring term, Marjorie's family wrote that she would not be returning in the fall. Before leaving in June, Violet advised Sophia that she also would not be back. She thanked Sophia for giving her a Temple education, but said she wanted to concentrate on her bridge game. She asked if the King of Sweden offered a Nobel Prize for bridge. Sophia did not know. If so, Violet declared, "I intend to win it. You will be proud of me, Sophia."

"I am always proud of you, Violet."

Though Sophia believed bridge games beneath a Warrior Woman, she tried not to begrudge Violet her passion. For Sophia, this was an article of faith; she tried not to begrudge any passion. And so, when, at the back of the library, she came upon the desk and found there, elegantly finished, beautifully carved, and carefully inked in, *Wavril,* she did not begrudge that passion. But she did not misjudge it either.

Chapter 21

On these short, pale summer nights, the window in their room open, the curtain blowing back, Waverley often lay awake and wondered how she could ever have lived without Avril. They were the only two students in the school now, together constantly and in all undertakings. Unlikely sisters. But for the war, Waverley and Avril would never have met. Sometimes Waverley kept herself awake, wondering if she could thank the war for giving her Avril. How could she separate her joy in being Wavril from a need to be grateful to Hitler? A vexing moral problem. She broached it obliquely once to Sophia, who told her not to be silly, and so she was no longer vexed. That was simple.

Waverley had further reason to be grateful for the ongoing wartime emergency. In early June the central operator rang the school announcing a long distance call for Waverley Scott. She took the phone with some trepidation. Rhoda's voice far away, crackling on the wires, coming from Halifax, asked, implored: Would Waverley mind terribly, would she be brokenhearted if she had to spend the summer at the school? If she couldn't have a summer holiday with Rhoda? It was the war, you know? Mr. Gerlach was burdened with many cares and obligations, lots of contracts. He needed Rhoda with him. Her voice wavered: Mr. Gerlach had wanted to call Miss Westervelt and enroll Waverley in the summer session without even asking her consent, but Rhoda had insisted, no, they must talk to Waverley first. Rhoda made herself sound firm, protective, almost like a North American Woman of the Future.

Holding her elation in check, Waverley said, Yes, she would stay at the school this summer. She would be happy to stay.

How happy, Rhoda had no idea.

She rolled over now, comforted by the sight of Avril's dark head on the pillow beside her, sleeping peacefully, mouth open, her hand curled against her chin. Waverley stroked her short hair and then lay back. Listening. She knew Temple School so well, its every creak and whisper spoke to her like a foreign language she had long since learned. She listened hard, caught a distant stuttering, sputtering. Sometimes she fell back asleep and then woke again, jarred to wakefulness by a vanishing sound.

Waverley thought the sounds were nocturnal animals, the island's myriad rabbit population, the possums, racoons or deer trying to get into the wire-enclosed vegetable garden. But their room did not face the garden. Nor did it face the chicken houses, so even if a fox were tormenting the chickens, she probably would not have heard it. Her window faced Assumption Island. And though animals lived in the tangled thicket at the bottom of Useless Point, the sounds that woke her seemed more rhythmic and staccato than animal sounds.

And then one night, it came to her: the sputtering of a motorcycle. Distant. But not a dream.

On this night she quietly roused Avril, finger to her lips, and motioned for her to follow. She picked up their sandals and checked round the door in case the insomniac Sophia still trod the halls. Seeing no one, she offered Avril her hand and led her down the broad staircase, through the hall, into the kitchen and out to the mudroom door. She managed to open it slightly and scoot through so that it did not make its customary squeal. Sophia, of course, knew every creak and rattle in Temple School too.

The nocturnal life of Useless Point did not like being disturbed, and there was stirring in the nearby woods, and rabbits darted all across the yard, startling Avril, who clapped a hand over her mouth. They made their way to the toolshed, where Waverley opened a drawer and found a flashlight, which she did not turn on till they had left the school grounds and garden altogether and had come to the wooded path that led down to the beach.

Keeping her flashlight on the ground, she pulled Avril behind her. They bumped into low-lying branches so often that Waverley was reminded of Hector Lomax's awful death. The bracken and nettles, the blackberry vines with their cruel thorns tugged at her nightdress and scraped at her hands. But once on the beach, Waverley stopped, smiled, pulled Avril close and pointed, down some distance to where the beach curved. There a small fire snapped in front of the sole lookout hut the students had built.

"It's Sandy," said Waverley.

"How do you know?"

"The motorcycle. I heard it in my sleep."

Still holding hands over the rocks, they used the flashlight to evade the beached logs scattered around like dinosaur bones. From a distance, seeing the light, Sandy picked up his flashlight and met them halfway down the beach.

"I've been expecting you." He grinned. "I keep coming here, expecting you."

"Why didn't you tell us?"

"And how should I do that? Use the telephone so the whole island knows? No, I knew you'd come. Sooner or later."

He had built the fire out of driftwood, and a salty smell rose with the smoke; kelp and barnacles snapped in the heat and sparks flew up. The ice blanket lay behind it.

"Well, if Sophia's right and there are Japanese subs out there in the Sound, we are a perfect beacon for them," said Waverley with a twinge of guilt. Not enough guilt, however, to put out the fire.

He reached into the little hut and drew out a knapsack, winked at Waverley, and said to Avril, "I have a surprise for you. Close your eyes." He put a bag on her outstretched hand. Some sort of puffy white substance in little balls.

Avril squeezed it. She looked very dubious.

"Marshmallows," Sandy declared.

"What are marshmallows?"

"They're American. Just about as American as you can get."

"What do you do with them?"

"You eat them! Tell her, Waverley. Tell how you eat a marshmallow."

"I don't know. I've never had one."

"I cannot believe that a North American Woman of the Future"— he took out a pocketknife and began to trim a branch—"has never roasted a marshmallow. That's pathetic."

"They're on the List of Nevers," said Waverley. "Quizzer says you might just as well cut open a pillow and stuff your guts with feathers as eat a marshmallow. He said people could die of them and they have."

"Well, here's your chance to tempt fate." Sandy expertly trimmed the branch. He fashioned the end into a sharp point.

With that, he stuck the marshmallow, softly resisting, on the end of the stick and put it in the fire, turning it round and round as it browned. Once it flamed up, he drew it from the fire and close to his own face. It burned blue and lit his dark eyes oddly. He blew it out quickly and held it out to Waverley.

She plucked it gingerly, burning her fingertips on the charred sugar, and popped it into her mouth. The soft warm undersubstance got stuck in her teeth and melted against her tongue as she rolled it round in her mouth. Avril ate hers slowly and with much misgiving. She did not like it.

"Too American for you?" commented Sandy, holding another over the fire.

"I like American. I like you and Waverley."

"You like bananas and raspberries." Waverley stuck another marshmallow on the end of her stick and put it in the fire.

"They are not American."

"You like the Victrola and the music."

"The machine is American, the music is not."

Sandy pulled the flaming marshmallow close to his face, and the confectionary torch illuminated something in him Waverley had not seen before. "If you look carefully, you can see whole cities burning in this marshmallow." He brought his marshmallow close to his face, and when it had entirely charred, he blew it out. "Like London." He ate the mushroom in one gulp. "I've joined up, girls. I'm not sitting here on this rock while the world burns around me."

"The navy?" asked Waverley.

"I couldn't stand the army. They might send me somewhere without water. I can't live without water around me. Salt water."

"When are you leaving?" Avril asked.

"Soon. October at the latest."

Waverley blew out the flame on her marshmallow and ate it, feeling somehow as though the char and ash and sweetness had gone not between her lips, but between the chambers of her heart.

Avril and Waverley returned before dawn, just as the sky was beginning to leak light in the east, and they jumped into bed and slept briefly, dreaming, both of them, of fire and water and the sounds of the tide lapping at the beach. At 6 A.M., the school's usual rising time, summer and winter, Waverley rolled over on her pillow, which reeked of woodsmoke.

"We stink," she said, sniffing her nightdress.

They flung their nightdresses and pillows in the closet, shook the blankets out the window, and left them draped there. They spent a long time in the bathroom, washing up and washing off, but when they came down to breakfast in the kitchen, Sophia's expert nose wrinkled.

"Woodsmoke," she said. "Where could that be from?"

Avril and Waverley both looked perplexed as their jaws moved silently over milk and day-old biscuits.

As those June nights rolled into July, into August, they lay awake late, listening for the distant pop of the motorcycle. They crept out of the school, startling the rabbits and possums as they made their way down the wooded path to the beach. Driftwood logs, washed up on the beach, looked bleached and merely pale by day, but by moonlight, they seemed to glow. They formed a fort around the fire and lookout hut.

Sandy was always there before they arrived. He'd build a fire and lay out the ice blanket and have a bag of marshmallows or some other Untrue Food. He brought chocolate and was inducted into the Church of the Chocolate God, resurrected on the rocky beach. He didn't have many desserts to contribute, but he donated to the services some old Indian chants taught to him by his grandmother. He brought beer and tobacco and cigarette papers. Waverley learned to smoke, not with Sandy's easy gravity or Avril's insouciance, but smoke just the same. Before they left, they doused the fire, and broke it up, scattering the embers and rolling the last of the still-burning logs into the water where they sizzled and bobbed on whatever current they took a fancy to.

When during the long summer days Quizzer took his instruments and the two girls to the beach, he pondered over the charred remains. He commented that probably some Indians were using the beach for their fishing. "We must get word to them not to build fires on the beach at night. They will be beacons for the Japanese. Sophia is certain there are Japanese subs in our Sound and I personally have never known her to be wrong."

Waverley and Avril exchanged a look of complicity and went each to her own tide pool and with her own bucket.

And if there were Japanese subs plying the waters of the San Juan Islands, they might, those summer nights, have seen the fire on the beach, might have heard Avril teaching the other two the dirty verses to the "Mademoiselle from Armentières," might have seen Waverley with marshmallow on her hands, her mouth and in her hair, running down to the water's edge to wash off with Sandy getting up, running behind her, tackling her, crashing into the icy water, and she crying out for Avril, who would come to her aid. The three of them, splashing, dunking, plunging and pushing till they were blue with cold and Waverley losing a sandal and they having to flail about in the dark water looking for it.

They ran back up to the fire, shivering, teeth chattering, cold. Sandy shook the blanket free of twigs and handed it to Waverley and Avril, who held it up like a curtain while they peeled off their dripping nightdresses. They hung the nightdresses on a branch and sat before the fire, wrapped up in the blanket. Sandy put his hands over the fire. "Your clothes are wet and cold too," said Waverley, opening her side of the blanket to him. "Take them off."

So he stood, peeled off his shirt, slid out of his pants and got inside the blanket, making it stretch over all their backs, and they all three put their feet as close to the fire as they could bear. Waverley, between Sandy and Avril, could feel the difference between their bodies, the bulk and muscle of Sandy's, the fragility and smoothness of Avril's, her small bones, his thick joints. Waverley's own body was literally somewhere between them, neither as slender and light as Avril, nor as muscled and well formed as Sandy. Waverley reached out and put her arms through each of theirs, pulled them closer to her and rested her chin on her knees, on the rough stubble of the ice blanket.

When Sandy made his next delivery, he brought the ice into the kitchen as he always did, using the blanket as a sling and bent double under the weight of the ice on his back. Waverley wondered why the ice didn't melt immediately once touched by that blanket, which smelled powerfully not just of smoke and sticky marshmallow, but secrecy and salt water and desire, so pungent, so wonderful that she felt rather weak-kneed there, holding open the lid of the icebox so that he could lower the ice into it.

That evening while they were all at supper, Sophia remarked that the icebox smelled like woodsmoke and Quizzer said she was mistaken. Ice and fire don't mix. Waverley and Avril both asked for more cornmeal pudding.

The ice blanket became more imbued with fire and smoke, with secrecy and salt water and desire as the summer wore on. Inevitably there came that night when dashing back up to the beach and the fire from the freezing water, they did not use the blanket for a curtain. Avril peeled her dripping nightgown off and flung it on a branch. Waverley bent down and picked up the hem of hers, pulled it over her head, dropped it on the stones.

"Avril's breasts are like flowers," she said as they locked arms and stood, nude before him. "Mine are like fruit."

"You are both so beautiful. So beautiful."

"You have to love us both," said Avril in a thick whisper. "We are Wavril, and you have to love us both. And we both have to love you."

"It can't be like the ark," said Waverley. "I love Avril, and we love you, and we must always love each other, all three."

"I could not love just one of you. I love Wavril, the both, the two."

Waverley smiled. "Forever."

"Forever," said Avril.

"We have to swear on the Chocolate God."

"We don't have any chocolate."

"Swear anyway. That's what faith is," said Avril.

Sandy so swore and then slowly, carefully peeled off his wet pants, his white boxers. He cast them off and sank, kneeling on the blanket. Waverley and Avril came to him and he wrapped his arms around their hips and pressed his face into their bellies. The damp from his lips and heat of his hands stroking their hips, their buttocks, the long swath down their thighs to that tender place at the back of the knees. He wrapped them in warmth as the woodsmoke enveloped them, and they wrapped their arms around one another. They had been numb with cold, their nipples rigid from icy water. Their nipples stayed rigid, but nothing was cold.

Sandy's arms reached around the curves of their thighs, his fingers tucking just under the buttocks, pushing farther, meeting no resistance. A groan escaped from Waverley, emerged from deep, dormant within her. Avril gave little cries and wilted to the blanket, drawing them both down. Sandy lay between them, the stem, the root of him upthrust entreating their hands. He closed his eyes. He took their two hands and joined them, brought them down over the thick hair curling at the base of his penis, more beautiful than any garden statue, more beautiful than the murals, the nude men prancing about the practice room walls whose lilylike manhood bore only metaphorical comparison to this. Waverley whispered to him, needed to hear the words, murmured without euphemism as they stroked Sandy's legs, the swollen, upthrust beauty of him. She wanted her own low voice to counterpoint the tempo of his tightening breath, coming faster and harder as their hands bestowed such pleasure on him, on each other. Avril and Waverley plied his legs farther apart, and Sandy sought the contours of their breasts, stroking as though he would commit them to memory, the fruit and the flower. In all that heat on the ice blanket, Sandy cried out and erupted, spurted, his whole body tensed toward a single moment, his every muscle straining. He released and then relaxed, the girls on either side of him, their arms looped over his chest, their heads on his shoulders, the scent of him thick in their nostrils and on their hands. The fire died down and only the plume of smoke curled over them like a cover.

Night after night that summer they learned by doing. Sandy's body was so clean, so upright, so without secrets, so hard and willing to let them draw from him such pleasure. Waverley, pleased to have been an instrument of his pleasure, to have bestowed pleasure, rewarded him again and again with her voice and her smile and her complicity with Avril, their shared sense of delight in him. He absorbed their tempo and transformed it; music into a sort of movement, coming to a breathless crescendo. Avril's tempo, her tune were altogether different. From Avril, Sandy and Waverley had to elicit bright cries. Waverley could have bathed in Avril's cries. Avril's cries had to be teased out from all the hidden tender places; Avril's cries had to be found, discovered, unearthed and were the more gratifying for their secrecy. When Waverley lay between them, Sandy coaxed her too, in some tactile tongue, seeking and finding; Avril gentle but insistent, spoke with her fingers, whispered *Wavril, Wavril* and pulled from Waverley such quickened tempos, such rough breaths, like music once ingested, emotion helplessly expressed.

In the daytime they never spoke of these nights. But sometimes in the ordinary course of things, of weeding the vegetable garden, or tying up the tomatoes or mending the wire fence, of chores in the chicken house or scrubbing down the vast iron cooker after supper, Waverley's fingers brushed Avril's. A current passed between them, sometimes a jolt, sometimes a tingle, so much so that they reflexively, imperceptibly leaned toward each other, like Chou-fleur and her red geranium. Standing together, they might pick up a piece of lint from a tunic, or stand so their hips touched as they hung up the dripping laundry, or sit so close at the school table as to brush each other's shoulders or legs. At night they sometimes whispered, lay arm in arm, beside each other in nightdresses that smelled of smoke and desire, on pillows that smelled of smoke and desire and sheets that reeked of it: the chemical union of smoke and desire and the scent that Sandy left indelible on both of them. They came to know him as they knew no other. They came to know each other as they knew no other. No more could be unseen and no more remained unspoken.

Chapter 22

*A*vril swore in French. With rags tied round their heads and over their mouths to protect against feathers, dust and dried chicken dung, Waverley and Avril scraped the henhouse roosts with wire brushes. Chickens clucked and quarreled at their feet, annoyed at their presence and pecking their sandals. Waverley kicked at a chicken that had mistaken her toes for worms. She might have chased it, but she heard the sound of a vehicle wheezing up the hill. Their rhythmic brushing ceased. Today was not Sandy's delivery day. They untied their masks and the bandanas on their heads and used them to dust feathers from each other's tunics, so they could at least look presentable for him. At the sound of the Dodge, Nijinsky barked and bounded into the yard.

Stepping from the dimness of the chicken house, they squinted in the sunshine spilled everywhere about the yard, glinting off the green leaves. Quizzer emerged from his brain-testing lab and straightened his bow tie, smoothed down those strands of hair that gleamed along his balding pate.

Sandy turned the motor off and got out. The truck shuddered pleasurably. He did not return the greetings from Waverley or Avril or Newton. He said nothing but went round to the passenger side of the cab and opened the door. Rhoda Scott stepped out.

Waverley gasped and grabbed Avril's arm. Avril asked over and over what was wrong. Who was this woman who came toward Waverley with her arms open and her face wreathed in smiles?

"Waverley, dear!"

Rhoda wore a smart suit of pale gray-blue and in her gloved hands she carried a clutch purse. She had silk stockings with perfect seams and blue high heels and a gardenia in her hair, which was longer and more elaborately styled than Waverley remembered. But then, it had been a long time. A year. All of that. More. A lifetime. Waverley backed up against Avril. She rubbed the bandana over her face, down the front of her tunic. She shook it out and tiny feathers danced.

"You better not touch me, Mother. I'm filthy."

"Mother?" exclaimed Avril. "Mother?"

"How you've grown, Waverley. How tall you are and brown, and healthy I suppose. Yes, you look very healthy."

Quizzer introduced himself to Rhoda. He greeted her with his usual flourish and hyperbole and waxed on about what a talented student Waverley was and how the school was so fortunate to have her. He might have gone on, but Sandy interrupted him.

"Excuse me, Professor. I have to get back to Massacre. They need me at the emporium. Can you bring them back to Massacre in the Packard?"

"Oh, certainly."

Rhoda turned to Sandy, opened the purse and pulled out some bills. She thrust them into his hand. "Thank you for bringing me on such short notice. No notice."

"That's too much money."

"Keep it. I insist." Rhoda pressed it on him and he took it. Without another word, he got in the truck and left. He did not look back.

"Do you have any bags to be carried in, Mrs. Scott?" asked Quizzer.

"We're not staying." She looked positively radiant, bathing in beatitude.

"We?" Waverley could feel sweat prickling along every inch of her body.

"We?" Avril breathed out in one long rasping syllable.

Newton held open the mudroom door, and ushered Rhoda in. "I assure you, Mrs. Scott, we don't usually take our guests through the mudroom and the kitchen. But then, we don't usually have guests. Sophia will be delighted though, I'm sure. Come along, Waverley, Avril."

She held Avril's hand and they wordlessly followed Quizzer into the library, where Sophia sat at the desk beside the map with its pushpins. She wore spectacles. Newton introduced their guest, and Sophia rose, removed her spectacles and made an impromptu speech, what a delight it was to meet Waverley's mother. "I would not have guessed you to be mother and daughter. Waverley must look like her father." Sophia towered over Rhoda. "I wish we had known you were coming, Mrs. Scott. We would have had a program ready in your honor. We would have had some sort of—"

"This is not a visit. I'm taking Waverley home with me." Rhoda turned to her daughter and her face lit. "Home, Waverley." She lingered over the word as she brushed a few feathers off Waverley's tunic. "Mr. Gerlach and I, that is, Waverley's guardian—you met him when he made the arrangements for her—"

"I met no one, Mrs. Scott. I spoke with him on the telephone."

Rhoda's face fell slightly and a moist little *Oh* issued forth. "Well, it doesn't matter. We're getting married. Waverley will have a real family."

Waverley edged slowly toward Sophia, as though to take shelter in Sophia's shadow, to ensconce herself behind Sophia's dignity and conviction, the bulk of her body. "I have a home. This is my home. This is my family. These people, they are my family. I love them, and I'm not leaving."

Rhoda tugged on the fingers of her gloves and removed them. "You don't understand, Waverley. You have a mother and a father now."

Waverley linked arms with Sophia. "I have Sophia and Quizzer and they are better than any mother or father. I have Avril!" She reached and pulled Avril up close against her. "Wavril! We are Wavril!"

Rhoda regarded the small dark-haired girl quizzically. "And you are who?"

"*Wavril*," Avril breathed their name out, "Wavril, Wavril . . ."

"Avril Aron is a student from France," said Sophia in her even voice. "Staying with us for the duration of the war. For as long as is necessary."

Rhoda approached Waverley, took her hand, drew her gently from Avril and Sophia. "You haven't heard me, Waverley. You'll have a wonderful home. In Asheville. You know how we love Asheville, North Carolina. The mountains are so healthful, and Mr. Gerlach has bought us a house there and we're getting married, and—"

"What did he do with Mrs. Gerlach?" Waverley burst out. "Did he kill her? I'll bet he killed her."

"Waverley!" Sophia exclaimed.

"How else did he get rid of her? He has a wife, Sophia! He's married! He has a wife and he has daughters and she's been sleeping with him all these years, a married man! How can he marry Mother if he has a wife? He must have killed his wife!"

"He's getting a divorce," snapped Rhoda, her face flushing as she explained to Sophia and Newton. "There was a first Mrs. Gerlach, but she is living in Reno now. For a divorce. It won't take long. Another few months. Then we'll marry and Mr. Gerlach will adopt Waverley."

"Never!" Waverley doubled her fist and beat it on Sophia's desk. "Never! I won't be adopted! I'm not a baby! I'm a Warrior Woman! Tell her, Sophia, tell her I'm a Warrior Woman! I'm a North American Woman of the Future! And I won't be adopted like a baby or a pet!" She beat on the desk till Sophia silently closed her hand over Waverley's fist, conducting courage through her body like a current. Waverley hushed, trembling, then vowed, "I won't be Waverley Gerlach. What the hell kind of sonofabitching name is that?"

"What are they teaching you here!"

"We do not teach profanity, Mrs. Scott, I assure you."

"Profanity," Newton explained, "results from congestion of the stomach and there's none of that here. We feed our students True Foods."

Sophia rested her hand on Waverley's shoulder, and while she wept Avril wrapped her in an embrace, their dark heads together.

Rhoda looked around. "Where are the other students?"

"It is the summer," Newton offered, "and many of our students . . ."

Sophia shook her head. "A school is not judged by its numbers, Mrs. Scott, but by the achievements of its students. Our students will have dinner with the King of Sweden one day."

"But I always thought, I was under the impression—"

"Nothing was kept from you, from either of you. If Mr. Gerlach had inquired how many students were here, I would have told him. He did not inquire."

"Sophia," Waverley pleaded, wiping her nose with her hand, "don't let her take me. Please. I'll do anything. I'll stay on the antiprofanity diet. I'll do the chickens every day. I'll turn Music into Movement, I'll cook and clean and do the laundry and scrub the pans and mop the floors! Every day, Sophia!"

"What sort of work is that for a student? Don't you have servants here?"

"Our school is a democracy," Sophia replied. "The work of the world is the work of our students."

"Mr. Gerlach was paying a lot of money for an exclusive school."

"I hate Mr. Gerlach!" wailed Waverley. "I'm a bastard, Sophia, it's true. He sent me here because it was remote and far away from everything! He just didn't want anyone to know. Mother doesn't want anyone to know that I'm his bastard! I'm a bastard, Quizzer! He never married my mother!" She began dancing, turning anguish into movement and flinging herself about the library. She waved at Rhoda. "She's not even Mrs. Scott. There never was a Mr. Scott! She—"

"Shut up, Waverley." Rhoda's mouth had pursed like a string bag. "You ought to be happy Ed has acknowledged you." She turned to Sophia and Quizzer. "My husband, that is, Mr. Gerlach is a very rich man."

"I hate that sonofabitch!" cried Waverley, running back to Sophia, running headlong into her, pressing her head against Sophia's ample shoulder. Sophia held her, held Avril as well, who was dazed, stunned, as though she had been slapped.

Sophia allowed Waverley to weep for a while, then she released both girls. "Stop crying."

They both gulped and swallowed, held hands, choked back sobs.

"Wipe your nose."

Waverley used the sleeve of her tunic.

"You are a North American Woman of the Future, are you not?"

"Yes."

"Then act it. You are a Warrior Woman. Such women do not cry. Or if they cry, they do so in private."

"They save their tears," said Avril miserably.

"If you keep to the things you have learned here, they will serve you. They must serve you now." In a gesture of tenderness, Sophia reached out, stroked the dark curls of Waverley's head as she buried her own heartbreak. What was the good of having a vision if you could not invoke it in a crisis? "The test of adulthood, of maturity, is in how you handle the unexpected." Sophia stepped back and drew Avril with her, leaving Waverley alone in the center of the library, her gaze on Avril, whose features contorted in mute pain. "Now, hold out your arms." Sophia spoke clearly, slowly, as though her voice could carry across time. As indeed, finally, it did.

Waverley flung her head back, looked overhead, the old well-known mottos painted across the ceiling beams. *Waste Not Thy Hour. Form Is to Function as God Is to Nature. See the Unseen, Hear the Unspoken. Learn by Doing. Fear Nothing Save Ignorance, Untruth, Ugliness. Transformation.*

"You must be transformed and you must be transformed now. Lift your arms. Out. Parallel to the shoulders. Your spine, Waverley. Remember the spine is the Corinthian column of your whole body. Chin. Yes. Close your eyes. Can you fly? Can you imagine flying?"

She started to blubber, nodded though she could not speak.

"Can you see the Unseen? Hear the Unspoken? Ingest the music and express the emotion. Can you discover the tempo inherent in any given day or activity?"

"Yes."

"And will you keep time, Waverley, always, feel it, recognize the tempo, discover and develop, and direct your life accordingly?"

"Yes."

"Very well then. You are Transformed. I will send your Certificate of Transformation in the mail."

"I'll give you our address, Flint Street in Asheville, North Carolina."

Sophia ignored Rhoda. To Waverley, she said, "Put your arms down, Waverley. Dear Waverley." She glanced at Newton, whose cheeks were wet with tears. She bit her lip. "She is your mother, Waverley. It's her right." Newton was so overcome, he had to retire to his laboratory.

Waverley vowed to Rhoda, "I will make you regret this."

Up in their room, Sophia pushed open the door and Rhoda gave a short, surprised snort of disapproval to see the beds pushed together. She rebuked Sophia for allowing girls this age to sleep together. Sophia replied that she had not known they slept together.

Rhoda went to the bureau and began opening drawers, but Avril flung herself against the dresser. "This is our room. You cannot do this! You cannot. We are Wavril! Oh, don't do this to us! Oh Waverley, no!"

But Waverley, unable to reply, powerless to stop Rhoda, watched her mother go to the closet and open the door. There rose from within, reveling after its long confinement, the smell of woodsmoke, which blew through the room like a banner. Waverley and Avril held their collective breath as Rhoda reached to the floor and drew out the two white nightdresses, which seemed to dance of their own accord and to their own tempo, wafting the scent of beach and smoke, salt water and desire, of the forbidden.

"What is that smell?" asked Rhoda.

"Smoke," said Sophia woodenly. "Woodsmoke." Her gaze rested on Avril and Waverley. Her mouth tightened into a seam. "I think you both have lied to me."

"No, it's not what you think. Honest," Waverley protested. "All right. It is what you think, but you never did outright ask, Sophia. You never did. I would not have lied if you'd asked," she lied.

"I should not need to ask outright if Temple students are breaking the rules. But now I shall ask outright. What have you been doing that this smell"—and she didn't wholly mean the smoke—"should be so present here?"

"We went to the beach at night. We sneaked out and went down to the beach and built fires. It wasn't so very terrible. Was it?"

"Breaking trust is always terrible. Moreover, you know very well there may be Japanese subs in the Sound. You have been aiding and abetting the enemy."

"Are we at war?" asked Rhoda.

"Warrior Women," Sophia informed her, "do not need war to be strong, to be true, to be loyal." She rested her grave gaze on the girls. "You have both broken faith with the school."

"It was my doing, Sophia. My idea!" Waverley cried. "Don't punish Avril. Just like the Church of the Chocolate God, that was mine too. She just followed me. They all followed me. Avril only said the Chocolate God was hers because she couldn't be expelled."

"The Church of the Chocolate God?" inquired Sophia, befuddled for the first time in twenty years. "I thought it was just a box of candy."

"We made a god of chocolate," murmured Waverley, her eyes on the floor. "I made it."

"You made a church? You worshiped chocolate? After all we have done to spare our students the freight and weight of crippling religions and Untrue Foods, and you made a—chocolate god?" Breathing hard, Sophia sat down on their bed and from those sheets rose too, the scent of woodsmoke. "All this," she glared at them knowingly, "has been going on while I have been trying to educate you? You have been making a church and alerting the enemy submarines while I have been trying to groom you to have dinner with the King of Sweden?"

"Who is the King of Sweden?" Rhoda demanded. "And why does everyone keep talking about him?"

"Punish me for sneaking out at night, for the fires on the beach. I am guilty, not Avril," Waverley whimpered. "But honestly, Sophia, it's just like you've said, like in the library, Fear Nothing Save Ignorance, Untruth or Ugliness. It was none of those. I promise you that."

"It was subversion. Deceit."

"No! No, really. It was discovery, Sophia. That isn't breaking the Temple rules. I will always live up to what you've taught me. I will never disappoint you. I promise. Never again."

"We promise," Avril wept. "After the war, Sophia, we are going back to Paris, and make a school like this one and to make Warrior Women—"

"Well, as of now," said Rhoda bluntly, "Waverley is going to North Carolina."

*H*er clothes were an obvious metaphor for what had happened to Waverley Scott. Nothing from her old life fit her anymore. Her old blouse strained at her breasts and the skirt was too short. She was taller, fuller-bodied, brown and well muscled, strong, broad shouldered. And so, Waverley Scott left Temple School still wearing the regulation tunic, leggings, socks and sandals. In her suitcase she carried pitifully little, another tunic, her nightdress, a toothbrush, a hairbrush, her pillowcase with the Temple logo, a few pairs of underwear.

Standing in the school's yard, the Packard running, Avril wept as Sophia held her, and Quizzer put the suitcase in the Packard.

"Get in the car, Waverley," Rhoda called out, "we're leaving at once."

Waverley leaned toward Avril. She burbled and bubbled with promises. "I will come back for you. I love you. I will always love you. You won't forget me?"

"Never."

"Sophia—"

"I will never forget you, Waverley." Sophia's gray eyes were bright with unshed tears. "I will go on loving you, though you have taxed me, you know that. I will not say good-bye. I did that in the last war and it proved false."

At the Massacre dock, the *Nona York* awaited them. Rufus barked a greeting for Waverley, his tail wagging, and he ran up to the Packard when she got out. But Captain Briscoe was solemn. He was polite to Rhoda, called her Ma'am as Quizzer handed him Waverley's single valise, and Rhoda followed him down the dock toward the *Nona York*.

But Waverley held Quizzer in an embrace, wept against his shoulder, Quizzer unabashedly weeping too, till at last he kissed her forehead and bade her farewell and got in the Packard. Waverley stood in the cloud of its exhaust, her feet planted apart, looking up toward the Marine and Feed while her mother called her from the dock. The Captain fired up *Nona*'s engine.

High in a window at the Marine and Feed, a thin curtain moved and Waverley saw a pale broad face. Sis. And then the door opened and Sandy walked out. A measured tread, moving toward the dock, down the dry unpaved street.

Mrs. Torklund burst out of the door and stood, calling after him. "Sandy! Sandy Lomax! You go down to that boat and you're finished at the Marine and Feed. I won't have it! You'll be out of a job! You leave them girls alone! You—"

Sandy took off the Marine and Feed's leather apron, dropped it, walked on it, and came to the dock where Waverley stood. He opened his arms to her and she ran to him, brought her face up to his, her body up against his well-known body. She wrapped her hands around his back, splaying her fingers across the smooth muscles in his shirt and pressed her face against his chest, breathing in the smell of him, sweat and oil, metal and fish, woodsmoke. She opened her mouth to his.

They kissed, long and hard and to the snickering delight of the Massacre locals. Rhoda Scott drew a sharp, incredulous breath to behold her sixteen-year-old daughter in what was clearly an adult and practiced embrace. Mrs. Torklund went back inside and slammed the door. Sis dropped the curtain in the upper window.

Sandy stood on the dock while the *Nona York* chugged away from Massacre, into the waters of the Sound, which shone copper-green in the afternoon sunshine. Waverley stood on the deck, watching till the *Nona York* rounded a curve perhaps of land, or perhaps a curve of time, and he was lost to her view.

Then the Captain called out, told Waverley to come inside. Her mother sat primly on a bench, her smart shoes cloaked with dust, her gardenia sadly browned and wilted. She regarded Waverley with a combination of distrust, dislike and ridicule.

Waverley went to the table and put her head in her arms. Rufus curled at her feet. Captain Briscoe left the wheel for a moment and poured a cup of his grit-ridden coffee, quickly sweetened it from his hip flask and gave it to Waverley. She declined. But he pressed it into her hands. He said the shot of whiskey would dull the pain. He said he knew what it was to lose someone you loved.

Part Four

The Time Being

Mankind is
answering to the
Spirit

I cannot breathe
the body nevertheless
Nolan.

Chapter 23

The life to which Rhoda aspired was made manifest in the house that Edward Gerlach bought for her. A fine old frame house, high, wide, with a roofed porch, it met the world with rectitude that passed for dignity. There was a tidy garden in the back and lace curtains in the windows and a cherry wood dining room set and an overstuffed couch, canopy beds. Here she would be Mrs. Gerlach. After the divorce was final, of course. This last little consideration, so minor, really, as to be truly trivial, was dispensed with, and Rhoda presented herself to the world of Asheville matrons as Mrs. Gerlach.

Waverley detested the house. On sight. Never having had a settled life, she did not cherish its icons, and the house on Flint Street seemed to her crushing to the spirit, claustrophobic to the body, and death to spontaneity. Asheville, with its ring of mountains, affected her like a choker at the neck. Sometimes she could not breathe.

Over cups of tea and little sandwiches (prepared by the black hands of Elsie, hired to help), Rhoda made friends with the ladies she had met at church. They were plump pleasant women who moved in a cloud of blue talcum. Rhoda poured tea and told her newfound friends that she had just brought her daughter back from a private school in Washington, suggesting by evasion that her daughter had been educated in the nation's capital. Rhoda explained that her daughter was shy. That's why she wouldn't come downstairs. And yes, her daughter, Waverley Gerlach, was the image of her dear father. Mr. Gerlach, she said, (cream?) traveled all the time. Business. Steamships. Railways. (Sugar?) And leaving the rather tetchy subjects of husbands (one lump or two?) Rhoda moved along to ill health, of which there was plenty in Asheville. This was a town of chronic sufferers, people seeking cures in the air, the water, the medical miasma. Ills and ailments were a favorite topic of conversation. For this reason, Rhoda had adored Asheville and had wanted to live here, though Edward had picked out (and paid for) her house.

Waverley refused to be properly introduced to the blue talcum ladies. She tucked her hands in her armpits, planted her feet apart and declared she would not do it. That was just the beginning of what she would not do. She wouldn't eat Elsie's cooking because it wasn't True Food. She refused to give up cropped hair, her tunic, trousers and Roman sandals, would not change her underwear. In all these acts of rebellion and willful hatefulness she felt entirely justified, elevated, even somehow heroic, certain this is what a Warrior Woman would have done. And in her letters home to Temple School, to Avril and Sophia and Quizzer, it was in this noble light she presented herself.

Rhoda had furnished the perfect girlhood room for Waverley, complete with canopy bed and a dust ruffle, rosebud wallpaper, and a closet full of new clothes for school. The closet stank. It smelled of mothballs and camphor, and not woodsmoke, marshmallow and desire. The clothes stank. The room stank. Waverley detested especially the little vanity with its ruffled skirt and vials with stoppers and powder puff boxes. She ripped the sonofabitching skirt off the vanity. She flung it down the stairs for Elsie to pick up. She tore off the sonofabitching dust ruffle and opened the bedroom window and threw it out on the roof of the porch, scrambled out after it and kicked it. She crawled back in through the window and went to the vanity and gathered up the little glass perfume vials. She stood at the window and tossed them across the porch roof to the street, enjoying the sound of their smashing on the sidewalk. She dumped the powder boxes, puffs and all, on the floor. She refused to go to church with her mother. She took up serious smoking. She took money from Rhoda's purse and bought candy and cigarettes, stamps for her letters, paper and ink and envelopes. She cried herself to sleep.

But nothing prepared Waverley for that first day at the high school, where she found herself amongst hordes of foreign strangers—hundreds of them swarming in the halls and classrooms. Amongst these Asheville students, Waverley felt less like a Warrior Woman and more like one of the dead seals whose corpses would sometimes wash up on Sophia's Beach, buffeted by the tides, ugly, flyblown and inert. The Asheville youth regarded Waverley Gerlach—her cropped hair, her tunic, her Roman sandals and her leggings—with a sickening mixture of mirth and hostility. They whispered behind their hands, they laughed in low chuckles. So bizarre was Waverley that on that very first day, the girls' vice principal sent her home, saying such a costume was unacceptable to the school. Girls must wear dresses. Return in a dress.

Wearing a dress, Waverley's terrors were much exacerbated. She was constricted at every turn. Congested. The clothes itched. Not merely homesick in an abstract, lonely way, she was devastated by the rites that all the other students here subscribed to, unthinkingly, cheerfully. In the gym, in horrid little cubicles, girls got into shorts and blouses for classes that demanded strange undertakings called field hockey and calisthenics. Waverley stood stupidly by while people intent on throwing or catching a ball ran into her, knocked her down, whistles blowing randomly and without any sense of timing whatever.

Science labs held many more tools than a telescope and a microscope and there was no talk of chickens. The smells in the science lab made Waverley sick. Formaldehyde. Gas from Bunsen burners. She could not bring herself to look at the lab shelves, on which stood jars of preserved dead things, pickled like Untrue Foods. There was no *Form Is to Function as God Is to Nature*, no List of Nevers, no lectures on universality or the principles of the tides. No tides. Landlocked.

Ignorance, untruth and ugliness were all around her. She was besieged. The teachers (a few males, many females) were small, pinched people who had been rolled in chalk dust and set out to dry. They lacked all enthusiasm or any eloquence. They had no stride, any of them, but walked in little mincing steps, as though their ankles were looped together. The faculty reeked of congestion in their bowels, constriction in their clothing. Waverley could smell it in them, on them, like she could smell how tired their hair was, bound in buns, or flaking dandruff. They had no interest in asking questions, or the universals; they expected only silence and neatly done homework from their students. Waverley refused to do homework, but silence, well, that was easy. All day she was silent as a nudibranch, terrified of speech. Her words were not their words. She could not understand them when they spoke. Her own voice was like something from the wilderness.

At night, her words on paper, these were eloquent. Waverley wrote passionate letters home, begging Avril's belated forgiveness for the way the Temple students had treated her when she'd first arrived. Waverley knew now, understood, oh yes, what Avril had suffered, that colossal loneliness, how it could just ream out your heart. And poor sweet Marjorie. Waverley now knew how the world outside of Temple School would treat Marjorie, because Waverley's math teacher had pronounced her retarded. Waverley had been moved to a class for the hopelessly inept. Here the teacher snarled, smoked out the window and kept a ruler close by to smack offenders. The other students ignored Waverley as they ignored everything. They put their heads down on the desks, slept and drooled. They had slack jaws and vacant eyes. Not at all like dear cheerful good-natured Marjorie, whom Waverley also missed with a poignancy that verged on passion.

Students in her history and literature classes laughed at Waverley's confusion, at her accent, at her weird phrases, her lack of understanding. No one had ever heard of Sir Walter Scott, much less read him. No one had read anything that Waverley had read, women authors, past and present. The teacher was instructing them in Silas Marner, whom Waverley thought one of the great boobies of literature. The teacher said that George Eliot was actually an authoress who wrote under a man's name. Waverley groaned aloud and flung her head down on her desk. The teacher asked if she was indisposed, and Waverley did not understand the euphemism. The girl beside her asked if she needed to go to the powder room.

No one here seemed to have any notion of women. Only girls and ladies. No one seemed to have any understanding that properly fed and educated, women were far better than men, and would redress the great mess men had made of the world. Just look at history. But in history class there were only men, generals and soldiers. No maps of the whole world with pushpins, scarcely any mention of the conflagration abroad, just the recitation of dates and places from the War Between the States. Why would anyone care about that while a war raged in your own time?

Eventually the girls asked Waverley if she had such short hair because she had been sick, if she did farmwork to have such muscles. "I am a North American Woman of the Future," she retorted to their giggling delight, their clucking chuckles. They sounded like chickens. She thought of these girls as chickens who pecked and scratched and sometimes went broody and turned cannibal and had to be fitted with the killing collar. She wished she had a killing collar.

The boys were nothing like Sandy. These were herds of males: ogling, lounging, making snide remarks, commenting on Waverley's loping walk, the way she twisted constantly in her clothes as if they chafed her at every turn. They did chafe. She hated them. She hated everything and everyone.

Worse, she grew to believe that though she might well be a North American Woman of the Future, there was no future in it. Certainly not here. She had been educated to anomaly. What could she do?

Sophia's letters counseled patience and a higher, deeper, wider wisdom to withstand these mere slings and arrows. The assaults on Waverley were nothing, Sophia declared in her neat, precise hand, and testified only to the vulgarity, the ignorance, untruth and ugliness of the people who dispensed them. Sophia did not seem to realize that this was the entire school. The entire town. For all Waverley knew, the entire world outside of Useless Point.

Avril was no help. Avril just wrote passionate letters of longing, scrawled and often incoherent, French and English expressions fighting for space on the same page. Sandy wrote little, except on postcards from Long Beach, California. Quizzer vowed to send Waverley some short pamphlets (which he would very shortly write) about the North American Life-Enhancing and Perfecting Diet of True Foods, so she could help these poor benighted souls toward health and freedom.

A solution came, oddly, from Irene. Waverley had barely stayed in touch with Irene since her Transformation, a note now and then at best. Irene did indeed have an apartment in Philadelphia. And a job. And a lover. She had made good on all her promises, and now Waverley wrote imploring her advice: *Help me. How can I live here? How can I live at all if I am to stay here?*

Irene's reply was a model of brevity, clarity and direction:

My new lover is a nice boy, but too refined to Learn by Doing. My roommates are Miss Butler girls and too refined by half. It's all rot. You should come here. Come to Philly and live with me. There's nothing in North Carolina. The longer you stay there, the more miserable you will be. It will not get any better. Waste not thy hour. If you want to escape, there's only one way. Offend them beyond all belief. I have learned this. They'll leave you alone after that. They'll shut up. I had to do this, and I can promise it works. For real offense, I have discovered that men do not like to hear the word penis from a woman, never mind if she is from the future.

There was a particularly odious boy in Waverley's history class, much sought after by the female population. That much was clear. As a punishment for sending notes and talking in class to the pretty girls, the teacher had set him beside Waverley Scott. And so, Waverley fastened on him the unfaltering gaze, the look she had learned from Sophia herself. She said in a clear, distinct voice, "Your penis is just like your brains. They're both pink and shriveled and ugly."

The success of this outrage (she was sent instantly to the girls' vice principal, who called her mother and assigned her detention) inspired Waverley. If a refusal to employ euphemism could get her suspended, imagine what profanity could do. Irene was always so clever.

The following day at lunchtime, Waverley took out a bag of tobacco and papers and rolled herself a cigarette. She lit up. A woman teacher came over and told her to put it out this instant. Waverley dribbled her ash on the teacher's sensible shoes and puffed away. Then she said, "You sonofabitching old sow."

A short expectant hush fell over the lunchroom as the woman teacher gave a gasp and went in search of a man. When he came to upbraid her, Waverley continued to smoke and then she called him a sonofabitching pig and a damned fool who kept his brains in his scrotum.

Two male teachers escorted her forcibly to the principal's office. She went with a terrible struggle, screaming, so there should be no question but that Waverley Gerlach was an unhinged menace. In the principal's office she called them all sonsofbitches, and she threw in a few observations on the principal's penis and his secretary's buttocks. She tucked her hands in her armpits and glared at them. They called her mother to come get her. She was suspended for a month with the threat of expulsion should there be any further incidents.

In the cab Waverley said to Rhoda, "If you try to send me back there, I'll tell everyone I'm a bastard and my name is no more Gerlach than yours is."

Rhoda bristled, hoping the driver had not heard. When they got to the house, Rhoda pulled off her gloves and paid him without looking at him.

In the front hall, Rhoda unpinned her hat and removed her coat. "I'm going to discuss this with your father. He'll know what to do."

"No he won't," Waverley called from halfway up the stairs. "He won't have any damned idea." She slammed the door to her room.

Rhoda did not usually telephone Ed. He always telephoned her on Sunday night and Wednesday night. She kept his appointments and travel schedule in a neat, daily diary on a little writing desk in her room. She always knew where he was, just as if they were still traveling together. She knew that he preferred appointments, not spontaneity, and ordinarily, she would not have upset their scheduled conversations. But this situation was dire and she must discuss it with Ed. The phone was at the foot of the stairs, and closing the door to the kitchen (so Elsie should not hear) she lifted the receiver and pressed it to her ear, her lips poised over the mouthpiece. She asked the operator for long-distance.

When finally she got through to Ed, she rendered an account of what Waverley had done at school, without personally resorting to profanity.

"She's your responsibility," Ed remonstrated from Chicago, shouting over the static in the wire. "Can't you control a sixteen-year-old girl?"

"She didn't used to be like this."

"She didn't used to be sixteen."

"It's your fault, Ed. You sent her to the awful island school where they taught her all these awful things. She wears her awful clothes, sandals and pants, pants, Ed! She smokes cigarettes and calls people names. She's rude to my friends and thoughtless of the servants. Now she's got herself expelled from a perfectly nice school."

"What can I do about it, Rhoda?"

"You're her father! You're supposed to help!" As soon as she spoke,

Rhoda knew she'd made an error. In the ensuing silence, that error ballooned between them. She ought never to have indicated that a life in Asheville with Rhoda and Waverley, his wife and daughter, could be, would be anything but pleasant, cheerful, cozy and domestic. "It will be better when you're with us, Ed. When are you coming?"

"Let me talk to Waverley."

Waverley ambled into the hall, there by the foot of the stairs, and picked up the receiver. Into the round black snout of the phone on the wall, she offered a laconic hello.

Mr. Gerlach made a sound, a cross between *Aha!* and *Ahem!* and then accused her of smoking cigarettes and being rude and purposely getting herself expelled from school.

"When are you going to marry Mother?" Waverley asked in a loud voice, especially for Elsie's benefit. "Have you got your divorce yet? Mother's already told everyone she's married, so you better make an honest woman of her. Daddy." She spit out this last, like gristle, and dropped the receiver and walked away as it banged against the wall, silence on the other end.

School effectively dispensed with, Waverley's days that autumn settled into a routine. She would walk to the library for books by the armload, to the post office for postage and to mail letters, to the mom-and-pop grocery store at the corner for cigarettes and chocolate. She walked into town for paper, envelopes, pens and more than one bottle of ink. She returned to her room, sat at the little vanity (minus its frilly skirt and perfume bottles) and she wrote. Daily, passionate, endearing notes to Avril, to Sandy, sometimes writing the same thing to both of them, as though the letter for one was but a draft of the letter to the other, especially now that Sandy was in the navy. Though they were all three far apart, Waverley wrote that at night, in bed, she reached her hands to either side, hoping to find their hands, to smell again the smoke and salt and sweat, the sticky remains of burned-up sugar-sweetness, thickly perfumed, pungent scent rising, dripping from their bodies and the ice blanket. She loved them both, Sandy and Avril. They must both love her. They must always love one another. She was amazed, shocked really, that the writing itself suf- ficed to assuage her loneliness, at least while she was in the act of writing.

The act of writing letters gave way to the act of reading letters. To her surprise reading was not quite as gratifying. No one responded with a passion equal to Waverley's. Or at least no one could put their passion into words. Letters usually arrived in an avalanche, because postal ser- vice on Isadora was irregular. When these paper bouquets arrived, Wa- verley plunged her face into them, ran back upstairs, flung herself on the bed and opened them randomly with no thought to any order, just to breathe deep the words, if not the air, of Temple School, the voices of Sophia and Quizzer, the scent and sweetness of Avril.

Sandy did not write. He sent a few postcards from California, which Waverley pinned to her wall. His messages were about the weather (hot), the navy (demanding), the food (great). He signed himself "with love." Waverley brought her lips to these words, murmured over them, but they remained dry, unsupple.

In late November Waverley got a letter from Bessie Lomax, a mad, garrulous, ranting letter. Bessie had found Waverley's letters to Sandy after he had left for the navy. Bessie swore if Waverley ever wrote such filth to her son again, she would summon the headless ghost of Hector Lomax, the spirits of all of Hector's ancestors, the slaughtered Indians from Massacre, to say nothing of the wrath of an Old Testament God to come after Waverley in the night. She wrote that the girls at Temple School were all filthy whores and that French girl was the filthiest whore of all and if Bessie ever caught Sandy with her again, she'd wring her French whore neck and throw her body off the Massacre dock.

And that's when Waverley knew she had lost them. Or would. The eliminating tide had carried Waverley away, and after she had gone, the accumulating tide had swept up Sandy and Avril together. She had lost them. To each other. Never mind that they were all three separated now, clearly Sandy and Avril had shared something that excluded Waverley. Bessie knew it. Now Waverley knew it.

The jealousy that swept over her was, in its way, as powerfully hot and unstoppable as the sweet thump of love. The letting-go of a groan in pain was as deep and audible as the letting-go of a groan in pleasure. But then, slowly, the anguished spasms eased. And Waverley wondered perhaps, since she was going to lose them anyway, then maybe it was better to lose them to each other. In having each other, maybe they would also have Waverley. Even if she could not have them. Sometimes the ability to let go of a dream is as important as the ability to hold on to it. With a sickening sort of certainty, Waverley fathomed that she would be one of those who would see what dreamers come to. Mrs. Torklund, for all her narrow asperity, had predicted Waverley's future.

Chapter 24

$\mathcal{I}$n the weeks that followed the attack on Pearl Harbor, even sleepy Asheville roused. Galvanized by the scope and destruction of Japanese aggression and Hitler's declaration of war, all Americans plunged into patriotism. Asheville's civic leaders and citizens (including the ladies of Rhoda's acquaintance) gave up bridge and took up knitting, sewing, organized committees in defense of their country. The war effort touched every life. On the radio they announced voluntary restrictions; there would be no playing of requests on the radio (they could be enemy codes) nor would they announce the weather any longer in case enemy pilots used the information.

Rhoda alone seemed impervious to the thick, high headlines declaring *WAR!* For weeks after Pearl Harbor, Mr. Gerlach did not call, and Rhoda's life went into a sort of clumsy abeyance, as though she could have no opinion, take no course of action until she heard his voice. She sat in the living room near the phone, which did not ring.

Waverley on the other hand, already an all-around Warrior Woman, went to work with real gusto. She exhumed an old sewing machine from the basement of Flint Street, oiled it, greased it, got it working. She worked the treadle expertly (feeling the rhythm, finding the tempo) and sewed blackout curtains for their house, enough for every window. Then she sewed some more, stacks of them, and gave them to Elsie to give away.

Late one afternoon Elsie called Waverley into the kitchen as she was preparing to leave. "Your supper's in the oven. Chicken—"

"You know I hate chicken."

"Well, your mother likes it and she pays my wages, only I'm quitting. Today's my last day."

"But—" Waverley stammered and cast about, slowly absorbing the implications of Elsie's announcement. "Does that mean I'll have to do everything here? Take care of Mother and . . . everything?"

"That's what it means. You heard the radio these last two weeks. They say the war needs every pair of hands. Well, my husband and me, we figure that means black hands and white. We're going to Detroit. Going to get good jobs and good money. Better than here."

"Oh Elsie, take me with you! I can get work in Detroit."

"You got your work." Elsie nodded meaningfully upstairs. "You got your mama to look after."

"I don't want that work."

Elsie scoffed. "Most folks don't get to pick their work in this world, Miss Waverley, and you are no different." She placed in Waverley's hand the instructions for Rhoda's medicines, all of which were kept on a silver tray on the kitchen counter. The bottles reflected in the silver, a little rainbow of pink and blue and white. Elsie showed Waverley where she had pinned to the cupboard the list of when and how and what was to be administered to Rhoda.

Waverley collapsed in a kitchen chair, faint with apprehension. "I can't do this. I can't be taking cold compresses upstairs to an invalid all day. I'm a Woman of the Future. I'm going to have dinner with the King of Sweden."

"You'll pardon me for saying so, but you go on like you are, Miss Waverley, trashy talk and disrespecting everyone, you are more likely to be having trouble with the judge than dinner with the king." Then Elsie put on her hat and coat, buckled her galoshes and walked out of Waverley's life forever.

That evening, as Waverley was listening to the evening radio broadcast, moving her own pushpins around the map of the world she had bought, the phone rang. Waverley answered it while Rhoda hurried downstairs, hanging on the banister, her bathrobe flapping open.

"It's him," said Waverley unsympathetically, adding with special invective, "Your husband."

"Give me that phone." Rhoda stood very close to the phone, her arm over it, as though she and the phone might dance. "Oh, Ed," she said, her face wreathed in smiles. "It's been so long, two weeks, I've been so worried. I didn't hear from you. And now, there's the war and all. Yes, yes, I know there's been the war for years, but now we're in it. Just a minute, Ed." She turned to Waverley and asked her to turn off the radio and go into the kitchen. "This is a private conversation."

Waverley didn't know what could be so private about little exclamations of *Oh, Ed!* And sympathetic murmurings about the service Ed was rendering his country and yes of course Rhoda knew how important his work was. The war effort. Transport essential in the fight against worldwide evil. She heard Rhoda say *Divorce. What about the divorce, Ed? Has Margaret got the divorce?*

There was a long silence after that, some mumbled observation about Christmas being in four days. Another long silence, then farewells and the sound of the receiver going back on the hook. And Rhoda's tread back up the carpeted stairs.

At bedtime, according to Elsie's instructions, Waverley was to administer the condiments of convalescence to her mother. The stairwell was lit only by a single light at the top, and all the blackout curtains were over the windows. On her tray the hot water bottle sloshed with every step and the little bottles chattered together. A cold compress lay on a saucer like a nubby slice of pudding. Waverley turned on the lamp beside Rhoda's bed, and the room glowed pink.

Rhoda rolled over, startled. "Is it morning?"

"No. It's night. It's December twenty-first, the winter solstice, the longest night of the year." Waverley picked up the cold compress and slapped it on Rhoda's forehead. She put the hot water bottle at her feet. She performed all these ministrations and antidotes in a brisk and unsympathetic fashion. She handed her a pink bromide in a small glass. "Drink this."

"Ed can't come to Asheville for Christmas." Rhoda sipped her bromide slowly. "Ed says he's certain it is a comfort to me to have my daughter with me for Christmas. With me all the time. I do not like to contradict him, but you are not a comfort to me, Waverley."

"I can't help that."

"You are an unnatural daughter. You have no natural feelings anymore. That school, that horrible island changed you completely. They didn't educate you, they turned you into a freak. If I had any idea of the kind of place he was sending you, if I'd known the sort of school—"

"Take these." Waverley handed her two tablets and a glass of water.

Rhoda took her pills and lay back down, exhausted. "You had an unnatural relationship with that French girl at your school. You slept in the same bed with her. You did unnatural things with her."

Waverley poured medicine into a spoon. "You shut up about Avril. We are Wavril. We are one and the same."

"So you admit you had an unnatural relationship. A Sapphic relationship."

"Sappho was a poet. I am not a poet, but I fear nothing except ignorance, untruth and ugliness."

What might have been a laugh caught in Rhoda's nose and came out as a snort. "Ignorance, untruth and ugliness? You are all three. That nose of yours, it looks fine on Ed, but on a girl! It's terrible. You are not beautiful. You have no charm. You are not very smart. You're ignorant as can be, though that school cost Ed thousands. Thousands! You might have had something, money anyway, Ed would have recognized you as his daughter, he would have given you money—"

"I don't want Ed's money."

"Well you won't get it whether you want it or not. Ever since you got yourself expelled, he wants nothing to do with you."

"He never did." She slid the spoonful of medicine between Rhoda's lips.

"Who will you marry? Have you ever thought of that? Who in the world will you marry?"

"What do I care? I'm not a bunch of grapes at the market to be weighed and bought. I'm a North American Woman of the Future."

"Is that what women of the future do? Have Sapphic relations with other girls and shameful relations with boys? What about the boy? Were you having a shameful relationship with him as well?"

"You can just shut up about Sandy too. He is not a boy. He's in the navy."

"You certainly kissed him like a sailor's delight. Shocking, that shameless embrace, in front of everyone there on the dock. Shameless and indecent, that's what you are."

Waverley capped all the bottles and put them on the tray. "And what is so decent, so fine and upright about waiting for a man who's shoved off on you?" She spoke calmly, controlling her rancor. "About clinging to a man who has cast you off? He's bought you off, Mother. Bought you this house, and set you up here, just like you wanted, but he's not going to marry you. Even if he divorces his wife, he won't marry you. He'll never come here and live with you and be the husband you want. He has someone else."

"Ed loves me! What makes you say such awful things?"

"I can see the Unseen. Hear the Unspoken." And she could. That same instinct that had allowed Waverley to envision a chocolate god allowed her to see Mr. Gerlach with a trim woman. This woman followed in his wake, notebook, clipboard in hand, efficient, respectful in public, adoring in private. They swept through hotel lobbies and dressed for dinner, the woman smoking as she screwed her earrings in, sitting at the vanity as Rhoda used to do. Someone younger than Rhoda. Someone unencumbered with faltering health and a grown, unlovely daughter who looked just like him.

Waverley turned out the lamp and took the tray and closed the door behind her. The spoon clanked in the glass on her way down. The stairs, though carpeted, creaked under her feet and from the living room, the clock ticked. The civil defense siren sounded, wailed its warning: *Turn out your lights!*

All over Asheville—all over America—lights were going out and lives were changing. Men leaving, women coping. Some men would return. Some would not. Nels Torklund, for instance, would not. Waverley had learned that Nels was one of those on the *Arizona*, bombed at Pearl Harbor. Isadora's first casualty. All of Isadora Island mourned with the Torklunds, embraced them in their sorrow. Sophia forgot their old quarrels, took over True Foods, fresh eggs, and Newton brought bottles of magnetized water for washing the pain away. They and Avril joined the whole island population in the little church for a memorial service for Nels. Nels's death at Pearl Harbor had nearly killed Mr. and Mrs. Torklund. They shut down the Marine and Feed, and the whole of Isadora was cut off from the world. Isadora Island went crazy without the post office, message center, or supplies, without this hub of island life. Finally, about ten days later, though her parents remained comatose, immobile with grief, Sis rose to the island's needs and reopened the emporium. The whole responsibility of running it fell to Sis, but she declined Avril's offer to help. Sis declared she didn't need help from anyone at Temple School. Waverley imagined Sis sitting at the cash register, her back to the wall where Nels's Pearl Harbor postcards crumbled, right beside the postcards Sandy had sent.

Waverley put the silver tray down in the kitchen, pulled on a coat and buttoned it, took one of Rhoda's Lucky Strikes and a match. She stepped out to the back porch where she was protected from the snow, but not from the cold. Shivering, she lit her cigarette. She smoked like a man, hands thrust in her pockets, cigarette dangling between her lips. Snow crinkled listlessly as it fell, mantling the yard, the trees, the roofs of all the neighboring houses which, however dark and unseeing their windows, oppressed Waverley with their very presence. She longed for the percussive thump of rain, the smell of low tide, the moan of salt wind rousing the wails of ghosts from the Indian burial ground at the beach. She wished for those short lavender dusks after short gray days. The solstice. The longest night of the year.

She imagined them, Sophia, Quizzer and Avril in Temple's kitchen, blackout curtains against the world, and a fire snapping, Nijinsky lying before it dreaming of rabbits. There would be a supper of True Foods, caramelized pudding for dessert. The gramophone would be wound up, playing something by Saint-Saëns, Ravel, Debussy or Satie, Fauré perhaps. They would have cups of strong coffee warming their hands. Quizzer would recite "The Convergence of the Twain." Sophia would start a round of "Sur la Pont." Avril would sing "Mademoiselle from Armentières" (if she could think of verses that were fit for adult ears). And if she couldn't, then she'd sing "La Vie en Rose." On this darkest night, they would declare themselves on the side of light. However dark it was, they could look forward to the light. Temple School celebrated not the enveloping darkness, but the certainty of light. From this day forward, the earth climbed toward light, sought its old balance. War or no war, folly or no folly, death or life, light and time happened outside history. That was how Sophia had educated her students. That was what they had learned.

Waverley took a last drag and stubbed out her cigarette, took it inside and dropped it in the ashtray. She locked the door behind her, though against what she could not imagine. She went up the dark stairs toward her room, the ticking clock in the parlor striking fear, marrow deep: *this is, this will be, this will become, the very tempo of your life. . . .* Counterpointing the tolling of 10 P.M., Waverley felt as though her tread had already lost the elasticity of youth. In her mother's service, she would become an old woman. She would act as handmaiden to Rhoda's life and Rhoda's losses. Shackled to them. Waverley's own losses, loves, dreams would grow each year more insubstantial.

There was irony here, Waverley thought. Not humorous, but irony just the same. She remembered Sophia that first day in the Marine and Feed, holding her arms out and asking her to imagine flying. Well, what about fleeing, Sophia? Would that do, Sophia? Would flight suffice for flying? If truly, Waverley's Temple education had endowed her with anything, if truly Waverley had been transformed, then she must now imagine fleeing.

Not winged flight. Train fare.

In her room at the top of the stairs, Waverley closed the door behind her. The darkened room still smelled like camphor and claustrophobia. If I stay here, Waverley told herself, I will die without ever having lived. I will not be a North American Woman of the Future because I will have no future. I can stay here for the time being, but no more than that. No longer. I will get out of this awful room, this house, this town, these mountains. I will get a job and earn some money. With all the men joining up now, there must surely be jobs. Asheville is full of men in uniform. What about all that work they once did? Tomorrow, Waverley vowed, I will find work. No matter how low or ill paid. I will stay here only till I've earned the fare back to Isadora. If I cannot fly, Sophia, I will take the train.

But Isadora Island seemed to Waverley so far away as to be another world, like earning the fare to Jupiter, or asking for a ticket to the Trojan Wars. To get the fare to Isadora would take forever. Waverley could die inside before she made that much money; worse, Rhoda could engulf her in an accumulating tide of guilt, inertia. Philadelphia was closer. Cheaper to get there. Irene had told her to come, *Come to Philly and live with me.* She'd move in with Irene, and earn her own living in Philadelphia and save her money to go back to Isadora, to Avril and Sophia and Quizzer. Home.

Waverley turned on the small desk lamp, uncapped her pen, took out some paper. She wrote to Avril, but for herself. She wrote, in a passionate amalgam of memory and imagination, of that very longest night, the winter solstice, and how she could so vividly picture snow powdering the island mountains, and at Useless Point the sleet silvering down. She described the school garden, all stalks and brittle stems and fenced against the deer who shivered in the woods and rabbits shaking in the underbrush. She saw the Unseen fox watching the henhouse and the chickens roosting, cackling, sleepy in their feathered darkness. In the school's kitchen, Avril, Quizzer and Sophia sat together, warm, drinking branade, their voices, the laughter, their remembering Waverley. She smiled to bring them all to life in words.

In this she was like any writer, taking up the pen not out of surfeit, but out of pinch, not out of plenty, but from want. She wrote to make vivid what lay beyond her, whether in the past or the future, to make articulate that imaginative amalgam of wish and memory, to make the lost laugh once more. Her words chased one another across the page, her pen flew just ahead of them, as though calling out all over again, *Avril! Wait for me! Wait for me, Avril!*

Chapter 25

Paris
21 Decembre 1941

Madame,

It is the most long night of the year. The most long year of my life.
How many times I have write to you, Madame? You are my companion.
We must surely be companions, you and I, loving the same man, loving
too the same girl, Avril. Often, many times, since my mother dies, what I
cannot say to Denis, he is a man and he is always with his work, and so I
say to you. I speak to you, like Chou-fleur and her geranium speak. No
words.

But tonight, now I will write. It must be. I imagine your hands opening this letter. Avril nearby. I can see your school, your island and my
beautiful Avril there. Denis always say you still have Indians there. Denis
say you are surrounded by mountains and water on this island and you
are protected from the past. He says to live in such a place, apart from the
past, is foolish and he will never go there. And this is true. He will never
go there.

I write to you now, not from the rue de la Grande Chaumière, our
apartment. But in his studio in the rue Delambre. I am alone in the studio. I write this on the table where Denis works, where his paints sur-
round me and paint is everywhere on the floor and the table. I like the
smell here. I have one lamp and no fire. I have bring with me Chou-fleur
and her lover, the red geranium. I wear the sweater Denis paints in. It
smells like him. I have a few of his cigarettes. Black market. Everywhere

1988 I was 30 — 16 yrs ago

*around me there is work Denis finish over this year and the work he leaves
unfinished. This letter will not be unfinished. No, God willing, I will put
on this paper what I have lost.*

To send Avril to you, this is not my idea. It is not the idea of Denis.
It is the idea of my mother. I do not want Avril to go at all. My mother
will hear of nothing else. When it is clear the Germans will occupy us, my
mother wants all of us, the family to leave Paris, even before the Nazis
march in our streets. No, says Denis, he will not leave. The Germans
come. Occupy Paris, and my mother implores to me, now while there is
still confusion and it is still possible to get to Spain or Portugal, to Liver-
pool or New York, we must leave. Ah, New York, that was her dearest
wish, but Denis says to her he will not hear of this. He says even if the
Cossacks and the Mongols occupy Paris, no. If Genghis Khan marches in
the Champs Elysées, Denis will not leave. I tell her, I cannot abandon my
husband. I will stay with Denis.

Very well, Judith, my mother say, you stay. I will take Avril. She
says this though she is not well. She has no thought for herself, only for
Avril. But then the doctor tells my mother, no, Madame, the next journey
you make will be to the country with no name. You will be going there
soon. It is the cancer. It is very advanced.

When I weep to hear how sick is my mother, she tells me to save my
tears. I will need them. She says if I do not send Avril away, I will kill
her. She says I will kill them both. My mother says she cannot die in
peace until I send my daughter from Paris. I hate her for this. She tells
Avril to save her tears and shut up.

We do not always like each other, my mother and I. (And she does
not like Denis at all.) But we are cut from the same cloth. She has lived a
loveless life, Madame, a watchful life. A harsh life. She tells Avril the stories, the ones everyone knows, terrible stories. The Germans marching in
the Champs Elysées in 1870 and the Siege and Paris Commune. She says
no one can forget what they did. Not what the Germans did. The French.
The Germans are swine, of course, but the French, she says, beware of
your very neighbors. It was the French who bloodied the streets to end the
Commune. Not the Germans.

She is all the time telling us stories, not from the past, but now, the
stories she hears because she is the concierge and all the concierge in the

city of Paris, they have their own communiqués, they know all. These stories fill us with fear. The Germans are making people vanish. Every day, my mother says: Empty. The apartment of Mme and M in the next building, empty, they are gone. . . . And my mother looks into her empty hands.

Denis calls her a stinking old woman, and says she goes through the garbage and knows every *pissoir* and listens to every low grunt of a whore and makes all of this, tales of fear and calls them truth. In anger, Denis leaves our apartment. Does not come back for days. My mother says the Germans have got him and good riddance. How can she be so cruel? She says his arrogance will kill him. Kill all of us. She says fine, so be it, do what you wish, Judith, but not Avril.

Avril must leave Paris. For Avril, there is opportunity, relatives in Saint-Antoine who will leave, the possibility for Avril to go with them. My mother digs up every franc hidden in the apartment for Avril. She sells every piece of jewelry, silver, everything, so Avril may go. She makes Denis go to his gallery. He gets money in advance for pictures in the studio. He forbids Avril to go. But my mother says Avril must. Will go. Avril does not want to go. Avril cries and screams. I slap her. I dress her. I pack. I take her hand and go across the river.

Swiftly, soon after Avril leaves with these cousins, I see, I understand, how my mother is right. I bless God for my mother's wisdom and insistence. I bless God for my daughter's escape. I pray for her safe arrival at your school.

Under the Occupation, to step outside the apartment is to step into streets filled with fears, with rumors. Denouncings every day. Peoples need only write a note to the Kommandant to denounce. A complaint about a Jew, a Communist, about someone with money or a nice apartment. A jealous wife can whisper to the Nazis, write a small note and pouf! A whole family can vanish. The Germans are swine, but the French are worse.

Never mind, says Denis. I have the *croix de guerre*. We will stay low and quiet. They cannot touch our daughter and we will be safe. We will follow the rules and they will ignore us.

But the rules change all the time. There are so many rules and instructions. There are the statutes *des Juifs*. There is a census where all

Jews must declare your residence, your age, your occupation, where you
were born. So we go, we declare. We are French citizens. We are born
here. We will follow the rules and they will ignore us, yes?

Then the rules change again. The rules say Jews cannot work in these
jobs, teachers and professors and journalists, they are dismissed for no
other reasons than they are Jews. To this, Denis says, more's the pity, but
it will not touch us. He is an artist. No one can tell him to work or not to
work. He have the Croix de Guerre. He says all these rules and the census and the Jews cast from their work, he says it is disgusting, of course,
but it is temporary. Then the rules change again and there are to be no
Jews in banking, in hotels, in the sciences. They remove the Jewish judges
and lawyers. They need the doctors. Businesses cannot be owned by
Jews, so they must sell to the gentiles, for what the gentiles want to pay.
Jews must move from the apartments above their own shops. They must
move but no one can rent to them.

The dealer who sells the painting of Denis for twelve years, like us, he
is Jewish. His gallery closes and he leaves. Not so much as a word. We
know not where he is gone and we know nothing of those paintings in the
gallery. Where are the paintings of Denis? No other gallery will take
paintings of Denis. No paintings by Jews they say. Then there are no
paintings in the museums by Jews. Denis says they are dead Jews anyway. What do we care? He will find a way to sell his work. He goes on
working and we stay in Paris.

At the end of summer, August, I am living through my mother's last
days. I sit in the apartment and I listen to the drip of the water as I bathe
her face. The pain is terrible. The heat is terrible. The streets are terrible.
Here, in the rue de la Grande Chaumière it is quiet. But all Paris knows
that in the 11th Arrondissment, that day, they are screaming. The streets
are blocked and the metro exits closed. The peoples are being arrested.
Not all the peoples. But there are many Jews in this quarter and the police
know this. They have the census, do they not? They know where everyone live. They pull them from their apartments. For days after this, we
dare not go out. They are checking papers, arresting peoples. Some say
three thousand, some say four thousand peoples Jews and Communists
arrested, gone. My mother say—Save your tears, you will need them.

Denis say, these are foreign Jews, peoples who have come to France to work, maybe twenty years ago, who have children born here, but they are not born here. They have not citizenship papers. They are not French. We are French. Some of these peoples, Denis say, flee the Germans when they march into Poland or Belgium. These Jews come to Paris thinking they will be safe. They are not safe. Denis say Nazis can be taking these foreigners and Communists to labor camps in Germany. To make them work in German factories. Because their men are all soldiers, the Germans need workers, says Denis, so they take the foreigners. But the Nazis will not trouble the French, the Jews of France. Besides, Denis have the Croix de Guerre.

Denis have the Croix de Guerre that night as well, Madame, 12 Decembre 1941. Ten days ago? Twelve? I have lost the time. That night we are waked by a sharp knock at the door and we are greeted with flashlight in the face. There is a German in uniform. There is a car in the street. There is a German driving the German military car. They ask for Denis Aron. They tell him to dress, to take a blanket, money, cigarettes, food for two days.

He will return in two days? I ask the German, who repeats only what he has said. I ask where will they take Denis, and again he repeats what he have said. If this is for labor camps, I ask, why are you taking men as old as Denis? Look at him! He has more than fifty years! He is not fit for labor! He is a painter! Do you know who you have here? This is Denis Aron! This is the great artist. His work is known in all the world.

The German police again looks at his paper and says, Denis Aron, Juif.

I find the money we have, the cigarettes, I give it all to Denis. I give him pen and paper, but the German says no. He may not have such things. I put some bread and cheese, some chocolate, some apples in a valise for him. I roll blankets and I tie them. I tell him to put many sweaters under his coat. It is cold.

Denis stands before the German and he asks me to pin on his coat the Croix de Guerre. My fingers tremble. I begin to cry. I see at last how small it is. Too small to protect him. Denis stands before me like a soldier of the French Republic. He does not move. I hear my own mother's voice, save your tears, do not waste your tears in front of the German police. Denis take my face in his hands. He kiss me on the mouth. He kiss my hands. He whispers that he loves me.

The German tells him it is time to go.

To me, Denis say, do not worry, chérie, they are only doing this be-cause now the Americans are in the war. Now the Germans will be de-feated. Just like the last war.

The German policeman knocks Denis to the ground and kicks him. Opens the door. The car is waiting.

These twelve days, Madame, dawn to dusk, I am in the streets of Paris, looking for word, for understanding, for news of my husband. I walk everywhere. I go to the other artists who are his friends. I go to the homes of the women who are his mistresses. I go to the wealthy who have his paintings on their walls. I go to the rag pickers who go through the garbage. I go to the French fleas who live on German dogs.

I learn that many mens are arrested that night, 12 Decembre. They are mens like Denis, old men, not fit for labor. Many, like Denis, fight in the last war. They are Jewish bankers and rabbis and lawyers and mer-chants, men of learning and substance and repute. They are notables. And they are gone. Where? I fear Drancy, a camp north of Paris. We hear terrible things of Drancy. But no, I have learned they have gone to a camp near Compiègne. I have learn also there is no heat nor electric nor water at Compiègne. How will these men live? It is winter. What is their fate? Have they a fate? If these men are not for German labor camps, what are they for?

Madame, you see my hand shake. I have fear. Do I stay here in the studio? Do I return to the apartment? I have no friends there. Maurice, he is a friend to all of us, always. But he is gone. Maurice is gone because he have a woman in Bordeaux. That's what Denis say. Peoples who are in his apartment, say he goes to England. Then they say he goes to Switzerland. Then they say he is in Bordeaux. I know only that one day, they are there and Maurice is not. I am now the concierge. I must report them, but I do not. I tell the Nazis nothing. But to live here in this city, to breathe is to collaborate, Madame. No one can hide.

So now, this night, I am alone in the studio where Denis work. My husband is gone, taken from me. My mother is dead. But I will save my tears. Death and the Nazis, they have not got my daughter. The hope of my soul is with my daughter and with you. I trust your strength and your wisdom, my friend and companion. I trust you will tell Avril of this, in

*your own way and your own time. Tell her of the death of her grand-
mother and her father gone with the Germans. Gone to Compiègne. To
camps in the very forest where the Germans surrender in 1918. Do not
tell her to save her tears. Let her cry.*

*I am alone here and not alone. I have Chou-fleur and her geranium.
I have you, Madame. I trust you will love my beloved girl. I trust you
will tell her that I love her. Please tell her I wish her to be like you. Not
like me. Like you. American. Denis always laugh at the Americans. He
says Americans have escape the hands of the past and turn into the arms
of money. He says the Americans have much spirit and no soul. If he
stood here before me, I would say to him, Denis, I will trade my soul in a
minute—so that my daughter may have spirit. Denis always say Americans have no past. I beg of you, Madame, make of my Avril a girl with
no past. How else can she be free of this sorrow? And of all that sorrow
yet to come. And when the war is over, as it one day must be, and the
Germans defeated, as I pray they must be, I have some hope, I take some
small soupçon of pleasure to think you will return, bring Avril home, that
I may embrace you both and we may all rejoice together.*

*With the most affection and regard I am
Judith Aron*

Part Five

Time after Time

Chapter 26

Nona York always thought of November as some vast silent symphony, which she applauded, glad to see October gone, all that death-masquerading-as-glory. November's moment of cold truth, served as an antidote between October's disguises and December's insincere *ho ho ho* (for which Nona had no use whatever). Throughout October the island chestnut trees glowed themselves into a rich and burnished bronze, then, all at once, on or about November 4 every one of them shed its leaves all at once, dropped them in a sort of choral unison. By November 5 they lie on the ground, a dry and dirty pool. Poplars, likewise: throughout October their leaves go golden and on November 5, as if attending to the tap of some grand baton, they release their hold and crash to the ground. If leaves may be said to crash. Thus, in two movements, no more than a day apart, all branches lay bare, the cold truth awaiting winter.

And now November 6, Nona was driving to Massacre for her own moment of cold truth. To meet Avril's daughter. Judith Denise, the daughter of Sandy and Avril. For better or worse, Nona knew, this would be another anniversary she would reflexively keep.

Nona had never asked Becky to meet Denise. She didn't want to look too interested, too desperate, too curious, or any combination thereof. Besides, she knew it would happen. It must. Isadora is an island after all. All roads dead end into the sea. Still, every time she'd gone into Massacre, Nona had regarded the faces of passing strangers with interest. Perhaps one of these faces was Denise. Judith Denise Lomax. Nona cared nothing for the string of married names and all the bad judgments they implied in their sorry wake. But *Denise? Judith Denise.*

Nona had flustered and dithered and worried over this meeting in a manner very unlike herself. She was not the dithering sort. Should she bring the doggies? Should she not? She decided against the doggies, but now the unaccustomed silence in the car oppressed her.

It was her habit to "write" dialogue out loud for her characters; she did so now for herself, as she drove to Massacre considering the various dramatic possibilities. Feigning surprise? Feigning indifference? Saying nothing at all? This last option had some appeal. After all, if she once began—if she once said *Avril*—it would be like launching a small boat into the eliminating tide. Returning to dry land would be difficult.

Pulling her Land Rover into the unglamourous Blue Dolphin Motel, Nona parked right next to Becky's Toyota. To the Toyota's foibles Nona owed this opportunity. Becky had called and said she would be late. The car would not start. She'd have to ride the motorbike. "In this rain?" Nona had replied. "No. I will come collect you."

Rain sluiced over the windows when she turned the motor off. Pulling up her hood, Nona got out, nodding only briefly to Carlene, the nosy manager, who watched from the office window. Carlene pointed upward like some derelict annunciation angel. The Lomaxes' apartment was right above her office. Nona dashed for the stairs. Rain fell in sheets off the overhang and her feet splashed along the walkway. In the empty apartments, the drapes (burnt orange alternating with avocado green) were closed. She came to the last apartment. The drapes were open. She peered in to see a woman curled on the couch watching television.

The woman looked up. Her long hair was unkempt, her eyes red-rimmed and apprehensive, and no laugh lines radiated out from these eyes. On the contrary, long incipient furrows traced along her cheeks. She pulled the chenille bathrobe more tightly around her and came to the door in threadbare slippers.

"You must be Nona York. Well don't just stand there with the door open. That bitch downstairs charges us double for electricity. This place is so shitty, the heat all goes out the windows and the walls anyway." Denise shuffled back to the couch, plopped down in front of the television, where a talk show host tried to keep peace between a husband and wife. "Miss High and Mighty is in the bathroom. She'll be a while. You might just as well have a seat and watch TV. You like the Shopping Channel?"

"I don't know. I can't say. I've never watched the Shopping Channel."

"It's my favorite, but I've seen this hour's segment, Crafts for the Holidays. So I'm waiting for their next segment. Talk shows are the next best thing. This guy's been cheating on this wife. For years. The bastard. Look at him. Thinks his turds come out in a tutu." Denise shook her head. "I'd watch the soaps, but I can never remember who's screwing who, you know?"

"I have that trouble myself."

"Besides, these talk shows are better than soap operas. These are real people with real problems."

Nona unzipped her rain jacket and sat down. She had expected a great *thump* of recognition, to see Sandy somehow transformed, and Avril reborn before her eyes. But looking at Denise, her hopes curdled. Time had dealt an unkind hand to Judith Denise Lomax. She was gaunt without being slender. She had, or might have had, Avril's dark coloring, but her hair was growing out gray at the roots and her dark eyes had not a glint of Avril's merriment, her implied secrecy, a quality that in itself had underscored intimacy. On Denise, Sandy's olive complexion looked to be of the green-olive sort. The nose: Nona considered the nose. It might have been Avril's nose. Then she wished she'd brought the dishtowel and could beat herself for being a damn fool. Sandy and Avril would always be young. Denise was old. Pushing sixty if she was a day. Still, the mouth. That stubborn pout. The mouth pursed over a sullen sense of injustice. Good Lord, thought Nona. *Bessie Lomax*. Bessie Lomax all over again.

The television talk show host was trying to patch together the doomed union. The studio audience booed the unfaithful husband. Denise plucked a frayed Kleenex from her pocket and blew her nose. "The guy's a bastard. Men are all bastards and children are all ungrateful brats. Words to live by."

"I couldn't say. I don't have any children."

"Well, you must have had a few men." Denise dug around in the couch cushions and drew forth, baubled with bits of upholstery foam, a battered paperback, *Love Shadows*. She read the cover critically. "You write all these books about sex."

"Books about romance," Nona corrected her.

"Well, I've read some of your books. And I just have to tell you, they are really stupid. All that True Romance and Great Sex. These people, all beautiful, they fall madly into one another's arms and one another's beds and they come again and again. And after that, everything's fine." Denise gave a sharp snort. "That is a true crock of shit."

"You're mistaking form for function," Nona replied, to Denise's dismay, since Denise hadn't any idea what this meant. "In romantic novels people are tested, but they are only tested once. Twice, max. Then the woman gets the man and the book is over. In life, even if you get the man, the book is just beginning. And if you don't get him, then another sort of book is beginning. Real people are tested time and again. To get through one test successfully doesn't mean you can endure another. Each time you have to regain your balance, and that becomes increasingly difficult, the older you grow. I mean, you can testify to that, can't you?"

Denise looked perplexed at the turn the conversation had taken. She said defiantly, "If I wanted sex, if I wanted to have a lot of orgasms, I wouldn't read about it, I'd go out and have it."

"An excellent choice. I commend you."

It had been so long since anyone had commended Denise Hermann on anything, that she warmed to her subject—sex—and her ex-husband, Jerry. If she had just stayed in California, she told Nona, she and Jerry Hermann could have worked things out, even if they were divorced and it was final. Pretty final. Soon to be final. But *no, no, no,* Becky had dragged her up here, against her will, insisted she come to this godforsaken island. Denise lowered her voice and added that Becky was jealous of Jerry. Becky always hated Jerry because Denise loved him. "But now, because of Becky I'm stuck on this godforsaken island. I hate the weather and the people and the dead-end roads. And I'm sick to death of being surrounded by all this goddamned water. No wonder Mom wanted out of here."

Nona replied obliquely, "I knew your parents. A very long time ago."

"Lucky you."

"I guess I best remember of Sis how competent she was."

"The CEO of Antiseptic. When I was a kid, if Mom came home from work and found the toilet brush dry, there was hell to pay. I had to wash and bleach the trash can—not the kitchen trash, no, the garbage trash—so the garbage man will think we're tidy. Sis would vacuum at midnight and wake everyone up, and bitch us out for not doing it during the day. She is a piece of work, that woman. I got bitched out for every little thing. She bitched me out in my own house from the day I got married," Denise offered with a doleful shake of the head. "But she gave me a good deal on the rental house. One of her fixer-uppers. Cheap rent and we'd fix it up. I asked my dad to help us do the work. But he never lifted a hand for us. He didn't like my first husband, and I couldn't be fixing-up. I was pregnant with Josh," she added, and her face radiated with a milky glow. "That's my son. That's his picture over there next to the television."

Nona picked it up and studied it. "He must look like his father."

"The image. You can see how good-looking he is. Becky's dad wasn't that good-looking."

"Tell me about Sis. Is she still in real estate—wasn't it? Didn't Becky say real estate?"

"My mother does real estate like some people play Monopoly. Always looking to buy Park Place and put some hotels on it. Sometimes she'd list a house, but then, no, she'd have another look through it and she'd just have to buy and rent it out. She never met a house she couldn't rent to some poor sucker, or buy it herself and fix it up and sell it again. I get tired just looking at all the numbers by her phone. All the tenants."

"Still formidable, then? Sis always was."

"Becky's worse," Denise offered confidentially. "Demand. Demand. Demand. Becky's always bitching me out. Get a job. Get dressed. Turn off the TV. Clean up. I had enough of that with Mom. I've told Becky, I'm not lifting my finger to this shitty apartment. But Becky acts like just because she's working and I'm not, I ought to be the dogsbody here. Oh, everything Becky does is right. Becky's got a job. Two jobs, now that she's at the bookstore. Becky's taking a class through University of Washington Extension. Whoppeedoo. Becky's signed up for yoga. She's exercising and eating right. I say to hell with it all."

"And do what?"

"What do you care?"

Her confidential mood shattered, Denise pulled the robe closer and the sleeves fell back from her wrists. Her scars were still discolored welts, thick and bluish. Denise tucked her hands in her armpits in Avril's old gesture when she was hurt or alone. Nona was so touched, she could only turn back and look at the television.

Finally she asked, "And your father? What about him?"

"What about him? He's still in the garage, his own little fixit kingdom. He fixes cars, fussing over them like they were about to have puppies. He's everybody's sucker. Everybody in a ten-mile radius brings him their cars. He'd never charge for labor, only for parts, and if he couldn't find the part, he'd rig one up. He loves anything that moves, especially old sports cars, but any car will do."

"I didn't mean that. I meant, what was he like as a father?"

"Dad was deep under the hood of someone's '64 Valiant while my sisters were smoking in the bathroom and stealing my clothes, and my brother's playing hooky and shoplifting, and I was smoking dope at the bus stop, and having sex in the backseat of cars. He never saw a thing. He never said a thing. My dad?" Denise plucked at the chenille on her robe. "He was good to everyone, except us."

"I hope you're not talking about Grandpa like that, Mom." Becky came out of the bathroom followed by a banner of steam. Her hair was still damp. "Because you know very well that's not true."

"Oh, and I guess you were around in those days? Miss Know-it-all."

"Say what you want, Mom, you broke his heart. Is it his job to snatch the cigarettes from your lips? Was it his job to see you didn't get knocked up? It's your own responsibility and it's time you took it."

"And I suppose my sisters and my brother all took responsibility, fine upstanding adults."

Becky pulled on her socks. "No, Mom, I didn't say any of the rest of them were having dinner with the King of Sweden."

"The King of Sweden?" asked Nona, her lips dry.

"Oh, that's a phrase of Grandpa's. Hard to explain. If it's any comfort to you, Mom, they broke his heart too. It's just that you broke it first. You were the oldest." She turned to Nona. "I don't want you to get the wrong idea about my grandfather. He is a wonderful man."

"To you," scoffed Denise.

"Yes. To me. He picked me up at school every day and drove me home in his sports car. He'd talk to me like I was someone of real merit or importance. We never talked about Mom and her boyfriends. Grandpa cared what I thought." She cast Denise a look of consummate disdain. "He came to the science fair. He came to the soccer games. He helped with the homework. He bought ten boxes of Girl Scout cookies every damn year and gave them away." Becky reached for her shoes, pulled them on and continued without looking up. "And I know for a fact Grandpa warned you about Jerry, told you he was a loser."

"I never asked for my father's opinion. Or his permission."

"Once you got in the sack with Jerry, you didn't care what anyone thought. Even when the law came after him for not paying child support."

"You are so cruel to Jerry! You never gave him a chance."

"A chance to what!" Becky's voice still trembled with remembered passion. "My grandfather taught me how to drive the car when I was twelve, Miss York. He made a duplicate of the key to Mom's car and he told me to keep it with me at all times, and if that bastard Jerry ever raised his hand to me again, that I shouldn't wait to call anyone, I should take this key and get in the car and drive to my grandfather's house."

"And did you ever have to do that?"

"Tell her, Mom. Tell her about your precious sweet Jerry. The love of your life Jerry. You tried to kill yourself over a man who doesn't deserve to lick your feet."

Denise hunkered down on the couch, rolling her shoulders forward and pouting so that Bessie Lomax looked to have been resurrected and returned to Massacre.

"The answer to your question, Miss York, since Mom is having a senility seizure here, is that yes, three times. The last time I was fifteen and my grandfather drove me home and he told Jerry and Mom if Jerry ever hit me again, if he caused me to cry, if he was ever so much as rude to me, or made a face at me or asked me to pass him the salt without saying please, my grandfather would kill him."

"He didn't mean it."

"Who didn't, Mom? Jerry or Grandpa?"

Denise lapsed into a funk.

"The next year I was sixteen and my grandfather gave me my own car and I never had any more trouble with Jerry except that he was an asshole, and I might have pitied him except I could see the suffering he inflicted. So just shut up about Jerry Hermann, will you, Mom? You and he are not exactly Rhett and Scarlett."

Denise turned on her savagely, clutched her robe against her bosom, rose and stalked around the room, shouting at Becky. "You're happy when I'm in pain! You love it when I'm miserable. And now, now you bring this old bag who writes scum, smut, trash and porno here to my own home to laugh at me, at my unhappiness. Yes! I loved Jerry! Is that so very awful? Am I the only woman who's ever loved a man? Am I—"

"Oh please, save it for the stage!" cried Nona, who had to put some kind of brake on Denise Lomax or let her forever sully the memory of Avril, of Sandy. "Let me see if I can guess, Denise. Your love story goes something like this. You and Jerry really had true love, a little rocky now and then, but a really good life together, until some little thing went wrong, something that can be put right again and it all will be fine. But in the meantime, you are suffering. No, wait, you're both suffering. But for you, your suffering is commensurate with your love for him. The further you sink into abject depression, sink into mental and moral squalor, the more it proves you love him. Yes? Something like that?"

Denise frowned. "What's *commensurate* mean?"

"It means that you equate suffering with love. If you're not suffering, you don't know what love is. Without suffering, you wouldn't recognize love. And that is just really unbelievably dim and destructive. Stupid in fact. Absolutely stupid. Laughable if it weren't so pathetic."

Denise was struck breathless and even Becky's eyes grew round. Denise looked at Becky as though she expected her to intervene, but in this she was disappointed. Finally Denise asked Nona, "Are you telling me I'm stupid?"

"You're a damned fool. You remind me of your own grandmother, Bessie Lomax. I knew Bessie. Her husband died and Bessie suffered because she loved him, oh yes. Bessie mourned, and drank and carried on suffering. She puked her guts up drinking cologne. She had to be looked after, Sis or Sandy had to look after her like a big baby. Would you like to know how your grandmother died? Bessie went to bed drunk one night during the war, and woke up with all the lights on, and she was sure that the Japanese had invaded Isadora Island, slunk up through Moonless Bay just like the Indians, that the Japanese were coming after her. People heard her crying out, *The Japs! The Japs!* The neighbors were running toward the house when they saw her fall out of her own second-story window. In truth, not very far from where we stand, Denise. That woman was your grandmother, and if you want to go on in that pathetic and disgusting fashion, fine, but don't expect your daughter, or anyone else, to feel sorry for you."

"You can't talk to me like that."

"Who but a damned fool goes on like you have?" Nona insisted. "If you want your ex-husband so bad, then go back to him. He's not dead, is he? Is he dead?"

"No, but I don't have any money. If I did—"

"If? To hell with *if*! *If* is the sort of word that might do very well in a chocolate truffle of a novel—but in life? No. *If, should, might,* those words will take you nowhere but to a great stinking slough of unrealized hope. So do not speak to me of *if* or its equivalents," concluded Nona in the regal fashion she had learned from Sophia Westervelt.

Denise, mystified, returned her gaze to the television talk show, where the wife and husband were ready to duke it out. She regarded the scene wistfully. "I want to be married again. I want a man coming home at night. I want a man next to me in bed. I want Jerry."

"How bad do you want him?" asked Nona. "In the books I write, when a woman wants a man, she finds a way to be beside him, even if she can't quite admit that's what she's doing. She'd never let him down. Is that how you feel about Jerry?"

"I'm not talking about a fucking novel! I'm talking about my own life!"

"Ah. Your life. What romance. Jerry is breaking his heart for you too, isn't he? He knows he's lost without you. He knows that without you, his life is empty. He knows it was a mistake, the divorce. He can't live without you. When you attempted suicide, he was frantic, at your bedside night and day. And then to keep you two true lovers apart, your daughter cruelly brings you here to this island far away. Jerry calls here all the time, begs you to come back and live with him and make a life together so he can be faithful and give you lots of loving, orgasm after orgasm. Is that your life?"

Denise glared at her daughter. "How could you tell a stranger all about my private life?"

"Mom, when you slit your wrists, it just wasn't private anymore."

Nona insisted, "Is that a fair description of the Jerry who waits faithfully for you in Anaheim?"

"Jerry doesn't know what he wants."

"Oh yes he does, Denise. And you've got the scars to prove it."

"He never hit me. Almost never," she murmured.

"Good God. I meant your wrists."

Even Becky looked shocked.

Nona stood. Walked. Calmed herself. "This has got to stop. You have been making your daughter's life a misery and your own life worse. That is what Bessie did to Sandy, to herself."

"Who is Sandy? And who are you? What do I care about my fucking grandmother? Get out!"

"Turn off the televison. Get up, get dressed, Denise. Take a shower and get dressed." To Becky she said, "We're not going to work today. We're going on an outing."

"I'm not trekking off to Chinook fucking Point or whatever the hell it is. Becky's taken—"

"Those are sacred places," Nona snapped. "And you will not talk about them like that. Go on, Denise, get dressed. We'll wait."

"Shit," said Denise to no one in particular. She got up, though, and disappeared into the bedroom, slamming the door.

"Don't get your hopes up," Becky cautioned after Denise had left the room. "She's stubborn. If she wants to rot and wallow, you can't change her."

"Yes, well Bessie Lomax wanted to rot and wallow too. And Sis let her. Sis encouraged her. I didn't think so at the time, but I do now. Now I think that Sis despised her, but she looked after Bessie only so that Sandy should be grateful to her. Sis wasn't being kind at all. But I didn't see it like that. Then. Neither did he."

Becky turned off the television. "How well did you know my grandfather's family?"

"I'm Waverley Scott." In the silence, she let the admission rest. It was like saying *Avril*. She had not said her own name in years. Not since she had returned to Isadora to live: Nona York, the well-known romance novelist. She had left Waverley Scott behind. Far behind. With Avril Aron. With Sandy Lomax. With Captain Briscoe and the *Nona York*, with Sophia Westervelt and Newton Faltenstall. "Sandy told you to find Waverley Scott. It isn't the name of a boat. In fact, *Nona York* is the name of a boat, but Waverley Scott was a real person. Is. That's my real name. I don't use it anymore. I've become someone else, just like your grandfather has become Al when he was once Sandy."

Becky sank uneasily into one of the plastic kitchenette chairs. "He wanted me to find you. That's what he said. Find Waverley Scott. Did he tell you I was coming up here?"

"I have not seen him or heard his voice for forty years. More. It was a terrible shock to me when you showed up. It's still a shock."

Becky's young face clouded with confusion. "I called him, when I first got the job and I said, 'I'm temping for Nona York, the dowager queen of Romance,' and he still didn't say anything at all to me."

Waverley sighed. "Was Sis on the line?"

Becky couldn't remember.

"If she was, that might account for his silence. Or maybe he didn't need to speak. You said he wasn't in the habit of speaking much. That he was a silent man. He didn't used to be."

From the bathroom they heard the high nasty whine of the hair dryer.

Becky said, "I could have lived here for years and never met you, you know. Why didn't my grandfather just tell me where to find you? Why didn't he just say, *Go find this old friend of mine, Becky.*"

"If we had not met, he might have."

"So, Waverley Scott." Becky mulled the strange name. "What is it you're supposed to tell me that's so amazing? He said I'd be amazed."

"I don't think I can tell you anything yet. Before I could tell you anything, I'd have to take you somewhere. You and Denise." She drew a deep breath and resolved again to give up cigarettes.

The shower, getting dressed, had not transformed Denise Lomax, but she was improved. Bessie Lomax's sorry pout had not been altogether washed from her lips, and her still-damp hair hung close to her face, accentuating the nose. Avril's nose, Waverley decided. Yes, freshened up and a little eagerness for the outing evident in her eyes, there was visibly a bit of Avril Aron in Denise.

Behind the wheel of her Land Rover, as she drove up along the island's main interior road, Waverley Scott again vainly tried to imagine her own dialogue. She had known for months, since meeting Becky, that she would make this journey. Perhaps she'd known for longer than that. Perhaps she had known for forty years she would make this journey. And with these women. Not Becky, perhaps, but Denise.

The island church came into view, a chapel originally built by the Westervelts for the spiritual reclamation of hard-living loggers. Once it was the only church on the island, though now there were many. This small acre, however, was still the only cemetery. Land on Isadora Island was too precious to be wasting it on the dead. Waverley pulled into the graveled parking lot, facing the prim white church, the leafless poplars. A chain-link fence to keep out the rabbits and the deer encircled the unkempt cemetery. There were very few families still on Isadora with people buried here. Everything had changed. The place was tended now by an indifferent lawn service. Waverley herself had not been here in a very long time.

She stopped the Land Rover but left the windshield wipers going, heeding their steady tempo. "Wait here," said Waverley, "I'll get the big umbrella out of the back."

But still she did not move.

Chapter 27

TEMPLE SCHOOL
ISADORA ISLAND, WASHINGTON
ISADORA 123

August 5, 1947

Irene, dear,

I send this note to you so that you shall be there with Waverley when she opens the enclosed letter. You must be there. There has been an accident and you must give Waverley this letter, this news. You must stay with her. I fear for Waverley when she hears Avril has died. Avril is dead.

Avril Aron came to Temple School after you had left us, but I'm sure you know of her, of Waverley and Avril, who called themselves Wavril. They loved each other. They loved the same man. Sandy Lomax. You remember Sandy. Avril and Sandy married. Perhaps Waverley told you. Perhaps she did not. No doubt she will tell you now. After you give her this letter.

I know that in the true Temple spirit, you will help Waverley. God bless you, Irene. You will wonder that I who have spurned all traditional religion invoke God. I might have been wrong about many things.
Your teacher,

Sophia Westervelt

"Hello, Harry."
"Does the doorman just let you come right up like you live here, Irene?"

"Beauty has its privileges."

"You mean money."

"I mean what I say, Harry." Irene walked past him and sank gracefully into the couch. She took off her hat and laid it on the coffee table. She lit up. "Where's Waverley?"

"Getting dressed." He closed the door and followed her into the living room. "My wife and I are going out tonight. You're not invited. Even if Waverley invites you, you're not invited."

"I expect Waverley won't be going out. I think you better leave though, go get some cigarettes and not come back." Irene never had given up her Ginger Rogers affectations and she did them very well by now.

"What's wrong?"

"I have some bad news to tell Waverley. She'll tell you later, if she wants. But not now. You'd be in the way."

"This is my apartment, remember."

"Don't be tedious as usual, Harry, just go away. Go ring the Liberty Bell. See the sights. Drink yourself into a stupor. Just don't come back tonight."

"What kind of bad news?"

"None of your business. If it was your business, you could stay. But it's not. You're not up to it, Harry. Believe me, you're not equal to helping Waverley through this. You're not equal to Waverley at all, but if you're really nice to me, I won't tell her."

Harry muttered something, breathing harshly through his nose. He was a lithe young man with a thin blond mustache above a mouth that lacked an upper lip and gave him the air of perpetually wounded surprise. He had the sort of body much enhanced by an airman's uniform, which is what he had worn when Waverley married him. He always spoke with an implicit sneer that she had mistaken for a clever and sardonic approach to life. And as he straightened his tie in the mirror, he observed sarcastically, "You girls are all alike, you North American Women of the Future. I don't know what future you're living in, but where I'm from, women don't go around giving the orders, telling men to leave their own apartments and what to do. They don't—"

"Form is to function, Harry. We're going to have a Temple School reunion. You do not want to be here. And I certainly don't want you here. And probably Waverley doesn't either."

Irene sashayed over to the cabinet, got out one glass and a bottle of Scotch. She put them on the coffee table. Harry took his jacket and left. He slammed the door. Irene finished her cigarette in front of the window, watching the traffic nine floors below. From her handbag she took her lighter and the rest of the pack and laid them beside the Scotch. Outside the traffic noises thickened in the early evening and the fan whirred, moving the humidity through the apartment in sluggish, unvarying patterns.

"Where did Harry go?" asked Waverley, coming out of the bedroom. She wore a foamy negligee over her slip and she carried her stockings in one hand, her earrings in the other.

"I sent him out for cigarettes."

"We have cigarettes. Why did he slam the door? We were going out." She screwed the earrings to her earlobes, one at a time, and sat across from Irene. Her hair was long and carefully coiffed (the old Temple cut long since grown out). Powder softened her olive complexion and rouge blushed along her cheekbones. Her lipstick gleamed. Waverley would never be a beauty like Irene, but she had grown into a handsome young woman with fine posture, and an air of observing the world intelligently. Charm was not her forte, however. Never had been. "I can only stand Harry when we go out."

"What about when you go to bed?"

"Oh yes, going to bed with him is fine. It's just the rest of the time." Waverley looked at the coffee table. "Why the bottle of Scotch? You've only poured one glass. What's in the envelope, there beside the glass?"

"It's a letter from Sophia. She asked me to deliver it." Irene pushed the glass toward her. "It's very bad news, I'm afraid." Irene spoke with unaccustomed tenderness, a sentiment so unlike her that Waverley knew, before she even began to read, that someone had died. But she could not have guessed who.

TEMPLE SCHOOL

ISADORA ISLAND, WASHINGTON

ISADORA 123

August 6, 1947

My dearest Waverley,

There has been an accident. I wish for a euphemism. I wish for a metaphor. I wish I could control my shaking hand. My heart cannot absorb it. I cannot put words around this awful fact, but it is true Avril is gone from us. Avril is no more. Can this be? Can Avril Aron, who came to us with such courage and such pain and such beauty, can she be dead? Can we have buried her in the plot that Newton and I have reserved for ourselves in the island churchyard? How can it be that Newton and I should be standing beside the graves we will one day fill ourselves, saying farewell to our girl, our own, our only daughter. For all our students, Avril was our only daughter. We were a family. We lived as a family lived. Her daughter was born at our school. We stood witness to her marriage. And now we stood witnesses to her death. We small band of mourners, before an open grave. God mocks us with this weather, a brilliant sunny day. The air was like wine.

Captain Briscoe brought Newton and me to the church in a borrowed wagon pulled by a borrowed mule. The church is still closed up. No preacher here anymore. We went to the grave, which Captain Briscoe and Mr. Torklund dug. We waited. There was no hurry.

They put her coffin in the back of the delivery truck, and Mr. Torklund drove from Massacre. Mrs. Torklund and Sis and little Judith were with him. Sandy rode in the back with the coffin, sitting beside it, his head in his arms. Sandy and Eugene and Mr. Torklund and Newton carried Avril's coffin from the back of the truck to where we stood.

Newton rose to this terrible occasion. The church has no preacher since the war. No one to say farewells for Avril. Anyway he was Christian. We have no one to say Jewish farewells. So Newton spoke. He spoke above religion and beyond it, but I cannot remember what he said. I have never been more proud of his greatness, his grace, his consummate bravery, though I cannot remember what he said.

Little Judith cried and fussed and called out for mama. She broke away from Sis, who had been holding her, but Mrs. Torklund caught Judith before she ran off. She slapped the baby. Oh, Waverley, I cried out against such cruelty and I snatched my baby back from Mrs. Torklund. Never! Never hit my girl again I told that miserable woman. I held Judith in my arms. I patted her back, comforted her, promised her anything, save that I could find her mother for her. I would not promise her that. I held my sweet little girl in my arms till it was over. Sis took Judith from my arms. She said they were going home now. They left.

Newton and I did not leave. We could not move. Captain told me we should, we must leave now. It was over. There was nothing we could do for Avril now, but I said, Oh Eugene, that's not so. That's not so, Eugene, and he said, all right, it wasn't so, but there was nothing we could do here. Nothing at the church. I looked up and saw the rest of them all walking downhill. I watched their backs. A few fishers, fewer wives. The last of the farmers. Some of Sandy's cousins from remote and wild parts of the island. The loggers are gone. The island is deserted, not just lonely and isolated as it has always been, but whole farms are untilled, sheep graze there and of course the rabbits. Whole farmhouses are ingested by vines, whole barns engulfed in blackberry, whole boats askew at low tide, their hulls rotting. The Massacre dock crumbles into the stagnant bay.

August 7

You were there, Waverley. Though you did not know. You were there. You were part of the Unseen and part of the Unspoken. Perhaps I should have spoken. Called you on the telephone. But I could not speak. How could I say such things, Waverley? How could I say that now Newton and Avril and I, we will all be together, but not in the way we imagined.

August 9

I have never seen Avril so happy as that day. Avril and Newton and I sat together on the front terrace of the school, drinking bran-ade and watching the distant waters sparkle and wink at us. She was tanned and relaxed, and her long hair tied at the back of her neck. Laughter came from deep within her, from a well of contentment that few of us experience. Newton and I just basked in her happiness. Her happiness was our happiness. She was telling us about little Judith and how she wouldn't go to Sandy's arms when he came off the fishing boat, because Daddy smelled bad. Avril said he did smell bad, but when he'd had a bath and a shave, the baby went right to him.

Finally she hugged us both and thanked us for the eggs and cooked chickens and produce and said good-bye. We would have brought all these things into Moonless, to her and Sandy, but the Packard doesn't work anymore and we cannot afford to fix it. I told her, even then, I told her, the motorcycle was dangerous, Newton said so too. She shrugged, like she always does, she said one day Sandy would build them a car. That he was smart, he could do that. But in the meantime, the motorcycle.

August 10

You will wonder why I did not call you with this terrible news. I could not speak. Newton and I can neither one of us bring ourselves to speak or we weep. I can scarcely write. You see how the pen trembles in my hand. I have been writing this letter for days. Days and days.

August 10

I return to this letter now, read it and see that I must ask you to forgive me for expressing my own grief, and not offering comfort. What can I offer? What can I say of your loss? You and Avril were, truly and forever, Wavril. I know how you loved her, Waverley. I know this. I understand it. I know too you were both in love with Sandy. When you left here, Sandy and Avril were left to love each other.

Newton and I delivered Judith Denise into this world. There's not even a vet on the island anymore. So this sweet girl was born here at the school, the first child born at Useless Point, probably in a hundred years or more. Born in that little back room off the kitchen. Sandy was still in

*the navy. Who knows where his ship was? I know where his heart was.
Here with Avril, with baby Judith. I wrapped her in warm towels and
gave her to her mother. Denis's granddaughter. How strange are God's
gifts. Newton and I, parents and grandparents to Denis's family.*

August 13

After the accident they put the motorcycle in the back of the Marine
and Feed truck and brought it to the shed behind Sandy's house. They say
that he emptied the gas tank, and stepped outside. Lit a match and threw
it in. The explosion knocked him backward. It singed his eyebrows and
eyelashes and some of his hair. They heard it all over the Sound. He might
have been killed. The house might have burned. A change in the wind
alone saved the house and the Maid of the Isles.

Sis tells me Sandy must be told to eat, to sleep, to breathe almost. He
cannot work. He looks at little Judith as if she is a stranger. I begged Sis
to give me the baby, that Newton and I will care for Judith, but Sis refuses. She says that the family must be kept together and that Sandy's one
chance of recovery is to feel and to be responsible for his daughter.

And in this she is of course correct. But I confess to you, Waverley, I
do not like Sis. I do not like her parents. I never have. All the Torklunds
have narrow pinched souls, and no imagination, no inner strings that
might quiver to beauty or thought. At least Sis is a miracle of competence.
Sis will marry Sandy. Of course she will. I suppose that's as it should be.
Sis says they will move to California. She says the future is in California
and that Isadora is dead. Perhaps she is right. Temple School is dead.
After all, my beliefs have come to naught. My work, my values, my
school, my hopes have failed. But still it pains me to know that Sis's values, not mine, will be the ones to steer my little baby granddaughter
through life.

August 16

I must, I shall mail this letter today. All these pages and look what I
have not written. I have not even given you the most ordinary of informa-

tion, the most banal facts. Avril was on her way home from Useless. The motorcycle accident happened at the top of the hill, the same hill where you and Sandy had your accident, and we think for the same reason, though we do not know altogether, since Avril was alone. She hit at least one rabbit. The motorcycle went off the road and into a ditch and flipped and Avril was thrown against a tree. We think she died instantly.

At least her parents did not live to see Avril die. Judith sent me their daughter so that Avril might live and now she is dead and I failed them all. Judith and Denis. Avril. Little Judith. I have failed everyone. I did not do what Judith Aron asked of me. I did not keep Avril safe. I must believe that Avril is reunited with Denis and Judith.

I know Judith Aron is dead. The Germans must have taken her as they took Denis. Had she lived, she would have written. There would have been word. She would have found Avril. The war is two years over. The Liberation, what did that mean, one wonders, to the dead? Avril said she would wait for her parents to find her. If they lived, if either one of them lived, they knew where she was. She was here. She would not give up hope. None of us gave up hope.

I reminded Avril, many times, how once before, everyone believed Denis was dead. And yet, he returned to Paris. I remind Avril that her mother is strong, stronger than any of them, stronger than the Nazis and stronger than their hate. Avril and I often talk about Judith and how she might one day ask the Captain for passage to Isadora Island, to find her daughter. How Avril would be here on this island, waiting. Avril will introduce us and we will embrace. We loved the same man and the same girl, and now the same baby. And now, truly, Avril will always be here waiting. The Maid of the Isles.

Forgive my incoherent letter. I am Transformed, but not in the way I expected to be. I embrace you, my dear Waverley. And like Avril, I shall be here. Waiting. I am not the Maid of the Isles, but I am here, on this island and of it as well.

Your loving teacher,
Sophia

Part Six

Defying Descartes

Chapter 28

She did not like to see things move. Mice, flies, spiders, moths, they all provided her with a sort of kitchen safari. Even her cats (great leonine creatures named for goddesses, regardless of their sex) knew not to dash too quickly; in her presence they moved with measured steps. For a long time Sophia had a steady hand, but as she aged, her eyesight (as opposed to her vision) faltered, and she had been known to shoot at rolling dust bunnies, those diaphanous bodies that had accumulated sufficient girth and grit to migrate, gossamer legions led by a light wind. The kitchen walls especially were pocked with holes because bullets ricocheted off the huge stove, off the fry pans, most of them unused, that still hung suspended from hooks. Outside she was equally dangerous. What had been the sloping green had gone to the wild, a twisted tangle of blackberry bramble, overgrown lilacs and enormous rhododendrons under which small creatures, birds, squirrels and legions of rabbits scrambled. She especially detested the rabbits. In firing at them, she often mistook the dancer for the dance. Her reflexive aversion to movement was a peculiar epilogue for the life of the founder of Temple School, a sorry coda for the woman who had spent her energies reconciling body and spirit, defying Descartes.

In 1959 when ferry service came to Isadora Island, the widowed Sophia still lived at the school with her cats. The chickens were gone, but she kept a small garden in a desultory fashion, that is if the weather was agreeable and the slugs didn't overrun her efforts. She had simplified life by selling all the furniture, keeping only a few beds and desks and chairs, the kitchen table, the grand piano, the wartime radio, the windup Victrola and all the old heavy records. She had given most of the books to form the core of the Isadora Island Public Library, so the library shelves were empty, though the great beams overhead still bore their mottos. *Waste Not Thy Hour* had less meaning now than it once had. She almost never went upstairs. She slept in the small room off the kitchen where Judith Denise Lomax had been born.

She talked to herself and to the framed photos of her students in their togas. Sometimes damp crept in under the glass and nibbled at their artful extremities. Still, Sophia kept the school's old schedule, rising early. She wore the school's old uniform, Roman sandals and woolen socks, tunics and trousers. She no longer wore togas. For one thing, togas had no pockets and she kept her pistol with her always. It was a small, ladylike pistol, nickel-plated, mother-of-pearl-handled and with a silver trigger. She bought it in Paris in 1909, and had used it only once, to break up a duel between an avant-garde sculptor and an art critic, a duel in which she had tangentially figured.

She had been the model for the sculptor's *Venus,* which the critic had likened to a fish being dragged from the Seine rather than a goddess emerging from the sea. There was some truth to this. Sophia's body was broad shouldered, long limbed, big boned and muscular, not the best model for Venus. But the critic had gone on to characterize the sculptor's work in general with phrases most unflattering and suggesting the artist's talents could be better spent plastering walls. To this the sculptor responded with his own ungenerous aspersions on the critic's taste and masculinity. Not in that order. Insults exchanged in Left Bank cafés escalated, resulting in the challenge. Dueling was forbidden in France and went on all the time. For the most part these affairs were shows of bravado without serious consequence, but the American, Sophia Westervelt, did not know this. She genuinely feared for the life of the sculptor, with whom she was having a torrid affair.

The duel was set for dawn. The weapons, pistols. The place, near the bicycle racing track at the Parc des Princes at Porte de St. Cloud. But there was some confusion about the exact spot agreed upon and so the contestants (and their seconds and hangers-on) were farcically stumbling about in predawn darkness looking for one another. Full dawn illuminated the sky by the time they finally took their places and observed the formalities. Full dawn suited Maurice Fleury, who had brought his camera to record the moment. He had no sooner framed the duelists in his sight when a taxi rattled up and Sophia Westervelt jumped out, firing into the air, shouting, "I will kill the first man who shoots!"

Perhaps they believed her. She was American after all and Americans were unpredictable. She was, in those years, a sort of Girl of the Golden West, the daughter of a great fortune in timber and shipping in Washington State, a woman well funded with high spirits, and a great appetite for life. Her money could be relied upon from her ever-obliging Pa, who continued to send her a generous allowance, to keep her comfortably in Paris even after she escaped from the maiden aunt the family originally sent to chaperone her. In a prim snit, the aunt had returned to Seattle.

Sophia Westervelt remained in Paris, discovered that the hub of the artistic universe was in Montparnasse. Eventually she moved there, renting a three-story house on the rue Notre-Dame des Champs with a light-strewn studio on the top floor and a walled leafy garden behind, with gates and a courtyard that permitted her, some years later, to keep her Ford there after it was shipped from New York. Sophia was of the opinion that only the Americans could make cars and only the French could make art.

She herself engaged in many of the arts. She had no native genius, but her enthusiasm, her pealing laughter, her energetic sexuality and her intemperate use of money made her many friends and brought her into the life of Montparnasse, into the studios and cafés and clubs where painters and poets, musicians, writers, dancers, composers, their mistresses and models and mentors all congregated. Eventually she became famous for her Wednesday afternoon teas at the rue Notre-Dame des Champs. These were not the sort of teas her mother would have recognized, nor any of her family for that matter. The austere, prosperous, Presbyterian Westervelts denounced Sophia (all except Pa) when word of her many antics drifted—eventually, inevitably—back to Seattle.

For these Wednesday teas Sophia kept on hand boxes of Turkish cigarettes. She had hired a fine Breton cook recommended to her by her friend Alice Toklas, another Girl of the Golden West, from San Francisco. She stocked the bar and brought in an impeccable waiter from the Café Voltaire to see that her guests' glasses were never emptied. Her tireless servant, Jeanne, saw to it that the ashtrays were always emptied. On Wednesdays, all Montparnasse, and much of Paris, came to the rue Notre-Dame des Champs. Here Isadora Duncan (another Girl of the Golden West, also San Francisco) danced one afternoon, impromptu, to a Debussy piece, Debussy himself on the piano. When Isadora had finished, breathlessly holding her final pose as Debussy struck his final note, Sophia threw herself at Duncan's feet.

She absorbed all she could of the Great Isadora's magic. Her methods. Her fluid grace. Sophia practiced till she dropped. She flung herself into the world of Isadora Duncan with tireless passion, but Sophia was too much her own woman ever to be a disciple. Besides, Isadora often traveled, on tour, on holiday. Sophia saw no reason, had no wish, to leave Paris. Why should she? Did she not have here, truly, the artist's life? She radiated a moneyed élan and her vitality could be envied but not equaled. Her French was never excellent and her English peppered with vulgarisms.

It was in both languages, French and English, that she tongue-lashed the duelists at the Porte St. Cloud. She strode onto the field of combat, hatless, berating the critic and the sculptor, their seconds and the coterie of onlookers, well-wishers, partisans and Dionysian die-hards who had all come to cheer or commiserate, it little mattered which. As the sky suffused with light, Maurice Fleury caught all this on film: the sculptor bleary with drink, the critic gray with anxiety, the American woman striding in with her pistol raised, firing into the air, the others stunned or annoyed at the intrusion of such a woman, and Denis Aron watching it all with his characteristic amusement and detachment.

By the time she put the pistol back in her bag, Sophia had talked them out of the duel and into the taxi—the principals, that is. Others followed in cabs hailed at the Porte St. Cloud and she offered to treat everyone at the Les Halles café, where the finest onion soup in Paris could be had at dawn.

The crowd of them took up several tables. Maurice and his friend from Arles took seats across from Sophia and the two contestants, whose bonhomie was contagious, all aspersions forgotten, good spirits restored by the soup, by the wine and bread. As the sweat ran down the windows and steam from the cooking mixed with cigarette smoke, Sophia Westervelt turned to make the acquaintance of Maurice's friend, Denis Aron. They could not believe that in the small world of Montparnasse, they had not met before.

Thus, Sophia considered the pearl-handled pistol a piece of her own personal luck, the instrument by which she first met Denis Aron.

He was not at this time the well-known painter he came to be in the 1930s. In those prewar years he was a talented rebel, a serious painter, but that described many. He had no particular movement to be affiliated with, still finding his own way. He had only just arrived in Paris the year before, following in the footsteps, advice and example of his childhood friend, Maurice Fleury. They were both eager to escape the suffocating respectability dominated by banker fathers and pious mothers, homes where life progressed according to unvarying bourgeois tempos: eating, sleeping, making money. In 1909 Denis Aron was slightly younger than Sophia, a big man, broad chested, dark, intense eyes, broad brows and broad smile. Like Maurice, he was well educated though he had been an indifferent student, rebelling against the school and against the bank in Arles where his father first made him a clerk. Finally his father agreed to support him as an art student in Paris for one year only. That year came and went. The family withdrew the allowance and told him to come home to Arles. His response was an emphatic no, and ever since, he'd been living the cramped, hand-to-mouth life of a Montparnasse artist, alternating weeks of serious, furious endeavor with days of debauchery and café trotting.

Within a month of their meeting, Sophia's affair with the sculptor was finished, as were Denis's off-and-on liaisons with two or three other women. For a time, Sophia's Wednesday teas came to a halt, so absorbing and creative was their love affair. The early nudes he painted of Sophia were the beginnings of the work that was later recognizably, unmistakably, Denis Aron. They lived together at the rue Notre-Dame des Champs. Working, playing, eating and sleeping, night and day they absorbed every aspect of each other, cobbling their life together in French and English, a patois that came to be their own language, as much physical as verbal. Their love affair was turbulent and exclusionary, monogamous, and in the raffish and insouciant world of Montparnasse, their friends made fun of their intensity, their breathlessness. Sophia little cared, and Denis had never minded what people said. Their love opened to both of them sensation, experience and emotion they had never known and never expected to know. Curse or blessing—they sometimes could not tell the difference—they flung themselves into each other. In five years they never spent a night apart.

In the summer of 1914 they packed up the Ford and made their way north, Denis painting as they went, Sophia writing a book about French art for American readers. They stopped whenever they felt like it and stayed as long as they wished. In August 1914 they were in Reims in a rumpled hotel bed, the windows open to catch any miscreant breeze. In the courtyard below came the voices of the landlady berating the groom, who told her to stuff herself, he was joining the army: war had been declared. The slow languorous tolling of the cathedral bells rang out, joined by the sounds of celebration in the street. Denis sat naked, reading a newspaper and smoking, Sophia curled beside him, sleepy and fulfilled.

"I don't understand," she said, yawning, "all this gaiety, their joy in going off to fight the Germans. People ought to be grave and thoughtful when war is declared."

"You don't understand because you are American," he replied without looking up.

"I understand perfectly well. I don't approve. That is what I am telling you."

"What do we care for your approval?" He looked over to see her eyes wide with hurt. He shrugged. "Don't take it so, *chérie*. It's true. You are an American. You can't understand. We French have two choices here, revenge or forgive. Forgive is impossible, so we must revenge, you see?"

"Revenge what?"

"We will avenge Sedan."

"What's Sedan?"

"The defeat that allowed the Germans to march into Paris, to humiliate us in 1870." When she looked perplexed he added, "The Franco-Prussian War! Can you imagine, Sophia, the Germans marched in Paris? Unthinkable! Our enemies marching through the Arc de Triomphe."

"But that was"—she figured quickly—"more than forty years ago.

You weren't even born. How can you revenge yourself on events before you were born?"

"You see, you do not understand." He flung the paper down and smoked for a moment. "Forty years, four hundred years, it's nothing, but you are an American, you do not know that. Americans have nothing to remember. With nothing to remember, you have nothing to forget. Nothing to forgive or revenge. Americans conquer nature. You grow money. You are like clean children after their baths and none of the grime and dirt from the past is anywhere visible. So you cannot understand this, *chérie*, but that's just how it is. It's simple."

"It's not simple," she protested. "It's murderous and disastrous!"

"The Germans are all dogs and cowards. They have no honor. They are as fleas on the back of a dog. They will be taught a lesson. We will be home by Christmas."

"Not you! Surely you're not going? You're an artist, Denis, you're not a soldier."

"I am French. That's enough."

They made love that afternoon to the toll of the great bell in the Reims cathedral. Sophia's body responded to the rhythm, the slow thrust of Denis's union with her like a knell, and when he held her at the last shuddering moment of his release, she was filled with a dread so intense and visceral she could not even admit it to him, to anyone. He slept, his arms around her, and Sophia pulled his hand to her mouth, moving her lips against the dry, paint-stained palm. The bells ceased at last.

She kept him from joining by any means she could, successfully, until the spring (by which time Christmas had come and gone and the Germans had not been taught a lesson, and moreover had moved perilously close to Paris itself). That was when some old compatriots from Arles showed up in Paris to have a fling before they enlisted. They stayed with Denis and Sophia. She regretted her hospitality, and with good reason. When they left, Denis and Maurice Fleury left with them, arm in arm, singing all the dirty verses from "Mademoiselle from Armentières."

When Denis left the rue Notre-Dame des Champs, Sophia's Wednesday teas ended altogether. She let the Breton cook go. She lived alone with Jeanne, her faithful servant, in a Paris that was gray and dangerous, expensive, full of refugees and want. The thud of bombardment sounded persistently. The air raid sirens blared at night. People wearily marched into their cellars. And just as wearily marched back out. Quarrels erupted amongst friends, and the old artistic cadre broke up: the bright circle of youth, irreverence, wit and genius that Sophia had thought would last forever, that was gone. She found she resented those men who were not in uniform, but at the same time she would not have wished war on anyone. Then she resented Denis for wishing it on her. Sometimes she spent the day in his studio, just to be surrounded by his work. She wore the sweater he painted in. She wandered amongst his canvases, the finished, the unfinished. She smoked. She looked out the windows. His presence here was at least more vivid, fleshly and tactile than his letters. These were all heavily censored, leaving only his declarations of love, and over time those grew more stale, repetitious, thin, unconvincing.

Perhaps Denis was right and perhaps Sophia had no sense of forgive-or-avenge, but as an American she chafed under inaction. She was impatient with her own sullen sadness. Finally she packed up the Ford, and taking the reluctant Jeanne with her, she volunteered herself and her car to the Red Cross, following the northern route she had taken with Denis two years before. She and her terrified servant carried supplies, messages, medicine, ammo, telegrams; they carried the wounded—and the dead, as it turned out. They ferried doctors and dressings and morphine between field stations and behind the lines. Sophia learned to sleep amidst incessant shelling, to eat when and where and what she could, to pee by the side of the road, to change tires and haul petrol, to hold the hands of dying men and listen to their prayers and curses.

In a hospital in Reims she was called to the bedside of a man whose ear had been shot away, who bellowed at her, *massacre, massacre*, describing, so Sophia thought at first, what he had seen, beheld as a soldier. But no: Massacre was a place in Washington, a place he longed for and had left behind. Eugene Briscoe was an American who had joined the Canadian army when the girl he loved had jilted him.

At dawn, when at last Eugene Briscoe slept, Sophia stumbled out of the convent that was serving as a hospital. She was delusionary with lack of sleep. Yes? She was dreaming. No. She was dead perhaps. She might be dead, in heaven or hell, but she saw Denis Aron waiting for her on the running board of the Ford. He leaned there, legs apart, chin resting on his chest, mouth open, snoring. Sophia moved cautiously to him, believing she had created this apparition from the sheer needing of him, from love. She knelt between his knees and put her arms around him, murmuring, *My love my love my love*, not caring if he was real or some wish incarnate.

He had thinned and wasted, his cheeks and eyes hollowed out. The hearing in his left ear was seriously impaired and he carried scars whose origins he could not even remember. The muck and mud of trench life had left him with an awful fungus growing over his feet and his buttocks. At least he was not wounded. But as Sophia discovered, he was not whole either.

In Reims, the hotel where they had stayed that August was gone, bombarded, blasted. The cathedral whose somber tolling bell had seemed so terrible to her, that was gone, bombarded, blasted. But Denis was not gone and she clung to him and he to her, more fiercely even than in the early days of their passion. Sophia recognized this as hunger of a different sort. This was not a lust for, this was a lust against. Lust against time, against death, against everything they would be denied. They had three days.

Two months later in the midst of her Red Cross duties, Sophia miscarried a child and the doctor who attended her hadn't slept in four days and botched the repairs. Sophia thought she would die of the pain. Morphine was reserved for soldiers. Women had been having babies or losing them without morphine for centuries.

And then, Jeanne was killed. She had been waiting for Sophia in the Ford and it was hit by a shell. Of the Ford, there was nothing left. Of Jeanne they found precious little, a bit of skull tufted with hair, some bone, a crucifix. Struggling with sorrow, suffering, loss, ill-nourished, unkempt and sleepless, her health seriously impaired, Sophia left the battlefields. She made her way slowly back to Paris, to the rue Notre-Dame des Champs. She collected her ration cards. She waited it out. Alone.

During this long, chill winter in Paris when all life—from coal to wine, from soup to shelters—was rationed and miserable, when the ink sometimes froze in her pen, Sophia Westervelt put aside her book on

French art for Americans. A fatuous book, as she now saw it. And instead, she first began to formulate, to codify, write down the ideas that would become principles of a new education. She wrote volumes, tearing up, tossing out, reworking, rethinking, rewriting, not a book, but a plan. Moreover, a plan of action. She was, after all, American. And Denis was right: yes, as an American she had nothing to remember, nothing to forget, nothing to forgive and nothing to avenge, but in the face of what she had seen at the front, was that not an advantage? Was it not possible that people like her, Americans, women, could set an example before the world, lead men away from the cruel sectarian hatreds strewing graves worldwide? Might there not be a way to jettison all the old ways of learning, the thinking, the old education that had clearly led to this debacle? This assault on humanity of biblical proportions? Hers was not a Wilsonian political insight or endeavor, not a League of Nations, but the vision of an educated spirit, an informed body, an inquiring mind that would question (and then reject) murderous traditions, ancient hatreds hoary with time and inimical to sense. Men made war, fought war, brought war. Women could be educated to prevent it. North American women, attuned not just to different drummers, but a whole different tempo.

Chapter 29

People greeted the Armistice, the end of the war, much as they had the beginning: with the tolling of cathedral bells and jubilation in the streets. Sophia had not joined the first revelry and she did not join this one either. She was past thirty. Her hair was nearly gray. All revels were behind her. She closed her shutters against the noise and picked up her pen and went on working on her Curriculum for Temple School. By now it had a name.

In December Eugene Briscoe showed up at the rue Notre-Dame des Champs. He wanted to thank her again for her kindness to him in Reims.

Sophia smiled and asked him to stay for dinner. "Though it won't be Christmas dinner, I'm afraid. I've decided not to do that anymore. Not any of it. I've decided to break free of history and tradition and religion altogether."

"That's fine by me, Miss Westervelt." Eugene Briscoe rolled his hat in his hands and felt where his ear used to be. "Christmas was three days ago."

"Ah. You'll stay anyway, I hope."

Sophia was delighted to listen to Eugene Briscoe speak of islands and inlets and passages and points, coves and beaches, to bring in to her darkened Paris home the gray-green mornings, the softening fog, the lilac twilights of the Puget Sound. She was cheered to hear Indian names she'd not heard for years and years roll off his tongue, *Snohomish, Stillaguamish, Swinomish, Duawmish, Snoqualmie*. To form these words on her own tongue was to relearn the old language, the names as ancient as the timber, whole forests the Westervelts turned into shingles and shakes and silent lumber.

"If ever you decide to return to Washington, Miss Westervelt," Eugene said, as if he guessed at some of her longing, "you just call on me. I'll take you anywhere you'd like. Me and my boat, we'll be at your service. Just write me at Torklund's Marine and Feed, Massacre, Washington. There's only the one. I'm taking my army pay and the money I saved to build a house for Nona, and I'm buying a boat, a fine sturdy craft. I'm joining the Mosquito Fleet, gonna be wonna them little boats darts all round the Sound, mail, supplies, passengers, livestock. It'll be a good life."

"I'm sure it will be, Mr. Briscoe. Thank you for coming. I will never forget you."

"Nor I you, Miss Westervelt. I hope you'll forgive all those terrible things I said about your family. I can't remember 'zactly what I said, but I know it was terrible."

"The Westervelts are a reprehensible tribe, except of course, for my dear Pa."

"Amen, Miss Westervelt."

"*Au revoir.*"

In February Maurice Fleury returned to Paris. He too came to the rue Notre-Dame des Champs. He sat with Sophia in her study, which was the only room she kept warm; she worked here, ate here, slept here. Maurice too was thin, hard, and his essentially lighthearted, convivial nature severely altered, but not perhaps destroyed. Though he had joined up with Denis and the boys from Arles, his skills as a photographer had plucked him from their company. His orders were to photograph what could never be described. The boys from Arles were both dead.

"And Denis?" said Sophia. "What do you hear of Denis? Surely, your family and his family, you knew each other at school, you would have heard if . . ." She poured him coffee so weak it was known as the juice of socks. It was all she had.

Maurice was clearly pained to tell her what he had heard from Arles. The assault on a German machine-gun nest in which all of Denis's unit had perished. Certainly none had returned, all presumed dead, rotting still in No Man's Land. Denis would receive the Croix de Guerre. Posthumously. Sophia had not been contacted by the Aron family. They were very strict, very pious, very unforgiving; they did not recognize her. She was not French, not Jewish. She was not Denis's wife.

*I*n the spring of 1919 Sophia Westervelt lived like a nun and worked like the devil. She wrote furiously, thinking, rethinking, perfecting, enhancing, weeding through and adding to her curricular design for Temple School. She fused her own ideas with those of the Great Isadora, and absorbed (edited, altered, expanded) all the notions of art derived from the milieu in which she had lived for more than a decade. She melted it all down and annealed the whole into precepts that could be expressed as aphorisms. *Learn by Doing.* Oh yes, that one she knew by heart. *Waste Not Thy Hour.* She'd learned that in Reims, hadn't she? Both times. *Form Is to Function as God Is to Nature.* Sophia had given up altogether the faith of our fathers, and though she did not deny God, she had no patience with His heavy, implacably masculine hand, His bad temper and petulance. Just look at Abraham and Isaac. Look at Noah and the ark. She much preferred a deity of art, a uniting of all the arts that could combine form and function, gods and nature, and create some lasting *TRANSFORMATION.* That was the goal, the dream. That was as well the concluding chapter of her curriculum.

That spring she worked, half in the hope that the influenza that was sweeping Paris, carrying off the rich, the poor, sainted and sinner alike, would kill her. Then she chided herself for this un-American sentiment. She worked, half in the hope that Maurice was wrong and she would come upon Denis as she had that day in Reims, asleep on the running board of the Ford. It had happened once. Magically. Unexpectedly. Against all the odds and possibilities. Why not twice? Then she chided herself for delusion. She must attend to her school. She must return to America and begin her school.

In the meantime, the old cast of characters—those who lived, those who had fought, those who had fled, those who had stayed—they re-assembled in Paris. But nothing was the same. Nothing and no one. She felt like a ghost. As much a ghost as Denis. Some of the old cadre came to call on her, to draw her into the new world, a brave new world they said, better, more free than the old. Sophia knew, though, she could only survive in the New World. She booked passage for New York.

On Bastille Day, 1919, France belatedly, officially, celebrated the Armistice as only Paris could. The whole city lined the Champs Elysées to exult, to cheer Victory! All the dead were glorious, the wounded were glorious. The lame and the eyeless and the limbless were glorious. The palsied and shell-shocked were glorious. The gassed were glorious. The orphans were glorious. The widows and sonless mothers were glorious. The parades and flags and bands were glorious. The wine was glorious.

But in the rue Notre-Dame des Champs, Sophia rattled amongst her trunks and packing cases, valises, going through the last of what little she would take, arguing with Maurice, who continued trying to convince her to stay.

"I could never be happy here, Maurice, no matter what comes next. All that gives me life or hope or any happiness is my work. My school."

"And Denis's work? Are you taking none of it?"

"I give it all to you. His clothes and brushes and tools, everything, the finished and unfinished, everything of Denis's is on the third floor, his studio. You take it all to your apartment in the rue de la Grande Chaumière. Keep it, sell it, do what you want."

"My apartment? There's no room there. The concierge in my building, she is an old dragon, truly, and I have no space for them."

"Then sell everything. I don't care."

"You're not even taking the paintings? Those are all that's left of him, Sophia!"

"Don't you see? If I took one brush, one tube of paint, one scarf he liked, the sweater he painted in, one canvas, anything of him, I could never be free."

"Do you want to be free of him? I thought you loved him."

Sophia paused thoughtfully. Finally she turned to him, and with the cold clarity of a woman who has willfully stripped herself of delusion, of illusion, of everything in between, she said, "I loved him. You loved him. And we need to be free of him. You want to be free of him too. Don't you? Don't all of you? Denis is dead. No one will put their hands into the void of death, will they? New people, new things, new laughter, new music, new wine, these are the things of life. Denis is part of death."

"The work is not dead." Maurice stood in front of a particularly vibrant picture.

She moved slowly amongst the framed and unframed paintings while the sunlight thickened and absorbed their reflected brilliance. "Maybe his work was before its time. Poor Denis, he was perhaps before his time. I wish he could have lived to find his time. Keep the work, Maurice," she insisted, regarding the canvases stacked all around the studio. "There might yet be some miracle, I will give you money to rent space somewhere to keep these things. Maybe you can find a dealer who will offer them."

"And if they sell?"

"Send the money to his mother."

Chapter 30

As penance for her sins and the freedoms she had snatched in Paris, Sophia endured a grueling reconciliation with her family on her return to Seattle. Only Pa was delighted to have her home again. The others inflicted on her all sorts of retribution. Her eldest brother, Jethro, was especially malignant, intolerable and mocking. The rest of them were merely prim, and insufferable. The Westervelts as a tribe took their places in church, each Sunday, with Presbyterian pride, certain that God loved them. Hadn't He proved it? Look how rich they were. Sophia refused to go to church. She did not tell the family she had decided to forswear all traditional religion. She said instead that Denis Aron had convinced her of the Jews' ancient wisdom and she would wait for the true Messiah. At home.

While she was suffering (and contributing to) the family's ire, Sophia was not idle. She wrote to Captain Briscoe and met him in Anacortes. She drove there in her father's Benz. Eugene Briscoe was happy to see her, to escort her onto the *Nona York*, a trim vessel, built in Eagle Harbor. She had never left the Puget Sound. Painted black and green, fitting colors, with carefully polished brass fittings, the *Nona York* was up-to-the-minute. There were oil lamps for the running lights, of course, but in the cabin, along with oil lamps, two electric lights.

The exploratory journey took several days, during which Sophia and Eugene became fast friends, for life, as it turned out. From a distance they beheld Useless, a wild point that sloped down to a large cluster of rocks swarming with seals. The Captain told her how Useless had got its name. "Too dangerous. Too isolated. No natural harbor. Not enough feed or forage for farmers and not enough timber for the Westervelts. Useless."

"But," said Sophia, "has no one noticed how beautiful it is?"

Dear old Pa gave Sophia outright the acreage at Useless Point for her school. Since he was the principal landowner on the island anyway, he petitioned and received from the state an official name change: Isadora Island. Sophia explained to Pa how Isadora Duncan herself was a North American Woman of the Future and should never have gone to Europe but stayed in America, on the West Coast in fact, to meld form and function, god and nature, to learn by doing and discover the inward tempo, effect Transformation. *I'm sure you're right, Sophia,* Pa replied, chuckling, *Oh yes, Sophia, I do love to hear that kind of talk. Just like poetry. Like Old Testament Hebrew or something.*

But even Pa was shocked to discover how expensive was the simplicity Sophia imagined. Temple School was built entirely with Westervelt timber, hauled down Westervelt logging roads milled in Westervelt mills and floated on Westervelt barges. The school was erected with Westervelt labor (including Hector Lomax). Eugene Briscoe and the *Nona York* became—and remained—the school's official transport. Sophia paid for everything, wrote checks that her father funded while she lived in a small, hastily erected clapboard at the back, behind an apple and pear orchard that she had planted with her own hands. The trees were brought to Massacre on Westervelt barges and brought over from Massacre on a trail that became a road, hewed by the hands of men her father paid. Sophia Westervelt had never worried about money, and she did not worry about it now.

While the school building and grounds were being erected, Sophia began the search for teachers to share—and dispense—her vision. See the Unseen. Hear the Unspoken. Sophia herself would teach Music into Movement on the model of Isadora Duncan, adding her own improvements. To begin with she hired a disaffected professor from the University of Washington to teach history and geography. The vast library she installed at the school (many books by women authors, as well as the usual men, everyone from Sappho to Willa Cather, from Hildegard to H. D.) would support the study of poetry and literature. She hired a poet, a graduate of Bryn Mawr, to instruct and expound on literary matters, and sharpen the students' written expression. The other arts—in all their richness and display—were taught by notable musicians, painters, playwrights, singers and sculptors, to whom she gave freedom, opportunity, and not inconsequentially, shelter and studio space in small cottages scattered about the vast school property. To the delight of the impoverished island, she hired ten housemaids (including Bessie Lomax, later dismissed for theft) and six groundsmen, and a cook, sadly unlike the Breton cook in Paris.

The trouble came in finding a scientist who shared her belief that North American Women of the Future must be versed in science, yes, but not shackled to it. That science itself must serve the spirit. She interviewed or corresponded with dozens of men in the course of the twenty months it took to build the school, and when she spoke with them they replied, "Yes, Miss," as though her last name was Muffett, that she would of course sit on her tuffett and be frightened by spiders and the rest of the natural world.

That was before she began a correspondence with Newton Eads Faltenstall (University of Chicago). His eclectic background in biology, botany, and the new science of psychology, his interests in chemistry, electricity, magnetism, and nutrition and physiology, all clearly fitted him for the task. He had a searching mind and an inquiring spirit. His theories on diet were very persuasive. Once the school got under way (thirty students, ages eight to eighteen) Sophia sacked the cook and Newton hired a new one, instructed her thoroughly according to his own theories in the proper care and cooking of True Foods, ideas taken from his eight-hundred-page manuscript. Half, he said, of the book he was writing, *The North American Life-Enhancing and Perfecting Diet of True Foods*.

Science for Newton was both form and function, god and nature, accumulating, eliminating, timing being all. His teaching methods (even the constant quizzing of students) were in absolute accord with *Learn by Doing*. He taught architecture and engineering by having the students build chicken houses. He taught the cycles of nature by having them maintain a flock of poultry. Eggs were a True Food. Egg whites were an absolute True Food. Chicken wasn't too bad either as long as it wasn't boiled. Newton objected to anything boiled, even water for tea. Sophia found his enthusiasm infectious, his ideas stimulating, his courtliness endearing. He came from a Virginia family who, he said, had long dissipated themselves in drink, a fate he did not intend to share. He loved teaching and metaphors.

He was nothing like Denis Aron. For Sophia in these busy years, the pain of losing Denis had receded like an eliminating tide, the love she still felt for him exposed like rocks stubbled on a beach, barnacled with emotions she did not ever expect to feel again. And she did not. What she felt for Newton was not what she felt for Denis. Her love for Newton was an accumulating tide. There was none of the need to model and fold herself into another person. With Denis she had taken positive, pervasive pleasure, both as his model and as his lover, in living in the shelter of his shadow. With Newton she lived in the shelter of his substance. She took pleasure in their shared enthusiasms, Newton's unflagging capacity for wonder.

His proposal of marriage, when it came, was in a letter on cream-colored paper left for her on her desk with a bouquet of wildflowers.

> . . . *Not only do I love you for better or worse, but I love everyone who has ever loved you. I embrace your joys and sorrows. Your heartbreaks are my heartbreaks, your moments of glad triumph, mine. In asking you to marry me I do not tread on the ground you have hallowed with others, nor to deny Denis Aron what you may yet feel for his memory. I ask only to be able to offer you my strength, my courage, my loyalty and love, as long as we both shall live. I solemnly promise you will never have cause to regret it.*

In June 1923 Eugene Briscoe met Sophia and Newton at the Massacre dock to take them to Anacortes on a Monday morning. And thence to their wedding.

Eugene Briscoe was all but amphibious, his time as a soldier in France the only time he'd stayed that long on land. On land he could not breathe well. Now and then Captain Briscoe rented a room at the Isadora Inn when he felt the need for someone's cooking besides his own, or, in the winter, for a bath. (In summer he just jumped off the boat into the icy water.) But he lived on the *Nona York* and could not sleep well unless the sea rocked beneath him. He lived not only on, but with the *Nona York*, establishing a peculiar intimacy, as if he lived with Nona York, the daughter of an Anacortes ship chandler whom he had loved. They were engaged. He had an engagement picture to prove it. Nona York was pert, petite and had a space between her front teeth that drove Eugene Briscoe wild with desire. In April 1915 Miss York broke the engagement, writing him a note in which she declared only that she could not marry him: she was leaving Washington. She was sick of ships, sick of the Sound, sick of the smell of tar and fish. Heartbroken, Eugene Briscoe joined up in Canada, went to France to fight the Hun, fully prepared to die. When the war ended, and all he had lost was an ear, he took the money he had saved for Nona York, invested it in the *Nona York*, and in that regard, he married her after all.

Unrequited love had not soured him on romance, however. He was flattered when Sophia and Newton asked him to be a witness to their marriage, along with Sophia's father, whose Benz awaited them at the Anacortes dock. Captain Briscoe was not quite prepared to ride in the same vehicle with Mr. Westervelt. Like most islanders his reactions to the Westervelts were complex, woven of resentment and necessity. But he would not have thought that this slender, diffident, bearded old gent was the ogre he'd always imagined.

"Ma didn't come," Pa explained to Sophia. "She is ill, unable to travel."

"Of course, Pa. I know Ma wouldn't approve of a wedding in a judge's office." Sophia's mother had not approved of anything she'd done since she was about six.

So they were a strange quartet. The bride in her lilac-colored voile dress, tea length, a smart cloche over her short gray hair, her gray eyes shining. Newton, bow tied and beaming. Eugene floating in his own indelible bodily bouquet, stroking his beard and slicking his red hair into some semblance of grooming. And Pa, clipped, trim, dapper, well dressed, white haired and shrewd.

Pa was not impressed with Newton; he distrusted a man who cared nothing for money. But clearly, Newton adored Sophia and actually seemed to understand what she was talking about most of the time. If it was just money, Pa could supply the money. Pa was dedicated to Sophia's happiness. As they waited for the judge, Newton assured Pa, as he had assured Sophia, she would never have cause to regret marrying him.

There arrived from Paris, some months later, from the rue de la Grande Chaumière, a letter from Denis Aron. He had not died. Wounded in that last assault, he'd been taken prisoner and sent to Germany to work in their labor camps, fortunate to have lived at all. There were days when he had not wished to live, and only his great innate strength and a body like a remorseless engine kept him going. The vision of Sophia Westervelt, his love for her, had kept his heart alive, gave him the determination to escape. Which he did. He went into hiding for months, living in the woods, stealing by night, hiding by day, not even knowing when the Armistice had been declared.

In his letter to Sophia, he did not explain the four years it took him to return to Paris. Dead, he had been awarded the Croix de Guerre. Now the honor was given him in person. He had a veteran's pension. Maurice still had his brushes, tools, unfinished canvases, and the sweater he had always painted in. He was living with Maurice. *Please return to Paris, Sophia.*

Sophia Westervelt was not a woman sensitive to irony. Irony appeals to more purely cerebral people and Sophia was too physical for that. When she read this letter, she went into the practice room, wound up the Victrola and put on Sibelius's *Valse Triste*. She danced to this until she dropped to the floor, which is where Newton found her. She gave him the letter, and he read it gravely.

"If you wish—" he began.

"No, no—"

"Sophia, my dear. It must be said now. If not, one day the Unspoken will be a barrier between us. Something you'd regret. I will never hold you here against your wishes or against your heart. You thought Denis was dead and now you discover he's not. If you want to go, you are free."

"If I am free, then I choose to stay. I love you, Newton. I love the work we are accomplishing here, the school and the students. There can be no dualism for me. I'm not that sort of woman."

TEMPLE SCHOOL
ISADORA ISLAND, WASHINGTON
ISADORA 123

Knowing that you live, Denis, however terrible the events you have lived through, will comfort my every hour. Knowing you are in Paris, that your friends have been restored to you and you to them, will gladden me, when I used to think of you only with regret, nostalgia and despair, or some lethal cocktail of the three. Your talent, your genius will return to you. You will paint again. You will love again. I have loved again. I have married a fine man.

I am not returning to Paris. Do not mistake my decision for the mere letter of the law as a married woman. This is the choice of my head and my heart both. My life is here with my husband and my students. I have a school now for North American girls, where they will be transformed into North American Women of the Future. They will become teachers and in this way I will help to transform the old corrupt world that deprived so many of our friends of their lives, their nerves, their limbs, their well-being.

I say au revoir in the spirit of my love for you, Denis. In the old days you would have accused me of bringing simple loyalty to a complex situation. Perhaps you are right. But if I am not loyal, I cannot live. I must be true to my husband, my students, Temple School, my island and my hopes for the future.

Chapter 31

*L*ate in life, widowed, alone at Temple School, brandishing her
nickel-plated pistol and terrorizing the rabbits of Useless Point,
Sophia wondered if loyalty wasn't an overrated virtue. After
all, a dog is loyal to his old shoe, isn't he? Was it not merely visceral,
then, and not especially noble at all? Maybe that was true of all the
virtues. Maybe there was only reflex, innate character and guilt that
moved people to do what they did. None of those could be construed as
noble.

Waverley Scott was reflexively loyal, like an old dog with a shoe.
Sophia recognized that this virtue (or at least this reflex) united her to
Waverley, as if they had been mother and daughter, rather than teacher
and student. Neither time nor even death much altered Waverley's loyalties. Sophia would not leave Isadora, but Waverley took upon herself
Avril's task, made the journey Avril would have made had she lived. For
a month in 1957 Waverley lived in Montparnasse. She wrote to Sophia
almost daily as she searched for Avril's family. For a remnant, some shard
of recognition, memory of that family.

No one in the rue de la Grande Chaumière remembered them. No
one in the neighborhood, in the whole *quartier*, it seemed, could much
recall the Arons. Waverley stopped in cafés she recognized from Avril's
descriptions. She wept to see the meringues. She spoke to merchants
and matrons. She tried to break through the old communal crust of for-
getfulness, the collective amnesia during the Occupation. Avril's grandmother seemed to have made some small dent in Montparnasse memory.
The concierge? Ah yes, a dragon. But she had died before the Occupation, no?

Judith, her daughter? Judith, if she emerged at all, was shadowy as smoke. What had happened to Judith Aron? Who knows? You say that one day, 1942, you think, but you're not certain, she disappeared? You're certain she disappeared? 1942. A bad year. Very bad. People sometimes left without a word. Who could remember everyone who left Paris in those days? People left. They didn't shout out their whereabouts, their destinations.

No one could remember Avril, the daughter, at all.

And as for the famous painter, Denis had ceased to exist. Surely people would remember the work if not the man. Waverley explained that there had been many paintings. Where were the paintings? The gallery on the rue Luxembourg was no more. The studio on the rue Delambre, well that was gone. But the work? Surely, the work of a famous painter does not simply vanish. In the 1930s, Denis Aron was a painter of such renown. . . .

Could she not see that Montparnasse was full of painters? If Waverley wanted a painter, she had but to glance in any direction.

No, said Waverley, I am looking for the work, for the wife of a man I believe to be dead. Denis did not just leave Paris. He was taken by the Germans. Arrested. December 12, 1941. I have a letter with this date.

They pressed upon Waverley another coffee, another *apéritif*. They said the Nazis were swine. The Occupation was terrible. Everyone was in the Resistance.

*W*averley wrote to Sophia throughout this ordeal. Waverley wrote to Sophia through all her ordeals: the anguish and uncertainties of jobs she had lost and men she had left, of men she had lost and jobs she had left. She wrote through a dozen different love affairs and many addresses. Two marriages, two divorces, one illegal abortion. After she bolted from North Carolina, she wrote from Philadelphia until she moved to New York and thence to Washington, D.C. For four months she wrote from Asheville while she dutifully tended Rhoda in a final illness. After that, she moved to Boston.

In all her travels, however, she did not return to Isadora Island.

Not even for a visit. As a grown woman Waverley wasn't certain she could go back and face the girl she had been. Her job writing advertising jingles seemed unworthy of her Temple education. She had begun to suspect she wasn't a Woman of the Future after all. More than that, and though she never voiced such doubts in her letters, she had begun to suspect that Sophia was wrong about the future, about what the future would require of women and what the future would reward.

In 1961 Waverley Scott achieved (if not dinner with the King of Sweden) anonymous fame with her catchy praise for Deodora soap. It was a deathless jingle, and for a time, the whole world wanted to *Be Deodorable!* The following year she wrote immortal lyrics for Bugban (to be set to *Begin the Beguine*). Her reward for all this brilliance was that her immediate supervisor took the credit for the Bugban lines, and the agency allowed him to do so. Waverley quit. She sat in her Boston apartment and smoked and fumed.

And then there came a letter from Sophia. Could Sophia borrow Waverley's writing talents for the summer? She needed a writer to help finish Newton's book. Had this request, the praise for her writing, come from anyone else, Waverley would have suspected mockery. But not Sophia. Sophia indulged in no false flattery, no sugared euphemism. Sophia was reliably straightforward.

Except that this time she wasn't.

Sophia Westervelt had no hope whatever of finishing Newton's book. Working steadily since his death, she had got to page 456. There were fifteen hundred more to go. No, Sophia needed Waverley for something else entirely. Sophia must put her past in order. Avril's things must go to Waverley. The little café photo of Judith had vanished. (Sophia suspected Sis had destroyed it.) But the desk with *Wavril* painstakingly carved, the three paintings by Denis Aron, the letters from Judith, those must go to Waverley. And too, there was this last chance Sophia might have to right what simple happenstance had denied Waverley Scott. And if Sophia could give her that opportunity, then Sophia's own life would somehow be ordered. Timing was everything.

Part Seven

Tempo

Chapter 32

*D*riving her green rented Ford onto the ferry reminded Waverley of driving into the belly of an enormous white wedding cake. She parked the car and then climbed the stairs to the top tier, wandered the ferry, astonished that all these people were going to Isadora Island. And of course they weren't, not all of them; there were stops in between and there were stops after Isadora. She bought a cup of coffee and went outside, looking westward. In the bright breeze, her immediate past and all its disappointments peeled off her like varnish, long strips of unwanted identity that blew away across the Sound.

In 1962, twenty years after she had left Temple School, Waverley still wore a version of the school uniform. No Jackie Kennedy pillbox hats for her. No cinch belts, spike heels, narrow sheath dresses constricting motion. She wore trousers, a plain cotton shirt, ironed, a rain jacket and oxford shoes with wool socks. She'd packed her Roman sandals. Her nose still dominated her face, but her mouth was full and mobile and her gaze intelligent, direct. She wore her hair short, not the old Temple regulation short, but with enough curl to frame her face. She looked younger than her thirty-seven years. Perhaps the North American Life-Enhancing and Perfecting Diet of True Foods had in fact destroyed old-age deposits. More likely, her youthfulness was allied to the wistful look of a woman who has not yet found what she's seeking in life. There is a point at which such a look hardens into disappointment, but Waverley was not there yet.

The ferry drew toward Dog Bay, and "Isadora Island!" rang out over the public address system. Waverley went down to the car deck, got behind the wheel of the Ford and lumbered off behind a trail of other cars with flying tailfins and hood ornaments

The island landscape remained, but it was no longer familiar. What had been a geography imbedded in the heart now had signs vying for drivers' attention. RESTAURANTS! GOLF! FISHING! MOTELS! CAFES! The Useless road—paved, and with a line down the center, amazing!—went up and over hills, turned, hugged the woods, the farms and orchards, passed round meadows, and here and there came near the sea, where pleasure boats and huge ferries dotted the Sound. All the cars were too big for the narrow island roads, and the drivers too impatient. Dead rabbits, possums, dotted the pavement like punctuation and made her queasy, uneasy. Just before the rise where Avril had died, Waverley's car got stuck behind an Edsel with a backseat full of unruly brats. The eldest gave her the finger.

She followed the narrow track to the school, and parked in the yard not far from a black limo where the uniformed driver sat, door open, reading the sports page. He nodded at her, nothing more. He and the shiny limo were a complete anomaly amidst the vegetative ruin. Quizzer's old labs were overcome with blackberry bramble, and the laundry shed had succumbed to belladonna. Grapevines Waverley herself had helped to plant had tangled badly with wild roses and crawled over the old chicken houses, obliterating them altogether. The garden, gone, and the high fence that had kept out deer and rabbits had fallen over into patches of tough grass and thistle. She went in through the mudroom and called out for Sophia in the school's kitchen. There was an unpleasant waft of cat food gone bad and a litter box unemptied.

The table had been pushed against the wall, piled high with papers, newspapers, unopened mail. An enormous Underwood typewriter kept watch beside stacks of what was no doubt Quizzer's book. Yes. Waverley turned the pages and recognized his neat hand. A huge tabby roused off a chair, sauntered over to Waverley, purred and rubbed against her legs. Waverley shooed it off. She couldn't abide cats. She called out again for Sophia.

The Sophia who embraced Waverley quickly—as if two weeks instead of twenty years had separated them—had thickened. She looked worried and tired, though she still had her Corinthian carriage. Her gray eyes were slightly filmy with incipient cataracts. Her hair, no longer neatly clipped, radiated out in a wild white halo around her head. But her clear voice was unchanged. "Jethro's here. Making an awful nuisance of himself."

"Jethro, the brother who—"

"The very one. It's his biannual buyout offer, June and January. His timing never varies."

She pressed Waverley's elbow against her side, letting camaraderie conceal her infirmity, and they walked down the dark hall. The school had been almost entirely shut up, except for the library, where the windows and curtains were all open and June sunlight washed in. Emerald shadows mottled on the parquet floor as the foliage outside trembled in the breeze. The shelves were empty, the furniture gone, except for a few desks. Ensconced at these, like churlish schoolboys, were two men, one clearly Sophia's brother, Jethro, who nodded curtly. The other, younger, rose when they entered.

"Ian Ellerman, a lickspittle lawyer like his father before him," said Sophia by way of introduction. "Now go on, Jethro. Where were you? I know your speech so well I could recite it myself."

"It's different this year."

Sophia literally looked down her long nose, indifferent and not amused.

"The ferry's here now," he added.

Jethro looked very like Sophia, at least he had the same high thin-bridged nose, but he had spindled in old age, and with his white thatch of well-groomed hair, his stooped shoulders and high cheekbones, he had the look of a bird of prey, still dangerous for all his years. Perhaps more dangerous. Jethro nodded to Ian Ellerman, who handed Sophia a sheaf of documents which, after pulling her specs from her pocket, she commenced to read. Now and then she would grunt, though whether approving or incensed, Waverley couldn't tell.

Waverley looked overhead at the familiar mottoes cobwebbed on the ceiling beams and felt herself thrust back to being fourteen and cowed by the weight of the words overhead. The old wartime map of Europe still hung from the wall. No pushpins, though the map was pricked and pocked and stubbled where they'd been. The huge radio still commanded its place of honor in the corner. The fireplace was cold and dry and the sound of scuffling caught Sophia's attention.

She pulled the little pistol from her pocket. "Birds," she said to no one in particular. "They get caught in the chimneys and sometimes fly into the library. I have to shoot them before the cats get them, or it's really grisly." Sophia put the pistol on her desk and finished reading. "This is a lot of money, Jethro. More than you've offered before."

"Three times more. You'd be a fool not to take it."

"The only way I go out of here is in an urn. Like Newton." Sophia nodded toward the fireplace, where on the mantel there sat a porcelain urn with a brass plate.

Waverley found it impossible to believe that the enormous physical bulk of Newton Eads Faltenstall could conceivably be contained in that urn, much less his large spirit, his constant quizzing, his absolute certitude, which coincided oddly with his always questing mind. So vivid was Quizzer that he seemed still present to Waverley, so palpable that she drew a quick gasp to see something dart past her. One of the cats roused and meandered to a dusky corner to await the advent of the next mouse.

"I won't sell. Not the land, not the clapboard, not the orchard, not the school."

"This is not a school! This is a relic! Isadora's not isolated anymore, and soon there'll be zoning inspectors out here. You'll never be up to code. You'll be condemned."

Sophia rose, returned the papers to Ellerman. "I have been condemned before."

Jethro laughed mirthlessly. "You think yourself ill-used by the family, but you are the one who has ill-used the rest of us. Pa supported you all those years in Paris. He set you up here, he spent millions—yes, millions in an era when no one even said that word!—millions on you and then he still put you in his will? That's a crime! Ma tried to talk him out of it, just like she tried to talk him out of letting you go to Paris in the first place. Study art? Ma knew what you were up to. But you could always beguile Pa, just by telling him that the low-life wastrels you set yourself up with were artists."

"Isadora Duncan was not a low-life wastrel, you moneygrubbing Philistine."

"And that Jew painter you lived with! A sponger! A gigolo!"

Sophia lay her fingers lightly on the pearl-handled pistol. "Denis Aron was a genius. I will not hear you defame him, nor speak cruelly of the dead."

"When Ma found out you were living with a Jew, it about killed her."

"Martyrish hogwash."

"You broke her heart. Ma couldn't show her face in Seattle for fear that someone who'd just got back from Paris would come up and tell her stories of you, nude dancing, nude posing, nude photographs, nude picnics. You did it all. And you know what, Sophia? I wouldn't care, except that you were still squeezing money out of Pa that should have been mine. Ours, I mean. Ours. Mine and the rest of the family's." Jethro pulled a white handkerchief from his pocket and dabbed his upper lip. "I'm offering you a decent price. Better than decent. And you, by God, ought to sell."

Sophia spoke with her old unflappable correctness. "Temple School is the only good the Westervelt money has ever achieved."

"Say what you will about moneygrubbing Philistines, Sophia, you have never earned your living. You've lived off Westervelt money. We've made your life possible. And we've done it living good, clean successful lives without going naked and living in sin. You are the hypocrite. And a failure. Who has had dinner with the King of Sweden?" He gave a bitter laugh.

"Actually, Violet came very close. There was a world masters bridge tournament in Stockholm, and she won. She sent me a postcard. It's around here somewhere." Sophia opened the desk drawer and rummaged.

"Never mind the postcard! What about when you die? Think on that! What then?"

"Is this a theological discussion about the hereafter?"

"I'm not talking about the afterlife, dammit! I'm talking about property!"

"Ah. When I die, I shall leave everything to Brave Eagle."

"Who in hell is Brave Eagle?"

"Your grandson, Henry Westervelt."

"Oh him. He'll never amount to anything either."

"When Henry was just a boy, he'd come here, stay with me all sum-

mer and be Brave Eagle." The line of Sophia's jaw softened and a brightness bathed her face as she explained to Waverley that in the years after
Newton's death, Henry had spent every summer with her, brightened
her life. He was a young man now, and he would be here this summer
too, in August. Sophia mused, "I sometimes marvel that Henry and I can
be related to the rest of the Westervelts. You in particular, Jethro. You
lust after money like a dog in heat."

"One day you will go too far, Sophia." Jethro's voice lowered to a
growl. "This land is not yours in perpetuity."

"I'm afraid it is," Mr. Ellerman interrupted. "My father drew up the
initial documents back in 1919, and set up the trust for this school in
1920. The property was deeded to her in no uncertain terms. My father
was extremely particular. He would not have been careless. In fact, I
checked all those old·documents myself before we came here."

"Then why in hell didn't you tell me that?" snarled Jethro.

"Because I was under the impression we were coming here to discuss
selling with Mrs. Faltenstall, not to bully and threaten her."

"You're fired, Ellerman. Wait for me in the car."

Ellerman extracted himself from the desk, closed his attaché case,
bid Sophia and Waverley a curt farewell and left. They could hear his
footsteps echoing down the long hall. Jethro too rose from the confines
of his student desk, and Waverley hoped he'd leave, but instead he wandered around the empty library, leaving paw prints in the dust.

When he turned to his sister, Jethro spoke in the ingratiating tone of
an insurance salesman. "Sophia, make your peace with us. You've had a
small stroke, Sophia. You could have another. Sell this great wreck of a
school and come back where you can have medical help, where people
can look after you, where you can be with family. You can see Henry
more often if you live in Seattle. Wouldn't you agree?"

"I wouldn't agree with you if you told me my ass was on fire and I
could smell the smoke."

Waverley gave an involuntary gasp to hear this from Sophia, just at
the same moment that a little mouse darted from the corner and the cat
bounded and Sophia picked up the pearl-handled pistol and fired in its
general direction. She missed.

Jethro left without another word.

Sophia put the pistol back in her pocket and her mouth resumed its old pensive line, but she did not stir. "There's a cane over there"—she nodded—"on that high shelf. Would you get it for me? I couldn't let Jethro see me with a cane, could I? Gossip would get back. People would think—well, whatever it is stupid people think."

With the aid of the cane she walked back down the long hall. Waverley linked arms with her in the old way, though there was no whistling anymore. She was dismayed to see great festoons of cobwebs hanging from the corners and the slick slug trails remaining along the wallpaper, much of which had bloated with the damp. Waverley listened to Sophia talk about Newton's book, and nodded now and then, assuring her that she had all summer here and they would get the book finished.

"Oh, I don't imagine we can finish! Newton worked on it for forty years without finishing."

"Well, there are two of us, Sophia, and I can type."

"Oh, please, Waverley, don't demean your gifts. You write, you know. You write well."

"Deodora? Bugban? It's commercial tripe."

"That's true of course. But it doesn't actually diminish the fact that you have a gift for invention."

Waverley flushed slightly under the compliment. A compliment from Sophia always had this effect on her, and momentarily she thought more kindly toward Deodora soap.

"And of course," Sophia added, as if reading her thoughts, "you were absolutely correct to quit when that simpleton took credit for your work. A Temple student never surrenders her dignity, and she does not allow herself to be bullied. Especially by men."

They came into the kitchen and wordlessly considered the mounds of paper on the table, the upright Underwood, the work before them. Waverley thumbed through the two-thousand-page script and groaned inwardly.

Sophia sighed. "I try to be like Newton and think of the process. Not the product. If I think like Newton, I don't get too discouraged. The North American Life-Enhancing and Perfecting Diet was his life's work, poor dear."

"It must have been terrible for you both when you found out how sick he was."

"I think Newton suspected for a long time, but he couldn't say it. It meant failure, you see?"

"Of course."

"But finally I insisted we go see a mainland doctor. They gave Newton some euphemistic claptrap, but they told me he hadn't a chance against the cancer. He had perhaps six months to live. I told the doctors, we despise euphemism, you must tell Newton everything. But now I wonder if I wasn't overly hasty in that. So principled, we were."

"Well his death always seemed to me to be true to those principles, Sophia. Not exactly the way he stated them, maybe."

"Newton was true to his beliefs till the end. Don't let anyone tell you anything different, Waverley. He always thought if you followed the North American Life-Enhancing and Perfecting Diet you could die when you felt like it, like buying a train ticket for a specific departure date. And that's exactly what he did. Newton chose his date and time and he went. He bought a gun at the Marine and Feed, and wrote a note to me, left a note for Eugene Briscoe to come to that empty cottage in the afternoon and collect his body. It was astonishing, really."

"Shocking."

"I meant that he could have been so organized." Sophia filled up the kettle and turned on the stove. "Have you seen Sandy yet?"

Waverley paled. "Sandy's here?"

She watched from the corner of her eye. "He comes here just about every summer for a week or so. This year he's here for the whole summer."

With a patently false brightness, Waverley said she'd completely lost touch with Sandy. "The only thing I know about him is what you tell me. Let's see, he married Sis and has a few kids. He teaches high school math in California somewhere. Sis is in real estate." She felt as if she'd recited correctly for Quizzer.

Sophia gave an eloquent grunt. "Oh yes, Sis Torklund. She sold the Marine and Feed and moved her own folks into Sandy's Moonless house, just months after Avril died. Her parents were not happy about it, but what could they do? They couldn't resist her. Few people can, not when Sis sets her mind to something. She wanted out of here and she got out. Off to

L.A." Sophia plucked a couple of tea bags out of a canister and put them in the pot. "Her parents didn't last too long, and when they went, Sis told Sandy to sell the Moonless house. But he refused. Then he let Captain Briscoe live there. Sis wasn't happy with that. But now he has sold it. Jethro wasn't kidding about the land values here since the ferry came. The ghosts of the Indians are counting their greenbacks, these last few years."

Waverley watched apprehensively, tempted to shout out Rule 14 about the lethal tea bag. "Do you see Sandy often?"

"Every summer. At least once or twice. He's always been a big help to me. He still is."

Waverley cleared her throat. "I've never heard a word from him. He didn't even answer my letter after Avril died." The kettle shrieked, and using her cane, Sophia moved to retrieve it from the stove, but Waverley got it first, hoisted the heavy kettle and poured the hot water into the pot. Sophia seemed content to let her. Clearly, in some fundamental way the interview with Jethro had winded her. She had bested him once again, but it had cost her.

"When Eugene Briscoe's health failed, Sandy moved him into the Moonless house. Eugene lived there for years, and every summer Sandy comes up for a week and does what Eugene needs doing and sits on the porch with him. Only this time, it's different. Eugene's been moved to a nursing home in Anacortes."

"I can't imagine Captain Briscoe on land."

"Yes, well you probably can't imagine him senile either."

"When Sandy comes up here, does he bring his children?"

"No. He's always alone. Sis wants nothing to do with Isadora, and the kids live so close to Disneyland, they don't need anything else."

"I wouldn't think Disneyland would answer for experience."

"It would if you knew nothing else. Cups are where they've always been, Waverley. Give them a rinse out."

"You drink tea now, Sophia?"

Her gray eyes twinkled. "Not in the library, where Newton's ashes are, of course, but the truth is, I never cared one way or the other for the North American Life-Enhancing and Perfecting Diet. Newton believed in it, and that was good enough for me, but since he died . . ." Sophia drew herself up with her old intrinsic dignity, perhaps the only thing utterly unchanged about her. "It's been . . . I have been . . . I am alone. And we were always together, Newton and I, in our work, in our lives, in everything."

"You had an enviable marriage. I often think about you and Quizzer, especially since I've made a botch of it. Twice."

"Well, that first one doesn't count. You and Irene were just girls, and I'm sure all the soldiers were telling all the girls they had to go to bed with them, or marry them, or whatever they wanted, because they might die and never come back. Something like that."

"Something like that." Waverley poured her tea and pushed the cup across the well-known scars on the kitchen table.

"That doesn't count as failure. That was Learn by Doing."

"Well in my case, it was learn by undoing." She watched while Sophia heaped sugar in her tea. "At least, as I recall, sugar was not on the List of Nevers."

"Ah, but chocolate was! You girls just about broke Newton's heart with that chocolate escapade. Newton was so passionate and inspiring. He so believed in his theories. And then, the work of his lifetime, the North American Life-Enhancing and Perfecting Diet, betrayed him. All false," Sophia sighed. "All false."

Waverley remembered that moment on the beach when she had suddenly understood that in fact, yes, Quizzer's great wobbling theory of the interconnected universe was probably rot. And yet, as she grew older, her judgment had softened. Quizzer might not have been wholly correct, but only imaginatively so. In any event he was so vivid and graphic and explicit that Waverley still could not endure the thought of sausage, anything ground up for that matter. She could not eat hamburger. But she loved chocolate, radishes and French cooking. She did not like chicken. She admitted to Sophia that she smoked cigarettes, hoping she would say it was perfectly all right to light up inside.

"A bad habit you got from Sandy and Avril. A very bad habit."

"Yes," she replied, disappointed.

"And marshmallows?" Sophia inquired over the rim of her thick mug, steam from the tea obscuring her expression.

Waverley replied at last, "The very smell of marshmallows makes me sick with longing for Avril. I've had two husbands, many lovers, lots of friends, but I have never been so close to anyone in all my life."

"Have you forgotten everything you learned here? Can't you imagine flying?"

Waverley sipped pensively, and with her tea swallowed a great white lump of tears. You could not be successful, not in a man's world or a man's business (and they came to the same thing) if you allowed yourself to cry, so she had schooled herself against tears, not so much saving them, as Avril's grandmother had counseled, just against showing them. Showing undue emotion of any sort. As she looked around the school kitchen, she knew that for the first time in twenty years—since she had been forcibly removed from Isadora Island—she could speak the truth, confront even fear without euphemism or metaphor. "I'm thirty-seven years old, Sophia. I'm sick of marriage. I never want to marry again. I will never have children. I'm tired of living with men and having to make everything nice at home, and working with men and having to fight them in the office, all the time pretending that I'm not a threat. I'm afraid that I won't find another job, that I have a reputation as a talented troublemaker in a business where talent is cheap and trouble is expensive. I'm afraid that when I die, all they'll put on my tombstone is Deodora soap. I wonder how different my life would have been if Avril had lived. Yes, I know, she had Sandy and Judith, and I didn't. I'm always outside, Sophia, always the outsider. I always have been, except when I lived here." Waverley took Sophia's hand; her skin was papery, thin and dry. "I'm afraid no one will ever love me again."

"Stand up. Go on. Stand up. Hold out your arms. Steady. Straight. Remember your spine. Your Corinthian column. Turn slowly." Sophia made vague noises of disapproval. "Oh, Waverley, truly, you are in need of Transformation. Do you think it's possible I might still have something to teach you?"

"It's possible."

"Very well then. Your first lesson. Go see Sandy Lomax. He's out at the Moonless house. You have this one summer. Waste not thy hour."

Chapter 33

Waverley followed all the signs to Massacre and did not recognize it when she got there. The old main street (now called Main Street) was lined with electric lights, telephone poles and new buildings. Sidewalks ran like concrete ribbons. The Marine and Feed was gone altogether. Waverley spotted three attorneys' offices, two banks, five Realtors, an accountant, a funeral home, four doctors and two dentists. The scent of exhaust, new wood and enterprise, of frying hamburgers and gas fumes from the Richfield mixed uneasily with the smell of low tide. In the past the sounds of Massacre were the wind moaning, the rain falling, the gulls quarreling and the lisp of the tide at the dock. Now hammers clanged percussively and a cement truck ground its gears and churned noisily. The town had an actual stoplight where pickup trucks with the Westervelt logo chugged and rattled, and tourists, behind the steering wheels of their enormous cars, licked ice cream cones that dribbled down their wrists.

On the Moonless side, perhaps a third of a mile from Sandy's, a set of tourist cabins were half built. She parked the Ford near the remains of the old shed. Nearby there was a '56 Chevy with its hood open, tools and a transistor radio on the fender. The radio played a tinny pop tune. The *Maid of the Isles* still sat beside the house, all but buried in thistles, grass and red clover. Waverley turned off the radio and came slowly toward the front of the house. The roof concaved dangerously and shingles lay all around on the ground. But there on the front porch with its broken rails, facing the stone-stippled expanse of Moonless, Sandy Lomax looked up from his newspaper.

He wore glasses. His hair had gone gray at the temples. His hazel eyes, the shock of unruly hair, the slow curvature of his smile, those were as they had been, though his face had altered. He rose, called out her name. They shook hands swiftly, awkwardly, like people who have forgotten how, and mumbled a stunned exchange. Sandy had no idea she was coming to Isadora. Sophia had not said.

They sat down on the steps, side by side, looking over the low-tide flats of Moonless, and talked inconsequentially of Massacre and how it had changed and how long it had been since Waverley had been here and where she was living now. There were long silences and uneasy laughter. A family in the distance was digging clams, a grandfather teaching the children where to dig, one of them holding a large umbrella over the old man's bald head. Their voices carried in the wind.

The old man reminded Waverley of Captain Briscoe and she took refuge there. It would be easy to inquire after Eugene, to speak of him.

"He lived here, alone, just fine for a number of years." Sandy lit up and offered her a cigarette. "And I'd come up in the summers, and I could see a change in him. I guessed what was coming. He'd talk to Bessie and Hector a lot, and that was pretty harmless. He was always looking for Rufus and for the *Nona York*. But then, he started fighting World War I all over again, crouching and hiding and screaming about the bombs and the barbed wire. The police, or the Island sheriff or whatever they're calling them, they had to come out here a number of times, and finally there was a public health nurse who called me, maybe in February, and said he could not go on living alone, and what did I intend to do with him."

"He has no one, does he?"

"He has me. He has Sophia, but she can't be looking after him. When he thinks he's back in the trenches, he can be dangerous, violent. This summer I moved him to a place in Anacortes."

"It must have been terrible for you too."

"He doesn't know where he is most of the time anyway, Waverley. I don't say that he's happy. I just don't know. He's safe."

"Is it a veterans' home?"

"The VA wouldn't have him. Can you believe that? No, they told me absolutely, Captain Briscoe fought with the Canadians, so the Americans don't count him a veteran. Probably just as well. Some of those VA places are real nightmares. The place I found in Anacortes is clean, and cheerful, modest. There are people around, but I'm his only visitor. And sometimes he doesn't recognize me. Thinks I'm my father. Sometimes he thinks I'm his father. Sometimes he thinks he's already dead. But as long as he's got left, I can keep him there. I'd no sooner moved the Captain to Anacortes than I had a dozen offers for this old place. Waverley, you wouldn't believe what they've given me for this scrap of land. They'll tear down the house of course."

Waverley turned, looked up at the house, a simple-enough frame, up on blocks, two rooms downstairs, a bathroom added off the kitchen, one large bedroom upstairs under the eaves.

"My father built it, God knows how he even came by the land, but they tell me the title's all fine. He probably paid about eighty-five dollars for the whole thing, and suddenly this little bit of beach is incredibly valuable. It's almost comic. Suddenly, Isadora Island is a piggy bank and people like us, like my family who clung here by their fingernails for generations, they're all rolling in dough."

Waverley said, "It makes me wish I had come back a long time ago, before the ferry, when Massacre was still Massacre and I could still ride on the *Nona York*."

"The boat's gone. Sold. Scrapped."

"It must have broken the Captain's heart to lose her twice."

"Twice?"

"You remember that story, the Miss York of the mainland who broke their engagement and broke his heart. Do you think it ruined his life, staying true to someone who had spurned him?"

"There are all sorts of ways to ruin your life. That's just one. Would you like a beer? Come on in."

Waverley put her cigarette out in a nearby ashtray. But she lingered at the front door, not quite able to step through. This had been Avril's house. Avril had been happy here. Avril's slender frame had filled up the doorway, and Avril's smile had shone behind the windows. Avril's body had warmed the overstuffed chair. She listened for Avril's laughter coming from the kitchen. She listened for Avril's voice in the little bathroom, all the dirty verses from "Mademoiselle from Armentières." She wanted to see Avril shrug and smile and declare herself to be a Woman of the Future. She wanted Avril. She wanted her with a great visceral thump of love and longing and loss.

"Tell me about Judith," she said when she'd followed him into the kitchen. "Is she like Avril?" The floor sloped and the linoleum buckled and the checked curtains had turned sepia with dust. The sink was streaked with rust and coffee stains. Sandy searched around the drawers and cupboards like they were all undiscovered country, looking for a simple beer opener. This was a man unused to the kitchen. She asked again after Judith.

"We don't call her that. She goes by Denise. Her name was Judith Denise, you remember."

"Well, yes, but she was Judith when she was a baby, wasn't she?"

"That was before we moved to California." He popped open the beers. "Sis said there were so many girls named Judith, Judy. They were everywhere. Sis said she should use Denise, that it was more distinctive. And I guess she was right. There's never been another Denise in any of her classes."

"Denise, then," said Waverley, thanking him for the beer. "Tell me about Denise."

"She looks a bit like Avril, dark hair, dark eyes, she's small. But she hasn't got that intensity about her that Avril had, that daring."

"Avril was obliged to be daring. How else could she have made that journey? Leaving home and walking across the Pyrenees when she was fifteen?"

"Judith Aron must have been mad with fear. Only now, as a father, do I understand what she must have lived through. Not until I was a parent myself did I understand Judith's desperation in letting her go half a world away to someone she didn't even know, in the hopes they'd take her in. My God."

"Her mother was right to do it though, to send her away. Avril lived and they didn't."

"For a while Avril lived."

Sandy's eyes met Waverley's directly and he took a long pull on the bottle, sat down at the small chipped table. Waverley sat opposite him.

"I need to know how it was," she said. "I have the letter from Sophia. But I need to know from you how it was this terrible thing happened."

He drank thoughtfully. "You remember the road, the rise and the turn there. The rabbits everywhere."

"Yes."

"That's how it was."

"Please, Sandy. Don't leave it at that."

"Why not? What do you want from me?"

"I will not ask you again. I promise. Please."

Resting his elbows on his knees, his fingertips pressed together, he said at last, "I taught Avril how to ride the Vickers-Clyno myself. I taught her how to drive it. For years I believed I killed her. Perhaps I still believe that. I only hope it was instantaneous and that she suffered no pain."

Somewhere distant there was the high whine of a power saw and hammers pounding in shattered, scattered tempos.

"Life goes on," he added. "It was a long time ago. No one remembers her."

"I remember her. Sophia remembers her." Waverley regarded the man before her, making a conscious effort to distinguish him from the boy she remembered; the mirth had vanished from his eyes, and he had none of his old easy physical spontaneity. It wasn't age, it was practice. Waverley fathomed that he had grown somehow accustomed to assessing consequences before he did anything, so much as raised a beer bottle to his lips. "Don't you remember Avril?"

"You should have come back when she died," he said in a flat voice. "You owed Avril that and you didn't come."

"How could I? Sophia didn't even tell me, write to me until it was all over. I called, two or three times? Didn't Sis tell you I called at the Marine and Feed? You never called me back. I wrote you a long letter and you never replied."

"I didn't know you called. I don't remember the letter." He closed his eyes, took off his glasses and rubbed the bridge of his nose thoughtfully. "I don't remember much of anything really. One day, I'm holding Denise and she was crying because she'd hurt her knee and I'd picked her up and kissed her knee, but she just kept crying for her mama. I heard footsteps on the porch and I looked up and there was Newton at the doorway and Sis right behind him. And I thought, that was pretty odd, that they would be together. Newton just sort of stood there, panting, like he'd run all the way from Useless. But Sis, she just came right in and took the baby from my arms. Newton told me to sit down. The next thing I remember thinking: the baby isn't crying anymore, I wonder how Sis got the baby to stop crying. That was maybe two years later." Sandy lit up. "By the time I finally came out of my coma of grief, I was a married man, a student at UCLA on the GI Bill, we had a place in married student housing and Sis was pregnant."

"That all sounds pretty final."

"There was no going back, that's for sure. I started out in engineering, but it was too rugged, too competitive, especially since I was working part-time too. The new baby never slept, and Denise was a handful. She was like Avril in that." He smiled. "So I got a degree in math and a teaching credential. California was desperate for teachers. I got a job in Orange County, bought a three-bedroom tract house with a yard and a detached garage. The year before, it had been an alfalfa field." Sandy chuckled. "You should have seen Orange County in those pre-Disneyland days, Waverley. You can't even imagine. But Sis could. Sis went to real estate school and got her license. She went to work for some cigar-smoking ex-Marine who thought she should be doing his typing. In five years she bought him out of his own business. Sis just rode that real estate boom, well, like those kids on their surfboards at Huntington Beach. They swim out, they stand up, they do the impossible, do it so well you don't even know it's impossible unless you try to do it yourself. Sis tried to get me to go to real estate school at night, but after about a class and a half, I walked out. Not for me, Sis, I told her, you are the family dynamo."

"She could always . . ." Waverley sought the word, but there wasn't one that would encompass everything Sis Torklund could do.

"We've moved three times in ten years. We'll probably move again this fall. Each house gets bigger, better than the last. We've got a pool now and a family room and a TV that has color." He gave a low chuckle. "Sis is such a go-getter, always straining after something, always got to have more and be better. She's always looking for what has to be done next, some new house sold, some escrow closed, some floor to be mopped or beds to be made or weeds pulled, the lawn edged, and not so much as a toothpaste glop in the sink. She keeps those kids hopping, but Sis got a bad bargain in me."

"Oh, Sandy, I don't think that's so." Waverley flushed slightly. "I mean that's being very hard on yourself, isn't it?"

"I gave up straining after things a long time ago."

"Do you like teaching?"

"It pays the bills. But I had wanted to make things fly or move. Well, I have a garage full of cars that don't run. Really, all in all mine is not a very inspiring story."

"At least you have kids."

"Four. And you?"

"None."

"Are you married? Do you mind my asking?"

"Ask anything you'd like." Waverley felt the accretion of years fall away from her, from both of them, and she relaxed. "A couple of years ago my second husband got transferred to Wisconsin. And I just couldn't bring myself to move to Wisconsin. So when I knew I didn't love him enough to move to Wisconsin, I knew I didn't love him. I didn't even love him enough to feel pain. I would have recognized pain," she added.

"You want to walk on the beach? Do you mind low tide?"

"I like low tide."

The clamming family had left Moonless, though there were several walkers on the beach, a young couple throwing sticks for a dog. There was a woman with two boys; she carried their bright buckets and shovels while they were sword fighting with driftwood sticks. Sandy and Waverley, side by side, not touching, rounded the Moonless curve and a curve in time as well, conflating the twenty years that had passed. Waverley told him amusing stories about Deodora soap, about being a North American Woman of the Future in ad agencies featuring Neanderthal men. She had tales about the cities she had lived in, her travels and the entertaining people, men and women, she had known. Walking beside Sandy she realized that in twenty years she had not known a profound contentment.

Diffidence had grown on Sandy Lomax. He seemed to be keeping his strength or resilience, even his laughter, in abeyance. There was about him a sort of syncopation, a beat dropped, missed, and then on the second beat he could laugh, he could let go, he could relax. Waverley wondered at his momentary hesitations, and why they seemed for him so reflexive. But she remembered too what he was like at the Marine and Feed, with Mr. Torklund lurking nearby, and Mrs. Torklund always eyeing the till. When he was behind the wheel of the truck, when he was at Useless Point, he was a different sort of person, relaxed and vivid.

Interspersed with Waverley's stories, Sandy told her how he and Sis had found ways of living around each other, as opposed to living together. (This was not Waverley's notion of a marriage, but she didn't say so. A two-time loser isn't an authority on marriage.)

Sandy and Sis's most fundamental contentions were over the last vestige of their island life, the Lomax house on Moonless. Sis had insisted on selling, and Sandy refused. It was perhaps the only thing he outright refused her, though it stood empty for years, until at last Captain Briscoe needed a place to live. Then Sandy and Sis quarreled bitterly over the rent—which is to say Sandy would not charge the old man any rent at all. And every summer, though Sis berated Sandy for going, he went to Isadora to look after the place, to replace the gutters, repair the wiring, things Captain Briscoe could no longer do, to sit on the porch with Eugene. Now, at the very moment when resolution between husband and wife ought to be in sight—the Moonless house sold for an unimaginable sum—their struggles over the old place intensified. Sis was furious that some of the money should go to keep Captain Briscoe in the Anacortes nursing home. Sandy reminded her—at his own peril—that the house was his and his alone. No community property. No joint tenancy. The only thing he had from the feckless Hector and Bessie. Sis Lomax told her husband that if he came home without the money from the house, then don't come home at all.

"The Torklunds never met a greenback they didn't like," said Sandy with a pale laugh. "It's just the way they are. Sis can't help it any more than she can help having blue eyes. I'm used to it. I go out to the garage and rebuild motors. But the truth is, Waverley, I'm surrounded by Torklunds. My girls are broad faced, blue eyed and fair-haired. My youngest girl is Sis's mother come back from the grave. It's scary. Even the boy, Nels, he looks like me, but he's Torklund inside. Sometimes, I wish one of them would do some daredevilish thing, like my old man, just do something foolish or funny. I wish they would laugh or cry or wring their hands, jump for joy, just for the hell of it, just because it felt good. But they aren't like that."

"And Judith? Denise, I mean. Surely she's not like that. She belongs to Avril."

They came to the end of the beach, turned and looked back at the sweep of Moonless. "No one belongs to Avril any longer, Waverley. Except maybe you and me." He skipped a stone out across the water. Expertly. Three skips.

"If Avril still belongs to us, then we still belong to each other. We made those promises on the beach. No matter what's happened, those are still promises. I don't care what you say," she added, suddenly aware of both time and tempo, the fixed, forever-in-the-past quality of the former, the ongoing, uninterrupted quality of the latter. Tempo had to be discovered. Time was a given, though not given equally to all. Waste not thy hour. "I never quit loving either of you," Waverley said. "No matter what. Even when I was jealous—and I was, very jealous, painfully jealous, especially when the baby was born and I was shut out of that whole experience, and your marriage and your being together—but I didn't quit loving you. Or Avril. After a while, when the worst of the hurt passed, I thought I could go on being part of your lives. If you had each other, you must both have me too. Like we never left the beach."

He stopped and rested his hands on her shoulders. "I don't think that's possible. I can't bear to think of Isadora, or that beach, or that summer, or you and Avril."

"Then you must have lost your imagination, Sandy."

"Maybe that's why I like fixing cars, because they can be fixed. But the kind of losses . . . Hearts, spirits, you can't just put in a new fan belt and have them be useful again. If I think about Avril, about you and Avril on the beach, it'll destroy me. Just like they're going to destroy this house."

"Then why did you come back? What was the point? You'd moved the Captain. Why come back here to live one last summer. You're not fixing up the house. It'll be destroyed."

"Some old loyalty, I guess. To my parents. My past. Sophia. Newton. Avril. You."

"A house can be torn down. Love can't."

"Could you still love me, Waverley? I'm not the boy you remember."

"I don't want a boy. I'm not a girl. I'm a woman and I want you. I want you to love me. I've always wanted you to love me."

He opened his arms to her and Waverley pressed her head against his shoulder, breathed deeply of his scent, pungent, heady with memory, but not the same old scent. He held her so close she could feel his heart thudding rhythmically in his chest. Waverley relaxed into his kiss, which was not what she remembered, but she believed nonetheless that the old, longed-for transformation lay within her grasp.

Chapter 34

Sexual Scrabble is a complex game, played with words instead of letters. The hope—not to say the object—of the game is to put these words together, horizontally and vertically, into sentences, not complete subject-and-verb sentences, but impressionistic, evocative pronouncements. More poetry than prose.

Problems of syntax are easily dispensed with. Subjects are a given: he, she, you, we, they—players are not obliged to supply subjects and possessives (his, hers, ours). Any combination is acceptable. Thus, all verb constructions are correct. And verbs are made easily singular or plural, past or present. Verbs and nouns are the most important elements of Sexual Scrabble. Any sentence will do, but as with sex itself the best sentences suggest action, reveal underlying currents of feeling and sensation, emotion, love. Words may double as verbs or nouns, as in *kiss*, *touch*, *suck*, *wiggle*, *tickle*, *thrust*, *shudder* and the like. An "ing" ending can be added just by saying so. The rules of Sexual Scrabble are fairly elastic and reflect often the mood of the players, *serious*, *intense*, *eager*, or *playful* and *teasing*. The vocabulary—limited only by imagination and experience—constantly expands. The more you play Sexual Scrabble, the better you get. Vulgar redundancies are just fine. The descriptive and correct *penis*, for instance, is part of the game; but so is *cock*, *dick*, *shaft*, *stem*, *prick* and so on. Brevity is the soul of foreplay. No one keeps score. Everyone wins. The game itself is the prize, and the inspiration derived from playing creates further inspiration. The players are *prompted*, *urged*, *enticed*, *seduced* into acting out the suggestions implicit in the game. In Sexual Scrabble, the more you play, the more words are added. Vocabulary *swells*.

This game, invented by Sandy and Waverley, had a vocabulary (by the end of that summer) of some 350 words, nouns, verbs, adverbs. The grammar of the game was exhilarating, and the adjectives! The *sweet*, the *strong*, the *sticky*, *damp*, the *dark*, *delightful*, *delicious*, the *forbidden*, *furtive*, *fulfilling*, *enriching*, *hungry*. Waverley could not believe she could endure such *lust* and *hunger* and *fulfillment* all in the same moment, that the *fulfillment* begat the *lust* and *hunger*, that she could be so brilliant, aware of her own body and simultaneously float far from it. She could *explore*, *anticipate*, *release*, *roll*, *relax*, *reveal*, *relinquish*, *surrender*, *achieve*, *impale*, *mount*. *Adultery* was a word in Sexual Scrabble, of course. An old word. They invented new ones like *sexhausted*, *sexcitement*, *sextasy*. They gave whole new meaning to *turnover*. Verb and noun.

Sandy and Waverley felt naked with each other even when they were not. People sometimes stared at them in the Island Grocery. They radiated that old, *musky* connection, *indelible*, *redolent* of *woodsmoke* and *desire*. They were unaccountably *gorgeous*. They bought *marshmallows* and the clerk gave them a gimlet-eyed wink.

The *pitch* and *intensity*, *spontaneity* of their love affair accelerated over that summer, and they sometimes lay in bed and listened to the tide ruffle up along the Moonless beach, or ebb, pull back, Waverley wishing she could stop, slow the moon in its courses, keep time from encroaching on them, knowing she could not. June eased into the great bay of July and July into the autumnal shores of August. Just before Labor Day the sale of the Moonless house would be final and the house destroyed. A restaurant was to be built here. Waverley & Sandy would be gone. But they laughed to think that from the *heat* they had created on this spot, when this restaurant was *erected*, the *meat* would fry itself.

One night Waverley got the box out and sat naked and cross-legged, writing out new words for Sexual Scrabble while Sandy grinned at her from the doorway: *transform*, *transformation*, *form* and *function*, the *fond* in *fondle*, the *hand* in *handle*, the *love* in *lovely*. She had discovered the *unction* in *function* and understood at last some aspect of the equation that had always eluded her. Progress.

$\mathcal{W}$hat did not make progress was Newton's book. The manuscript and the Underwood were cleared from the kitchen and taken into the school library, where now and then, Sophia and Waverley went at it. Those afternoons when she worked with Sophia, Sandy came to Temple in the evening, and she and Sandy cooked dinner for Sophia, Untrue Foods, a bottle of wine, and the three basked in one another's company. Then Waverley went home with Sandy. To Moonless. The house that had been Avril's now belonged to Sandy and Waverley. She lay in bed beside him and believed herself the Maid of the Isles, all the isles. The *intimate isles*.

Sometimes Sophia and Waverley didn't even bother with the book, but went directly to the beach. The path was difficult for Sophia, and she maneuvered the rocks with her cane and holding on to Waverley. When Henry Westervelt joined her in August, she leaned on him. He was, Waverley thought, so like Sophia, meeting him was like guessing what Sophia might have been like if she were a man. Waverley and Henry (he had moved beyond Brave Eagle) became great friends, and she was pleased that in him Sophia had found a son, a grandson, another sympathetic male.

Aside from their jaunts to Useless and the school, Sandy and Waverley went all over Isadora, places they had known and places they could not have gone before because the roads did not exist. But not until the summer drew to an end did they leave the island and go to see Captain Briscoe in Anacortes. They did not take the ferry but rented a boat. The ferry would have seemed disloyal to the old man and the inter-island routes he had plied for nearly forty years.

Waverley brought a small handful of wildflowers from Isadora, and the Captain, wheeled out to a sunny porch, held them, smelled them, pulled them so close to his nose that it was daubed with yellow pollen. He neither knew nor cared. He did not recognize either of them, but at least he wasn't in the trenches of World War I. He was utterly shrunken, everything except his great, rough, all-but-barnacled hands. He wore a cap at a jaunty angle covering the earless side of his head. He didn't hear too well out of the other one. He kept asking after Nona York and that sonofabitching Rufus, upsetting a bevy of old ladies nearby. He grew rambunctious and wanted to go up on deck. A male nurse took him inside.

Waverley burst into tears, and Sandy silently took her elbow and they walked away.

They sailed back to Isadora. Sandy held the tiller with one hand and Waverley leaned back into his other arm, resting her hand easily on his thigh. They listened to the wind, the sound of the water slapping the boat. In the months they'd been together, they had achieved much of the same sort of wordless unison that had made Wavril out of Waverley and Avril: they could communicate without speech. And unspoken, they had taken an implicit vow not to talk about the end of the summer, the end of their affair. Not to speak of what came after. To leave the present unsullied by the certainty of their parting.

Still, Waverley wrestled with questions that crowded in on her, the more insistent as their time together dwindled. She reminded herself over and over to live in the present, to be content with the present, but even then she had chronomania, an obsession with time that left her always with her feet in the past and her eyes on the future. Waverley always wanted to know what would happen next. These were the qualities and questions that would one day make her a very successful purveyor of Romance, but they also made her a difficult lover.

"What are you going to tell Sis when you go home?"

"I thought we weren't going to talk about that."

Waverley adjusted her dark glasses. She did not look at him. "I know, and I shouldn't, and I don't mean to, but I have to ask. I must. What are you going to tell Sis about us?"

"Nothing."

"There are some experiences that are, that ought to be indelible, Sandy. Like being a student at Temple School is indelible, something you can't erase or altogether conceal, and I thought love ought to be the same."

"It is indelible. You are indelible. You always will be. But honey, you know I can't walk back in and announce that I love Waverley Scott and I'm leaving home."

"I never wanted that." This was not altogether true; she had in fact constructed a fantasy life in the future for the two of them, so fantastical she sometimes thought perhaps Sis wouldn't mind sharing Sandy. "I don't want to be forgotten." She sulked.

He reached out and caressed the smooth dark cap of her hair. "Unforgettable Waverley."

This ought to have sufficed for her, but it didn't. She hated the whine in her voice, hated even the question, but she had to ask, "Do you make love with Sis?"

He pulled the tiller under his arm. "Every Sunday morning. Rain or shine. Like you'd take vitamins for your health. Regularly."

Waverley took a while to absorb this and everything it suggested and she might have pursued it further, but there was a leaden finality in his voice. In the distance a tug pulled a great barge through the waters of the Sound. Lesser boats, pleasure boats, tacked and evaded the tug and its wake. They reminded Waverley of swift blue dragonflies.

Sandy went on with a sigh. "I guess we should get this out and over and done with."

"I guess so." She was glad she was wearing dark glasses. She bit her lip so it wouldn't curl into a pout. She hated women who pouted.

"Teaching school, I keep pretty regular hours. Sis doesn't. She works a lot of evenings and Saturdays, showing houses, closing deals, things like that. I'm usually asleep when she comes home. Sometimes we don't see each other for days, she's a body in the bed beside me, that's all. And that's all I am to her. Anyway, when I get back in a couple of weeks, Sis won't be asking me if I did or felt or saw anything, met anyone, fell in love with anyone."

"What will she ask about?"

Sandy took a long thoughtful breath. He reached for his cigarettes, but he was out. As was Waverley. "Sis will ask if I brought all of the money for the Moonless house back with me and when I say no, that I will put some of it in an Anacortes bank account to pay for Captain Briscoe's nursing home, there will be hell to pay. We'll quarrel about that, probably as long as the Captain lives. Maybe as long as I live. I'll pay for this summer in any event. It will cost me. Even without you."

This was not what Waverley wanted to hear. "And if Sis should ask you if your heart is still on Isadora, if love and magic and happiness were all restored to you, if you went away for the summer and came back newly minted, happy beyond all measure, an indelible experience? What will you say?"

"I'll deny it."

"How can you live like that, Sandy?"

"How can I not? You ask too much of life."

"If you don't ask, you'll never get it."

"You'll never get it anyway. You're a born romantic. So was Avril. You were perfect together, but the world doesn't work like that. Marriage is only a way of getting through your days and nights. Sophia and Newton had something else, I admit that, but they did you a disservice if you grew up thinking that they were the model. They were the exception. The rest of us, well, we get by. That's all I want."

"Are you really so bitter?"

"It's just the way I'm living. Lots of people live like this. Maybe not you."

"I've been divorced twice. I'm not exactly the Nobel Prize winner in marriage."

"Yes, well, if you hadn't got divorced, think of that."

"I couldn't bear it. My heart would have shriveled if I'd stayed married to those men. My spirit would have died."

"Yes. Well, my heart has shriveled and my spirit's dying."

"I'm sorry I asked."

"I am too, but it's all right. We needed to say all this. We need to be honest with each other. It's the great thing we have, Waverley. We've known each other for so long. And so well." He pulled her close, rested his hand at the back of her head, massaging lightly as he knew she liked. "Who knows, it might not even have worked out with Avril, you know. All that was a long time ago. I can't even imagine it. It's like Newton always said, the tides wash over you and you have to respond. You have to change with them. But believe me"—he kissed the top of her head—"I won't forget you. Don't ever be afraid of that."

Effortlessly she adjusted her body to his when he leaned into the tiller. "Do you know about the pictures?" she asked. "Denis Aron's paintings that Avril finally gave to Sophia?"

"Yes."

"You know that Sophia has given them to me?"

"As she should. It's right that you have them."

"She's given me all the letters, too. The letters from Judith. Everything that's left of Avril, Sophia's given it all to me, but it's not mine. I want you to take them back to California with you. I want you to have them. I want you and Denise to have something of me, of us, of Wavril, something you can always see. Something indelible, like the pictures are indelible."

"I don't need Denis Aron's paintings to remember you."

"Please. Denise will need them. You can just tell Sis they're from Sophia."

"I can't do that. Besides, Sophia wants you to have them. You don't want to hurt her feelings."

"Sophia isn't as fragile as all that. And those paintings, they're all that's left of Denis Aron, of Avril for that matter. They belong to her daughter."

"You keep them, Waverley. You'll cherish them. Who knows what'll happen to them at my house."

"Denise should have something of her mother, something to remember Avril by."

"Denise doesn't know that Avril was her mother."

Waverley roused out of his arm and turned to face him, took off her dark glasses so that she should not miss or mistake his meaning. "That's not true."

"She doesn't know. Sis has built this whole story and if I pull out one little brick, well, she will never forgive me. Never forgive Denise either. Let Sis have her way. It's just as well." He adjusted the tiller to take advantage of the wind. "Avril's gone, dead. What can it matter to her?"

"You never told your own daughter that Sis Torklund is not her real mother! How can you be so cruel?"

"Cruel to whom? To the dead who don't know? To me? Maybe to me. But to Denise? It would be cruel to tell her. It would bring Denise a great boatload of grief—and I don't mean sadness, mourning a mother she never knew. I mean Sis would come down hard on her, on both of us, like the old ton of bricks. We, none of us in my family, need the misery. Believe me."

"So Avril . . . just never existed?"

"Avril Aron never existed. She was not a French Jew. There were no refugees at Temple School. Temple School itself hardly exists in the story Sis tells. I go along with it. For the most part. Why shouldn't I? Kids don't care about the past anyway."

"And what is this story?"

"Sis and I grew up together on Massacre. We have always been in love since I worked for her parents. We've always been together, except when I was in the navy. Sis and I got married just before I joined up. After our eldest daughter, Denise was born, Sis's parents wanted to retire. We wanted to go to California. I went to UCLA and the other kids were all born in California. It's a story tucked in with hospital corners. Tidy. Sis likes things tidy."

"And if it's not the truth?"

"You don't remember what it was like to try and resist her, do you? No one can resist her. Her own parents couldn't resist her. Sis always got her way. It might take a while, but she's relentless and that's sort of that."

"And your parents? Do Hector and Bessie figure in this tidy story?"

"Oh yes, I forgot that part. My parents are great for contrast. It's the famous Sons of Norway Torklunds versus the drunken Irish runaways who married Indians. Hector and Bessie make the hardworking Torklunds shine all the brighter. And you have to admit, for weeping and drinking, dying so drunk she fell out of her own bedroom window, there's no one quite like Bessie Lomax."

"You should speak up for Hector and Bessie!"

"And say what? You really don't get it, do you, Waverley? Why make trouble. No one gives a damn. No one gives a fisherman's fart about all this. The past, well either the past doesn't matter, in which case, why bother? Or it's going to shatter. In which case, why bother?"

"That's better than denying it."

"You say that because you don't live with us. Believe me, I know what's best for Denise. She's a teenager. She's already locked in pitched battle with her mom."

"You mean a battle with Sis."

Sandy ignored this. "Denise rebels. Every now and then I can see something of the toss of her head, some bit of defiance that's Avril all over again, but it's being squashed out of her. Not beaten. Just squashed. The others are squashed too, but it's hardest on Denise because she's not a born Torklund. Denise is the daughter of a girl with spirit and passion and courage, the granddaughter of a great painter, the great-granddaughter of a no-nonsense Parisian concierge. So Denise feels Sis's foot on her neck in a way the others don't. Denise suffers more than the others. She doesn't know why."

"But you do."

"If Denise knew about Avril, Sis would make certain she'd suffer even more. I am doing that girl a favor."

"And you?" Waverley paused. "Would you suffer?"

"Oh yes."

"She should know, Sandy."

"I'll leave a note when I die."

"That's terrible."

"No, it's just life. Denise will have to thrash through the usual teenage wasteland, fight with her mother and rebel her way into adulthood like everyone else does."

"How does she rebel? What does she do?"

"She cuts school. She's out late at night. Sis gives her a curfew and she ignores it, or she sneaks out after we've gone to bed. She hangs out with the wrong sort of kids. Whole bunches of boys sniffing around our place like foxes at the henhouse. I want to get out the BB gun sometimes and just scatter them. Makes me sick to think I might have been like that." He drew a deep, unwieldy breath, thick with exasperation. "She comes home smelling like beer and sex. I recognize it."

"You know all this and you don't try to stop it? To intervene?"

"To stop a teenage girl? You really have forgotten our sneaking out to the beach, haven't you? Beer and sex and marshmallows and fires to light the way for the Japanese subs?"

"That was different."

"That's what we all say, Waverley. But was it?"

"Maybe not," she conceded. "All right, if you can't intervene, then where are you in this picture?"

He considered. Tilting his face into the sunlight and listening to the rhythmic slap of the water on the hull of the boat, it was a while before he replied. "In the garage."

"Oh, how can you just bow out!"

"What good could I do?"

"You could protect Denise."

"Denise will come to me when she really needs me."

"You can't count on that."

"I don't. I just hope she will."

"Oh, Sandy. There has to be something else, something better."

"There is. You. This summer." He pulled her back against him, his arm flung round her. "All I had was the memory of Avril, the three of us on the beach, the Temple girls, the school, Newton, Sophia. I'd buried it all so deep that I'd lost it. I didn't hurt anymore but I'd lost everything that ever gave me joy, too. And you've given that back to me. I needed you and your love and this place and this time."

"This tempo," she corrected, swallowing the impulse to weep.

"I'll never come back here, but I'll never really leave either. I'll be like the ghosts of those Indians."

"I will come back," Waverley vowed.

"Watch out!" Sandy scrambled to his feet and braced the tiller. "Here comes the wake from that barge!"

He held the tiller firm, and Waverley clutched the side of the boat as they tossed violently in the wake of the long-past tug and barge. The roiling water passed beneath them, rocking swiftly, moving beyond, leaving behind a ripple. Pleasurable, actually, that ripple. Waverley resolved to add *ripple* to the Sexual Scrabble vocabulary. *Ripple*. Noun and verb.

"Let's go home," she said, though an element of her eagerness had diminished. She was disappointed in him. Sandy's refusal to tell Denise the truth betrayed, she thought, some fundamental lack of strength. And she was saddened that he had acquiesced wholly to Sis's insistence that Avril Aron had never lived. Hearing him talk reminded Waverley of the people she had spoken with in Montparnasse, people who had denied the Arons—not simply their tragic fates, but that they had lived at all. No doubt Sandy's garage was a fine and private place, quiet, away from the family strife, the noisy rebellion of a teenage girl against a disapproving mother, but shouldn't Sandy have tried to come between them? Shouldn't he have provided Denise with an alternative parent? Or at least invited her into the garage with him? He had let Sis alter the name Avril had given her daughter, but he should not have let Sis alter

Avril into oblivion. Did it pain Avril, her spirit, her memory that Sandy did not exert himself on behalf of their daughter? It pained Waverley. Pained her more than she could say, or would say. Not in the time left to them.

As they came upon Isadora Island, the darkly wooded mountain rose like a high gnomon on a sundial, to cast a shadow in the Sound. They sailed out of the shadow and saw the ferry in the distance. Closer to Massacre, the water went bronze with seaweed. Garbage floated, paper cups bobbed, the broken-off bits of lives, their own included, Waverley thought, adrift on silent currents, the accumulating tide simultaneous with the eliminating tide. Impossible of course. But that's the way it was, nonetheless.

Chapter 35

Sophia was wrong about many things and she believed she had failed in her mission. This was not so, even though most Temple girls grew up to be wives, mothers, club women, with comfortable lives, comfortable husbands, comfortable friends, women who as hostesses sent gusts of giggling through luncheon party conversations describing their eccentric education on Isadora Island: the whistling, the chickens, the togas.

But for a school that was only in existence some twenty years, and that never had more than forty students, the record of Temple alumnae achievement was actually quite impressive. The most celebrated, of course, was Violet, for years a world master bridge champion. The other students who left some mark on the world did so in fields that reflected upon Sophia herself. Temple School produced many teachers, earnest women whose lives were given over to process, to passing down wisdom, technique, instruction, even vision. There were assorted impassioned reformers dedicated to various causes (including a birth control activist who had gone to prison for failing to use euphemisms). There were dreamy poets whose works still lie in yellowing anthologies, and editors of little literary magazines, and women journalists writing courageously for small city newspapers. There was the occasional mystic. There were no wonderful singers, nor any but dilettante painters. The only Delphic Dancer was Lydia Fraser. There was (Waverley modestly thought) Nona York, who had certainly won renown as the author of romance novels. However, none of these were Women of the Future.

No, by the time Waverley Scott had arrived in the future Sophia had imagined (but failed to foresee) there was not a chance that women would be seeking out the tempo. Not a chance they would be looking to discover some inherent rhythm in any given life, much less the universe as a whole. Not a chance that the Unseen and Unheard should be thought worthy of notice, that expressing emotion should be considered an art form. No, truly, Waverley marveled, how could brilliant, prophetic, dynamic Sophia have been so wrong? How could she not have seen that the real Woman of the Future was Sis Torklund?

Sis Torklund had been ahead of her time.

Sophia Westervelt had misunderstood the way the world would go. She had misjudged what the world would honor, and who would make important contributions to society: women like Sis, who assumed leadership, responsibility, authority, who made lots of money, and demonstrated seismic sensitivity to the politics of power. With her unceasing ambition, Sis Lomax embodied everything on which North American Women of the Future would model themselves for more than half a century.

Sis invented *multitask* as a verb thirty years before it was coined to describe the obligations of ordinary life. Her energy was infectious and unforgiving, the sort of energy that both demanded and rewarded more of the same. Perpetual seeking. Sis saw clearly where she wanted to go. Went there. She advanced on the job, moving without charm or regret through a swath of what she would only recognize as obstacle or opposition. In choosing a husband, Sis had got the man she wanted, and when he proved wanting, she demanded little of him: that he bring home the paycheck and stay out of her way. In these things he obliged her. In her quest for Good, Better, Best, Sis took the whole Lomax clan with her, husband, four kids, disregarding their protests and rebellions, their bleating pleas for attention, affection or applause. Sis's houses had the cleanest counters, trash cans and toilets, the best-clipped lawn, and leafless swimming pools. She had a new car every two years, and a new and better house every three years. She had white living room furniture under plastic slipcovers which only came off when she decided to sell the place and had to show it. She kept her children awake at night while she vacuumed. Then they kept their children awake at night vacuuming, certain that if they did not, Mom would be all over them. Sis was critical, vocal and intrusive. She could not abide the unkempt. That Sis's children and her children's children had bouts of alcoholism, substance abuse, arrests for petty theft, forgery, and shoplifting, DUI's, bitter marriages, that they were contentious, backbiting and took grim pleasure in one another's misfortunes mattered not to Sis. She did not look back. She did not look around. She did not look inward. She looked forward. She tolerated no lapses, no day without its To Do list achieved. Sis Tork-lund Lomax was a tornado of motion in a void of emotion.

Though Waverley had long since suspected Sophia was wrong about the attributes of the Woman of the Future, after Becky Devere came to work for her, after listening to Becky's casual description of the swath and broth, the boil and ugly bubble of the extended Lomax family, she knew just how wrong Sophia had been. Sometimes after Becky had been at her house, Waverley had to take a nap. It was all too much for her. How, where had Sophia failed and Sis triumphed?

Clearly, both women both believed in practice and discipline (*Waste Not Thy Hour*), in courage and strength (*Fear Nothing Save Ignorance, Untruth and Ugliness*). But in freeing their students from sausage and tra-dition, Sophia and Newton also demanded inquiry: inward inquiry as well as outward. Discover the tempo. Transform. The telescope for as-sessing the vast Unheard. The microscope for assessing the teeming Un-seen. (The chickens probably had no educational value whatever.) That Waverley continued to practice what she'd learned at Temple School into old age testified to Sophia's powerful personality and Newton's en-thusiasm. She could never let go of *Learn by Doing*. And as for *Form Is to Function as God Is to Nature*, well, that one was antique to begin with; it offered her no end of trouble as she struggled to fit it round the vari-ous turns her life took.

Waverley's life, like any other, was a search for satisfactions, both personal and professional. Often she reached appalling dead ends. Friendships that waned for reasons she could not fathom. Husbands who left her. Lovers who betrayed her trust. Lovers who overstayed their wel-come. Husbands who were hard to get rid of. Skills that went uncred-ited. Situations where she had failed to grasp the political realities. Follies of which she was ashamed. Foibles she should have avoided. Op-portunities she had squandered. By the time she was forty, any long-standing union with a man was either behind her or beyond her. It came to the same thing. She remained outside the possibilities of love. In her professional life, despite her impressive résumé, real satisfaction had eluded her until the day she was on an airplane and had forgotten to bring anything to read.

In the pocket of the seat in front of her, there was an airsick bag and a copy of the advertising assault they called the in-flight magazine. Behind that she found a romance novel left by a previous traveler. This she found intriguing. Unlike Sir Walter Scott's novels, there was no Scots dialect and there was lots of kissing. Moreover, the novel seemed to suggest a world in which men and women were actually important to each other. This was a cheering thought. A world that recognized that love enriches life. This too was cheering. Waverley believed in love, believed in sex for that matter, passion too. But the author of this book had dithered about, and the heroine seemed unequal to the act of love, much less to love itself. The heroine was clearly not educated according to Temple principles, and so she was continually surprised by her own capacity for passion. The heroine (for all her violet-eyed head tossing) acted as though deep feeling itself was foreign and unseemly unless called forth by a man. No, Waverley thought, the book could have been better all-around: the story, the romance, the man—and certainly the woman.

So, in the time-honored tradition of Look It Up and Write It Down, Waverley began writing such a book. In her book the heroine feared nothing except ignorance, untruth and ugliness. The heroine asked too much of life. And earned it. She Learned by Doing. Waverley herself Learned by Doing, and finished this novel. Published it and many others of the same ilk thereafter. She took the name of Nona York, Captain Briscoe's false sweetheart and true boat, and developed a massive readership. Her books provided women with solace and hope, both things well worth having. In Nona York novels, good women found good men to love them. That these men were sometimes flawed, not always tall, dark and dyspeptic, made them more interesting. That the women were sometimes strong-minded but weak-willed made them more complex. The paperback covers were usually crimson or blue, suggestive though not in poor taste. The books were the perfect chocolate truffle: reliably rich, but textured.

But in becoming Nona York, Waverley Scott found herself in open opposition to many of Sophia's teachings. For instance, the relationship of metaphor to euphemism. Waverley discovered that metaphor and euphemism were very much allied, and not that one was an acceptable form of speech and the other a crass evasion of responsibility. They were root and branch, you might say, of the same impulse. In becoming Nona York, she explored that impulse in virtually every book she wrote. Eventually she kept a Rolodex of synonyms, most of them culled from Sexual Scrabble. The Rolodex was a no-nonsense way of improving her work. Sexual Scrabble: A Game for Lovers, she never played again, kept it tucked away, unopened, in the desk that said *Wavril*.

One particular element of Waverley's Temple education that served Nona York was, oddly, the Church of the Chocolate God: waxing eloquent on what had not happened to her. She had not found the right man and married him. After a while she just said she'd never been married at all. It was easier that way. But in Nona's books, these experiences of love and marriage were delectable, and, read back to back, fairly repetitious. Waverley did not think this necessarily detrimental, and clearly, neither did her readers. Love was by its very nature repetitious. Did not every generation discover it for themselves? Engage, indulge and ultimately become disillusioned with love? Some people (perhaps more fortunate, certainly more imaginative) discovered that love is a far bigger country than they ever guessed, that the tidy four-square, four-poster borders of boy-meets-girl are false and confining. In this larger country, love was expansive rather than nailed down. Love was both its own burden and its own reward. In this country a white cat could fall in love with a red geranium.

That Sandy did not have the courage or stamina to explore this country did not make him any less dear to her. Waverley could—and did—forgive Sandy Lomax his failures, though she remained disappointed that he had not stood up to Sis. He had not stood up for true love. For love at all. He had not stood up for Avril. In directing Becky and Denise up to Isadora, Waverley guessed, Sandy had finally acknowledged the wrong he'd done his eldest daughter. He could not directly redress this wrong, but he could hope that Waverley would.

As she sat in the Land Rover, that November afternoon, November 6, watching the windshield wipers beat, seeing the island church, the cemetery, the bare poplars waver in the watery autumnal light, Waverley was struck with pity for Sandy Lomax. She wondered what sort of man he might have been if Sis Torklund had not decided, early on, that he was the man for her.

Chapter 36

U nder the big black umbrella that Waverley finally fetched from the back of the Land Rover, there was room for all three of them. Denise did not want to get out of the car, but Waverley insisted. Becky pointed out that the rain had diminished. Still, their feet splashed along the gravel drive. Not surprisingly, they were the only people at the church. The doors were locked. Piles of leaves had wilted in the corners of the protected porch. Waverley ushered them in through the cemetery gate and closed it behind her. Becky and Denise put up their hoods and wandered off. Becky found the graves of the elder Torklunds and the marker for Nels, and called Denise over.

Waverley wandered to another corner, two headstones. Three names. Lomax, Westervelt, Faltenstall. Like the little family they had once been, Sophia, Newton and Avril were all together. Newton's ashes had been buried with Sophia in 1964. Waverley knelt and cleared the area of leaves, autumnal debris. She waited. The rain had dwindled to a thick mist, clouds rolling so close to the earth, the rain seemed not to fall, but to congeal.

"Who is Avril Aron Lomax?" asked Becky when at last she and Denise joined Waverley. "Did Grandpa have a sister who died young?"

With a sense of release, of expressing emotion worthy of Sophia Westervelt, Waverley said *Avril*. She repeated it a few times, and then in a still uncertain voice, she told them who Avril was. A French refugee from the Nazi Occupation of Paris. A student at Sophia and Newton's school, where Waverley had been a student. A girl of amazing courage and imagination. Sandy's first wife. Denise's mother. Died at the age of twenty-two or twenty-three. Young.

Waverley spoke without looking at her companions, but she registered the sharp inhale of their collective breath, the gasps, the hearts constricted, the minds congested with disbelief. Denise and Becky took each other's arms, held each other, crept closer under the big black umbrella. They protested that this small cemetery must be full of people named Lomax or related to the Lomaxes.

"That may be," Waverley interrupted, "but this Lomax, Avril Aron, is your mother, Denise. You are her daughter. She loved you."

Denise twisted her hands. "Dad's been married twice?" she said in a querulous whine. "No one ever told me Dad was married before Mom. I don't believe it."

"They lied to you," replied Waverley. "They both lied to you, Sis and Sandy, your father and the woman who raised you. She is not your mother and you are not her daughter. They should have told you. Your father should have told you, even if Sis didn't."

"Why would they lie? They are my parents," Denise insisted, hyperventilating. "Are you telling me my own parents have lied to me all my life? You expect me to come up here and believe you? Who are you to me that I should believe you? I never met you before today! You can't do this to me!"

"Sandy only acquiesced in the lie. It doesn't absolve him," Waverley reflected, "but Sis perpetrated it. Sis raised you, but she is not your mother. This woman, Avril, was your mother."

"No." Denise backed away, out of the protection of the umbrella. "Mom, is a, well, she's Sis, and whatever you want to say about her, fine, so she wasn't fabulous. So what? But this"—Denise wagged her finger at the stone—"she's nothing to me. A name. Not even a name I know. Someone would have said, in all these years." Her voice spiraled up. "Someone would have told me."

"No one else knew. Only Sis and Sandy. They left Isadora and moved to California. It was an easy lie to tell. Please, Denise," Waverley implored, "see if you can't find some small memory of Avril. She was dark and small, like you, she had brilliant dark eyes. She would have sung to you, yes, she would have sung in French to you. 'Mademoiselle from Armentières.'" Inexpertly, a shard of that old ditty crossed Waverley's lips. "Can you remember anything of Avril? Anything? They brought you to the funeral. Sophia held you all through the funeral, after Mrs. Torklund slapped you. You remember? Remember?"

Denise shook her head wildly, weeping, denying.

"How do you know all this?" Becky demanded.

"At my house I have some letters. I will give them all to you. I have the letter Sophia wrote me when Avril died. Maybe then you will remember that day. I have letters from Judith Aron, Avril's mother in Paris, letters she wrote to Sophia. I have three paintings by Denis Aron. No one remembers him anymore, his work has all vanished, but he was an incredible artist. That's how you got your name. You are named after Avril's parents, Judith Denise."

Denise mouthed the air, gulped, and finally she eked out, "Judith? You say there was someone named Judith? My name is not Judith."

"Your name is Judith Denise Lomax. Have you ever seen your birth certificate? Avril would be on there as your mother. Didn't you ever get a passport?"

"No. I've never been anywhere to need one."

"A driver's license then."

"I was sixteen or something. I can't remember. I think Mom went with me. Maybe she had it."

"Avril named you Judith Denise. She named you after her parents, who were dead by then. Denis had long vanished, but at least we know when they took him. December, 1941."

"Who took him?" Denise asked, her dry voice cracking.

"The Nazis. They came for him in a car one night and took him away and Judith never saw him again."

"And this . . . Avril"—Denise pointed toward the stone. "Where was she?"

"She was living here then. Her mother wanted her to be safe. She sent her away from Paris because she loved her. And Avril adored her mother. After the Liberation, Avril waited for word from Judith. But there was nothing. Judith did not come back to Paris. Judith just vanished. We don't even know when, really. Probably 1942. But there's nothing left to tell us anything about Judith, except that she was gone."

"Gone where?" Becky spoke into the void.

"My guess is when they first arrested Judith, they took her to Drancy.

It was a big camp outside of the city, and that's where they interned the Jews of Paris to begin with. From there, they went to Auschwitz."

"Auschwitz!"

"I've read whatever I could find about the Jews of France, and the books I've found all seem to suggest that yes, those Jews who were shipped out of Paris went to Auschwitz."

"Jewish? I'm Jewish? I have people who died at Auschwitz?" Denise stared at her daughter, both of them pale, stunned. "Who are these people that I should just be hearing about them? Any of them? I come from a family of French Jews? My grandparents were French Jews," Denise repeated again and again. "Oh, my god, how did . . . ? How could—" She pointed to the headstone. "How could she have come to this remote place?"

In a convoluted, rambling fashion, mixing up what she knew from Sophia, what she knew from Avril, what she herself had experienced both on Isadora and in Paris, Waverley tried to patch the story together, though she kept finding threads she'd missed, and weaving those. Denis and Sophia. Sophia and Newton. Judith and Denis. Maurice. The grandmother who saved her tears. Eugene Briscoe. Temple School. Judith and Sophia, who had loved the same man, sharing, finally, the same beloved daughter, Avril.

"Why did no one tell me?" Denise's voice quavered. She gaped at the grave before her and the enormity of the lie it implied. "And you? Nona York? Who are you to know all this?"

"I'm not Nona York. I mean I am, but before I was Nona York, I was someone else. Waverley Scott. I'm Waverley Scott," said Waverley, marveling for the moment that she could still be here, still have strength and stamina and time and tempo after all these years. And all these dead. "I was educated at Temple School. I loved Sophia and Newton. I loved Avril. Avril and I, we loved the same man. Sandy. I was jealous when you were born because Sandy and Avril had each other, and I had no one, but it didn't change my loving them."

"And Sis?" asked Becky, clutching her mother. "Did she love the same man too?"

"I can't answer for who Sis loved. Sis wanted Sandy. I know that. When Sandy got leave that first time, Sis didn't even tell Avril or

Sophia or Newton that he was coming home. Sis and her parents and Bessie met him at the Massacre dock and Bessie was drunk and started blathering on about some letters she'd found." Waverley considered momentarily. "Letters of mine. Love letters I had written to Sandy. Bessie started in on the Temple girls, how we were whores and so on, and how everyone on Isadora agreed with her. Bessie had read my letters out loud to everyone at the Marine and Feed, anyone who would listen to her. And when Sandy heard that, he just picked up his bag and started to walk to Useless. Sis tried to stop him, but she couldn't. He spent his whole leave with Avril and Newton and Sophia at Useless. You were born there some nine months later, Denise. Sophia and Newton brought you into this world. Sophia and Newton wrapped you up and put you in your mother's arms."

"Were they married?" Denise choked out the question. "When did Dad and—Avril . . . did they get married?"

"Later. After he was discharged from the navy."

"Oh God, isn't that rich? I'm a half-Jewish French bastard! Here I thought I was a Daughter of Norway! And now I find out my people were Jews who died in . . ." Denise bent double against Becky, like an old woman. Becky herself seemed in danger of collapse.

Waverley wanted to embrace them, to give, physically, something of the strength she knew she still had. But she did not dare. Their rage and disbelief made them the more fragile. The two clung to each other, Becky holding her mother while Denise wept and swore, cursed and moaned. Waverley held the umbrella over them. She said Avril had died in a motorcycle accident. "You can see why Sandy would never want you to ride that motorcycle. Avril died on the road to Useless. There is a hill. A high curve. Very dangerous."

Denise stumbled from the shelter of the umbrella and staggered over to the steps of the church, not even seeking the cover of the porch. She just sat there, rocking back and forth, groaning, head back, mouth open to the fine rain, twisting her scarred wrists in her hands.

Becky made no move toward her. In a thin, harsh whisper, she asked Waverley, "Why have you waited so long to tell me this? I've been your temp for months now. Every day I have come to your house and you have let me go on and on, talking about Sis and my grandfather and my mom, yet you never told me what you knew of my family. You know them better than we do, but you said nothing?"

"Timing is everything," replied Waverley obliquely.

"And what have you done to my mother? To me? Look at her! What am I going to do with her now? Look how old she is! And just finding out that her own mother wasn't her real mother? That she's been lied to forever? I've told you how easily she falls apart! Look at her wrists! How can I cope with this? On top of everything else, how can I possibly take care of her now? Mom could have gone her whole life with this lie, and been just fine."

"She didn't look fine when I met her."

"She's going to be much worse now."

"Perhaps," Waverley observed tartly, "but I'll bet there won't be any more phone calls to Jerry Hermann."

"What's going to happen when she calls home? When she calls my grandparents? What's going to happen when they hear what you've told us? How am I going to deal with that? With Sis? With my grandfather? He'll be devastated. Sis'll see to that."

"That's their problem. Not mine. They lied, Becky. They denied that Avril ever existed and that's not true. Avril Aron lit up the world while she lived."

"What was she to you?" demanded Becky.

"I loved them all." When Becky left her, going to the church step, Waverley added, "I loved Avril best."

Waverley walked over to the pair on the porch, where Denise sobbed in long inarticulate bellows. She put the umbrella over them for protection. Then she walked to her car, passing the graves of Bessie and Hector Lomax, two little stones that crumbled toward each other in a comradely fashion.

Rain pearled on Waverley's short gray hair as she opened the passenger's-side door on the Land Rover. She stood like a sort of sentinel there, listening to Denise cry and swear and pound the porch. Oh yes, she thought, November 6, I will remember this one. I will probably regret it. What I have done has been unkind to everyone. To everyone living. To Becky, Denise, to Sandy. Waverley imagined the abuse Sis would heap on Sandy's head when all this came out. Ah well. Sandy

would have to take his chances. Waverley looked back at Becky trying to soothe and smooth and placate Denise, who had rolled forward,
her head on her knees, a sobbing wad of humanity. Waverley was
stabbed with regret. Maybe in serving Avril's memory, she had con-
tributed to the destruction of Avril's daughter. Denise was not strong.
Maybe Denise could not endure this truth. Maybe it would just lay
waste to the lie of her life, to the rest of her life. What was it Sandy
had said all those years ago? The past is either irrelevant, or it can
shatter. One is as bad as the other. One demeans. The other destroys.
Waverley felt suddenly old, diminished, as the elderly are diminished.
Useless.

The two Lomax women lurched unsteadily toward the Land Rover,
the umbrella scarcely needed now. Denise was dripping wet, rain in her
hair, tears on her cheeks, all expression washed from her face. She
leaned on her daughter, but she seemed to have collected herself momentarily. She paused before Waverley. She did not get in the car. Her
rage had dissipated with the rain, and sorrow lined the furrows on her
face.

"I'm sorry," said Waverley, holding the door for her. "Truly." She
might have said more, something about her own noble motives, her loyalty to Avril, rationalizing the pain she had inflicted. But she didn't.

This gaunt, ungainly woman put her hand on Waverley's shoulder.
The petulance was gone from her eyes, the pout from her mouth. She
hunched over, like a prisoner just released who greets the world with little understanding and no great enthusiasm. She might have preferred
the prison.

"Thank you," Denise murmured in a voice surprisingly firm. "Thank
you for bringing us here." She got in the car. The door closed.

In the gathering autumnal dusk, Waverley stood momentarily trans-
fixed, chilled, shivering, as a past she had not experienced repeated itself, the dèjá vu of what she had not seen. Then it came to her: if Denise
could sink as low as Bessie Lomax, she could probably also rise to the
grandeur of Judith Aron. That night—Waverley could see the Unseen,
the apartment in the rue de la Grande Chaumière. Hear the Unspoken,
the pounding on the door—Judith rose, answered the insistent knock.
She opened the door. Yes, she was Madame Aron. *Juive.* She had known

all along they would come for her. She put on her coat, her hat, picked up a small bag. Already packed. Closing the door softly behind her, Judith went out into the rue de la Grande Chaumière, vanished into the night, dispersed into oblivion. And in the kitchen window, the white cat, Chou-fleur, sat purring beside the red geranium, the lovers alone in the otherwise empty apartment.